FALHORNE

By Tristan Dineen

Book One: The World is Burning

"Unhappy the land where heroes are needed." – Bertolt Brecht

Falhorne: The World is Burning

ISBN (print): 978-1-7779788-0-8
ISBN (e-book): 978-1-7779788-1-5

Cover Design by Anthony O'Brien
www.bookcoverdesign.store

Characters

The Falhorne

Vitus, Praetor of the Falhorne in the Grand Principality of Vinos

Tagus, Black Vinosian Falhorne and Vitus's former apprentice

Piso, Falhorne and Vitus's apprentice (killed at Fallonier Fields)

Porus, Falhorne (hanged by the Vinosian authorities)

Tarquinus, Black Vinosian Falhorne

Callidus, renegade Falhorne and leader of the resistance in Trastamere

The Asylum

Skarlos, Asylum Watchman and former mercenary

Remus, Asylum Watchman

Valens, Asylum Watchman and brother of Remus

Jesta, Speaker of the Asylum's Agoge Council, former armorer

Secunda, Councillor of the Agoge, former weaver

Nestor, Councillor of the Agoge, former leatherworker

Clodius, Councillor of the Agoge, former dockworker

Corvus, Councillor of the Agoge and member of the Association

Arbaces, elderly Old Believer and former soldier

Mia, Secunda's niece and granddaughter of Nestor

Fiore City

Sir Cosimo Gratano, son of Duke Sandro of Trastamere

Commodus Resti, Bailiff of Fiore

Cornelia ("Corrie"), Tagus's wife and local midwife

Callus, Vitus's serving boy and Tagus's informal apprentice

Nicco, gnomish member of the Association, former weaver

Gorgo, Samosian refugee and Association member

Meno, gnomish alchemist and brother of Nicco

Aileanor, Meno's mysterious companion

Agelaus, Captain of the prince's Gendarmerie

Arnim, Captain of the prince's Gendarmerie

Chero Julianus-Agricola, Grand Prince of Vinos

Theophilus, Bishop of Fiore

Maxim de Tolley, Guildmaster of Fiore

Owain Trevelyan, Tarnish Ambassador to Vinos

Giovanni Lechianno, Alchemist

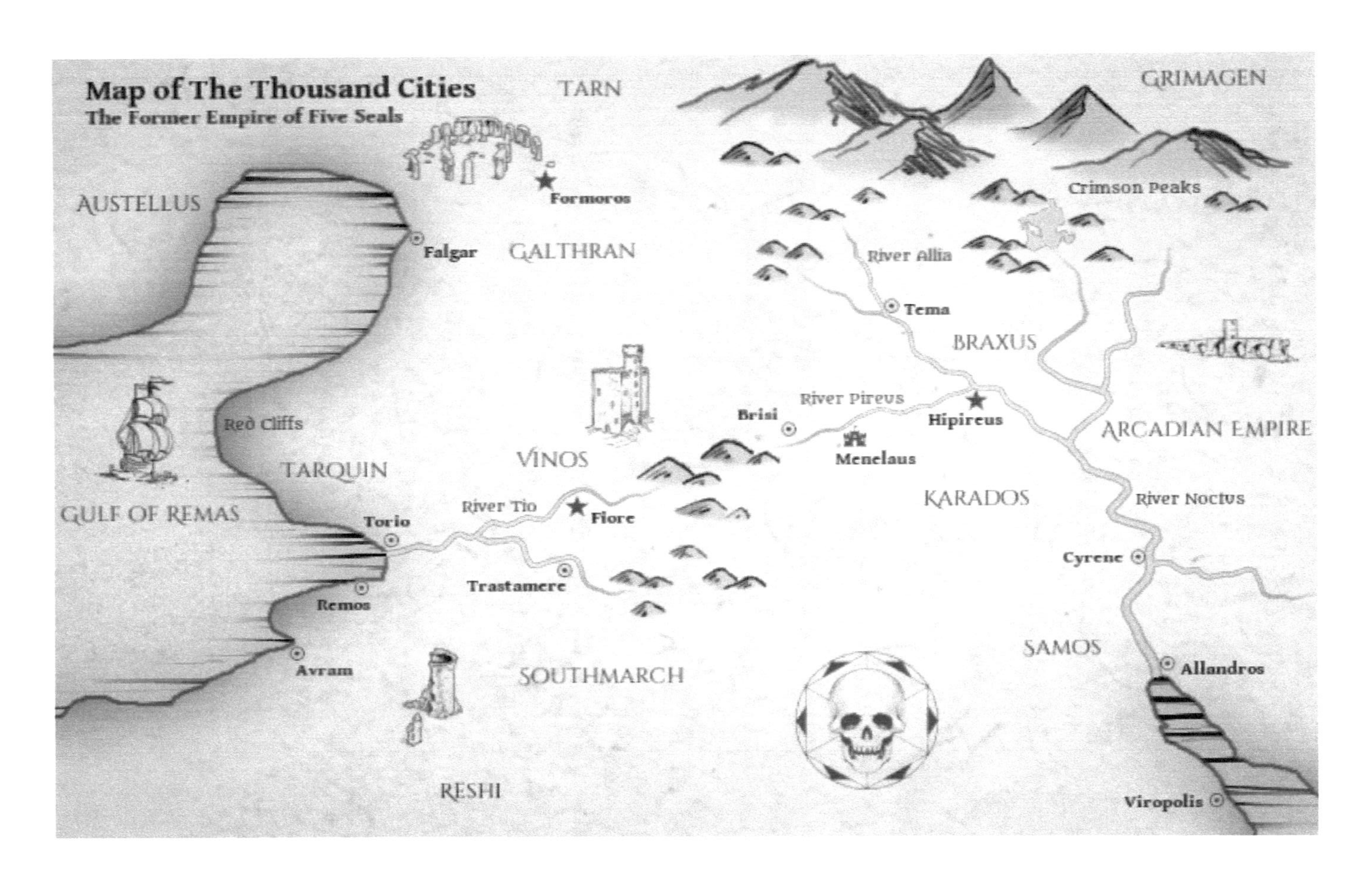

Map of The Thousand Cities
The Former Empire of Five Seals
TARN
GRIMAGEN
AUSTELLUS
Crimson Peaks
Formoros
Falgar
GALTHRAN
River Allia
Tema
BRAXUS
River Pireus
Brisi
Hipireus
ARCADIAN EMPIRE
Red Cliffs
VINOS
Menelaus
TARQUIN
KARADOS
River Noctus
GULF OF REMAS
River Tio
Fiore
Torio
Cyrene
Trastamere
Remos
Avram
SOUTHMARCH
SAMOS
Allandros
RESHI
Viropolis

Prologue – The Battle of the Fallonier Fields

"Advance!"

The Royal Army of Vinos lurched unsteadily into motion with a great groan of metal and the stamp of boot leather on hard baked earth. Noble knights, peasant pikemen and mercenary men-at-arms marched across the dry fields, preparing to enter battle while ignoring the hooded pariahs in their midst. The low, unearthly chant driving many of the prince's soldiers to hastily make the sign of the Almighty Sun across their chests for fear of being tainted. Whole battalions kept their distance from the dark figures as the opposing battle lines closed. For none wished to fight alongside the Falhorne. Only the infamous "Corpse Company" of the Royal Gendarmerie stayed close to the hooded warriors and they were dead men anyway. Dead men overseeing heretics on the wrong side of a holy war.

One heretic stood out from the others. His grizzled face cloaked in shadow above black plate armor. His eyes of blank white chalk staring into the mass of Templars, feudal levies and warrior priests, steadily approaching across the barren stretch of farmland. Vitus Bastarnae, praetor of the Falhorne of Vinos, was again defying the Church, along with the bounty that the Inquisition had placed on his head. Unlike the thousands of reluctant soldiers in the prince's ranks that day, he had no fear for his immortal soul. Fear meant nothing to the dead.

The morning sun had finally pierced the towering grey clouds, yet the praetor saw nothing but darkness as he spoke the final words of the chant and tightened the grip on his halberd. Ashen figures stalked forward in the shadow of a black mountain. He heard nothing but the moaning of a spectral legion. All was empty as the hand of death descended and the corpse-state claimed him, its voiceless call washing over the ranks of the initiated as the veil grew thin.

Mortis.

Vitus felt the Black King's summons. Felt it resonate in the minds of his apprentices. Tagus on his left and Piso on his right. He began to move. Nineteen others following in his wake, wicked polearms glinting with a deathly glow. Drawn forward by that which could not be foresworn.

Now he was running. They were all running. Black robes fluttering like carrion birds in flight. Completely subsumed in Mortis, Vitus was barely conscious of the half-seen shadows moving at his side or the crack of incoming arquebus shots left and right. He was a fleet-footed corpse alongside other fleet-footed corpses, dim shadow-wreathed eyes focused solely on what lay ahead. Everything was paling into insignificance: the low-hanging black clouds, the gunfire, the screams of the dying, the war cries, and the clash of steel. The world was closing in, everything blurring, merging, melding into a single image of a descending blade – he was in Barbarus.

Flashing, spasming images of formless clashing colors raced through an endless grey void. Ahead were white pulsating things, shrieking and writhing toward him as through murky water choked with dust. In this place between worlds, the only thing with a hard-edge, the only thing to have any solid definition at all, was the blade of his great halberd, that blazed with a sickly yellow flame yet gave off no heat. He could not see his hands, they had been swallowed into nothingness, but his weapon leapt forward at the white things like it possessed a will of its own.

One of the writhing forms noiselessly exploded under the impact, shooting rays of bright light in all directions that burned and dissipated into the void. The *damas* that was no longer his own crashed into a second white form and impaled a third, directed by forces beyond life and death. He had become a weapon of the gods.

The world, the screams, the cries, the crash of blades under slate grey skies, all of it exploded back into focus, as Vitus crashed into the man-at-arms in front of him like wild bull. The soldier fell back as the halberd's spike rammed through the breastplate of his neighbor with crushing force, impaling him like a stuck boar. Adrenaline and something more coursing through his veins, the Falhorne wrenched the spike free and swung the halberd's axe-head in a great decapitating arc, severing the fallen soldier's head in a fountain of viscera. Another soul for the Black King.

He did not pause, though his vision was dim. Ozone filled his nostrils, and he was only vaguely aware of the black armored figure of Piso, splitting the skull of another fallen soldier as he tried to rise to his feet. To his right, he recognized the uncertain outlines of similar black-clad soldiers as the second rank engaged the enemy with their pole-axes and bill-hooks. His body felt as heavy as a granite boulder, but the numbness of the enduring corpse-state soon enveloped these sensations once more. Without flinching, he parried a blinding sword thrust aimed directly at his face, his riposte sending the spike of his halberd through the soldier's right eye, before using the sharpened butt end of the weapon to disembowel his companion and delivering a savage kick to the crotch of a third enemy.

By then his eyes had rolled back into place and his senses had sufficiently returned to reveal the true extent of the carnage that he and his comrades had wreaked upon the foe. An entire battalion must have been destroyed to account for the piles of dismembered bodies strewn across the bloody grass. He saw Tagus slice a man clean in two with his halberd, the ruined halves flopping to the ground like sides of meat in an abattoir. Piso was pulling his weapon free from the unrecognizable remains of a hapless soldier whom he had literally crushed with one blow. And at the heart of the press, he dispassionately watched as his own weapon rose and fell in bloody arcs.

Most of the enemy pikemen were now fleeing for their lives before the onrushing black demons. The praetor's buzzing ears caught wind of terrified screams shouted in rustic peasant accents, "Malochia!" "Okampa!": unclean ones, foul things, monsters.

As the enemy's ranks thinned, he could see the Gendarme foot soldiers of the Corpse Company engaged in a frenzied melee, beset by foes on all sides. Of the mercenary battalions that had so zealously kept their distance from the Falhorne during deployment there was no sign. An entire wing of the Royal Army had seemingly melted away.

The outnumbered Falhorne were completely entangled with the foe. Everywhere armored men were cutting and hacking at one another with swords, axes, bills, and halberds. Pikes having been flung aside in favor of more brutal implements of close-quarter killing. But Vitus had no time to further survey the murderous panorama. The numbing effects of his momentary crossing of the planes had ended, and he could feel something of his human emotions returning: the animal fury of self-preservation, mixed with carefully cultivated rage against the ancient enemies of his people, who had been made to suffer through centuries of lynch mobs, gibbets, and Inquisitional torture chambers. He could only focus on the blood-soaked blade of his weapon. The way to Barbarus was closed, but through concentration, he could maintain the corpse-state detachment and channel its power.

His regained composure was tested at once. The Templar's white and gold tabard burst from the chaos, advancing to meet him through the thick of the melee. A Falhorne of the second rank attempted to bar the knight's approach, only to be casually impaled on the end of a lance. Vitus could not remember the man's name.

He stared blankly into the face of the onrushing Templar: the yellow-russet beard, gritted teeth, and hate-filled eyes; every detail spoke of a man secure in his own righteousness, a righteousness that hinged upon the utter destruction of the armored heretic before him, whose very existence was a blasphemy against the Most High. The holy knight wore a simple armored skullcap beneath his white hood, in stark contrast to Vitus's black robes. The bloodied lance hovered menacingly above the brutal insignia in the center of the bleached tabard which swathed the knight's plate armor – a four-pointed sun with an expressionless face.

The impact of the lance nearly forced Vitus to his knees. But he remained upright, holding his legs apart in "mora", the earth stance. Batting the thrust aside, he raised his weapon to shoulder height and delivered a thrust of his own from the serpent position. However, the Templar was no half-trained peasant. Snarling, he dropped the lance, and dodged the blow with a quick step to the front and side that brought him inside Vitus's guard. This warrior of the Church drawing his gladius in one swift motion, moving to strike at the narrow point between helmet and breastplate, aiming for a lethal blow. But the Falhorne's Mortis remained unbroken.

Driving cold precision against fanaticism, Vitus let go of his weapon with one hand, dropping down into the hunter's tooth position whilst grasping his opponent's wrist, staying the blade before it could strike home. Then with a twist of his forearm, he brought the butt end of the halberd up and over his enemy's guard, feeling the sickening crunch as it impacted against the Templar's unprotected jaw. The yellow beard was suddenly stained crimson. The hate-filled eyes glazed over and rolled back in their sockets, as the holy Knight of the Host crumpled to the earth in a jangling of useless armor.

Vitus dropped to one knee, narrowly avoiding being impaled by the pikeman directly behind the fallen Templar. He felt the weapon graze the plating on his left thigh and through the physical numbness of Mortis he felt a dull pain course through his body. Rising into serpent stance he brought his halberd down like a windmill upon the pikeman's iron helmet, sheering through the soldier's skull. He faintly felt blood trickling down his thigh.

To the left he saw another Falhorne fall, a Templar's lance embedded in his throat. The Knight of the Host who did this deed was summarily decapitated by Tagus, but it was a loss that the Falhorne of Vinos could scarcely afford as more and more enemies threw themselves into the melee.

As Vitus prepared to meet them, his tired limbs straining, he sensed something. Something very wrong. Something that could not be adequately described to anyone who has not heard the voice of the gods or plumbed the depths of inhuman emotions that bridge the divide between worlds; one who does not understand that the heavens above are as bloody as the earth below.

What Vitus felt was a sound, a scent, a taste, and touch combined into one force which pierced him with a thousand red hot needles plunging into his flesh at the same time. He doubled over as searing agony tore through his body, almost being impaled by another incoming pikeman as he sank to his knees. Teeth clenching so hard he thought they would shatter. He could not maintain a hold on his weapon and it fell to the trampled grass. Blinded by the pain, his fumbling hands grasped the shaft of the descending pike and he pulled as hard as he could. The air was heaving and pulsing, as though the heavy clouds were pressing downward, the sky falling to crush the earth and all life. It was all he could do to keep from losing consciousness.

After what seemed like an eternity, the pike came free from the grasp of an enemy that the praetor could no longer see. He toppled back with the broken shaft in his hands, looking up into the sickly yellow sky. The soldier's sword, drawn and plunging downward toward his chest, appeared as through a cloud of choking smoke. The sudden appearance of a halberd's blade, followed by the familiar and sickening "O" expression that consumed the soldier's features as he was disemboweled, all seemed unreal. Until Piso's strong arms pulled him to his feet and jolted him into full awareness of his surroundings.

The mystical assault was brutally apparent in the unearthly light staining everything within his field of vision with the vile tint of a desiccated body on an execution ground. It illuminated an apocalyptic scene. Vitus could see his brethren stumble and fall, clutching their foreheads as blood poured from their noses and ears, driven to their knees in agony – only to be run through or cut down by the enemy swarming all around. The Templars seemingly unaffected by the weight of a cruel sky. He could no longer see Piso amidst the chaos.

It was all Vitus could do to draw his sword; his primary weapon now lost beyond recovery amid the bodies. Fighting through the pain hammering through his skull, barely parrying the multiple blows aimed at his limping form, he struggled in the direction of Tagus, the dark form of his apprentice a beacon amid the madness.

"Brothers, gather to me!" The hoarse command barely escaped his cracked lips, yet by the grace of the gods his apprentice heard it.

Tagus launched himself forward, deflecting the thrust of a lance as he ran. Vitus half-smiled through the pain as he watched his youngest acolyte seize the Templar by the arm and drive his fist into the side of his enemy's helmet, before wrenching it aside and striking downward with his blade, not even bothering to look at the fanatic whose head he had just removed. His apprentice's face was contorted in agony.

Vitus felt some of the pain subside as they came together, as though he had entered some kind of protective aura. The surviving Falhorne rallied around their leader and were soon fighting back-to-back, ringed by Templars and their lackeys. Again, and again they struck back: hacking, thrusting, parrying, and blocking at a feverish rate as the blows rained down on them from all sides. The mystic agony continued to wane, although the ghastly yellow light remained, hanging like a pall over the carnage.

"Do not separate! Stand together! Piso! Where is Piso?" Vitus bellowed at his remaining Brethren.

"Praetor! He helped me to my feet, then disappeared!" Tagus hoarsely shouted back, parrying yet another pike thrust with the haft of his now broken halberd.

Suddenly the ranks of the enemy parted and Vitus could see the source of the deadly light. Through the maze of pike poles, flashing blades, and frenzied faces, he spied a lone white robed figure, arms upraised as though signaling the lower reaches of the heavens. Now he could hear the unholy chant, so low-pitched that it could have come from the throat of an ogre, penetrating the air around him and making it shake and heave with raw power. Neither he nor any of the others who beheld this sight had to speak aloud the evil name that hung in their minds like a body from a gallows tree: Inquisitor. There was no time to lose.

"Move brothers! Move! Toward the spellcaster! Now!" Vitus shouted and the survivors struggled forward, only to find their way barred by more Templars who engaged them in yet another savage melee.

Vitus saw a lance strike Tagus's armored shoulder and for sickening instant it seemed that his apprentice would fall. But the sturdy Falhorne did not even flinch and his devastating riposte cleaved the offending Templar in two.

The struggle was growing desperate. Vitus's leg bled from where he had been wounded while a crimson rivulet trickled from a hole in his breastplate. All the surviving Falhorne carried wounds of equal, if not greater, severity, as they formed a circle around Brother Tarquinus, who had fallen unconscious from blood loss. With the precision of the Mortis-state now shattered, doubt was finally creeping into the praetor's exhausted mind. Death was again outside their bodies, staring at them in menacing expectation.

In that instant, he saw a disturbance in the white-robed ranks of the enemy, a distant black shape moving through the armored throng. Though his eyes were rimmed with blood and sweat, for the briefest of moments, the mass of fighting men parted and Vitus beheld the tall, unmistakable figure of Piso striding forward.

His eldest apprentice appeared to be pushing against some immense force, like he was holding back a landslide. None could bar his way, his halberd licking out to sever limbs and smash bone, unstoppable and unrelenting. And Vitus gasped when he realized what was happening. Piso had re-entered the place between worlds in a feat that should not have been humanly possible. His apprentice had returned to Barbarus. The Mortis opened a gateway to the land of the dead, and to attempt to re-commune with this world before the rising of the new moon meant the certain loss of one's soul as forces beyond man's comprehension tore away the body's life force. Every Falhorne knew that. And yet Piso appeared unbroken. It was impossible. No Savant had emerged in one hundred years. It was madness, suicidal madness.

Even though he was fighting for his life, Vitus could not take his eyes away. He could make out only the rise and fall of Piso's halberd now, a dance of death hacking through that sickly yellow cloud until it was poised directly before the spellcaster at the eye of the storm. He could not see the face of the inquisitor but he could feel the wrath, the sheer hatred for the unclean being who had interrupted his mystical invocation of the Almighty Sun. All at once the haze appeared to bend inward, revealing at last the slate grey clouds that hung over the slaughter. There was an intense burst of white light, forcing Vitus to look away. When he looked back, he saw light and darkness intertwined. Piso's inert form wrapped in a bear hug around the mass of crumpled white robes. The flash extinguished. The haze dissipated. And they fell together.

****

Vitus refused to look at the dark-haired lady with the pale face, stubbornly keeping his gaze on the fire as he fought back tears, trying not to show weakness before his men.

"Fiore's flames embrace you, brother. May His sacred fire guide you through the Great Darkness. May the Fire Lord's brightness illuminate your soul before the Eternal Judge who weighs the worth of all men's lives. May the Dark Bird bring word of your deeds to the throne of the Black King, who shall honor you with a place on the heights of Barbarus until the splitting of earth and sky when you shall join Him in the final battle. Be worthy, brother, for one day we shall join you."

Vitus's chanted words trailed off into the syllables of the Old Tongue, words whose meaning was lost to the young men who had never trodden the halls of Cera Pelleus before its fall. Prayers that would one day pass from memory, never to be heard again, just as Kyros's mangled corpse was lost in the pyre's crackling flames. He remembered his comrade's name now, all too late.

The battle was over, and a bloody twilight of red and dark orange had broken through the grey masses of cloud, exposing the day's carnage. The bonfire burned brightly on the hilltop in the gathering gloom. Four dark figures watching their fallen comrades burn one-by-one. As each died away, more were brought forward, the pyre re-lit, and the rites continued; the weakened and exhausted praetor leading the Falhorne through the arcane passages of old prayers to forbidden gods, begging them to shepherd their brethren through the afterlife.

They had won.

Piso's sacrifice had broken the power of the Inquisition on the field, allowing Prince Chero to wheel his right-flank and lead a charge against the enemy center and Baron Martino himself. The mounted Gendarmes had broken through and taken the enemy in the rear, while Captain Brennus of the infamous Red Boars had successfully rallied the retreating mercenary companies into a renewed frontal assault. Martino, the would-be "Prince of Skaros" and the Church's chosen champion, had gone down fighting alongside his bodyguard of Templars.

With the baron's death, his army had collapsed, although the surviving Templars had fought on until they were overwhelmed, the Falhorne cutting down the last of them. It was finally over. The so-called "Skaros Schism", that had threatened to tear Vinos apart, had been crushed and Chero's wayward vassal brought to heel. Victory had come, but at what cost.

"Fiore embrace you, brother. May His sacred fire guide you through the Great Darkness…"

It was Piso's turn to burn. All heads were bowed, as the broken body of the Savant was lowered into the flames. The litany began again with Vitus invoking each of the gods of the Celestial Court in turn to watch over the soul of his heroic apprentice. Piso was the last of fifteen Falhorne that had died on the fields outside Fallonier village, struck down by lances, pikes and vile magic.

The column no longer existed. Of its vanguard of veteran warriors, only three still breathed: Vitus, himself bearing six wounds, leant heavily on a staff as he presided over his fallen sons; Tarquinus, who had almost bled to death from his many wounds; and Tagus, who had miraculously emerged unscathed. The mighty Rigo and the stoical Porus were the sole survivors of the second line and they could barely stand up.

Alongside the battered remnants of the dismounted *Gendarmes* of the ill-fated Corpse Company, the Falhorne had been the only force that had stood steadfast against the onslaught on the left-flank, effectively tying down an entire wing of the enemy army. Now five wounded *Gendarmes,* still clad in their bloodied suits of heavy plate armor and shredded blue and gold livery, stood with them on the hillock with heads bowed, not flinching in the face of the blasphemous funeral rites of heathens. They had endured the same trials and that was enough.

Among them was the woman. Pale-faced and dark-haired, she too wore the crimson-stained armor of Chero's elite guard. But her eyes, jade green and burning as hot as the pyre that consumed his apprentice, spoke of truths that the praetor did not want to know. That a woman would even carry a sword and dare to enter battle alongside men was alien enough for him, without the otherworldly stare that made him want to hide his face.

The night was closing in. In the distance, drunken soldiers sang, trying to drown out the echoed screams of fallen comrades. Wounded men groaned and suffered in their tents and under surgeons' knives. The

Falhorne had been the only ones disciplined enough to completely remove their fallen comrades from the field. The rest remained sprawled or crumpled in bloody silence as the last rays of light left their bodies.

Vitus's prayers fell silent as Piso was lost to view. All were in awe of him: he seemed beyond mortal. But Vitus could not forget the all too human words that haunted him and echoed down the passages of his mind as he watched the sun go down, wondering what new dawn his apprentice had died for, and what it would bring.

Chapter 1 – False Peace

"Terrence, you will fetch me my horse!"

At first the shrill voice in his ear seemed to be of no more consequence than the buzzing of a mosquito, one sound amidst a multitude of shouts, curses, the rumbling of wagons and the clattering of a thousand feet upon the cobblestones. Tagus barely registered the bellowed command that came from somewhere behind him in the early morning chaos of the crowded marketplace. He pulled down his hood and went on surveying the salted sides of meat, hanging from the old butcher's stall. He had much to do, and no time to listen to some pompous young knight yelling for his servant. The sound of the flies around the stall, combined with the loud-mouthed prayers of the nearby gaggle of white-robed churchmen, was more annoying. And yet something inside him was stinging, as though someone had just struck him with the flat of their palm.

The buzzing did not end. Louder this time, it burst upon Tagus's ears with the force of a whip cracking.

"Do you lack ears, boy? You will fetch my horse now!"

There was a slight pause, and Tagus could feel the indignant fury in the speaker's voice as they moved closer. There could be no doubt that its ire was meant for him.

"And if you polish the saddle to a mirror finish, you might receive but a light whipping for your tardiness…"

The voice was indeed polished. Filled with the natural ease of a man born to command; someone who felt power over other men to be nothing more than their due. Such people were dangerous, Tagus knew. And now the distinguished speaker stood directly behind him.

Tagus stopped eyeing the cuts of meat and calmly slipped on his gloves. He slowly turned his head, instinctively bringing his hands into *mora*, the ready position.

"Terrence! You stupid Reshian swineherd! Get moving or I'll see your worthless dark hide bloodied!"

The speaker's words felt like a tanned leather whip lacerating the flesh of his naked back. Tagus clenched his teeth as he rounded on the man.

The speaker's status was beyond question. His fine leather doublet, trimmed and inlaid with green velvet, had been shined to perfection. His fine leather gloves were inlaid with intricate designs that some master craftsman had intended to resemble ivy, although it was difficult to tell with all the lace trimmings that hung about it, spilling from beneath his wrists. Similar lacy frocks decorated his elbows and shoulders, hanging about his neck like a gossamer white cloud. All this was crowned with a crop of short golden hair, and a set of pallid features contorted with entitled rage. His red lips were set in a snarl. While his eyes, as brilliant green as the frilly white ivy-bordered doublet, were squinting in frustration. The young aristocrat was looking directly at him, and his words were not idle threats. Still, whatever his rank, he had crossed a line that Tagus had long ago drawn in the sand.

"Boy?" Tagus grunted, gazing directly into those furious eyes. The blue blood's insipid words making every sinew in his heavily muscled shoulders tense with anger.

"Do I look like a boy to you, sir knight?"

The black cloth of his rough-spun robe rippled slightly as he faced the fair-haired man with the full-brunt of his barrel-chest and battle-scarred face. His hands still locked in *mora*. His longsword in plain view at his hip.

The noble was taller than him by almost a head, but lanky. So much so that he marveled that the young aristocrat could bear the weight of that pompous suit without falling face first in the mud. The youth more resembled a marble statue than a living man.

Tagus, by contrast, was hardly youthful in appearance. Twin parallel scars marred the dark flesh of his left cheek, with another shorter scar cutting between his deep brown eyes. But the traces of these old wounds were eclipsed entirely by the disfiguring gouge that stretched from beneath his right temple to the left-side of his chin. The Braxian longsword that had pierced him at the Battle of Allia had nearly sliced his face in two. The treatments inflicted on him by an inexpert surgeon had guaranteed that the ugly wound would leave its mark.

For a split second, the noble's expression froze on his unblemished face. But just as quickly, the marble white cheeks flushed a deep shade of red, his eyes sinking into trembling caves of spite. Stepping menacingly forward, his irate voice hissed its way through clenched teeth.

"I am the Baron of Tamus, slave, and you will obey me, or I swear by all the power of the House of Gratano, that I will have your pig-faced head on a spike. Either way, you are getting a taste of raw-hide, Re…"

The noble had no time to finish before Tagus's weathered fist met his finely proportioned jaw, sending the haughty young man falling over backwards like a sack full of stones.

A hush fell over the noisy market air – shopkeepers, fishwives, beggars, diminutive gnome jugglers, finely dressed guilders and household slaves in their uniform black tunics alike seemed to lose their voices as the blue-blooded scion hit the ground amid trampled dirt and horse dung. The call of the doves that lined the tiled roofs of the fine stone and red brick buildings, and flew among the spires of the guild chapel, faded to nothing. The ancient aqueduct, whose waters had once fed the baths of the Emperor Lucius, but which now did nothing but gush into the marble fountain before the guildhall, seemed to retreat into another world. Even the ever-present groan and whine of the high gallows below the guildhall's tower, where the gibbeted bodies of the condemned swayed in the breeze, seemed distant and muted. The white-robed preachers held their tongue. While the mouth of the grizzled old butcher was frozen in a perfect circle.

But the uneasy silence was just as quickly shattered by shouts of rage and astonishment as the fallen nobleman found his voice.

"Rufus! Boros! Anthulf! To me, now!"

As if by pre-arranged signal, the pathetic fallen figure with the bloodied face was surrounded by three heavily armed men. Their brutish features were shaved, and their partial suits of steel field-plate were covered in the green and white livery of their master, but Tagus recognized the look of a mercenary when he saw one. These were simple thugs in armor, gripping brutal looking hand-and-half swords in their gauntleted hands.

The butcher had ducked behind his stall, while the common folk nearby remained deathly silent, staring at the spectacle of a solitary man of obvious low-birth, dark-skinned and dark-robed, facing down the wrath of an aristocrat and his armored henchmen. Several pike-armed city guardsmen lined the wall of the guildhall, but none of them made the slightest move to intervene. A haggard-faced old beggar, the ragged shoulder of his clothes marked with the required yellow "B", seated in his assigned place at the corner of a shop, glanced at the spectacle before dejectedly turning his grime-rimmed eyes away.

Tagus stood his ground as he stared the men down. The sting, the whiplash, in the words of his supposed "better" had resurrected old memories, re-opened old wounds, and re-kindled old rage.

"Touch me, and I will kill you," he said with all the bluntness of a cornered bear, the darkness of his features as impassive as a steel blade…three of which were now pointed at his chest.

With seasoned hands Tagus seized the hilt of his sword. Stepping forward, he was preparing to strike at the incoming mercenaries when a second thundering voice stopped him mid-stride.

"Stop brother! Stand down!"

The deep and commanding voice was like a cannon blast amid the general silence, so powerful that it froze the mercenaries in place. But every shopkeeper and beggar, no matter how ignorant, could recognize the aged black-clad figure that was now striding purposefully through the haze of smoke from roasting pigs and chickens toward the confused scene. Even the clerics beneath the gallows shrank back as he passed them, expressions of fear and loathing on their faces.

Taking his hand from his sword, Tagus practically snapped to attention as his mentor and commander, Vitus, strode into the narrow space between him and the retainers. Their swords were still leveled in his direction, yet visibly trembling.

"What is this foolishness? Sheathe your swords!"

The men stepped back, obviously intimidated. But they did not put their weapons aside as they clustered about their master, who was still in the process of struggling to his feet, gripping his bloodied jaw in one hand and letting out muffled curses.

Vitus threw back the hood of his dark cloak, turning his bald, heavily scarred head back and forth, casting stern glances between his apprentice and the disheveled young noble. His wrinkled cheeks, studded with white stubble, resembling an ancient castle wall. The old, yet finely wrought suit of jet-black leather armor worn over his robes making it appear as though he had just stepped from another time.

"Brother, I trust there is an explanation?"

Tagus had no time to answer before the noble sprang to his feet, set a hand to his sword, and lunged at him.

"Curr! Reshian dog!"

But just as quickly, Vitus's strong hand was on the young man's sword arm, and his frenzied attack was stopped dead.

"Ah, so I have the honor of addressing the noble Sir Cosimo of House Gratano. Very many greetings, sirrah."

Vitus spoke as though he were a high-born nobleman addressing a junior member of his own house.

Perhaps it was the formal bearing in his voice, but the features of the knight seemed to relax slightly, though his finely chiseled face lost none of its fury.

"I will not be insulted by common mongrels, like this Resh," he spat, "stand aside Falhorne, your kind have no place here. I will take my vengeance, as is my lawful right!"

He started forward again, but Vitus immediately gripped Sir Cosimo by both shoulders, forcing the young man to look into his piercing deep-set blue eyes.

"Your right ends where mine begins Cosimo. This man is Falhorne. He has my full protection, as is guaranteed by the Treaty of Trastamere in perpetuity for as long as men draw breath in the land of Vinos. Duke Sandro would deplore your lack of legal knowledge, for it was signed within the hallowed halls of your father's very castle in the springtime of your tenth birthday…do you remember now?"

Cosimo snarled and backed away, shaking Vitus's grip from his shoulders.

"You dare to speak of my lord father, black dog…take this Resh mongrel out of my sight! I will not forget this insult…damn it! Where is Terrence? That insolent slave…I will have him flayed alive for this…"

Wiping blood from his battered cheek and casting a last hateful look at Tagus, he stalked off, followed clumsily by his retinue. The market day crowds parted before them and they were soon lost from view among the other finely dressed nobles, guilders and merchants, along with their hulking armored bodyguards and retinues of slaves in black tunics – some of them bearing their masters aloft in sedan chairs over the common scrum of the marketplace crowds.

The collective silence rapidly fell away as the usual bustle drowned out the memory of the incident that had threatened to spill blood on the cobblestones. The head of the cowering butcher slowly crept back into view behind the stall as the flies buzzed around the cured joints of dangling meat. From beneath the gallows, the furious sound of prayers once again mingled with the flies.

But Tagus continued to stand, wordless and rigid, as his mentor turned to him. He felt no shame. He had his own honor to defend, regardless of what blue-blooded fops might think. He was no one's slave. Still, his praetor's look of reproach was humbling.

"Well young lion, perhaps you should save your ferocity for when it truly matters. Angering excitable young nobles is a waste of your time, and that of your brethren. Clearly you have not outgrown this crucial weakness of yours. Come. Fetch that last joint of pig and make haste to the Asylum. I will send young Callus for the rest. We are wanted at the festival and I have a message for the Agoge."

Vitus's features fell back into shadow as he raised his hood. He turned away, his black carapace shining in the sun that had momentarily broken through the grey clouds, and began to walk away in the direction of the aqueduct's arches and the paved expanse of Thresher Street.

Without a word, Tagus faced the fearful eyes of the butcher, his finger already pointing at the cut of meat that his mentor had indicated. Nearby, a moon-faced gnome in a ridiculous leather hat marked "E" in yellow, cautiously began tossing brightly colored balls from hand to hand in his lawfully designated place under the eaves of an enterprising maker of fine leather goods, all under the watchful eye of a nearby guardsman, whose hand rested on the pommel of his sword. Above them, the bell of guildhall's tower began to toll, drowning out the distant voice of the town crier as he once again began shouting out royal decrees to the autumn sky.

****

"By Fiore's flame!"

Tagus nearly staggered to his knees as the stout stave cracked against his skull, and all his senses chimed like the bells atop the city's spires as they rang down the hour. Squinting his eyes through the throbbing pain, he could clearly see the grin on the young boy's face – a grin that could have easily stretched several leagues and more. It was the "lucky shot" kind of grin a student makes when he thinks that he has mastered the world and believes his teacher to be a doddering old fool. Tagus felt his cheeks redden with embarrassment in the hot, stuffy air as the heat of the sparring bout passed and he remembered where he was.

"Coo! Looks like Master Tagus could use a lesson or two!"

It was true, as much as he would never admit such a thing to the young scoundrel, certainly not in the thick of the Fire Day festivities. He was badly out of practice. It had been three years since he had last engaged in soldiery, four since he had last seen a real battlefield, and he had trained only infrequently since then.

"Heh! Looks like our not-so-young lion's been turnin' pages more than sword pommels these days, boys!"

Brother Tarquinus's remark cut like a blade through Tagus's throbbing skull, letting the laughter of the assembled men and boys seep inside to throttle his ego as he spat out a mixture of saliva and blood.

Gods damn them…

First the outrage with that cretin of a noble, and now he was being made to look like a fool in front of everyone…and by a mere child!

"Aye, and the poor fella's belly is getting a little paunchy too…"

Of course, Skarlos, the biggest and most heavy-set among the Asylum's watchmen, would add a shot of his own into the mix.

Gods damn them all…

There were days when he cursed the fact that he was the most literate of Fiore's Falhorne. At forty years, he felt more like a humble clerk than a soldier. From handling Vitus's correspondence and papers, to poring over the endless, fruitless pleas for a hearing that his mentor sent to the royal court each week. He could almost feel his muscles atrophy with every stroke of his pen.

Young Callus's mocking jest felt something like a bee sting, hot sand, and itchy straw bedding rolled into one. The cocky look in the little fellow's dark flashing eyes as he glanced around smugly at the admiring onlookers was a challenge that could not go unanswered.

"Impudent roguish youth!"

The chuckling black-haired boy had no time to block the sudden sweep of his teacher's staff before it smashed against his shins, sending the bewildered Callus tumbling head over heels onto the hard-packed earth of the old inn yard.

The barrage of jibs and laughter rang through the air, as Tagus forced a grin onto his face, in spite of his lingering irritation and throbbing skull.

"You know cub," he said, rising groggily to his feet and planting the butt of his staff on the ground as he looked down at the dazed and somewhat shocked youth. "I am living proof that not all blows to the head are lethal. You may wish to remember that, especially if you really do want to be a dragon slayer…dragons have big heads, or so I am told."

There was a second eruption of laughter and much clapping of hands from the gathering as Tagus rubbed his bald cranium with calloused fingers. He reached down to help Callus to his feet, ignoring the general noise and continuing with his hard-won advice.

"A lucky hit does not make you master of the battlefield. I and some others I could name found that out the hard way…do not let a lucky strike get you thinking that you are ready to face the nightmare lords single-handed or something stupid like that."

The dazed youth meekly nodded in response. Tagus felt the flush leaving his face as he inwardly thanked the gods for his own dark visage – at least it made embarrassment a little less obvious. Callus's pale skin seemed practically ablaze.

"I…I'm sorry sir…" the boy gasped at last, fumbling to pick up his own staff whilst brushing the dust from his sweat-sodden linen shirt.

"Don't worry, son, even the best of us starts with his face in the dirt!"

Tarquinus was still there, tall and lean in his black cloak, with a jovial smile on his face. Skarlos and the others had moved off to observe the other bouts.

Tagus sighed, ignoring his comrade's admittedly apt remark, as he leaned the staff in the corner of the yard, pressing his aching back against the dirty mud and thatch wall. But his eyes never left his apprentice for a second.

"Cub, just count yourself lucky that you learned not to be a cocky bastard in a practice yard rather than a battlefield. I think we have clobbered each other enough for one day. Go and join the others. Get some food in you."

"Yes…yes, sir…"

Callus's dark eyes were chastened and downcast as the formerly victorious youth staggered from the yard, almost tripping over his own feet more than once as he withdrew. Tarquinus shook his head as the boy vanished, before re-joining the crowd.

Tagus forced air into his exhausted lungs, breathing hard. The shut-in air of the innyard, with its nearly one-hundred occupants packed together, felt like the interior of a brickworks kiln. His head continued to ring from the blow that he had received and he shut his eyes from the fiercely grappling forms of the two wrestlers that the onlookers had crowded around. This was Fire Day, the festival of the Lord of Flames, and, by Fiore's burning holiness, he felt it.

"Brother Tagus?"

He opened his eyes at the familiar voice, and saw young Remus standing there in his rough leathers. Unlike his twin brother Valens, the former soldier had been explicitly prohibited from taking part in the contests by the praetor. Somebody had to run errands after all, and, after the near bloodshed at the marketplace, Tagus had been let off the hook from his usual duties. Although now he was somewhat regretting it.

"Yes?"

His voice had a slight wheeze to it as he replied, which he immediately felt ashamed of.

"The praetor wants you at the sacred fire…now."

A sweaty strand of brown hair fell across the young watchman's normally stoic face as he regarded his elder with concern.

"Are you…alright?"

Tagus felt the flush return to his cheeks.

"Fine…I am fine. I will go to him."

His head was still on fire as he stumbled from the yard, cursing the spectators and their shouts and jeers as the glorified brawl behind him continued. Glancing over his shoulder, Tagus even saw old Arbaces enter one of the wrestling bouts, the elderly watchman eager to prove himself against much younger men in the traditional feats of strength that marked the Fire Lord's day. For the Lord of Flames was the patron of warriors. The men of the Asylum seemed to be enjoying their time off; grappling, swinging fists and wooden cudgels rather than toiling on the docks for money-grubbing merchants. Even if the prizes for winning amounted to little more than bragging rights before their peers. Tagus turned away and entered the street. It was a far cry from the ancient days when bloody gladiatorial contests would be fought in Fiore's temples to win his favor.

The normally drab and muddy lanes of the Asylum were alive with streamers, ribbons and makeshift banners of bright red and orange. Normally grim and downcast faces were brightened, in spite of the overcast sky. For the spirits of the ancestors walked amongst them. Cookfires had been built in the tiny yards of ramshackle hovels, from which the rare scent of roasting meat rose into the sky, tended by the hands of mothers whose children were used to thin gruel and biscuits. For them this was a special treat to be savoured only a few times a year. Women and children alike sang old songs in happy voices, gleaming bone white in freshly laundered linens. It was in contrast to the dark figure who stumbled down the street before them toward the river, offering muffled curses while clutching his forehead and drawing their curious gaze. He made his way to where another crowd had assembled and a low chanting had begun to rise over the humble thatched rooftops.

The bulk of the old port authority building soon swelled before him and the smell of burning wood overpowered the scent of roasting meat. Tagus saw the tongues of orange and yellow shooting over the heads of the faithful gathered about the great bonfire. By now, drums had joined the chanting, each borne by a woman in a faded red skirt, standing at each of the four corners of the fire as the barefoot crowd moved amongst them in a thousand-year-old rhythm. They were almost all women, although a number of children bore torches and even a few lighted candles as they circled the flames alongside their mothers. All of them bore strips of crimson cloth around their otherwise plain linen dresses and skirts, some of which were blackened from contact with the great heaps of ash. The fire would not be permitted to go out until the last flicker of twilight that evening.

"For we shall rise with His fire!"

The crowd parted as the leader of the chant broke into view, a black-haired woman with a spritely step, wearing threadbare wrap of bright orange that did little to conceal her slender figure. Jesta, the central figure of the Agoge council and speaker of the Asylum, was fulfilling the same spiritual duties that her ancestors had since the time of Five Kingdoms, long before the rise of the Empire. On Fire Day, it was the women who prayed while the men fought.

"For His flames are within us!"

The dancing headwoman's thin fingers turned over a tiny clay vessel from which hot coals fell upon the packed earth beside the drummer. Tagus could see similar smouldering piles alongside the other three musicians, whose beat had increased in tempo and in energy as Jesta energetically led the others in hailing the elemental lords of creation.

"Fiore, Sol, Mora, Viro! Bless us, oh Masters of the Celestial Court!"

As Tagus continued to follow Remus toward the circling mass of faithful revellers, he saw another dark figure silhouetted against the flames. Vitus's back was to him, but his mentor's appearance was unmistakable, the "Ash Crown" having long ago left its mark in his flesh. In his dark robes, he stood alone and apart from the others, his booted feet planted firmly in the dust of the narrow street. His hands were clasped behind his back, as though he were a general, tensely observing the movements of his troops on the battlefield, while pondering the anticipated maneuvers of his enemy.

"Hail, good Remus," the praetor said, without turning his head. "And I welcome your timeliness, Brother Tagus, my young lion. I have already dispatched Callus to fetch the others. There has been a disturbance at the Silo Street gate. It demands the immediate attention of both the Watch and the Falhorne. Come."

The old man spun nimbly on his heel. His grizzled face and blue eyes stood out against the bonfire as he began to march purposefully down a narrow lane that led between uneven rows of cramped hovels. With Tagus and Remus dutifully falling into line behind their commander.

Passing between the modest, yet well-tended, back gardens, which hung heavy with the scent of herbs, they soon reached another street of hardpacked, rutted earth. The cobblestones began scarcely a few feet away, and continued uphill in the direction of the vast gateway of grey stone that stood between the Asylum and the Ox Guts beyond, looming beneath the sullen sky.

The source of the "disturbance" met his eyes as soon as they had exited the lane. Tagus's head abruptly ceased to throb as his brow creased in a heavy frown.

The high archway's iron portcullis had been raised and one could see through to the gallows, with its dangling rusted gibbets creaking in the wind, sitting ominously at the crossroads of Silo Street. But it was not only the menacing bill-armed city guardsmen, charged with sealing off the Asylum during the "heretical" Fire Day festivities, who stood in the gateway. Clad in the blue and gold livery of Prince Chero, the sentries had clearly made an exception to the general quarantine imposed on the Old Believers on those days when their celebrations might "corrupt" or "mislead" the more upstanding inhabitants of the Vinosian capital. The white robes stood out like the funeral shrouds of the church-goers. And Tagus thought that it was fitting that the raiment of these deluded priests should resemble the vestments of the dead that they chose to bury rather than purify.

The unholy prayers met his ears almost at once. There were at least a dozen churchmen in the gateway, all of them crying out praise to their false god while proclaiming damnation and death upon the "disbelievers" within the walls. But between their furiously waving arms and the celebrating heretics that they sought to condemn in the name of the Great Betrayer, whom they worshipped as their one and only god, a thin black line had formed in the street.

Tagus fell in line beside Tarquinus, his fellow Falhorne in black, who stood shoulder to shoulder with the brothers Remus and Valens of the Asylum's Watch. The only difference between the twins was the missing left eye, now covered by a leather patch, that the latter had lost during the Braxian Civil War. Valens in turn stood by stood by Skarlos – the great Samosian gripping the haft of his great double-axe as he held the mighty weapon horizontally at hip-level. All three watchmen wore leather jerkins. The five of them stood with swords at their hips, facing the gaggle of priests with uniformly grim expressions as their Praetor Vitus strode forward.

"There! The black demon himself dares to show his face!"

A gilded staff was thrust accusingly at Vitus as he stopped at the center of the street, standing before the would-be invaders of the Asylum. His expression was stern as he locked gaze with the short thick-set priest of Solar Dominatus who stood at the head of the others, still crying down divine vengeance.

"How dare you bar the path of His divinely appointed servants! Cease your unholy transgressions blasphemer and kneel in the name of the Most High!"

Unlike the others, this churchman had his hood down and his shaven head was fringed with red flaming hair, his fat face contorted in righteous indignation at the armed heretics before him. His ornate staff was still pointed accusingly at Vitus, while his other arm was raised toward the band of Falhorne as if he were trying to ward off some impending landslide with his bare hands.

"The Divine Word commands! Cease your unholy revelry infidels and hide your unclean faces from the light of the Almighty Sun! Fall to your knees in repentance and extinguish your evil fires! For His Holiness illuminates the shadows and filth in your souls!"

The golden-trimmed robe and gold and azurite talisman dangling from his neck revealed the clergyman's rank, and Tagus's heart leapt into his throat. He knew the man. He had only seen him a few times before, but his features were unmistakable. The man's face was proud, as befitted someone of power; who carried the authority of the Hierophant in Hipireus and spoke with the divine right of his god. Such men were dangerous. Every Old Believer, from child to elder, knew that. Whether the danger came from summoned mobs of zealots, baying for heretic blood, or from disciplined soldiers and retainers driven by duty and the promise of plunder, the outcome was the same. The lords of the Church were to be feared. The man who stood beneath the gateway with his entourage was Bishop Theophilus, the highest-ranking clergyman in all of Vinos.

But Vitus appeared completely unmoved by this. His ice-blue eyes were calm, even as his chin jutted proudly forward. He remained silent in the face of the tirade directed at him. Indeed, his arms were crossed over his black leather breastplate, as though he were a patient father looking over a child throwing a tantrum. Then Tagus saw the praetor's eyes move away from the thundering priest, to where a short, wizened figure could be seen standing among the guards.

"Many Fire Day greetings to you, my honorable Bailiff."

When Vitus called out to the man, it easily sounded over the bishop's stream of invective. The same voice that had cut through the clamor of the battlefield so many times.

"The honor is mine, good Praetor."

The man's high nasal voice too sounded over the bishop's as he stepped forward. His pale face was lean and eagle-beaked, with sharp hazel eyes. He was dressed in a finely tailored azure blue robe surmounted by an equally expensive-looking jerkin of black leather, studded in bronze and emblazoned with the golden lion of Prince Chero. A gaudy broad-brimmed leather hat shadowed his face slightly, but did not hide the severity of his eyes. Those eyes told Tagus all he needed to know about the identity of the newcomer. It was Commodus Resti, an altogether infamous enforcer of royal law. He could not have been more than five feet tall, but the eight muscle-bound city guardsmen surrounding him, saw-toothed bills in hand, more than compensated for his lack of stature.

"I trust that you and your men come among us with good intentions on this lawfully recognized holy day," Vitus said, still ignoring the bishop, who had by now ceased his tirade and was gazing at praetor and bailiff with daggers in his brown eyes.

Bailiff Resti, in his turn, gave a half-smile and held out his hands to his sides.

"I merely uphold the Prince's Peace. I trust that you remain familiar with the particular measures that must be taken this day to ensure public safety."

"The public safety of all would be better upheld if the word and spirit of the Treaty of Trastamere were respected in full and without fail. Provision thirteen stipulates clearly that the agents of the Church are not to enter the sovereign territory of those who remain faithful to the Old Gods. I trust that you remain familiar with your obligations to enforce this provision under the fundamental law of Vinos. For it permits no exceptions."

The half-smile on the bailiff's face instantly vanished at these calmly spoken words.

"I do as my royal sovereign commands, Falhorne. Do not tell me my business."

With that, he produced a parchment roll from a satchel in his fine leather belt, the royal seal clearly displayed in red wax.

"His Majesty is concerned about reports of Old Believer violence. The Grand Prince saw fit to provide His Holiness with official protection, duly requested of course, on this day of heathen celebration. As you know, his word carries the force of law."

"There has been no violence, Resti. None but the violence that these charges of yours see fit to bring to our doorstep. The word of the sovereign does not override the provisions of the Treaty, duly guaranteed to my people in perpetuity so long as any man draws breath in this realm. By allowing these churchmen to enter the Asylum, you and your men stand in violation of the law you claim to uphold. As stipulated in provision five, this grants the Falhorne, as appointed protectors of the Old Believers in this land, the lawful right of armed self-defence. Do you deny us this right?"

As if on cue, every Falhorne and watchman in the line set his hand to his sword. Two of the guardsmen nervously edged backwards as Skarlos raised his axe into full iron door, the ready position for attack.

The bishop's round face was flushed red.

"Treason! The blasphemer defies the rule of Prince Chero himself!"

He immediately rounded on the bailiff.

"Why are you standing there? I uphold my right under Church Law to preach the Divine Word to these heathens on this occasion of blasphemy. By royal decree it is your duty to enforce the Holy Canon in full! Now remove these disbelievers from my sight and allow us to proceed!"

But Resti did not move. His wry smile had returned.

"I would not have a confrontation on this fine morning, Praetor. None of us wants that. Least of all you. Law and order must always be our primary concern. Your Holiness…"

He turned his prominent, curving nose toward the raging Theophilus.

"I believe that you had made your presence felt and satisfied your divine commission for the time being. With your blessing, me and my men shall take our leave."

At this, the bishop resembled a keg of powder about to explode from a slow burning fuse. But no words left his furiously frowning lips as he abruptly cracked the butt of his staff against the ground and turned away, casting one last hateful glance at Vitus. The hooded priests, confused and startled expressions on their shadowed faces, quickly followed their leader as he silently stalked away down Silo Street in the direction of the Temple District.

"I must return to the palace now," the bailiff said in a calm, business-like tone. "I suggest that you take your concerns to the royal court when you are able. Naturally some of my men shall remain to seal this gate as His Majesty's regulations demand. Obey the laws of this land and you shall have nothing to fear from me. Good day."

He did not wait for a reply. Snapping his fingers, Resti turned, with six mighty guardsmen following in the small man's wake as he marched in the direction of the gallows. Another six remained, polearms in hand, barring the way between the Asylum and the world outside.

The praetor stood for a moment, watching them go, before returning his gaze to the stalwart line of defenders; their hands still firmly placed on the hilts of their swords and awaiting further orders from their commander.

"That is all, comrades and brothers. You may return to the festivities."

Tagus could not help but notice the weariness that filled his mentor's eyes.

The festivities went on into the evening, the flames of the bonfire leaping high into the darkening sky. The grey clouds had cleared and the sagging steeple of the port authority building cut the sun in two as it sank low over the distant rooftops of the Mill District beyond the river. News of Theophilus's retreat had caused the gathering to erupt into wild cheers that echoed across the Tio's waters.

By then the ceremonies and ritual blessings were complete, but the people of the Asylum continued to dance about the flames, some of the faithful clasped in each other's arms as they moved to the joyous rhythm of the drums and pipes. Tables, laden with cooked meats and steaming pots of rich herb-laced stew, lined the street leading to the bonfire as normally hungry bellies celebrated with the feast laid out before them.

Tagus stood among them, the fat from a cut of roasted pig dripping painfully down his clean-shaven face and working its way into its many scars of war. He ate his fill regardless, striving to forget the earlier troubles of the day.

He was about to leave the table, when a pair of strong arms suddenly grabbed him from behind and a shrill girlish voice shouted in his ear.

"Oh, come on you big black bear, you should be dancing!"

At this, the badly startled Tagus did something strange. He smiled, a wide grin that made the scar tissue on his face strain and bend outwards like a garment about to burst apart at the seams. He turned to see Mia's beaming young face and happy dark eyes looking at him from beneath that familiar mop of messy black hair.

"So handsome…"

"You are such a silly girl," Tagus chuckled, putting his arms gently around her notably wide shoulders.

Mia might have had the face of a teenaged girl, but she had the body of a stevedore and her embrace was enough to make his ribs strain.

"Just trying to keep you in shape, old man!" She giggled, pulling her arms away before clapping him on the shoulder, like she was an old soldier friend greeting him in the middle of an army camp.

"Will you dance with me?"

Tagus hesitated at the question. He had known Mia ever since she was a child, had seen her run through the narrow lanes, playing with the other kids, happy and covered in mud. As a Falhorne, he had kept his distance from the people of the Asylum, dwelling apart from them. Yet even as an eleven-year-old girl, Mia had insisted on following him whenever Vitus had sent him with messages for the Agoge, conversing with him in her lighthearted way whenever he was sent to reinforce the Watch at the Asylum gates. She had grown so strong, becoming the breadwinner of her family with the decline of her ailing father. Even now, her spirit was contagious.

Still, for a moment he worried about what Corrie might think of his cavorting with a girl not yet twenty years of age, but Mia's happy smile dissolved his inhibitions faster than ice under a summer sun. His wife would not mind. Although she might have if she had been able to get past the guards. Had she been able to join in the dancing herself, she would surely have driven away all interlopers like a jealous goddess as she spun her man to-and-fro, as she had done at their wedding three years ago. But today they simply could not be together, and, as they had long ago established, when apart their lives were their own.

"Just try not to break my leg this time."

"Oh please, you made it through Fallonier without a scratch and you've been stepping like Antillia in her garden for years with that old Allia wound! Come on, you geezer!"

He swore that the girl's grip on his hand was as strong as that of ten men. As they danced together, the heat of the flames sending sweat dripping down his skin beneath his robe, Tagus felt the day's troubles burn up in the music and in the bare feet that rose and fell upon the earth. He recognized the driving melody of the *Relentless Pursuer*, the light-footed motion of the *Shadow Fox*, and the defiant exuberance of the *Goddess Flower*. As the ancient songs of his people poured out, and as Mia's strong arms clasped and whirled in his own, all thought of his old injuries passed from his mind.

It was only when Mia had finally led him from the revelling throng and back toward the tables that he stumbled and, again, nearly sank to his knees.

"Tagus!"

Her powerful arms quickly seized him by the shoulders, dragging him over to a simple wooden stool that was hastily vacated by a startled looking man.

"I am fine…stop fussing…" Tagus gasped as she lowered him down onto the crude seat.

"Antillia's tits you are!" She sharply replied, her girlish features full of concern. "You could've stopped me at any time, silly man…"

She shook her head as Tagus starred at the ground, ashamed of his near fall.

"Oh, stop it! Look, I have so much to tell you."

Mia crouched beside the stool, looking up at him as she proceeded to pour out the recent details of her life, bubbling over with youthful spirit.

"Grandfather's been so busy of late. The council's appointed him and Clodius to talk to the merchants. He goes to the docks every day and tries to speak for us. But he keeps saying that those Tarnish fellows have nothing but gold in their ears and not a single ducat they'd ever part with without a fight. Gods know, my father wouldn't argue. Mother and the little ones can barely get by on the few coppers the bastards give him for a day hauling those cursed bales of satincane…damn them, he can barely leave his bed now…"

Mia was the grand-daughter of Nestor, one of the eldest members of the Agoge, and the niece of Secunda, another aging councillor of the Asylum. Her father, Baltus, was one of hundreds among the faithful to toil on the riverport's docks.

"But you'll never guess what that red-bearded fellow Corvus got for me! You know the Day of Blood's coming up, right? Well, the foreigners will still be in the marketplace while the church-goers go prayin' and one of them, this Avram mercer they call Mela, offered me two whole ducats for a day's work! I practically fell on my knees to thank the lucky goddess when I heard! That'll be two months of food, a salve for father's back…something for little Jano's cough…"

Tagus did not want to interrupt the girl's happy outpouring, even as his heart sank with dread at her words.

Gaius Sanguinus, "The Day of Blood", would forever haunt the dreams and memories of those dubbed "Old Believers" under the law and common parlance of Vinos and the Thousand Cities. It was on this day that the Betrayer had crowned himself emperor over what was then the Five Kingdoms between the River Noctus and the Red Cliffs. He had drowned the land in fire and blood, casting down the temples of the true gods in favor of his own. The city of Fiore had been razed by his armies, its population slaughtered, and the fire god's sanctum at Cera Infernus destroyed. Thus, had the Empire of Five Seals arisen, along with the Church and its Inquisition. Heralding the beginning of seven centuries of brutal persecution: *The Time of Devouring*, named by the faithful in homage to the Devourer of Souls that was Tylo, dread Lord of Gormani, the underworld.

For seven centuries the followers of Solar Dominatus, the "Most High" whose hateful message the Church would see spread throughout the four corners of the world, had celebrated the mass murder of their "heretic" foes as the Day of the Almighty Sun. Alongside the emperor's birthday, it had been the Empire's main holy day. But even the downfall of their beloved Empire, amid chaos and civil war, had not stopped them from celebrating it for one hundred years more. It was a dangerous time to be a follower of the Old Gods. Tagus knew that the hostility earlier displayed by Bishop Theophilus was child's play compared to what the Betrayer's followers were capable of.

"Mia, you must not take such a risk," he finally said. "What if something happens to you? You should stay here. Do not leave these walls while the white-robes are in the streets."

"I know," she said, her smile remaining although the merriment in her voice had gone. "But I've got mouths to feed and I need this job. I know the dangers, but Corvus promised that we'd be protected. I have to trust him."

Tagus shook his head, struggling in vain to keep his fears at bay. The Church and its zealots would be out in force on the day after tomorrow, but it was also one of the rare opportunities for an impoverished Old Believer to make money. With all followers of Solar Dominatus ceasing work that day, foreigners alone maintained their businesses. Many would be willing to hire heretics if they could not afford slaves. The Tarnish merchants at the riverport had long employed, and abused, the men of the Asylum, regarding Church law and holy days as mere obstacles in the way of profit. Mia would not be the only one trying her luck that day, offering prayers to Antillia for divine favor. He would have to trust her judgment.

"I'll be fine," she smiled at him, her eyes taking on a peculiar shine. "Come on, I'm sure you still have an appetite, black bear…"

As it turned out, he did.

Chapter 2: Blood and Fire

"Merciful Mother of All Things…"

Corrie had to cover her mouth to keep from saying more, as she knelt down beside the body in the low lantern-light. The sickly-sweet scent of death had not yet set in, and she smelled the blood that ran in tiny rivulets down the narrow lane. Strong enough to drown out the odor of garbage and filth. The mutilated corpse lay between two six story tenements that looked about ready to fall over on top of each other.

"D'you know her?"

The voice of the thickset hooded man bearing the dirty-paned lantern was dry as strong wine and lightly accented in Samosian. It seemed to join with the muggy pre-dawn air.

"Yes. It's as I feared."

Corrie went through the exercises once more, focusing her breathing and calming the blood in her veins as she looked down into Ella's lifeless eyes. They were flung open and staring in abject terror at the declining face of the half moon as it shone between the Ox Gut's diseased buildings of sagging wooden beams and dank, decaying thatch.

The second hooded man, tall and rail thin, rasped out a Braxian curse as he kept watch at the alley's mouth, long fingers gripping a square-headed iron mace. Common thugs, city-guardsmen or crazed fireweed addicts, the list of potential threats was long. Their tiny band in the shadows might have been smugglers, bearing crates of the drug to stash in a dealer's deep cellar or in the backroom of a safehouse. If they weren't footpads waiting for their next victim to stumble down the dark lane, before robbing them of their meager possessions and leaving them to the dogs. None of the locals would raise an eyebrow.

Corrie turned to the third member of the group, the one that had led her to the murder scene. He was by far the shortest of the bunch, and clearly a gnome, though his face was hidden behind a mask of black cloth. The high collared coat rendering his squat body almost shapeless. Even his eyes were lost in the shadow of a wide-brimmed hat.

Corrie had lived in the slums long enough to recognize members of "The Family". What had once been an underworld criminal syndicate was now all that was keeping the non-human population of Fiore alive. This gnome could have been the head of a merchant league before the laws had changed to bar him and his kind from respectable work.

"When did you find her?"

"Not an hour back, me lady."

It was the lanky Braxian man who replied to her question in his heavy rasping accent, briefly turning from his vigil and working his nearly toothless gums as he spoke.

"I waz at the Gate, helping some of the lads there pleading for back wages from their bossman so they could keep their place on the Boards…"

The man, nervous and on edge, glanced repeatedly over his shoulder into the narrow street as he related this information. Corrie understood his guttural slang well enough, as distinct as it was from plain Vinosian. The Ox Guts was a hodgepodge of foreigners, many of them refugees that had lost everything in the Braxian civil wars or the Samosian "troubles", it was inevitable that they would try to exercise some creative control over their oppressive new surroundings.

"The Gate" was their name for the city's main market beneath the guildhall, where hundreds of slum dwellers lined up each day in search of work. Some boss opening his door to you might mean the difference between eating and starving that night.

"The Boards" referred to the vermin infested flophouses where the migrant workers lived. Most were landless peasants, with wives and children back in their native villages. They had come to the city seeking any sort of employment that would keep them and their loved ones from starvation or the debtors' prison.

"I was headin' back to Pedlar's when I found the lass," the man went on. "Ran to get you and the boss right away. Wermut be bloody tonight."

He shook his head sadly, a look of resignation in his eyes.

"Wermut" was common slang for the Ox Guts as a whole, echoing the Braxian epic of the same name. In it, a valiant hero, chosen by the gods, fought to stave off the end of days. It was ironic, Corrie thought, given that the world had effectively ended for many of the northern refugees; whole families of them left at the mercy of unscrupulous slumlords who were not above renting out filthy cellar corners to the highest bidder.

The Vinosian and Samosian migrant workers, crammed together on wooden platforms in the dingy flophouses, had another name of the slums: "Gormani", the underworld.

"Ya say ya saw her before she left the whorehouse?" It was the hooded Samosian speaking.

The three men had approached her after she had finished seeing to Polla and her unwanted pregnancy at the Billy Goat. The brothel on Pedlar's Square where so many of her local clients eked out a living from the paltry wages of horny homesick laborers returning from "The Work", as they called the half-finished cathedral that cast its long shadow from the nearby Temple District. She had followed them in spite of her exhaustion, thanking the All Mother that Octa's baby would not have her "watering" until the day after tomorrow. Though the reason for the postponement was hardly anything to celebrate. Church holy days were never anything to celebrate in her line of work.

"I saw Ella leave the Goat at the ninth bell," she replied, struggling to keep her voice calm. "When the churchgoers started crowing down by the cathedral. I didn't get a good look at the man she was with, but I remember he was better dressed than most of the clientele. His jerkin looked well-tailored and had some kind of design on it. I wish I remembered more about the bastard."

The Samosian let out a long sigh in response and got to his feet, scuffed boots scraping in the dirt.

"That'll be the second corpse we've ad' in three days then. At least this one ya can sorta recognize."

Corrie looked down. Ella's long dark hair was now matted with blood. Her neck had been torn wide open, almost to the point of decapitation. Her lace-frilled black dress had been shredded down the front and her guts looked like they had been torn apart by wild dogs.

Corrie breathed slowly, in and out, remembering the calming exercises that Soyga had once taught her. This was the part she hated most. Dipping her hand in the cold thick liquid, she followed the trail of blood from where it flowed at Ella's feet. Keeping her finger in the now rapidly congealing mass of red, she drew it through the gory mess of entrails, up to where the woman's ribcage had been cracked open like an egg, ferociously torn open and exposed to the elements. Finally, her blood-streaked hand descended into the dark hollow where the young woman's heart once beat. It was gone. The shuttered lantern cast enough dim light for her to see the teeth marks in the mangled flesh of the chest cavity. It was indeed like the others.

She steadied herself, focusing her mind on the blood that ran through her fingers, on the residue of the life force that had once flowed through Ella's body, and on the Stream of Life which flowed through all things. She felt it. The backlash of emotion was so strong, so palpable that she nearly toppled over backwards.

It was terror. Raw like that of a trapped animal. Raw like the claws and teeth of a beast ripping into its chosen prey. And then there was only blood, a river of blood beneath the uncaring night sky above an uncaring city and its overlords. One more murdered whore.

Corrie cursed under her breath. There had been fifteen victims in the last month alone: migrants, beggars, refugees and prostitutes, all considered expendable by the powers that be. The guards would show up in the morning, cordon off the alley, and stand around all intimidating with their pikes and bill hooks before taking the body away to an unmarked grave without bothering to alert any next of kin. The bastards weren't paid enough to care.

"Did you get anything, sister?"

The masked gnome finally spoke, for the first time since their arrival, his voice muffled into a dull drone by his disguise.

"It's the same as before. Terror, pain and blood. All I can sense is the killer's hunger for these things; a hunger worse than a fireweed fiend. But the sight fails me. It's as if the monster wears the darkness itself for a cloak."

Corrie let her back slump against the warped boards of the wall behind her. She had not bothered to keep the frustration from her voice. Her increasing sense of hopelessness in the face of what the locals were now dubbing "The Monster". Every few days a new corpse turned up, torn to shreds by what could only be some sort of monstrous animal, and, so far, none of her training in the Craft had been able to offer any real insights into its nature. Like the others, she was still jumping at shadows.

"Blast it all…"

The masked man cursed as he fumbled inside his long coat, grey as storm cloud, that stretched down to his stout black boots. There was a sudden clink of glass. In a gloved hand he produced two small vials, before carefully kneeling down beside the corpse in an almost reverent posture.

"Another one for the Companions…"

Corrie sighed. Faceless and unknown, the so-called "Companions" were members of The Family who had developed a social conscience as of late. Doing more for the slumdwellers than smuggle drugs and pimp out slum girls to high-end brothels in the market district. Supposedly, they bankrolled the Association of Journeymen, which, like The Family, was illegal under royal law. Men and woman had faced the gallows on the mere suspicion of membership. But it was the only force that really seemed to give a damn about the lives of migrants, refugees, whores and beggars alike.

The gnome carefully dragged one vial through the spilled blood of Ella's chest cavity, before wordlessly stoppering it and securing it beneath his coat. With a small knife he then cut a piece of flesh from the same area, before placing it in the other vial and securing it as well.

Corrie stared at the grisly spectacle.

"I hope your Companions haven't gained a taste for such exotic foods," she said. "That cutlet looks a little too small for sharing and besides, there's barely enough to go around for us witches as it is. You know from the tales how we poach all the meaty ones anyway…only twiggish folk left around here. So, you'd best stick to tamer meals, lad."

A wry smile clung to Corrie's lips, before she burst out laughing at her own joke. She had deliberately made her voice high and squeaky, like that of an enthusiastic little girl. Hypnotized by the antics of one of the travelling circuses that occasionally passed through the slums to add some color and a momentary glimpse beyond the squalid rough and tumble of day to day existence. It was ridiculous, but a little humor went far to dull the pain. Here in this rat-infested alley, crouched over a mangled corpse of a girl who deserved so much more, it seemed the only appropriate response apart from uselessly bawling one's eyes out.

The gnome, to his credit, seemed to share that sentiment, along with the dark humor; chuckling even as his human counterparts exchanged bewildered glances.

"It's good to know you witchy women can laugh along with the rest of us burning our asses in Gormani's flames."

His chuckle quickly became a laugh, echoing along the alley and off the rotted beams of the dark tenements. His companions flinched nervously and glanced wildly about, as if every street tough in the district were about to bear down on them.

"God's tits, lady, we shorties have lived underground and underfoot so long that we've turned getting our backsides burned into an artform…a kind of entertainment, really. Glad to know some of you big'uns can appreciate the pain too."

Corrie's silly smile clung stubbornly to her face as she allowed her laughter to join that of the little gangster.

"Heh…biggest understatement I've heard in all my days, gnome," she responded, putting her hands on her hips.

"I've patched up enough folks that I can chuckle over a split skull, giggle over an addict in a death spasm, and manage a laugh after watching a baby die of the pox in its cradle. And now I'm laughing knowing that we'll have to abandon my friend here to an unmarked grave in a shit-stained hole by the Tio. I'll have to attend a whore's funeral on the morrow with no family, just a crying group of girls gathered at the back of the damn Billy Goat, paying their respects before the owner screams at em' to get their lazy hides back to work. But at least we poor stupid bleeding hearts can share a casual jest, right?"

"Heh, why do you think I joined the Association in the first place?" He grunted, wiping his eyes. "So I can patch up wounds inflicted by others and laugh about it. But that's old news to you."

It was a true enough statement. The Association of Journeymen had begun, as far as Corrie had been able to gather, as a loosely knit group of laborers who had stood up against Guildmaster Maxim de Tolley in an effort to retrieve unpaid wages. That had been three years ago, at the same time that her husband had returned from Braxus. The new group had been so successful in organizing laborers, quickly adding domestic servants in the market district to its ranks, that it had been forcibly disbanded by the city guard and two of its leaders hanged. Their bodies left to rot in the market square for months on end.

But the Association hadn't gone away. It had only swelled in size when the laws were changed to exclude women and non-humans from most forms of work. Three years later, almost all of its members were in the slums, but oppressive laws and naked force had not stopped them from making their presence felt through strikes and sabotage along the docks, in the marketplace, and at the cathedral.

The latter had gotten so bad that the Church authorities had reluctantly ordered the contractors to raise the pitifully low wages of the migrant workers as a "gesture of charity". On the riverport docks, called "Brokeback" by the workers that toiled there, they had just sacked the whole lot and brought in slaves and desperate Old Believers from the Asylum to fill the gap. But that hadn't stopped the agitators from making inroads among them too. In the Ox Guts, the Association ran soup kitchens for starving, tried to help the sick, and provided needed goods to the desperately poor – even if a lot of it doubtless consisted of leftovers from "The Family's" black-market operations. It was no surprise that they were the only ones who were truly interested in getting to the bottom of "the monster" murders.

"It would seem we're fond of pain."

Corrie continued to wear the mask, the smile that was her protective ward. But it was nothing to joke about. She remembered the worst cases: the stillbirths, the gaunt and haggard mothers weeping inconsolably over their little ones in some airless garret room; the children who succumbed to disease or infection before their fifth year, forcing their grieving parents to hide their faces and move on while their remaining kids played in courtyards and filthy rooms crawling with the same diseases that made new deaths and renewed heartbreak only a matter of time; the man beaten to a pulp and left for dead by a gang of street toughs willing to kill a humble laborer for his day's wages, plunging his family into a panic when they found out their breadwinner would never walk again; the raped women, battered and bruised, their pride laid open along with their bodies by their attackers, begging for her to terminate their unwanted pregnancies…just as Polla had. Corrie remembered the state of the young woman's throat. She had barely been able to speak such was the bruising. Lying there, disowned by her family and only given shelter by a boss who wanted to preserve her as a piece of marketable flesh.

And there had been more, so many more besides. Each of the men and women who came to the foul lanes of the Ox Guts had a story to tell; a place they came from, people they loved. And for too many it would end just as Ella's had, in a dingy back alley on alien soil, far from home. Only Corrie, healer and mid-wife to the wretched of the earth, remembered them.

It had been five years since the prince had quarantined the Ox Guts to stop the spread of the pox, leaving the slum dwellers to die in their hundreds. The Association did not yet exist, and it had been her and a rag-tag band other women with healing knowledge who had come to the aid of those whom authority had abandoned; even her former teacher had come out of her isolation in the Asylum to help set up the makeshift infirmaries. By their efforts, they had saved many lives, but had also lost many. Too many. Too many bodies, their remains lying together in what was now known as Ash Lane, where Soyga had burned them to save the others from infection.

Many of the fireweed fiends to whom she had subsequently granted mercy were men who had lost their families in that horrible epidemic and had sold their souls to the drug after drink had failed to drown their sorrows. Thus, they had made themselves into beasts, animals of frenzied lust, to avoid to pain of being a man. Once the addiction had passed its critical stage, there was nothing to do but give them release and lay on hands until their muscles stopped twitching and stillness came to their orange-tinted flesh along with their hearts. She always remained, bent over the body, when the quiet came.

No self-respecting physician of the respectable classes would stoop so low as to tend to the unclean and the discarded, and so it fell to her and those like her. "Witches", "wisewomen", "harlots", they had been called by so many names, only the All Mother knew how many. Fate had bound them to the lives of the downtrodden.

The gnome finally stuffed the knife and the vials into his oversized coat, its folds drooping in the fetid air, and stood up. As his companions continued to nervously grip the handles of their weapons, fearing attack at any moment, he turned to her and she could feel the broad, sincere smile beneath the mask.

"Jokes aside, the common laborer learns to laugh even after their closest friend has fallen from The Work and smashed every bone in his body. The Association is here so their children won't have to learn such lessons and can laugh a little easier."

He looked at her one more time, and she could make out his wide dark eyes in the shadow of the hat. They were hard eyes, but the emotion was there; sorrow and rage mixed together with single-minded determination. So much like her Tagus, she thought. She still had to ask him about how the Fire Day celebrations had gone.

"I think it's time we took our leave, sister. The guard will be here soon."

"Aye," she said, finally letting her wry smile slip into a hard frown, "You know where to find me. I want to know if you find anything more about her and who, or what did this."

They parted ways. The little band of Association men vanishing in the opposite direction into the shadows of the alley.

Corrie picked her way through the maze of darkened lanes back in the direction of Silo Street. Her former confidence was gone, and the sudden cry of a stray cat from the shadows caused her to jump, her heart racing. The shouting of drunks from an all-night gambling den, the shattering of earthen tankards and the sound of brawling fists meeting flesh, sounded to her like screams of pain and bodies being torn apart. A loud argument between a man and a woman, sounding through the thin walls of another slum dwelling with rotting support beams, punctuated suddenly by a slap and a yelp of pain, became the final desperate gasps of struggle before a horrible death.

Corrie froze at the sound of the distant cry, resounding faintly along the claustrophobic confines of the alleyway before being swallowed up by the night. Then there was only the insane cackling, somewhere down a narrow street, of fireweed addicts on a short-lived high…that would soon fade into the desperate moans as withdrawal set in. Nearby, a ragged beggar huddled against the wall of a squalid flophouse that they could not afford to enter. They did not move as she passed, following the moon, picking her way forward through the cruel shadows toward the hard embrace of her attic room and its one bed, where her sleeping husband awaited, unaware of her absence. Only when she saw the tumbled four-story rooming house that she shared with so many other poor and starving souls, did she feel the tears wet her cheeks.

****

The world was burning.

Clouds of ash and cinders choked the air of the black city and its dead streets. Everything was on fire. Hovels blazed like flaring torches, while tall tenement houses were transformed into towering infernos against the dark sky in which no stars shone. The moon, full and massive, shone a crimson red.

Far below, a lone shadowy figure flitted through the burning streets, stopping briefly at each house before passing on, trying in vain to staunch the flames consuming everything. But the figure was alone and could expect no help. For the world was cruel and unkind.

The figure stopped as the black mountain came into view, its titan bulk silhouetted in the moon's bloody light, as it loomed above the city. Something moved upon its summit. Twin orbs of yellow light pierced the gloom. It was like the furious eyes of a god starring down at a damned and wretched soul locked in the infernal pits of Gormani.

Suddenly the dark summit was ablaze with light – flaming yellow, orange, and red – swirling about the crowned black titan whose divine form blotted out the moon and whose shadow fell across the pyre of a city below.

The summit was Mount Barbarus, and there the Black King stood, crowned in flame as he appeared in the legends. His mighty weapon, a jet-black halberd, miles high, resting atop the mountain's pinnacle. His awesome gaze fell upon the tiny figure, its mortal insignificance nearly lost in the inferno below, like an ant caught in brush fire. There would be no mercy.

An inhuman roar split heaven and earth. Was it the end? Had it all been for nothing?

Tagus awoke, sitting bolt upright in bed and nearly hitting his head on the ceiling of the small garret room. His breath was coming out in harsh gasps in the stale air, the flames of his nightmare fading into the grey beams of morning sunlight that passed through the dirty panes of the single tiny window. The thunder in his ears dimmed, but did not vanish, and his muscles tensed as he thought he heard the sound of distant bells through the thin wooden walls.

Tagus let his head sink back onto the crude pillow of stuffed straw as his naked body was made conscious of the movements of the bed bugs beneath it; the tips of the straw bedding jabbing at his wet skin, feeling like pins and needles. Somewhere in the corner, a fly was buzzing annoyingly, while failing to drown out the bells that continued their maddened chiming in the depths of his mind. He had to squeeze his eyes shut, telling himself again and again that the Day of Blood had not yet come.

"Damn them."

It was only then that he became fully conscious of his wife's presence beside him in the small bed that was barely wide enough for the two of them. Cornelia's form stirred and Tagus felt her thin hand creep across the sweaty flesh of his broad chest. She held it there, feeling its labored rise and fall. Soon her face appeared from beneath the blankets and her gentle dark eyes met his.

"Cursing the world already today, darling?"

She smiled girlishly, draping both her arms around his shoulders and resting her head on his chest, letting her tangled hair fall around him. Her voice, soft yet at the same time strong and comforting, continued.

"Did you dream of the war again?"

He had not. Although the visions of war had troubled this old soldier for years, and she was so used to helping him face them. Tagus did not reply, putting his arms around Corrie and holding her, feeling her breathe, feeling the life of the one he loved. She did not speak further, but clasped him tighter and with more insistence.

At first, the nightmare vision of his dream, along with the press of her body, obscured the rhythmic knocking on the room's half-splintered wooden door. But his eyes shot open as he recognized the familiar pattern. Quickly, he slipped from his wife's arms and snatched up his clothes from where they lay on the floor.

Tagus had only just pulled on his rough linen shirt and woolen trousers when Corrie arose from the bed and again embraced him, her slender naked body gripping him with real strength as she pressed her lips to his. It felt like an eternity before their kiss ended, and his wife's dark eyes again drew level with his own. He suddenly felt shame at his hasty departure.

"It's Vitus again, isn't it?"

"Yes, he has summoned me. Hardly a surprise after yesterday. I must go."

"Duty calls you again," she sighed, her small breasts pressing firmly against his chest, "Then promise me that you'll give that greedy praetor my warmest regards for stealing away my husband."

"You know I cannot promise that," Tagus grinned.

"And you'd better not," Corrie's lips had again formed a girlish smile, "Otherwise I could never keep you. I hate liars."

They both laughed, Tagus playfully scuffing up Corrie's tangled black hair, as she swatted at him. The knocking had ceased outside and they forced themselves to smile as they dressed and prepared to face what they both knew would be a difficult day.

"Do you have any calls this morning?"

"Three. The watering of young Octa's child has been delayed, but I've got a pregnancy on Copper Row and one of the ladies down by Pedlar's Square was just violated by one of her more brutish customers and needs my help. It'll be a full day…but so was yesterday when I hear that you had to act a mother to all those young'uns in the Asylum. I'm happy just to be a midwife today, so you be keeping the white-robes at bay, you hear? Don't go aggravating any bishops, at least no more than you have to."

"Fallonier Fields should have been the end of them," Tagus sighed, shaking his head, yet still smiling at her attempted jest.

Corrie grinned, touching the scar on his left cheek.

"Just promise me you'll be brave, my roguishly handsome Falhorne. What do you expect the boss man will want from you this time?"

"The usual. More reports to write. More letters to go over. More missives to answer. The only difference is that he will probably want more men at the gate in case the white-robes return. I do not…"

His face fell and he felt her arms draw tighter around him as he pressed his forehead to her shoulder. He had not told her about Mia. She had barely asked him anything about the previous evening and he had only offered up the barest of details.

Tagus fought down the guilt and focused on his wife's hand, as it guided him into his simple black robe. Together, they walked down the tenement's rickety steps and out the sagging front door. Memories of ringing bells, burning cities and evil chants spun in his mind as he descended. His worn boots and heavy frame making every step groan in protest.

Corrie, the local midwife, would have to be braver than he this day. Although they had been together for almost three years, he still could hardly believe that he possessed the love of such a strong woman. Descending from her attic room, for all his fears, a part of him felt like the fabled prince descending from the tower of his forbidden lover…to whom the slums bowed as queen.

The messenger was long gone by the time they reached the street. Having pushed open the flimsy door and walked out into the weak sunlight, Tagus found that the demonic visions of his dream came back to him in all their horror. Even at this early hour, a drunken wretch lay sprawled in the doorway of the tenement opposite. But Tagus had to shake his head to clear it of the vision of a blackened cadaver roasting in the fires that had consumed his former home.

He clutched Corrie's hand tighter as his boots met the cobblestones. In the lead up to the Day of the Almighty Sun and its restrictions on everything from trade to tavern-going, Silo Street was already alive with people. Muddied by the constant tramp of bare feet, lacking the luxury of even the crudest foot wrappings.

As they set out in the direction of the Asylum, a dozen dialects sounded in his ears; passersby conversing in their native tongues from every corner of the Thousand Cities. Migrant laborers from war-torn Braxus, their work on the great cathedral soon to be suspended for the holy day, made their way from the tenements and flophouses toward the Temple District. Others, either unemployed or shirking, headed in the direction of Pedlar's Square with its taverns and brothels, where the little coin they had amassed might buy a moment's pleasure and diversion from their endless toil. Their fair features were joined by dark-haired refugees from equally war-torn Samos, likewise tramping toward a day's toil in the docks or warehouses.

The general reek of alcohol from their unwashed bodies was enough to reveal their general attitude to religion; more interested in drowning themselves in a bottle of cheap ale than going to church…which was for women and children anyway in the eyes of most of them. The native Ceremus tongue of Vinos and the coastal lands of Tarquin was intermingled with Samosian Arkanoi, Braxian Grimagen, and everything in between.

We wanderers that tramp the earth,
Hey ya, oh ho.
Scattered wheat chaff from our birth,
Ai ya, oh ho.

We the tillers of the land,
Hey ya, oh ho.
Till torn out by liege lord's hand,
Ai ya, oh ho.

Some sang as they walked. Crude and unvarnished peasant songs, sung in dialects from the Noctus Valley to the highlands of Karados, rang in the morning air. All of the tongues and variations of the Ceremus and Arkanoi languages, and more besides, were strung together in a messy cacophony of discordant sound in a city that was once the heart of the old empire. The ballads of displaced and rootless people, torn from the soil of their native villages to fester in Ox Gut tenements where daylight never entered.

Through the masses thronging the streets, the squat forms of outcast gnomes could be seen. A few of them still wearing the ragged finery that they had once worn as guilders and tradesmen, back when non-humans were still permitted to engage in such professions. Now they sat among the drunks in the alleyways, or among the mad-eyed and orange-skinned ranks of the fireweed addicts on street corners, begging for enough coins to get their next fix. Their pride and skills rapidly fading amid the grey of the slums.

Among the pale and olive-skinned complexions of the passing crowds, one could see dark shadows moving to-and-fro. They were Black Vinosians. Their status at the bottom of imperial society not rectified by the Empire's downfall. Most walked with their heads down, not wishing to draw the ire or enmity of their fellow dregs of lighter skin tone, to say nothing of the authorities. Tagus, with his proud bearing and black hooded robe, was the only one among them for whom the crowds parted, drawing looks of fear, no one desiring to obstruct the path of an armed heretic about whom dark legends swirled and childhood fairy tales offered dire warnings.

But Tagus paid them no mind, nor did his wife. Unlike the decrees that hung upon the great arched gate, or the gallows that hovered like menacing phantom above the stinking garbage that lined the road, peasant superstition could be ignored.

The gallows stood at the great bend in Silo Street where it took a hard-left turn and was swallowed by the Ox Guts slums. In plain view of the

Asylum's hovels, several decayed bodies dangled in their gibbets, the stagnant air not allowing for the ghastly whistling noise that usually came from their empty eye-sockets. Tagus, sweat dripping down his cheeks, turned his face away before one particular body could catch his eye. One horribly decayed corpse that he had no intention of looking at right now. The rank smell of the passing crowds was not so strong as to drown out rotting flesh.

Nor was the press of bodies so great as to obscure the many royal decrees posted on the Asylum gate. Leaves of rain-damaged parchment outlining the penalties for breaking the laws restricting the movement of Old Believers and threatening particularly severe penalties for the bearing of arms:

Heretics bearing weapons shall die upon them.

Tagus steadfastly kept staring dead ahead. Twelve royal guards stood below the great archway, six on one side and six on the other. A two-fold increase from the previous day and wielding savage-looking billhooks in the place of pikes. Resti had evidently decided not to relax the measures he had put in place in the name of "peace".

"You be careful today."

Tagus forced a smile as he listened to his wife's parting words. He felt her grip on his hand tighten and then gradually release. The brightness of her smile equalled only by the sadness in her eyes as she turned back toward the slums.

Holding his head as high as he could, Tagus passed between the two groups of guardsmen. The proud golden lions of the guard's surcoats combined with their sneering contemptuous faces.

"Coming to the gutter to ply your trade, whore?" One shouted after Corrie's rapidly retreating form.

"Come here and I'll give you something hot between your legs, pretty bird!"

"Ha! I've never grabbed me some heretic tits before!"

The abuse kept coming as he continued down the lane, accompanied by a storm of sniggering laughter. Sweat born of a barely containable rage dripped down Tagus's forehead and into his eyes as his jaw clenched.

Chapter 3 – Burning Thatch

"Gormani take them…"

Tagus clutched the sealed parchment roll tighter in his hand and quickened his pace.

Behind him, the market had emptied and the bells continued to ring out over the squalid tenements of the Ox Guts and the Asylum's dank hovels beyond as the city's churches and the pinnacles of the new cathedral joined their hateful noise with the belfry of the guildhall. The Day of Blood had come.

He could hear the distant drone of hymns as he walked, dodging past the few people who remained on Silo Street. The enemies of his people would be out in force today, and, as had been the case since the days of Ishan the Founder, it would be up to the Falhorne to ensure their protection.

"I will be back, my love," he had told Corrie that morning, caressing one of her pale cheeks. "We have faced this day so many times, it will be fine."

"Too many times," she had whispered back, "More than seven hundred times. And how many deaths and losses over seven hundred days across seven hundred years. I don't want it to be my husband this time."

She had kissed him again before pressing her face to his shoulder. Tagus had kissed her on the forehead, and gently slid his fingers down the skin of her back. They were almost the same height, the two of them, standing barefoot on the splintered floorboards of her attic room.

"And I do not want it to be my wife, either," he had whispered in her ear.

"Then promise me we'll live," she had said sharply, "That we'll hold each other in a sleep without nightmares."

It was a promise that she knew he could never make. He might have died already on Fire Day if the noble Sir Cosimo, who had mistaken him for a wayward slave, had had his way. But now there were more lethal

53

threats to be feared. Vitus had given him the message before departing to the royal court. It was an urgent warning. And, as the mid-morning sun climbed high over the tenement roofs and shot blades of light into the dingy alleyways between them, he saw that the warning had come too late. Far too late.

The gateway to the Asylum pierced what was once the external wall of Fiore city, before the ancient metropolis had expanded its sprawling bulk down the gentle slope toward the waters of the River Tio. It was crowded with white robes. The pungent scent of incense blocked the filth of the streets from his nostrils and he could identify the hateful words of the *Gloria Invicta Solaris* rising into the stagnant air. Even though he could not see him in the press of bodies, Tagus knew that Theophilus had returned. Just as Vitus had predicted.

He forced himself to keep moving forward, though fear was rising in his chest. Squinting against the glare, he picked out a dozen priests of Solar Dominatus, their identities given away by the gilded tassels on their belts and the sign of the four-pointed sun emblazoned on their muddy white robes. But this time they had not come alone. They were leading their congregation in prayer, which must have been at least two hundred strong, strung out along Silo Street in a vast procession of hooded figures, some of them bearing gilded standards and richly patterned banners bearing the sign of the Almighty Sun, sagging beneath a windless sky. Sol, the Sky Lord, was making his disfavor plainly known to the servants of the Betrayer.

Now Tagus could hear the shouting from beneath the gateway. It was the Day of the Almighty Sun, and Church processions were to be held throughout the city. But this particular procession of the Most High's faithful was attempting to enter the narrow lanes of the Asylum, from which they were permanently barred under the terms of the Treaty. They had been attempting such an incursion for the past three years. It was the ultimate insult to the rights of those who remained faithful to the Old Gods, for whom the Asylum was their sovereign domain under royal authority.

A lone black figure, Tagus elbowed his way through the press of churchmen and their followers. The tall robed figure of Brother

Tarquinus and his gaunt olive-hued face soon came into view beneath the arch, standing at the head of a rough wedge of armed watchmen. The bulky leathered form of Skarlos could be seen at his right, while the lithe twins, Remus and Valens, stood to his left in their rough jerkins. Even old Arbaces was there, though he had officially retired from the Watch last year. His wrinkled face grim as he fingered the hilt of his ancient sword, an aging and tarnished breastplate hanging awkwardly from his torso.

None of the five defenders had raised their weapons. Yet they remained on conspicuous display, especially in the case of Tarquinus, whose great sword ran down his back, its tip almost touching the cobblestones. Skarlos held his mighty axe in full iron door, as he had on Fire Day.

Tagus noticed that the presence of the city guard had decreased significantly. Only two guardsmen, bearing long pikes rather than billhooks, and clad in the same golden lion livery of Prince Chero, stood impassively between the shouting Tarquinus and the irate priest that was facing him. Tagus had to force his way past three more of the white-garbed supplicants before he was able to stand beside his brethren and truly see what they were up against.

Almost immediately, he noticed two things: The bishop and the men-at-arms. Theophilus, as predicted, was standing at the fore, his staff of office taller than the man himself. Although this time he was letting his lackeys do the ranting.

But that was not what made Tagus's heart sink and every sinew of his body tense.

Amidst the throng of white-robes, the bright light easily caught the glint of steel. There were at least half-a-dozen men behind the bishop with armor under their vestments. A glance at the gilded sun talismans about their necks left no doubt as to their identities. They were Templars of the Host, the same knights of the Church that the Falhorne had fought ten years ago at Fallonier Fields. Now they were at the very gates of the Asylum and threatening its people. Far from the loud-mouthed priests and unarmed throngs of past years, this was an invasion.

Tagus glanced behind him, to where the road narrowed into a muddy unpaved lane between whitewashed wattle and daub walls, the cobblestones giving way to hardpacked dirt as they approached the banks of the Tio. Black rags drooped mournfully from doors and windows, hung there by the Asylum's inhabitants just as they had every year, marking the catastrophe of their ancestors. The air was silent, but heavy with the weight of fear. No people to be seen apart from the terror-filled eyes that sometimes peered furtively from the glassless windows over which crude drapes of dark wool or tarred leather had been thrown. The pressing mass of white-robes around the Silo Street Gate might as well have been the imperial legions that had massacred their forebears. Every child among the faithful knew the stories.

Run my child, run some more, when a soldier knocks upon the door.

"This land is the sovereign property of the Vinosian Old Believers. As guaranteed by His Majesty Grand Prince Chero and the Eternal Order of the Falhorne in accordance with the terms of the Treaty of Trastamere. You have no lawful right to be here, Priest!"

Tarquinus had to shout to be heard over the cleric's unholy tirade, but his simple statements of fact were doing nothing to calm the situation. He was not Vitus. The hoods of the formerly concealed Templars had slipped back, revealing the acorn-shaped steel helmets beneath. A dozen gauntleted hands grasped sword hilts as the Bishop of Vinos, brandishing his gilded staff, began to thunder.

"Silence your wicked tongue, blasphemer! The Divine Light of the Most High knows no boundaries and is confined by no earthly laws! You will not bar the passage of His chosen servants!"

Theophilus was now gesturing unsubtly to the armed men behind him as Tagus joined Tarquinus in the vanguard. He reached for the hilt of his own sword, only to utter a muffled curse as he felt the pain of arthritis shoot through his sword-arm, causing him to awkwardly switch to his left hand, gritting his teeth in the face of what was threatening to become a bloodbath. Six men against two hundred, Templars among them, was suicide. But if it was necessary to protect those faithful to the true gods, he would do it. He was Falhorne.

"Damn you, priests!" Frustrated and losing patience, Tarquinus spat these words in anger, letting his own hood slip back from his greasy black hair. "The Treaty of Trastamere mandates the Falhorne to protect our people, with arms if need be. You will go no further!"

As he reached for the hilt of his mighty sword, the two impassive guardsmen were visibly trembling, pike poles shaking in their hands. Poorly paid louts, they were caught in a situation that none of their scant training had prepared them for. Neither was prepared to risk life and limb to keep the two sides apart, as four Templars stepped forward alongside their leader, longswords half-drawn from their scabbards.

"Hold!"

The bellowed command cut through the tense air like a scythe. There was a commotion among the mass of Church-followers as numerous pike poles rose above the throng, advancing toward the point of confrontation. In a few short moments the crowd parted.

"Hold! In the name of Prince Chero!"

Commodus Resti was there. Lean as a wolf, his eagle-beaked nose turning as his sharp eyes surveyed the scene, like a conqueror looking over a newly sacked city. He was dressed in the same finely tailored azure blue robe that he worn two days before, but the black jerkin was now a steel breastplate, emblazoned with his master's golden lion. The gaudy broad-brimmed hat was gone too, and the severity of the bailiff's gaze was matched by a closely cropped head of steel grey hair. The blood had visibly drained from the faces of the two hapless guardsmen, as their diminutive commander, surrounded by no less than fifteen heavily armored soldiers, advanced with hands on hips.

Stepping forward with a truly pompous air of importance, the official took a roll of parchment from within his robes, bound with a gaudy red ribbon, and began to read in a harsh voice that rose to shrill levels of intensity, as if to emphasize the power behind his words. The wily fox and deal-maker of the past had become a lion and it was a lion's message that he brought.

"In accordance with His Majesty's *Decree Maximus* ordinance, concerning the regulation of private arms and irregular soldiers, I am charged with the gathering of all illicit weapons and militaria from this borough. So be it!"

Ignoring the half-drawn swords of the Templars, the mass of thick-set guardsmen immediately rushed toward the Falhorne and watchmen blocking the procession. What followed unfolded with mind-jarring speed.

Tarquinus was set upon by two of them; one restraining the thin man while the other wrested the greatsword from his back. Cursing furiously, Arbaces tried to intervene, but was immediately knocked to the ground, his dented breastplate clattering on the cobbles.

It took three men to pin Skarlos down. The tough former mercenary raised his battle-axe, only to have it caught by a billhook and wrenched from his grasp. The big watchman got in several blows from his fists before he was tackled to the ground and pinned there while his sword was stripped away.

The remainder came at Remus, Valens and Tagus. For all their experience, the twins were no heavy-weights, and were quickly overpowered.

Tagus grappled with the two guardsmen who had rushed at him, and managed to shove one bulky fellow to the ground, only to receive a punch in the face from one of the men who had just finished subduing Tarquinus.

He fell into the mud, his jaw stinging violently as the blue sky seemed to press down with its blinding light. By the time he rolled to his feet, his sword was no longer at his hip. He could only lean heavily against the stonework of the gate, clutching his injured face.

The defenders had been disarmed and unceremoniously thrown to the ground on either side of the gateway, with Resti's enforcers standing between them and the churchmen. The bailiff approached the bishop, who bore a smile of undisguised triumph on his fat face.

"My apologies, Your Grace. You may continue on your way. His Majesty extends his warmest greetings to you on this blessed day."

With that the hymns began again, and the procession passed by into the empty and silent streets of the Asylum. A column of guardsmen passed in their wake, but Resti and his men stayed where they were, to ensure that no one rose in pursuit. He kept them there, four guards being assigned to restrain Skarlos, who was struggling like an enraged bull as they punched him repeatedly in the gut.

Plumes of smoke began to rise over the hovel roofs in a snaking line that made its way toward the Riverport Gate on the opposite side of the Asylum. More guardsmen soon arrived, heavily armed with pikes and bills, until some twenty men were watching over the six disarmed men as the scent of burnt thatch began to fill the air.

"Are you mad, Bailiff?"

Tarquinus had at last risen to his feet after laying stunned for some minutes on the ground. His black robe dirty, a dark bruise spreading across his cheek.

"His Majesty shall hear of this!"

Resti stood unmoved, his features as cold and clinical as his response.

"Royal decree carries with it the letter and force of the law. You were found in violation and thus punished."

"No decree would allow His Majesty to strip weapons from those permitted to bear them under the Treaty! When was this decided? Why was the praetor not consulted?"

"Ignorance of the law is no excuse, Falhorne. Think yourself lucky. I could have had you arrested and thrown into the dungeons for disturbing the Royal Peace. But, in light of your generous cooperation, I shall be merciful."

The eagle-beaked official snapped his fingers, and every one of the assembled guardsmen snapped to attention and dutifully faced their leader. He made a quick gesture with his hand and the men fell into line behind him as he turned to go, throwing his former prisoners one last contemptuous parting shot.

"Now see to your fellow gutter rats!"

As if he had just received a direct command from his master, one of the guardsmen turned and spat a large wad of saliva directly at Tagus's feet. And they were gone, the procession of blue and gold uniforms winding its way up Silo Street.

"Wallow in your own filth, you bastards!"

Arbace's elderly voice, full of impotent rage, echoed uselessly down the empty street as he called after them. Some passersby turned to look at the six men, battered and as unsteady as drunks, before disinterestedly moving on. Skarlos remained collapsed in the mud where his captors had thrown him. He did not move.

"Do not waste your breath," Tagus gasped, looking up from his own mud-spattered boots. "It will do you no good. What the bailiff said is true. The praetor only learned of the decree this morning."

He held out the battered letter in his hand. At least the bailiff's men had not taken that.

"Stay here, watchmen, see to Skarlos. Come on, brother, we have to go after them."

Tarquinus, alarm filling his eyes, merely nodded whilst clutching his bruised cheek. This was the first time that the authorities had dared to do something like this. But Tagus was fixated on what the monsters might have done to the "heretics" of the Asylum in the absence of its guardians. His head throbbing, he stumbled down the lane toward the river.

The smoke from burning roofs continued to rise in thick columns, blanketing the thatched roofs of the quarter with spectral white haze, as though the procession's hateful robes had tainted the air with their passing. Tagus hobbled on through the choking smog, the old leg wound acting up amid the stress.

The smell of the fires was everywhere as the flames came into view through the gloom. Seven hovels had been set alight along "The Strand", the widest of the Asylum's lanes. The passing zealots had tried evidently tried to burn more, but the lack of wind had frustrated their attempts. The inhabitants, after cowering in their homes, had quickly formed bucket brigades and were drawing water from the river, the silence broken by shouted instructions and anguished cries.

Tagus and Tarquinus moved to join them, hauling the dirty brown waters of the Tio to douse the sputtering flames. Few of the hovel-dwellers turned to look at the black-robed newcomers and those that did wore masks of anger and sorrow.

The water hissed as it met the ruined thatch and wood, wheezing out more of that foul smelling smoke from the dying homes of grief-stricken families. Almost all of the folk gathered on the Strand were women and children, barefoot and dressed in ragged greys and browns, the color and vibrancy of Fire Day having vanished. The men had all gone to work before sun-up on the docks – taking advantage of the holy day and the opportunism of the foreign merchants.

Drenched with sweat and aching from his injuries, Tagus suddenly thought of Mia and her new job in the marketplace. Had the white robes gone there too? A powerless sense of dread set in.

Several members of the Agoge council could be seen among the swelling crowd, consoling those who had suffered damages in the now extinguished fires, and seeing to minor injuries and burns. Tagus saw the sooty face of Clodius emerge from the husk of a shack. The old and wrinkled Secunda trying to ease the shock and pain of a young mother. Old Nestor, Mia's grandfather, was moving energetically from one hovel to the next, inspecting the damage and yelling out commands.

Acts of vandalism, from broken down doors to smashed pots, became noticeable as the veil of smoke began to lift under the noon sky. Tagus thanked the gods that there were no bodies in the streets. A pompous show of force it might have been, a disgusting violation of the fundamental law of Vinos, but it had not become the massacre he had feared. The kind that had happened too many times over the course of the long and blood-stained history of his people and a Church that hated them as blasphemers in need of purification. It could have been so much worse.

The bishop's procession of hate and destruction was long gone by the time the fires were out. Tarquinus, still full of rage, had followed its trail all the way to the Riverport Gate, stopping only when threatened by the muskets of the Tarnish marines who guarded the way to the docks. Like Resti's men, these foreign mercenaries had let the white-robes pass unmolested.

"Bloody scoundrels," the lanky Falhorne had told Tagus upon his return, spitting into the mud, "They're holding the dockers at gunpoint down there. Stopped em' from going home when the flames went up."

Tagus looked at the ground and cursed himself for his own ignorance. For ten years he had dwelt nearby and yet the faces and names that he recognized in the streets were few. It had not seemed to matter amidst the revelry two days before, but now it felt like a gaping wound in his soul. Apart from the councillors and watchmen, only Mia's family stood out, her sickly infant brother sobbing loudly in his mother's arms.

Arbaces soon re-appeared. The aged ex-soldier, who had given a good account of himself in the contests on Fire Day, was stalking up and down the street between the charred hovels, as though he were on patrol, his old sword and breastplate now gone. He saw Tagus and stopped briefly, before dropping his gaze to the mud and turning away.

Tagus thought he heard the word "coward" escape the old man's lips.

It was Jesta, the headwoman of the council, who finally approached him with something other than stony silence and muffled curses. She was heavily veiled. He could not see the hardness in her eyes but felt them in her stern voice; the voice that had dominated the Agoge from the day of its founding.

Old Believer women only wore veils on three days of the year: the three primary holy days of the Empire – all of which inspired mourning. In contrast to the bright orange skirt that she had worn during the festivities of the Lord of Flames, the simple dress now enshrouding her lithe form was as dark as the rags fluttering in a low breeze from the hovels. He held out Vitus's letter to her; the futile warning that had arrived too late to save the homes of a dozen families.

"Falhorne," she said coldly, her words distorted beneath the veil's cloth mesh as she lowered her gaze from the battered parchment, "I trust that you tried to stop them."

On top of his war injury and stinging jaw, Tagus's limbs ached from the exertion of hauling water. He knew that he presented a less than impressive figure. Nor did he have an impressive reply to give.

"We tried," he said, not bothering to hide the bitterness and shame in his voice. "It was six men against hundreds. We tried to block their path.

But Bailiff Resti saw to it that we failed. I have never seen them violate the Treaty so blatantly before."

Jesta nodded in understanding. But he could tell that her eyes had lost none of their hardness.

"Does the praetor know?"

"He was due at court today, still trying to plead with the prince on behalf of Porus and his family. I doubt that he has been made aware of what…"

"Then you will send word to him," she cut him off, "at once."

With that, Jesta turned her back on him and walked away; a pillar of strength amid the chaos around her. She had no time for fools.

Tagus watched her stoop next to a weeping boy with a burned face, gently placing her hand on his damaged cheek as the child continued to cry, the rest of his face pressed into the grey folds of his mother's long skirt. She whispered something to the mother, their lips invisible in the darkness of their respective veils, before taking the child by the hand. She gently led him away, passing Remus who was trying to comfort a weeping woman whose home had been gutted by the fires and had lost almost all of her worldly possessions apart from her two daughters who stood by as though in a daze. She had wrenched off her veil and her reddened face was covered with tears.

Nestor and the other members of the Agoge continued to pass back and forth, ensuring the recovery was organized and coordinated. Just as they ensured the regular disposal of the Asylum's waste in a communal pit on the riverbank, they would guarantee that all those affected by the fires had beds that night and food in their bellies.

Jesta soon re-appeared, having retrieved some sort of powder from one of the huts. She was already applying it to the injured boy's wounds.

A sweating Tarquinus emerged from a hovel nearby, an armload of garments that had been partly reduced to ash clutched in his hands. He dumped them on top the heap that was slowly rising between the fire-damaged homes as the inhabitants and their neighbors searched through them, salvaging anything they could and discarding what they could not.

"Brother, come here…"

As he called Tarquinus to him, Tagus could not help but notice another slender veiled woman standing motionless in the street, the blackened remains of an idol of Syrus, the Blue Hawk and messenger of the Celestial Court, clutched in her hands. It looked as though it had become an incarnation of his more sombre brother, the Dark Bird, bearer of the slain. It was the kind of transformation he did not want to contemplate further.

"Yes, brother?"

Tarquinus's long face looked ashen, devoid of its usual good humor. His tattered black moustache drooped as mournfully as his surroundings.

"Councillor Jesta commands that we alert the praetor. Dispatch Remus and Valens together to the palace. Get them to take this."

Tagus pulled the red wax seal from the inner pocket of his jacket. It bore the Falhorne's ancient sigil: three spears thrust through the ashen crown of Ishan, the sign of his martyrdom at the hands of the Betrayer's servants scant weeks after the first Day of Blood. He only prayed that it would be enough to guarantee safe passage now that the highest authorities showed no respect for the Treaty.

"I'll see to it," Tarquinus nodded grimly as he took the seal from Tagus's outstretched hand.

"And make sure Skarlos gets the attention he needs," Tagus replied. "You will meet me at the Black Horseman afterwards. If this royal decree its to be believed, then we have work to do."

"And what of your wife, brother?"

Tarquinus was pointing to a slender woman with long black hair. She was barely in view behind a low rickety fence at the side of one of the hovels, kneeling and applying a poultice of herbs to a young girl's burned arm. She wore no veil. Tagus felt his pulse quicken.

"I shall go to her. Make haste now."

As Tagus crossed the lane, he felt the pain of his emotions rise and sting as badly as his injured leg and arthritic shoulder. Tears pricked his eyes as his mental defenses wavered and the full horror of what had happened swept over him like a wave of filthy river water, drenching him and clinging with its foul odor. What was he supposed to do now?

"Corrie…"

His voice was weak as he called to her. And tears rolled down his cheeks like a child as his wife's familiar brown eyes turned to him with a look of pained understanding.

After whispering in the young girl's ear, touching gentle fingers to the child's reddened face and guiding her thin right hand to hold the poultice in place, Corrie stood and came to meet him. The only fragrance he smelt when she embraced him, strong arms enveloping his shoulders, was that of sweat, effort, and caring. And, in that moment, it was all he needed.

"Be at peace, husband," she whispered with all the surety of a mighty soul that had seen far worse in her years spent healing the suffering. "There are many who need my help. I shall join you later at the inn."

The embrace ended, and Tagus felt the pain and confusion return as he reluctantly walked away.

****

"We should speak of other things," said Tarquinus. "Or we might just go mad and lose ourselves after a day like this."

Tagus grunted in agreement, taking another bitter swig of watery ale. They had already spoken enough of the dreadful situation.

"Baron Martino must be laughing in his grave."

He and Tarquinus sat together in what had once been the common room of the Black Horseman Inn, facing each other across a low trestle table; seated on benches with cups of Skarlos's sour millet beer between them. Their dingy surroundings were illuminated by the dim light of a single lantern that stood next to the beer keg atop the otherwise empty bar. The walls were of bare crumbling plaster, as devoid of decoration as the scuffed and worn-out floor beams below their feet. In their black robes, the two Falhorne might have been hermit monks huddled in a derelict monastery.

Remus and Valens had returned an hour ago, having managed to catch up with Vitus only after what had almost become a full-on brawl with the palace guards. Tagus had sent them to join Skarlos, who was now recovering under Corrie's care. If their story was to be believed, his mentor had only sighed in response to the news.

"The praetor insisted on returning alone to that dragon's lair," Remus had groaned. "He made some remark about knowing the nobility 'better than they know themselves'. For his sake and ours, I hope he does."

Vitus had been trying to visit with Prince Chero every day for the past week. With reports of assaults against the faithful and violations of treaty rights, the old man had set off to the palace time and again to protest to the royal court, alone, without delegation or bodyguard, taking the entire burden of negotiation upon himself. No doubt he saw the bishop's procession and its violation of the sanctity of the Asylum as just another point on a growing list. He only hoped that his aging mentor's health was not failing him through all this exertion, as his eyes wandered across the room's spartan interior.

The Black Horseman had become the unofficial barracks of the Falhorne of Fiore three years ago. Standing close by the Silo Street gate, its two-story slate-roofed bulk stood apart from the huddled surrounding mass of lanes and thatched hovels. Once it had been the only establishment of its kind within the boundaries of the Asylum. It had first begun to suffer when non-humans were barred from the trades, before closing down entirely when commercial enterprises were banned from the area by royal decree. The innkeeper had been a good-humored gnome by the name of Nicco, and the doors of his establishment had been closed to no one in the days when the Treaty was respected and when Old Believers had been free to work and trade without restriction, within the Asylum or without.

"Look after it, damn you," was all that the proud gnome could say, when he had handed Tagus the inn's great iron key on the day of its closure, his stubbled round face streaked with tears. Most said he had gone away to Tarn after that. He had not been seen since.

The Falhorne had taken up residence shortly after his departure. The only ale left in the place was a weak beer that Skarlos made based on a Samosian recipe he knew from his youth as a brewer's apprentice. It was the best he could do given that anything superior was beyond their means. The terms of the Treaty barred them from any and all commercial activities. The only money came in a trickle from the royal treasury and what the grasping royal officials would let slip through their purse strings was barely enough to keep the two of them fed and clothed year in and year out. But Tagus was almost ashamed that he had accepted any amount of money from the crown at all after the day's events.

"Well brother, how's your young charge doing?"

The tall man grinned, creasing the long conspicuous scar extending down his bruised left cheek as he looked down across the table at his stocky companion.

Tarquinus was the only other "Black Vinosian" among the faithful in Fiore, though his beige skin obscured his heritage. The native of the Tarquin west country had joined the Falhorne upon deserting a mercenary company. He had been tight-lipped out his origins, but Vitus had finally drawn it out of him that his parents were the children of freed slaves, and had lived little better than slaves as dockworkers in the great port city of Torio, where the waters of the Tio flowed into the Gulf of Remas. Still, the man's accent and mannerisms would have been at home on the plantations of Trastamere.

"Was I just seeing things, or did the little rascal land you a good one the other day?"

"That he did," Tagus responded, knocking back his beer to avoid savoring the wretched flavor. "And it was a good hit, no doubt he'll be boldly slaying dragons in no time and I shall be able to brag to the four corners of the old Empire that this wretched heretic gave birth to a hero."

Tagus forced a smile as he thought of Callus. The boy was a real spark, no doubt about it, dreaming big dreams far beyond what his lowly status could allow for: dreams of knightly virtue, heroic feats, great battles, and the monstrous creatures of legend.

He had certainly displayed as much when the Falhorne hosted the Fire Day contests in the yard of the Black Horseman. As much as he had been irritated at the headache he'd received, Tagus could not stay angry at the young scamp. Callus was a boy struggling to change his stars, which was something Tagus knew a thing or two about. For now, he was just content to teach him the rudiments of staff fighting, while entertaining him with stories he had heard from others. The tales that Tagus had first heard years ago from Orc fighters returned from the Red Marches left the boy spellbound.

"Heh, either that or the cocky bastard'll just leave you headless one day, brother."

The two men laughed together, wrinkles forming on their battered faces. They were not young anymore. Their rough features, further tarnished by the day's struggles, exposing them as men who possessed stories to tell. By remaining in Vinos's capital, they had been reduced to little more than beggars. Apart from their pitiful allowance from the royal treasury and what little savings they had left from their former days of mercenary work, they had nothing. The poor inhabitants of the Asylum could little afford to contribute to their sworn protectors between bread and taxes.

"Dragons," Tarquinus said, the creases of laughter yet to leave his scarred face, "if we could bring one of those critters down it might even shut Theophilus up for awhile. We haven't got the manpower to take on no wyrm these days though, even if we could stir one up from the legends. As it stands, we're lucky we can still afford the millet for Skarlos and his foul brew."

Tagus could only nod silently. All amusement leaving his dark face. Only five Falhorne had survived Fallonier Fields, and now the city held a mere three including himself. It made the twenty-strong force that had taken the field against the upstart Martino and his Church allies look like an army. Ten years ago, all of them had settled in Fiore's Asylum under the terms of the Treaty of Trastamere. Some, Tagus among them, had gone on to serve in the Royal Army. Some had also served in the ranks of other noble potentates across the region, particularly in the Braxian Civil Wars. As fighting men in the Thousand Cities – the divided, war-torn land that had emerged after the Empire's fall more than a century ago – this mercenary service had more than seen them through the first seven years after their bloody victory. That was before Prince Chero, the monarch for whom they had fought so bravely, had decided to ban servants of the Old Gods from such employment.

"We've been bleeding for too long. Losing too many brothers. Porus deserved better; he at least had the backbone to stay at his post when all the shit came down."

Porus.

The mention of that name made Tagus shudder in the darkened room. The passage three years ago of the initial laws restricting the freedom of Old Believers had led to the imprisonment of some Falhorne for violating them. Vitus had fought their cases successfully at first, employing the legal knowledge that came with being one of the original signatories of the Treaty with its guarantees of autonomy and respect. But the official harassment had continued and with Porus, their luck had finally run out.

"He was fully within his rights."

The grizzled veteran of Fallonier had intervened to stop of a member of the city guard from beating an Old Believer youth who had been found working illegally for a butcher in the Ox Guts, after the passage of the "Protection" laws heavily restricted where the inhabitants of the Asylum could work. The youth had been on his knees, bloodied and screaming, when Porus had intervened and wrestled the guardsman to the ground before taking the boy to safety.

"I remember Resti came for him the next day and charged him with outright treason for his lawful efforts to protect his own people…"

This time Vitus's legal arguments fell on deaf-ears and Porus had become the first Falhorne in Vinos to be hanged since the reign of Prince Cosimo had witnessed the Order's destruction in the infamous Great Betrayal. That had been three months ago, but the memory remained fresh. Even Porus's body, still dangling from the gallows beyond the Asylum gates, although horribly decayed, had not rotted as much as it should have.

In another time, it would have meant war. It would have been an affront that the Order and its grand masters would have never tolerated from any ruler, no matter how powerful. But, in their weakness, the Falhorne of Fiore had been able do nothing but ineffectually protest and demand the redress that they knew would never come.

"Porus had honor, unlike some."

After the prince's decree, not everyone had been willing to part with the potential riches of mercenary work and choose poverty in the name of duty. In spite of his commander's protestations there was nothing he could do to make Rigo stay when the veteran Falhorne refused to abandon his lucrative profession. He had migrated west to Tarquin, where the Inquisition was kept out by the domineering influence of Tarn and its merchants. Rumor had it that he had followed Nicco's example and migrated to Tarn itself, where the Church had no power and where established communities of Old Believers had existed for more than a thousand years. But Rigo was far from the worst.

"Do not mention the blasphemer's name," Tagus grunted irritably as he pushed his cup away.

Of the Falhorne that had remained in the prince's domain, most had abandoned their sworn obligations to defend the faithful. Most had joined forces with a turncoat who still dared to count himself among the defenders of the Old Gods, in spite of breaking nearly every sacred vow that a Falhorne could make. It was not without reason that Vitus blamed this man for their present predicament. Tagus, Tarquinus and Vitus were the only veterans of Fallonier to remain loyal, but that day's wickedness had made it painfully obvious how inadequate three men were in safeguarding a sacred agreement that many saw as being in its death throes.

"The apostate can be damned. Porus sure as hell ain't coming back, or Piso. And good luck getting the old man to initiate anyone new after all this time. I only wish we could afford some decent armor," Tarquinus spat on the floor and re-filled his cup from the squat stoneware pitcher.

Tagus hung his head as the afternoon sun began its descent outside the windows of dirt streaked glass, the only glass windows in the Asylum. Giving up military service had been painful. It had been his livelihood for the entirety of his time as a free man. He recalled the shame that had gripped him when he had been forced to sell his old suit of field plate five months ago to some lily-livered scrap dealer. So went the two battered iron greaves, replacements for the ones that he had frantically torn off and let drown in the swirling waters at the Allia Bridge during the campaign serving under Marshal Augustus Tilly in

Braxus. Most of the mercenary force had been wiped out on that savage day four years ago, with Tagus and his Falhorne brethren being among the few survivors…somehow the breastplate had survived with him.

Other stories had covered its polished surface. The breastplate had born a deep scar on its lower left side from where another lance had nearly torn through his stomach on the field of Pizana whilst in the service of Duke Piero Atocha in Tarquin. A similar deep scar had cut deep into the crown of the helmet where a battle-axe had nearly split his skull during Prince Chero's half-hearted campaign to root out the brigands and warlords preying on Vinos's southern frontier lands.

Indeed, that armor had displayed the complete map of his adult life, just as surely as it had been etched into his battle-scarred flesh. He had only parted with it at Vitus's express command: the faithful were facing new taxes and new tolls in equal measure, and the Falhorne were duty bound to support them. Even if it meant selling off their most prized possessions.

Perhaps it had been just as well. Before sitting down to their poor ale, he and Tarquinus had spent two hours hiding what little equipment they could still afford to keep, knowing that the bailiff would return. Their makeshift "armory" beside the bar, where his old armor had once hung, was now empty, apart from the dust. Stripped away to nothing, much like the Falhorne themselves.

"At this rate, we'll be relying on the Association for our defense. I hear they got some fancy contraband."

Tagus did not smile at Tarquinus's attempted jest.

"Accept weapons from the bastards getting the menfolk to sell their souls? Over my corpse. They are all criminals."

"Come on, brother. The number of slaves working docks is growing every day. The folk around here need to keep the wolf from the door, even if it means building temples to the Betrayer. The Agoge's got no money. And folk have to eat."

Tarquinus did not let his grin fade.

"That's why we should toast the Association's efforts to smuggle our people into the Church's heap of shit to taint their foundations and draw their wages! Better than joining some gang in the Ox Guts."

"Just drop the subject, brother. I do not want to hear it."

"Fine. Is Corrie still meeting you here?"

Little of the sour beer remained, but Tarquinus was relentless in his efforts to consume it.

"There are many who need help after what happened. I doubt she will make it."

Tagus thought about bringing up the dream he'd had the other night with his brother Falhorne, but decided against it. There were more important things and just thinking about that apocalyptic vision put him on edge. It had been all too real.

"I should be going."

Tagus waved away the offered pitcher and stood up.

"Just make sure Skarlos is fine and that the others get some rest when they return," he said, taking a step toward the door.

"Ha! You'd better tell the praetor the same thing!"

Tarquinus's face was red.

"And post someone on watch at the gate tonight. The white-robes should be too tired after their midnight festivities, but it would not surprise me if some fanatics decided to push their luck. Make sure that does not happen."

"I'll stand out there with my last sword drawn all night if I have to, brother. Chero's decrees can rot in Gormani. I mean what else do I have to live for, eh?"

Tagus was about to leave, when he remembered something. He returned to the table, silently cursing the alcohol clouding his senses.

Wordlessly, he lifted Tarquinus's rough hands and took them in his own.

"Blessings of the Black King be upon you, brother. See you in Barbarus."

"Ishan favor you, brother," he responded to Tagus's prayer, "See you in Barbarus."

The lanky Falhorne smiled widely, the blue and black bruise seeming to spread across half his face.

"Good diction there. The old man trained you well, you smart Resh bastard!"

Tarquinus was still laughing drunkenly as Tagus slammed the heavy front door of the inn and stepped out into the rapidly descending twilight that reeked of tar and burnt straw. Black Vinosian humor tended toward self-deprecation, the same went for every other downtrodden group of wretches in the Fiore slums, but he was hardly in the mood for such talk. "Resh" meant foreigner, outsider, and, even when it came from the tongue of a fellow outsider, it still stung.

The cobble-stoned part of the street, beginning just inside the gate before it slithered off into the mud of the Asylum's lanes, had once been a minor marketplace, where the enterprising among the faithful had peddled whatever wares they could gather at well-below market prices, drawing in a steady stream of poor slumdwellers from the Ox Guts. That had all changed when the merchants had complained. Few hovels remained close to the city wall, and they were all empty after new regulations had been put through a year ago, leaving the Black Horseman isolated below the battlements.

Tagus paused. It was a quiet night. The curve of the moon hung in a clear black sky over the old port authority building, its dilapidated frame hiding the endless noise and bustle of the docks. Above his head the wooden sign of the Black Horseman creaked in the soft breeze that blew in from the river and the tall houses of the Mill District beyond, where the rumble of the great water wheels could be heard. Upon the sign was the faded figure of a desert horseman of the southlands at full gallop, shielded from a blazing sun by a robe of white cloth and with skin like charcoal; as dark has his own.

Bells were still ringing in the distance, and, when he turned his gaze toward the gate, his eye caught the tail end of a candlelit procession of white figures disappearing down Silo Street in the direction of the Lucian Gate and the Temple District. Guards remained at their posts under circles of sickly yellow lamplight. For none but the Falhorne were permitted to leave the confines of the Asylum after dark.

Beyond the wall, the cathedral's skeletal half-finished bell tower loomed against the darkening sky above the sea of tenement roofs, the squalid dwellings of the workmen whose toil had made possible this grandiose icon of Church power. Not that any of that mattered to the ragged drunks stumbling along the road, shouting curses and making ribald jests as they enjoyed what little remained of their day off.

But neither the bells nor the drunks were loud enough to drown out the muffled prayers to the gods coming from behind the mud walls of a hovel across the street, where a crude wooden icon of the Blue Hawk loomed in a single window behind a tallow candle. A lone light of defiance in a place where the sound of boots on a nighttime street would trigger the nightmares of a long and bloody history. But they would endure, as the faithful always had.

"There you are, my darling."

The tired, yet happy, voice caused Tagus to spin about wildly while reaching frantically for the sword that was no longer at his side. There was Corrie, his wife, standing in the middle of the darkened street. Once more, Tagus wanted to weep. In the distance, the bells were still ringing.

Chapter 4 – Black Dog, Blunt Sword

Mercer Lane was an ox bow shaped thoroughfare arcing between Thresher Street and the Royal Way. Its entrance was not far from the towering edifice of the guildhall, the clocktower looming over Tagus's solitary form as he made the short trek from the intersection of Silo Street, its hateful tolling reminding him that this accursed day was not yet done. The soaring stone arches of Emperor Lucian's aqueduct loomed over his head as he passed beneath them. Built during the early days of the Empire, its snaking stone form, born high above the straight way of Thresher Street, carried pure water into the city from the hills to the east. While the poor of the city had to rely on brackish wells or even the filthy Tio for their water, the wealthy districts between the market and the palace reaped the pure bounty of distant springs, the great bridge of water cutting the city in two.

Vitus's home of seven years was identical to the proud stone townhouses of the merchants and high-class tradesmen which lined the short street on both sides. Its peaked roof and steep edges making it resemble a rectangular-shaped tower. A light was burning in the second story window, revealing the old man to still be at work in his study.

The praetor of Fiore's remaining Falhorne was truly a man apart. As "executor" of the Treaty of Trastamere, he alone among the Old Believers had been granted permission to establish a "household" beyond the confines of the Asylum. After their one-time patron Duke Atocha had seen fit to expel the Falhorne from Firente Castle and all his lands in Vinos, Vitus had been granted the well-appointed house by the city's main marketplace with the blessing of the guilds, which at the time still included followers of the gods among their number. The prince had at one time given the house city guard protection, but that had been withdrawn at the same time the Falhorne had been banned from military service.

After that, vandalism had become a real problem, with Tagus often being forced to act as a sentry against potential break ins, sitting up at night while his master slept. Security was normally tight in such an opulent neighborhood. With the lanterns spaced every ten feet, illuminating Mercer Lane in a dusky glow that showed the way for the ever-present green-coated men-at-arms, the merchant league's own hired muscle, who patrolled the marketplace and its environs. But that hadn't stopped the front gate from being torn from its hinges last year, nor the dumping of animal remains and offal in the yard two months ago.

Tagus sighed as he unlocked the gate that led to the narrow yard and its solitary apple tree. He would have preferred to stay with Corrie that night. But Remus had interrupted them with the praetor's summons, even as he had embraced his wife under the sign of the Black Horseman. There had been no time to talk or give vent to his churning emotions.

A single knock on the heavy nail-studded wooden door was followed almost immediately by the scrambling of young feet and the squeal of metal on metal as the bolts were drawn back. A bright ray of lamplight spilled out into the night, illuminating Callus's boyish features as the youth gazed up at Tagus with his characteristically wide and nervous brown eyes. The same mop of dark hair splayed outward in all directions and smelt of kitchen grease.

"Master Tagus, you're back! Praetor was gettin' worried…"

"Hello to you too, cub."

Dragging his tired feet, Tagus stepped into the narrow vestibule, shutting the door behind him. He had to shoo the boy away when Callus knelt to try to pull of his teacher's muddy boots.

"Son, I have told you many times, I can do that myself. Is the praetor in his study?"

"Yes…yes, he's waitin' sir. Do ya want food or drink?"

"No thank you."

The boy was as eager to please as he had been on the day when Tagus had first brought him in from the slums. Callus had been a beggar then, as a thin as a rail and jittery as anything, wild eyes scanning his bleak surroundings like a trapped animal. Even after nearly two years the boy was paranoid that Vitus would tire of him and throw him out. Reassurances to the contrary never seemed to count for much. Callus had no family and could not name his birth parents. Tagus had pressed him on it once, and he admitted that he had run away from an orphanage, but would say nothing else. Perhaps the boy would open up with time.

"Callus, lad, get some rest," he said groggily. "I will see you in the morning."

"Will we be training?"

The youth's eyes had taken on a pleading look.

"No, I doubt there will be time."

Tagus shook his head as the boy scampered away. Sometimes he rued the day when he had given in and begun to instruct Callus in the basics of swordsmanship. The eager lad had been flailing at everything from table legs to pots and pans for awhile before he had managed to bring him under some semblance of control. Still, as had been the case on Fire Day, there was something invigorating about the heart and soul the boy displayed in everything he did. It was the heart and soul Tagus wished he had right then as he cast off his boots and walked barefoot up the front hall stairs toward the study, the aged wooden boards creaking with every step.

Tagus knew better than to bother with the formality of knocking on the study's heavy oak door. He simply shoved it open and let it strike the wall before stepping into the small cramped room beyond. Vitus's time-scarred face smiled up at his old apprentice from behind a cluttered wooden desk.

The study was framed with great oak beams, the space between them taken up with walls of bare stone. A badly overflowing bookcase rested against one wall behind the desk. Beside it was a tiny iron-barred window through which the night breeze blew in. Outside the faint traces of the setting sun could be seen across a jumble of rooftops, gables, and spires that thrust skyward like the blades of a pike phalanx marching across the horizon. There was scarcely room for the simple cot that served as the aged praetor's bed. He still insisted on living like an encamped soldier, sleeping under the stars before battle. The large master bedroom down the hall sat empty.

Tagus closed the door behind him, gazing at his mentor through the jumping light of two candles that the old man had carefully kept clear of the jumble of papers before him. The twin flames cast flickering shadows on the walls, eerily dancing to music that was not playing.

"At last, the young lion comes forth from his den."

The weight of a lifetime of battle and hardship was settling over that stoical face as never before. Yet deep within those blue eyes a spark still burned, having leapt forth from truly ancient fires.

Those blue eyes, hard as ice or as soft as still water, the severe shaven head with its ritual scars burned into the flesh, and the wrinkles that resembled a weather-beaten cliff. He had seen that face through the flash of blades, whilst half-blinded by his own blood. He had seen it through the early morning mist of the training yard at Castle Firente, when the strain of exertion had driven him to collapse in the mud. He had seen it through murky water after the Allia Bridge gave way, drowning men and beasts alike in the swollen river. He had seen that face and clung to the outstretched hand that followed it until he could breathe again.

"Brother, did you respond to the Agoge's request?"

Tagus was the only Falhorne in Fiore, perhaps in all of Vinos, who dared to call Vitus "brother". All others referring to him by the august rank he had insisted on retaining even though the Order itself was no more and its hierarchy a distant memory. No doubt there were a few others, scattered between the Red Cliffs and the Noctus River, who remained true to the old ways, but their numbers could only be dwindling. Few Falhorne endured past their thirtieth year anymore, let alone the sixty-five years of his mentor's lifespan. Fewer still bore the mark of the Ash Crown, once burnt into the flesh of every initiate in the Order and which still wreathed his mentor's hairless skull in a dark circle. But their black robes were identical.

"That I did, young lion."

The wrinkles on the praetor's face were like twisting fissures in the candlelight.

"Watchman Valens brought me word of this outrage. I too have struggled to prevent bloodshed this day. Templar Varus, who insists on being the captain of the guard's shadow, would have thrown Valens and his brother into the dungeons had I not intervened. But yes, I dispatched my reply. I only received word of this *Decree Maximus* this afternoon, but apparently it has been posted all over the city…here, read the cursed thing."

He abruptly shoved a dirt streaked sheet of parchment across the desk.

"I taught you your letters for a reason."

Tagus lifted the document, which looked as though it had been recently torn from a wall, and did as he was told. The letters were large and bold, printed in fresh black ink.

Decree Maximus. By the royal command of His Majesty, the august Grand Prince of Vinos and Archduke of Skaros, Chero Invictas I of House Julianus-Agricola, all irregular armed groups within the Grand Principality and Duchy are to surrender their arms and militaria forthwith and without delay to the rightful royal authorities and upholders of the Royal Peace. His Majesty furthermore decrees that all citizens of Vinos lacking the Franchise are to be disarmed forthwith by the full authority of Crown and Church. From this day forth, any citizen bearing arms without royal sanction shall be stripped of them and face punishment as determined by the low courts, ecclesiastical courts, and high courts in accordance with social standing and the will of the arresting magistrate. Failure to immediately surrender unlawful arms shall constitute an act of treasonous rebellion against the Crown and all involved shall be punished in accordance with righteous laws, both earthly and divine, as outlaws and bandits. So be it.

The document bore the royal seal of a lion rampant in crimson wax.

Tagus looked up. His expression now as grave as his mentor's.

"There will be a council meeting on the morrow that I want you to attend, Tagus. I shall return to the palace and attempt to bring this flagrant abuse of the Treaty to the attention of His Majesty."

The idea of the Falhorne being forcibly disarmed at the same time as Templars were patrolling the palace walls made Tagus want to spit. But his bitterness was drowned out by a greater fear.

"Brother, you truly wish me to stand in your place before the Agoge?"

"Of course, young lion, who else would I send? I cannot be in two places at once."

In ten years, this had never once happened. Tagus had accompanied his mentor to the Asylum's governing council on many occasions, but he had never been asked to take the praetor's place before. Vitus was the Falhorne's diplomat and speaker. The thought of standing before the assembled councillors and being called to account for their complete failure to protect the Asylum that day was something that chilled his heart. Never before had such a responsibility fallen upon his shoulders alone. He thought about declining, of sending Tarquinus instead, but his pride stopped him; that stubborn soldier's pride that refused to show weakness or cowardice before his commander.

"Very well."

"Return to the Asylum first thing in the morning. Go to the Black Horseman, they will no doubt summon you from there. If Chero will not see me, I shall dispatch young Callus to the guildhall with an appropriate message for De Tolley. I sincerely doubt that the guildmaster wants religious turmoil obstructing his profits. Rest now, young lion. All will be well. The Black King protects."

Tagus felt the vision of the burning city fill his mind.

****

Walking down Silo Street in the direction of the Asylum, Tagus refused to meet the unfriendly stares of the guards and shopkeepers. Indignant that a Black Vinosian should walk the street armed. Even though he was fully aware of the prince's decree, he did not bother to hide the weapon at his hip as he passed through the morning crowds. Migrant workers, shabbily dressed and on their way to "The Gate" in hopes of securing a day's work in the marketplace, eyed him with a mixture of respect and suspicion. His wife's standing as a treasured midwife in the slums might have helped his cause in their eyes, but he remained a "Resh" and an outcast, marked as all Falhorne were by his tell-tale black robes.

He saw that the city guards had sealed off one of the many alleyways that threaded their way into the bowels of the slums. A ragged crowd had gathered there, most of them women in tattered shawls and ragged skirts. The air about them was alive with a pidgin dialect that blended

Vinosian, Braxian, and Samosian together in a confusing hodgepodge, more chaotic than a mercenary camp. The guards, ten of them that he could see, stood grim and commanding with their pikes, blocking access to the tiny lane and shielding whatever lay beyond from view.

Some of the women were pleading with the impassive guards in broken Vinosian Ceremus, their faces lined of pain and tears. Another murder. Tagus knew that he no longer needed to ask Corrie where she had been the night before. No doubt the authorities would bar access to the site and claim it was a simple case of death by stabbing, common enough in the violence-ridden slums of Fiore. His wife had told him little of the horrific wave of killings that were terrorizing the slums, but it was enough for Tagus to know better.

There were four pike-armed guards at the Asylum gate when he arrived. But all they could do was offer unfriendly glares as Tarquinus, re-armed and defiant, stepped from beneath the archway to greet him, four Asylum watchmen at his back. Skarlos was among them. Although the big man could only stumble along, hand clutched to his massive chest, his expression was as firm as any of the others.

"Resti showed up first thing this morning," Tarquinus said as soon as they had passed beyond the earshot of the guards. "He and his men tore the Horseman apart, top to bottom. Left it a shambles, just as we predicted."

"And?"

The lanky Black Vinosian grinned.

"The bastards never even came close."

Tagus smiled in return. He was rather proud of how the two of them had hid the Falhorne's remaining weapons and armor. And it seemed the stash was secure.

"Illiterate fools, indeed."

"Still gave us the usual horseshit," Valens grumbled, spitting out of the side of his mouth into the dirt of the lane. "The bailiff talked himself half to death about how he was 'just keeping the Prince's Peace' and all that. His men held us at sword point the whole time, just like yesterday."

"They should count themselves lucky," Skarlos's deep and jaded voice rumbled, "If this was proper battlefield and a proper war, I'd split their skulls for this."

They reached the former inn, and Tagus saw that the heavy front door had been brutally torn from its hinges. Glass covered the street where the barroom window had been smashed. The search had indeed been violent.

"Doesn't look like we'll be having any more of Skarlos's pig swill anytime soon," Tarquinus chuckled drily. "The brutes broke up the vats something fierce…how's that for an insult? Denying us our last beer! Unbelievable!"

None of them, amid their cynical laughter, noticed the little dark-haired girl arrive and none of them did notice until she was practically tugging at Tagus's sleeve.

"Falhorne Tagus?"

Tagus followed the hesitant high-pitched voice and looked down into nervous plaintive eyes. They were bright blue and almost as striking as Vitus's. The round olive-hued face betrayed her mixed blood. Perhaps she was ten or eleven years old. The girl was short and dressed in a simple brown linen dress. Her feet were bare and dirty.

Tagus forced himself to smile at her. She looked familiar, but he could not put a face to a name. Something about her reminded him of Mia when she was a child.

"I am he."

After a slight hesitation, as though the girl was trying to remember what she had been instructed to say, she continued.

"The Agoge requests your presence, Falhorne Tagus. I am Thea, please follow me."

Tarquinus and some of the others chuckled at the girl's strained attempt at formality, but Tagus did not join them.

"Of course, Thea. I will come at once."

He glanced back at his brethren before following the girl as she set off at a brisk pace. Tagus, the pain in his leg acting up again, found that he had to struggle to keep up as they turned the corner and proceeded along the narrow street toward the river.

The scene that unfolded around him was one of poverty and defiance. The roofs and walls of the hovels that had been partially burned down the day before had been patched with assortments of timber, thatch, and dried clay. Locals, all of them women and older children, were still carrying out repairs. Neighbors coming together to help one another.

Unlike the Ox Guts, in the Asylum there was neither chaos nor squalor amid the poverty. Unlike the flophouses of the migrant workers, or the shantytown spilling from the Lucian Gate into the surrounding countryside, the hovels were well kept and tidy. Their ramshackle appearance and constant repairs revealing the love and care of the inhabitants. There were no landlords here. The homes belonged to those who lived under their eaves, something else that had been guaranteed by the Treaty. Vitus had negotiated hard at the Castle of Trastamere so that his people would not be subjugated to rack rents or the debtors' prison.

Tagus could feel the pride of an independent people as he descended further into the shallow valley of the Tio; a people that had rebuilt and rebuilt again, devastation after devastation, but had always retained its self-respect. Even the small gardens and plots outside the hovels, where the people of the Asylum grew the majority of their food, were telltale signs of independence. The putrid stench of human waste, kept as night soil to fertilize the garden plots, was a small price to pay. Unlike the slums, full of displaced people, here everyone spoke the same language. The Asylum possessed the shared consciousness of a village.

This time however, Tagus did not feel welcome in this enduring community of the faithful. From the window of one hovel, its boards creaking in the light breeze that carried the stench of the Tio's stagnant waters, a dark faced woman stared at him. He could feel her anger. The anger of a soul caged, and a life held hostage. If she had a protector, it was her husband, her family, her neighbors, the Agoge, her humble garden plot, and her native wits…not him, and not the Falhorne.

In her daily trials and tribulations, fighting for enough bread or thin gruel to supplement her own meagre produce and keep her loved ones from starving, the fabled guardians of the Old Gods might have been a myth, cruelly spread to give false hope. And myths only protected those who could afford it. For all its resilience, this was still a place for unwanted and inconvenient souls. For all their proud endurance, its inhabitants knew what the outside world thought of them and how vulnerable they were.

The downward sloping road grew muddier. Idols of Syrus stared at them from the glassless windows of the hovels as they passed, some of them veiled by bundles of dried herbs. Symbols of the hope that the messenger of the gods would plead the inhabitant's case to the Eternal Judge who weighed all men's souls.

Children, their clothing torn and dirty, could be seen playing in the muddy streets, with one child racing off to conceal himself in a game of "Huntress", while others tried to elude each other in a game of "Runnings". Tagus knew the grim origin of these games – and why the children of Old Believers were so adept at running and hiding. He also saw youngsters gathered in small clusters and heard the haunting rhyme they sang. He had first heard it a year before, but now it was everywhere, and it chilled him because he knew its meaning:

Black dog, blunt sword, run, run, run!
Coward! Coward! Neath the sun, sun, sun!
You ran, ran, ran!
Stone around you! Stone around you!
Black dog! Black dog!
Turn to rust!
Turn to dust!

The children sang, and danced around one of their number wearing a black cap, dipped in tar. Tagus could hear their words in his sleep sometimes; reminding him how far his brethren had fallen. Mocked for their weakness. The men of the Watch, simple soldiers like Valens and Remus, would not understand just how much this stung the pride of a warrior of the gods. One who had stood on Fallonier Fields and fought his whole life for something – something he was now powerless to defend. Everyone knew it. He refused to look at them, but he knew that they were pointing and laughing at him amidst their games.

The old port authority building towered three stories above the surrounding hovels. It was not long before Tagus was walking in its long shadow, still trying to block out that awful children's song. It had been the centerpiece of the former riverport, its now rusty spire looking down over a great assemblage of warehouses and merchant wharfs, none of which remained standing ten years on. Its steep slate-grey roof thrust upward from the muddy shallows of the riverbank, perhaps in salute to the Lady of Waters herself, though Viro's power must have been miniscule indeed next to such an open-air sewer.

Fiore held the distinction of being the last navigable point on the River Tio that was accessible to sea-going vessels, making the city a major trading hub. But with the satincane boom and the growth of trade with the empire of Tarn, the prince had found that the city lacked the space to accommodate the larger merchant vessels sailing from Torio on the coast. It had not been out of charity that he had allowed the Old Believers to carve out the Asylum on the site of the old riverport, after it had been mostly demolished and a new and larger dockyard constructed to Tarnish specifications further upstream opposite the marketplace and guildhall. At the same time, the fortified island of Gladio had been strengthened and the new riverport completely shielded by its cannons.

Some merchants at the time had resented the ceding of the land to the Old Believers and there had been armed clashes between the Watch and some of the merchant guards before the prince's men had stepped in to uphold the Treaty. The port authority building, with its stone foundations and wooden superstructure was now the centerpiece of the Asylum and the seat of its Agoge council.

A regular stream of barges, galleys and other river traffic flowed past the aging building as Tagus hesitantly followed Thea up the flight of eroded stone steps that led from ground level to the first-floor entrance. He saw someone patiently waiting for him – her smile infectious, even amid the omnipresent grey of stone and sky.

"My man finally comes," Corrie said.

The weariness in her dark eyes did nothing to obscure the relief and happiness in her voice.

Tagus let his fears and worries drop away as he rushed to embrace his wife, holding her black cloaked figure close as they stood together on the threshold he feared to cross.

"They told you I would be coming?"

"I knew as soon as they said Vitus would be at court today. Octa's watering was delayed and the council has been chattering like a bunch of hens. About yesterday, I…"

"Do not apologize, love, you do not have to. I was the one who ran off when the old man called me. It was a bloody long day."

He ran a finger gently along one pale cheek, coming to touch the edge of that smile, but it had vanished.

"There was another murder. Did you not see the guards on the way here?"

"I did. Was it someone you knew?"

"Yes…"

"I am sorry."

They held each other in silence before Corrie finally let her arms fall away to her sides. Her face returning to a half-smile with some effort.

"Octa's girl is finally undergoing the watering now. I've done my part and now Jesta's doing hers. But I fear we do not have much time. The bailiff will be here again soon."

Tagus's expression became grim.

"When?"

"At the first bell," she replied, "word about town says that some new decree has come down from the palace, which cannot bode well for any of us."

"I know. Vitus showed it to me last night. They are tearing the Treaty to shreds."

"The Resti's not the only one. The collectors came around here first thing at sunup, demanding taxes that, by the Treaty, are not even owed. Jesta told me that she had to chase em' off. Don't expect any contributions to the poor box this week."

Tagus sighed and finally let his arms drop away from Corrie's narrow shoulders. He did not want to face them. He wanted to stay here with her. But if he had to enter, he wanted it to be by her side, just as it had been on the day they were married.

"We should go in."

Tagus's eye caught Thea's insistent gaze even before the word's had left Corrie's mouth. The girl stood expectantly in the doorway, her blue eyes firm beyond her years.

"Yes."

Cornelia merely nodded and drew open the rickety wooden door. Its flaking paint must have been fiery red at one time; a traditional Door of Flame invoking the blessings of Fiore, the Fire Lord.

By ancient custom, such doors marked the entrance to the council chamber of the Agoge – the gathering which oversaw the affairs of the Celestial Court's faithful in every community. But what would have been a Temple of the Sacred Fire in another time and age was now nothing more than a re-purposed warehouse that had seen better days. Fiore was a city named for the Lord of Flames himself, and had once been the seat of his greatest shrine, the fabled Cera Infernus, the ruins of which were now buried somewhere beneath the prince's palace, or so Vitus had told him. But whatever the squalor and primitive feel of the place, Fiore's flame still burned within.

Inside the door, in a narrow vestibule at the end of a dingy front hallway, Tagus could see the brazier, burning in homage to a defiant way of life that refused to die. He was sure to make the Sign of Sacred Flame over his chest and mouth as he passed the brazier's blazing coals that flared in the low-ceiled anteroom. He could hear muffled chanting from the council chamber.

He looked at Cornelia, remembering the last time they had passed through that final door together. Three years ago, it had been freshly painted, bright and welcoming. That day her dress had been just as red and neither of them had cared that it was but a simple second-hand garment of white linen, painstakingly dyed with the extract of blood root. She had looked beautiful in it. Her eyes had shone like black pearls, fire in her every step as she walked with him arm-in-arm. He, on the other hand, had been no more presentable then than he was now, the only real difference being that his black robe had been freshly laundered.

He fought to keep a straight face as the door opened. It had not been a fairy-tale, nothing like the legends of star-crossed lovers fulfilling some grand destiny by their union.

The two of them had fallen in love amidst the chaos of the Asylum's creation. At a time when the Watch had to fight off gangs of street toughs in the pay of slumlords irate about losing their properties to heretics, whether lawfully or not. They had met over the beaten body of a dockworker, fighting to keep him alive after the thugs had finished with him on a nameless backstreet.

Corrie was not among the faithful, and did not dwell in the Asylum. Back then she was simply a kind young healer who had stepped in when it mattered. Tagus had watched her pass through the gates time and again in the following months to deliver babies and see to the sick and injured unable to afford the services of a high-brow physician. She was five years younger than himself. He could not remember the first words he had said to her, nor when they had first made love, only the circumstances under which they met and the mutual respect it had spawned in their hearts.

It was still six years before he had agreed to marry her. Six years that had seen him away for extended periods, crisscrossing the Thousand Cities from Braxus to Tarquin as a soldier. All the while taking comfort in the arms of more than one of the desperately enterprising women who had followed the mercenary armies devastating the landscape. Likewise, he knew Corrie had been with other lovers in his absence. She had never hidden that from him. But that had not been the reason he had resisted marriage for so long.

He had been afraid. Afraid of undermining his oath to the Falhorne, and afraid of letting Vitus down most of all. He had known only one object of devotion, embracing another and keeping them balanced in his life seemed unthinkable. She had grown impatient with him, and it was only after a confrontation and a heated argument that he had finally given in, yet again out of fear: the fear of losing her. It seemed almost silly; now he could hardly imagine not being married to such a strong and beautiful woman. But at the time it had been the hardest thing he had ever done.

Many in Agoge had not liked it, one of the guardians of the faithful marrying an outsider. Vitus had his reservations. Even some of Corrie's own friends in the Ox Guts had questioned her wisdom in marrying a Black Vinosian "Resh". But with Jesta by their side, the two of them had found the strength to carry on. Tagus only hoped he could do so again. His wife could not protect him from his current responsibility, anymore than he could give her children: a "lion with a mule's cock", as his mercenary companions used to call him, and it was true. No bastard had ever emerged from this soldier's seed while on campaign.

Crossing the threshold, and in spite of Corrie's earlier warning, he was startled by the sudden shrill cry of the infant. Reminding him of a bawling baby in a burning village, whose name he did not know and whose location he could not even remember. He had to shake his head to clear it of the disturbing image, only going on when he felt the squeeze of his wife's hand against his palm. Looking to the source of the noise he saw a dark-haired young woman, in a common dress of patched grey cloth. In her arms she held the tiny form of a newborn child wrapped in a shawl.

The room Tagus had stepped into was a high-ceilinged square chamber that might have once served as the main office of the port authority. It was taller than it was wide, the ceiling rising to twin ridges like two tents placed side by side in a military camp. Skylights with cracked panes let in shafts of grey light. The air was heavy with the smoke of the braziers, another of which stood in the center of the room. The bare brick walls were blackened with accumulated soot. There was only one other exit, a narrow unpainted wooden door in the opposite wall.

The five figures that sat around the brazier at a low wooden table could not have appeared more different: a hook-nosed elderly lady dressed in a floor length skirt that, like the door, might have once been a shade of red but was now a burnt auburn; an equally old man in a long black coat and a worn rounded woolen cap that shadowed his grim unshaven features; a middle-aged man in black trousers and a badly stained white shirt of coarse cloth whose face was so heavy with worry that he might have appeared twice his age if not for his unkempt bright red beard; a man who might have actually been quite young, but whose grimy hairless face spoke of a life spent cleaning ash pits that made determining his age a difficult undertaking; and finally a younger woman in a faded blue dress whose dark hair cascaded over her shoulders in ragged tresses but whose eyes were as hard as black marble. She was standing before the young mother and slowly chanting words in the old tongue over the infant child.

Upon hearing the door open, her eyes shot in Tagus's direction, boring into him as he entered. In keeping with sacred traditions his mentor had long ago taught him to respect, he slowly dropped to one knee and bowed his head before the headwoman, who held a vial of a clear liquid in her left hand. Jesta did not stop her chanting, her gaze returning to the object of her ritual.

"*Invictas aquaticus Viro*. The Lady of Great Waters embraces you child."

She lowered the glass vial carefully until it was directly above the tiny hairless head of the infant and let several drops fall, landing in a perfect circle. The child kicked its legs, let out another shrill cry of protest, and then went silent, as if placated by some serene power.

Tagus continued kneeling as Thea rushed past him to the side of an adolescent girl, tall and skinny with dirty blond tresses, who stood like a steadfast soldier by her mother's side. Corrie had likewise left the kneeling Tagus and was now standing with Jesta over the infant, the councilwoman acknowledging her with a brief glance. The following words the two women said together, in perfect unison and with all the harmony of twin sisters.

"The Stream of Life flows within thee."

It was a blessing that Tagus did not recognize. But he did recognize the book that Jesta held in her outstretched right hand. Her voice possessed the same firm conviction as her eyes as she spoke the blessing of the gods. Tagus found himself holding his breath as the rough leather covering the ancient tome, held most sacred by the followers of the Celestial Court, was extended to the infant. This time she spoke alone.

"By the Lords of Sea and Fire, Heaven and Earth, the Hand of Damas the Lawgiver extends to you."

The Book of Damas, the very law of the gods, to which the Falhorne had once pledged their lives without exception during the glory days of the Order and Cera Pelleus. It was a tome of black leather bound in brass, the only written record of the old ways to survive the pyres of the Inquisition. It was the book compiled from a divine scroll that Damas the Lawgiver claimed to have received from the very talons of the Blue Hawk, and thus born of heaven.

The child's mother then spoke the words of the oath that Vitus had once made Tagus repeat until he had learned it by heart, before he had ever learned to read and write. The mother clearly could not do either, the roughness in her voice revealing a life of hardship spent in dark lanes and market stalls in search of whatever odd job could earn a copper for a day's meal of thin soup. Yet her soft voice spoke with the confidence and purpose of a spirit grasping at higher things.

"Lords of the Court, hear my voice and judge my heart, for I walk the paths of your design."

Her words were immediately followed by the chorused voices of Jesta and Corrie, once more in perfect harmony.

"The Stream of Life flows within thee."

The woman, Octavia, proceeded to reverently bow her head over the serene form of her infant daughter. She was the woman Corrie had most spoken of over the course of the previous week. Tagus was well aware of the kinship that his wife toward this young mother, now with a third child alongside her older daughters Thea and Anna, the latter whom she had bore when she was just fifteen years old. She would have died, so Corrie said, had Jesta not been by her side.

All three children had the same father. And this was the third such "watering" that he had not been present for: laboring on the "Brokeback" docks during the birth of his first child, and on "The Work" for the second and third. He was not among the faithful, being a refugee from Braxus and a former soldier in the civil wars. His marriage to Octa had caused a minor scandal in the Asylum, some being suspicious of this outsider's intentions with one of their womenfolk.

Looking at the faces of the councillors, he was not surprised to see Secunda, the hook-nosed old woman, wearing an obvious and disapproving frown as she watched the third offspring of this marriage undergo its first rite of passage. Vitus had told him that, prior to the Great Betrayal and the Order's fall, it had been commonplace for outsiders to marry into Old Believer communities, but that this had quickly died out after Prince Cosimo's efforts to destroy all traces of heresy in his lands. Now it was rare, and, hemmed in by Treaty violations and restrictive laws, the people were getting more suspicious of outsiders by the day.

Still kneeling, Tagus lowered his gaze to floor. Not out of respect but out of shame as a painful awareness stirred within him. The "watering" was a blessing that every child of the faithful received upon entering the world. The rite that invoked Viro, Lady of the Waters, who would embrace the child in life and bear away his purified body upon death. And it was a rite that he had never experienced.

"Rise Falhorne."

Startled, Tagus slowly rose to his feet, the raven-haired Jesta following his every move as he faced the council. The ritual was over, and all eyes had turned to him.

Octa, the young mother wore a smile of blissful tranquility as she passed him by, her infant sleeping peacefully in her arms as she gathered her children and bore them away into the hard streets beyond the Agoge's red door. And yet, when Tagus met her eyes for the briefest instant, he could see hope behind the struggle for life. A hope that he found hard to share.

For a second, Jesta paused behind the simple wooden chair that was the headwoman's seat. Her eyes went to Corrie, the two women locking gaze as though an unspoken conversation passed between them. His wife nodded, bowed her head slightly to the council, and turned away to follow the family, presumably to see them safely home, for her task here was done.

As she passed the rigidly standing form of her husband, a strong but gentle hand pressed down on Tagus's shoulder, and then she was gone. Tagus was alone facing the Agoge.

"I think we are done with ceremony," Jesta said brusquely, taking her seat at the table.

"There are important matters to discuss and, from what I have heard and seen, I am not about to go digging for miracles in Antillia's Garden…"

"You'll be digging graves if the Betrayer's servants have it their way…" Mia's grandfather, the black shrouded old man, interrupted in a voice as grim as his face.

"I cannot even remember the last time his lordship permitted us a pyre…telling us to bury our dead and thus pollute the good earth," he coughed violently before continuing his tirade, "denied the purification of sea and fire…obscene!"

He gestured violently with both his hands. A frantic pattern of criss-cross slashes through the air.

"Calm yourself Nestor," came a wheezy gravelly voice as the soot-covered man inclined his head. "Blasphemy may be distasteful but I'm sure the gods would prefer us to survive."

"The nightmare lords take your concerns Clodius. It's easy for you to say," Nestor grumbled.

"A man has his pride. A nation has its honor. The Devouring went on for centuries and yet we never lost our souls. Besides, odd-jobbers and scavengers like you wouldn't understand what being in a guild is like, or what it's like to lose one's craft because he does not forsake the gods! As if the art of stitching raw hides into armor was a monopoly of the Betrayer's faithful!"

"Well good councilman," the wheezy-voiced man called Clodius responded acidly, "I once again welcome you to the real world. Your bellyaching won't make the high and mighty leatherworkers take you back you know. Especially when you're too proud to do some honest work at the docks alongside the likes of me."

"Ha! As if I'd even get the opportunity now that you're all being replaced by slaves."

"That's enough, Councillor!"

Jesta, who had been tolerating the irritated banter between the two men, finally intervened. Her eyes raging with black fire as she turned on them.

"Both of you are out of order. This is neither the time nor the place. Control yourselves and do not interrupt me again."

Her voice was deadly serious and the two older men immediately fell silent. Tagus could see that both of them were afraid, their eyes like those of rabbits in the face of a she-wolf. There was relief in their faces when she finally turned away. And Tagus could not help but give an inward chuckle at the thought of Antillia, the Fortunate Lady Inspiration, bestowing her exhilarating boons upon such a dour congregation.

The headwoman was once again calm and businesslike as she focused her attention on the opposite end of the chamber.

"Gentlemen, you may enter!"

Tagus was startled by the command as its report bounced off the high walls and tented ceiling. His dark humor was quickly interrupted as the back door of the chamber creaked open and two men silently entered the room. In an instant, Tagus found himself frozen in shock, for he recognized both of them and had not expected to see either man alive again.

Chapter 5 – A Gathering of Heretics

Nicco was the first to enter. Nicco the gnome innkeeper. The same gnome Tagus had last seen on the day the Black Horseman closed its doors for the final time. His dark beard, once long and bristly, had been cut back to almost nothing, and his formerly colorful attire had been replaced by a long grey coat with a high collar, so long that it almost dusted the council chamber's floorboards. His broad face was wrinkled and creased, and his eyes appeared more deeply set and brooding. But there was still that tell-tale flicker of energy within their recesses as he crossed the floor to Tagus and firmly grasped the stunned Falhorne by the hand, shaking it warmly and letting a wide smile split his face. He said nothing, only removed his wide-brimmed hat to reveal an almost completely bald head as he turned to face the council.

The second man's appearance was far less welcome, and Tagus could not stop his lips from dropping into a sour frown as the tall man made his way forward behind Nicco. His was a face that Tagus had never wanted to see again. And when he spoke, the sing-song voice, the sincerity of the greeting, and its undeniable youthful energy stung like the back-end of a wasp.

"Very many greetings, brother."

The man wore a long black cloak, but it was open at the front, revealing the boiled leather armor beneath and twin wheel-lock pistols gaudily thrust through his belt, butt ends crossed over his torso. The cloak's hood had been thrown back, revealing the long and clean-shaven face, olive in complexion and oddly contrasted with the fringe of yellow-russett hair that crowned his head. His body was that of a soldier: lithe, but muscular. Bold green eyes stared down at Tagus, and it was nothing short of insulting that they were so welcoming and warm. His thin smiling lips did not return the frown, as he held up his left hand, where a familiar straight-sided rune was painted in black on his palm. The ancient Ormus sign for "oath-bound". Confirming that the man was Falhorne.

Callidus, the rogue of Trastamere, and Vitus's renegade apprentice, was still counted among his brethren. It had been ten years since Tagus had last laid eyes on him, when he had broken with Vitus over the Treaty and blasphemed against the old ways.

"Why are you here, apostate?"

Tagus's voice was snarling with surprise and hostility in equal measure. He momentarily forgot that he was standing before the Agoge.

"Falhorne!"

Jesta's sharp voice cut into him like a knife.

"Remember your place. We are not here to hurl insults."

Tagus bowed his head, tearing his eyes away from Callidus but not bothering to hide the scowl that consumed his face. Why by all the gods was he here? How did he even get here? What business did the Agoge of Fiore have inviting such a man? Someone who had turned his back on his own brothers in the name of alien ideals.

"Enough small-talk."

Jesta faced the three of them sternly, one of her hands placed firmly and authoritatively on the cover of the Book of Damas as she spoke.

"In the name of the gods and their benevolence, I have gathered you here because we are all in danger. Perhaps the greatest danger we have faced since the Skaros Schism. The multiple outrages that our community has suffered is recent days are not isolated incidents. And they demand unity if we are to overcome them. That is why I have gone to the trouble of inviting our brother from Trastamere to join us this day."

She gestured toward Callidus with her other hand, and the rogue Falhorne bowed his head in response.

"Along with our brother from the Association of Journeymen, whom Councillor Corvus has been good enough to summon."

Nicco flashed an odd hand signal that may have been a kind of salute, pulling back the thumb and index finger on his left hand and raising the other three digits beside his cheekbone. Corvus, the silent red-bearded councillor, returned the signal with an undisguised grin. Evidently their clandestine relationship was an open secret on the council.

"Praetor Vitus could not join us this day, in light of his pressing duties at the royal court. Brother Tagus has come in his stead."

Tagus bowed, as respectfully as he could amidst his anger and confusion. If Jesta's words were true, she must have dispatched an invitation to Callidus days before the outrages that had taken place on the Day of the Almighty Sun. That meant she had been planning this gathering for some time, trying to draw them together in the Agoge chamber. What would Vitus think of all this?

Both man and gnome stood silently beside him. But, while the formerly bickering men of the Agoge were now staring into space, the two women, young and old, did not break their iron-clad gaze on Tagus, and him alone. Jesta turned to the older woman and spoke.

"Councillor Secunda, you have a pressing matter to raise with Brother Tagus. I shall grant you the first word before we delve into more pressing matters. You make speak."

Secunda's hair was steel-grey, with the quality of a storm cloud. It more than matched the anger in those eyes that were as hawk-like as her beaked nose.

"I just pray that our protectors offer us more than words this time."

The old woman spoke gravely, her wrinkled face ghostly in the flickering firelight.

"The Betrayer's servants are coming for us again. My own niece was taken yesterday morning while helping the merchant Mela sell cloth in the market for a few coppers. For this crime she now lies in three separate pieces spitted on pikes in the marketplace."

Her gaze was cold as ice.

"And not a black robe to be seen in her defense. Why?"

****

Why?

The accursed question had revolved itself through his mind again and again. Vitus stood steadfast at his post; a lone black sentinel, isolated and reviled, but still standing tall and proud like the knight he had been trained to be. But even the most stubborn pride could not drive away the doubt that was slowly eating into his very bones as he stood in the midst of that long line of petitioners snaking toward the royal throne to plead their cases before their liege lord. It had come as a slap in the face, to be drawn to the palace in a state coach, only to be haughtily told by the lord chamberlain himself that he was to wait his turn with the others. His was not a petty appeal for clemency, nor cap-in-hand groveling for patronage, but a matter concerning the highest law of the land. And yet he was forced to play this stupid game again.

But Vitus did not allow his frustration to show. Ever since childhood he had known the importance of remaining in control and not giving one's enemies any opening through which to hurt or shame you.

His eyes followed the movements of the richly dressed merchants, well-to-do citizens, proud-faced aristocrats, and white-clad clergymen, who lined the hall and formed into their respective cliques; all vying for the royal ear, all looking for ways to cut down and subvert their rivals in the eyes of the prince. To show weakness before any of them was akin to prostrating oneself before a hungry lion.

He barely noticed the splendor anymore. The great throne room of the palace of Vinos, so much expanded by the grand princes since the days when it had been the seat of the imperial governor, resembled a giant amphitheatre cleft in two by a great axe stroke. The long straight aisle stretched two hundred feet from the great double doors. The latter sheathed in bronze and bearing a grand effigy of the first "Emperor of the Five Seals", Callus Invictas, King of Karados, and the first mortal ruler to earn the title of "Betrayer" in the eyes of those faithful to the true gods.

Vitus had to hide his disgust every time he passed through those doors, a tribute to the sacker of Cera Infernus, upon whose ruins the palace of Vinos had first arisen. Of course, the prince's murderous grandfather, Cosimo, another Betrayer, had lovingly restored the ancient doors after he had made his opportunistic pact with the Church, stabbing the Order in the back. His grandson had not had the taste to remove them, even at the height of the Skaros Schism when the Templars were marching on his own capital. The damned fool.

The line slowly moved forward. Vitus kept his eyes on the back of an absurdly foppish silk hat worn by the irritated looking young noble in front of him. The hall was lined with tiers of seating on both sides of the aisle. Here various cliques gathered and cast their predatory gaze down on the petitioners approaching the throne, keeping an eye on their chosen representatives, while sizing up the delegations of their rivals.

He was finally close enough to see the prince's face. Chero looked so small from this distance. The scion of House Julianus-Agricola, descendent of a major protagonist in the civil wars that had brought the Empire to its knees, sat on the mighty bronze, gold and amethyst-inlaid throne that his great-great-grandfather had stolen during the first sack of Hipireus. It had been taken as tribute from some eastern king beyond the Noctus centuries before it had caught the eye of Marcus Julianus-Agricola when he and his rebel legion were looting the imperial treasury. Its high back bore the words of the *Deus Veritas,* perhaps carved on this piece of war booty by the command of Emperor Lucius the Proud himself after his murderous campaigns of conquest that had stretched as far as the eastern mountains.

The prince's cleanshaven face was bored, his arms slumped over the throne's massive armrests. The golden diadem on his head only partially concealing his diminishing crop of reddish-blond hair as he looked down from the head-high dais as yet another ambitious noble begged him to give their son a place in the royal government; a place in the chancery for those with no legal training or a place in the Gendarmerie for those who could barely lift a sword and expected their blood and pedigree to do the lifting for them.

Then Chero stood abruptly. A hush fell over the courtroom as the cliques turned their gaze to the man whose every step, every word, every gesture, could spell victory of death for their schemes. But the Grand Prince of Vinos, resplendent in his robes of state, said nothing, merely descended the steps of the dais and was lost among the throng of guards and courtiers.

"The court is hereby adjourned," the artificially cadenced voice of the lord chamberlain echoed from the colonnades that held up the high ceiling, "Most High bless the Grand Prince!"

Vitus's heart almost stopped and he had to resist the urge to clutch at his chest. He surged forward with the press of courtiers, trying to push his way toward the throne, only to see the royal crown pass between another set of high bronze doors and vanish. Directly behind him stepped Bishop Theophilus, his mitred white robes appearing spectral through the crowd as he too disappeared into the inner sanctum of the royal apartments. Chero was gone.

Vitus fought through the tangled mass, wincing as someone elbowed him in the ribs, silently cursing his aged muscles that quickly began to ache, straining in a near melee. He reached the front, only to find the way blocked by a line of plate armored Gendarmes, forming a fence between the spurned courtiers and the chamberlain.

Protestations mixed with angry accusations tore through the air around him, almost drowning out the official's attempted reassurances. But Vitus was propelled by something more than petty grievances and entitlements.

"Chamberlain!"

His voice cut through the air with all the fury of one caught in the chaos of battle. Compared to that, the noise of this gaggle of disturbed and angered courtiers was nothing. Lawyers and nobles alike hushed their words and stared wide-eyed at the raging stubbled face of the black-clad old man in their midst. In their eyes, he could see some of the old fear, the old sense of uncertainty and dread of the unknown that the name Falhorne had once inspired, even in blue-blooded hearts. And he found comfort there.

"Excellency! By the highest laws of Vinos, by authority both royal and divine, I come on behalf of my people. The Old Believers of Fiore seek redress for the crimes and outrages committed against them under the sacred terms of the Treaty of Trastamere. As is your sworn duty, you shall admit me into the royal presence."

It was not a request, it was a command, and he spoke it in the same manner as before his soldiers on the battlefield. He was getting into that room. The Church would not monopolize the royal ear. This time the breach of the Treaty was beyond a crime. It was foul murder, an abomination, and its perpetrators would answer for it. She was scarcely more than a child…

The chamberlain's attention was now firmly fixed upon Vitus. His golden chain of office settled over the front of a long satin robe, done up in the style of the Empire in imperial purple. His clean-shaven face and piercing hawkish eyes flared, as though this dignitas had suffered an intolerable insult from a lesser man. His hard lips moved, the official's words were as cold, concise, and unfeeling as his responses had been to the others.

"His Majesty has made his will known. That is all you need know, petitioner."

He turned away, and Vitus was left staring into the faceless helmets of the immovable Gendarmes that continued to hold back the press as the chamberlain too passed through the doors to the royal apartments and vanished from view. He felt the rage rising within him, fueled the sour taste of betrayal, but that was nothing compared to the fear, the fear that he had failed. The faithful trusted him, and he had failed that trust.

Slowly the strength drained from him, and he felt like a tired elder, his head pressed against an immovable wall. Others soon swept passed him, calling after the departed chamberlain, and he was pulled back as a rip-tide pulls a drowning man, until he finally allowed himself to sit down on the hard marble of the hall's lowest tier of seating, not far from the main doors and their hateful image of the Betrayer. He let out a long shuddering sigh, bitter memories rising from the darkness to claw at him.

Vitus forced himself to focus. Remembering his teacher's words. The hard and unforgiving features of Praetor Pallas swam before his mind's eye.

"The greatest weapon is the void, young soldier. Never forget that."

The first stage of Mortis set in like a dull grey cloud on a sunny day. All of Vitus's emotions pressed down, down, and down until they were swallowed by the earth, with only the barest residues remaining. The echoes of his unworthiness and anger continued to sound somewhere in the depths, still heard, but far enough away that they would not interfere. So it had been since the days of Ishan, the Founder and Black King, when the gods had gifted their chosen warriors with power over death. Without the training that he had received in the days when the Order was strong, the corpse-state would be entirely beyond reach in a place such a this.

Here, with no other Falhorne present, his focus could only be weak and the corpse-state more of a calming caress than an all-encompassing embrace that could pierce the veil and open the lands of the dead. Even with the Mortis weighing down his emotions like lead, he could not shake the worries that stubbornly persisted. The knowledge of the Order's ways was fading. Knowledge of its disciplines, Mortis being one among many, had been slipping away for the forty years since that dreadful day at Valia when Cosimo the Betrayer had triumphed over the Order's last stand and Vitus had fled with the others. For all their defiance the Falhorne were diminishing. Night was closing in and Vitus felt the hollow echoing fears of an old man who has watched his world slowly crumble around him. What was left?

What was left for Tagus? His apprentice deserved so much more. He had no grandmaster above him. No brotherhood of dedicated knights to help him develop his potential to the extent that Vitus knew him to be capable of. He had seen the things that his apprentice could do, and only pride had held back his awe.

At Fallonier Fields, Tagus had single-handedly held the line when the Falhorne's charge faltered, remaining in Mortis longer than should have been possible. The young lion's powers of control, his focus, had rivaled that of the martyred Piso, whose final display of power that day had shocked his praetor to the core: an orphaned son of an executed "warlock" had channelled his very rage to break back into the lands of dead alone, something that hitherto only a trained squadron of veteran Falhorne had been able to do acting in unison; striking down a powerful inquisitor without so much as moving a muscle on his face.

Vitus had felt the seemingly fathomless strength within the man, as his former apprentice raised himself to the highest levels of Mortis single-handedly, offering himself to the gods as their champion. Tagus had the same potential. In the days of the Order, when the grandmaster's sword had rested in its rightful place upon Cera Pelleus, such exceptional warriors would be honored as "savants", blessed in the eyes of the Black King, honored both on and off the battlefield and groomed to be the greatest Falhorne of their day. Now they lived in a world that shunned them as freaks. Perhaps Piso had been lucky to die when he did.

Detached thoughts of worry continued to circulate as Vitus sat by the great doors, not looking at the angry faces of the petitioners as they filed out. He had sent Tagus to the Agoge in his stead for the first time. Had he been ready? Emotions would be running high and the events of recent days had surely embittered the hearts of the councillors. Would they blame him? Would they blame Tagus? Would they blame all the Falhorne who had failed them? All his efforts, all his struggles, all that had been accomplished through the Treaty, and all that had been betrayed, it had all been for his people. And for them he would continue to bleed.

"Fire tests iron as sorrow tests men."

Palla's final piece of advice was revolving in his mind, along with the faded image of his mentor's serene face as he lay dying in that peasant's hut after Valia, when the hand that Vitus had expected finally came to rest upon his shoulder and a voice he recognized whispered softly in his ear.

"Brothers to the end, Praetor."

He let Agelaus's strong arms pull him to his feet, both of them shielded from view by the press of exiting petitioners, before replying.

"Brothers to the end, Captain."

****

Why?

Tagus's heart sank as he looked into the depths of those cold blue eyes, like a stone cast into an abyss of ocean. An atrocity had been committed, one of the faithful was dead, and not one of the Falhorne, sworn defenders of the Law of Damas, had been there to save her.

Mia.

He could have stopped her. He could have stayed in the marketplace on the Day of Blood. He could have sent someone else. He had no good answer as to why he had not. Nor did he have the slightest idea of what Vitus would have said had he stood in his place. Vitus, who as a youth had selflessly risked his life at the sack of Brisi to protect the survivors among the faithful. But he, Tagus, was not his mentor. Damn, why did it have to be her? Why had he not been told? Surely Vitus would have known…

As a Falhorne he was guilty. His mentor had always told him that a warrior of the gods was nothing without honor. For ten years, these poor people had voluntarily given them contributions to ensure that they would have guardians, defenders who would ensure that such atrocities never befell their children. Yet he had failed to save a young woman whose spirit had burned bright and who did not deserve to die. What would happen to her family now? To her crippled father and sickly brother for whom she had taken such a risk? By Gormani's flames… There were no excuses. Only weakness. Weakness that caused water to well in his eyes and his muscles harden to lead.

The anger he had felt for Callidus and the welcome shock of seeing Nicco again fell away into darkness. Even his love for Corrie felt irrelevant and wrong. He wanted to fall to his knees, to beg forgiveness, to throw himself at the mercy of the Agoge and to accept whatever punishment they saw fit to give him.

But he had no words. He simply stood, a broken man, weak, naked, unarmored before the truth of his own frailty. As weak as the infant who had just received the "watering", and yet Tagus knew that his sin would not be washed away.

"The dark one has lost his tongue," Nestor remarked drily. "I suppose that would save him from telling us how our men and our women are supposed to get on with the business of buying and selling. Now that there is no market that won't see them murdered before sundown."

His eyes sank to the floor, a look of disgust on his wrinkled face.

"Is this why we continue to give what little we have to our great 'protectors', even when you only saw fit to repay us with your neglect?

Yesterday we were invaded and had our homes burned. Today our children are murdered in the streets, while you lot do nothing."

The soot-stained Clodius looked equally disgusted behind his ashen mask.

"I'd like to ask the dark one just how are we supposed to work and feed the mouths of our children with the Betrayer's servants swarming everywhere with murder in their eyes…no one there to stop them, even with our so-called protectors stuck in the city and not running around the Five Kingdoms like black dogs with a taste for mercenary gold. Your praetor talks of honor, Resh, but we on the streets know better."

Only the red-bearded man stayed silent among the councillors, looking gravely at Tagus as Secunda, vindicated by the response of her peers and with unquenched anger in her voice, launched into another attack. One that was far more personal.

"And just where is the praetor? Why is he not here instead of his black-skinned running dog? I told Cornelia she was a whore for marrying this stupid Resh…"

"That's enough, Secunda!"

Jesta's eyes flared once more with black fire as she rounded on the old woman. Callidus and Nicco, hitherto stoically silent, both flinched at the same time.

"Your personal losses have blinded you, sister. You have said enough."

She turned to face the other councillors.

"Nestor, you may go ahead."

Nestor, the old man, wore a mask of bitterness in the wake of his previous tirade, and his voice matched his face.

"For once I and Clodius agree on something. Ha! I remember a time when the sight of single black robe was enough to scare the Hierophant himself back behind the walls of Hipireus. But now you cower like wretches while his lackeys burn our homes…why should we give your kind what little we earn so you can waste it and watch our people die?"

He audibly spat on the dirt floor and scrunched up his eyes.

"Secunda is not the only one who grieves, black dog. Need I remind you that she was my grand-daughter, but what would be the use of explaining that to the cold heart of a soldier…"

Jesta sighed heavily as she saw the tears pricking Tagus's eyes.

"Clodius, you may proceed."

The grimy face rose again against the trembling "black dog" before him.

"And does not the Treaty demand that the Falhorne speak for us at the royal court? How do these murders and outrages happen when you lot have the ear of the prince? Answer me that. Or do you still lack a tongue? Truly the Devouring never ended…"

Tagus could offer no rebuttal for what he knew to be the truth. He stood before the council members a weakling, and all his fear of vulnerability, of having no defense, no means of resistance, no way of fighting back, was breaking on his mind like a rushing torrent as the tears began to flow.

Did I say you could speak, mongrel!

Tagus shut his eyes as the overseer Ranald continued.

Did I say you had a tongue, Resh!

He had to put his hand on the table and lean forward to steady himself. He could almost hear the overseer's footsteps and the whistle of knotted cow-hide through the air.

"Falhorne, have you nothing to say?"

It was Jesta again. Her eyes stone-hard, but now more akin to shale than black marble; a softer core behind a hard shell. He did not know why, but this trivial observation somehow calmed his racing mind, swallowing the image of the towering overseer and the bloodied, frightened boy at his feet.

"No, I do not."

He struggled to continue, wiping his tear-stained cheeks, choking as he spoke.

"Please, tell me of this incident. The praetor must know everything."

Jesta glanced at the downcast, hopeless faces of the others and sighed audibly, painful emotions cutting through her hard visage like tremors.

"Vitus knows, Falhorne, for we told him this very morning. But the scars remain deep, for we know that nothing has been done, and clearly you yourself remain ignorant. It was yesterday when Mia and the other youths left the Asylum and went into the market square to look for work among the foreigners. Their passes were in order, but that did not save them."

Tagus began clenching and unclenching his fists as the councilwoman continued. He had to fight to keep the tears from returning.

"From the account of the events that was told to me, it all started when some of the apprentice boys confronted the merchant Mela. Even on a holy day, they didn't like the idea of the faithful being given what they saw as 'their jobs', especially a girl like Mia, whom they accused of doing 'man's work'. Soon enough, the local guilders were complaining about this 'foreigner' underselling them with her cheap 'mongrel labor'."

Jesta paused, her face contorted with anger.

"Bloody hypocrites and liars! Most of them own slaves. But Mela stood her ground against the bastards, even when the guard showed up. But they weren't the only ones. The Betrayer's priests soon arrived with a throng of townsfolk they'd assembled to confront the 'invading heretics.' That's when the riot started: one dead, three broken arms, five smashed ribs, and fifteen stab wounds. Mia…was torn to pieces…"

Jesta stifled a sob as Tagus forced a reply from his dry lips.

"What about the survivors?"

"I can answer that, Falhorne."

It was Nicco speaking. Both he and Callidus had remained silent during the whole interrogation that Tagus had just endured. He had almost forgotten the two of them were present.

Jesta gave a wordless gesture and the gnome, looking almost wraith-like in his long obscuring coat, turned to face him.

"I was there. Mia was torn to pieces outside the Royal Exchange, with the houses of several merchant leagues behind her and the guildhall towering above. The tradesmen on the way to the guild chapel were the first ones to complain about the Tarnish merchants and their Old Believer laborers. A procession of churchmen and laymen then confronted the merchants and, when denied, became violent. Surely Ambassador Trevelyan will seek restitution from the prince for lost profits."

The former innkeeper allowed himself a faint smile.

"My boys arranged the whole thing, even passed coins to the market guards so the kids would get a chance to work for Mela of Avram. Being foreign, she never cared much for our local prejudices. I just want to emphasize that right now because some folk here seem to enjoy hurling abuse at black skin and robes. This man and his organization had no responsibility here. It was all on us. Bella was keeping watch and was quick to summon aid when the shit came down. But our gang was nothing against that mob, and the guards sure as hell weren't risking their skins."

Nicco's smile abruptly disappeared and he slowly shook his head.

"Sure, we brawled with the cloth-ears, tried to hold them back, but there were far too many. We got away, barely. The boys covering our retreat into the slums. But the girl was out of reach, and they were on her like a pack of slavering wolves. By the time they were through, she looked like a victim of the Low-Town Monster, hung up like some sick trophy. There was nothing to do but get everyone else out before there were more deaths…so if you want to scream at anyone for this, scream at the gnome. I'm long past due for some abuse."

No one spoke. Nestor looked downcast, staring at the table. Secunda's face was full of anger, but she said nothing.

Again, it was Jesta who broke the silence, speaking as she plaintively clutched the shoulders of her blue dress.

"Assigning blame means nothing now. I've been seeing to the wounded with what herbs we can spare," she said. "But such things that we cannot grow ourselves are in short supply now that the cartel his majesty forces us to buy from has raised its prices for the third time this month."

She leaned closer to Tagus and her voice grew quieter.

"I fear for what may come next. This is the eleventh incident in fourteen days. The fifteenth in the past thirty. The Betrayer's servants grow more brazen by the day, unmolested and unpunished by the law.

Young Aegeus was nearly beaten to death three days ago, after city guardsmen stopped him from running away from the mob chasing him down Smith's Lane in the Guilder District. He was just looking for work. Then Julia the maidservant was accosted while on her way to market, stripped of her clothes and pelted with stones while the guards laughed at her humiliation. But they have never gone this far before; invading our community and killing an innocent girl. Should things go on like this, the peace that we have known since Fallonier Fields will be at an end. I fear that the sack of Brisi may be our fate as well."

Jesta looked as though she were presiding over a funeral. Invoking the Eternal Judge for His blessing in a man's last rites. Her eyes resembled bottomless pools of still water, holding experiences that Tagus could not fathom.

"I apologize, Councillor," he said, trying and failing to hide the shame in his voice.

"I swear that I shall do my duty, as will my brethren. We have failed the faithful. I know I can speak for us all when I say that we refuse to take any further donations from the Asylum's coffers until this injustice has been avenged. I swear by the ascended soul of Ishan himself that we would rather die than let these foul deeds continue."

Tagus nearly choked on the last words, wondering if he could back up such promises with anything beyond feeling, and dreading the headwoman's response to their inadequacy.

Clodius gave a bitter smirk, he clearly did not believe a word of it.

But it was Corvus, the red-bearded man, who spoke next, raising his voice for the first time. There was a deep rumble in his throat, his every word spoken with pain and heavy with grief.

"Forgive me, Councillor Jesta, but neither the Falhorne nor Nicco are responsible for this calamity. It was I who made the arrangements with Mela and the Association, trying to get work for the youth here abouts. I did so without speaking with you or my fellow councillors. I did it because I thought Mia and the others would be in good hands. But I was wrong. All the Association people who tried to protect the young uns' are marked men now. The guards have already rounded up some of their family members in the slums. I won't stand here and let the Falhorne take the fall for what was my doing. Nestor, Secunda, I beg your forgiveness. I shall step down if the council wills it."

He bowed his head, as if waiting for the headsman's axe. But all that came was a sob, followed by tears as Secunda broke down, her mask of anger shattered as she rose from her seat and stumbled from the room, the door slamming behind her. Nestor said nothing, only stared sullenly into space.

"Let us go on," Jesta finally said, turning to the bearded man, who still sat silent, staring at his feet.

"I understand your feeling, Corvus, but now is not a time to fall on one's sword. Nicco, what more do you have to say about this incident? What did your men discover?"

Tagus continued to stand like a soldier at attention, despite his aching legs, trying to control his breathing. He wished that he could escape into Mortis. But it was impossible. He was full of shame, full of anger and grief for what had happened, but also that they would blame him for it. Deep within, a cowardly part of himself was relieved that the attention of the council had shifted elsewhere and whispered 'better you than me'.

Nicco's face was deadly serious as he replied.

"I speak as a foreigner, brothers and sisters, even though I was born here as were my parents and grandparents. Most people in this city would gladly see a runt like me hang, especially after all those Church proclamations against non-humans. We gnomes are used to being strangers in our own land. We were destroyed as a nation a thousand years before the Empire and its Church even rose its ugly head, not that it stopped them from using the supposed 'threat' we posed as a means of keeping the lower orders in line. When folk fall on hard times, the lynch mobs always follow."

"Some of you will recall," he went on, "The Great Fire that levelled half the city seven years ago. When the prince supposedly couldn't spare even a single guardsman to help us downtrodden souls. It was the journeymen and apprentices who fought to keep the fires from spreading to the Asylum."

Tagus remembered that hellish week. It had been a hot dry summer and the flames had spread like a forest fire through the thatched roofs of the Ox Guts. Forced demolitions by the prince's men had not saved the old cathedral from being gutted, its roof raining molten drops of lead. At the time, some of the faithful had praised the Lord of Flames for the incident.

Even then it had been clear that many followers of the Old Gods were looking to others for protection rather than the Falhorne: looking to men capable of defending their livelihoods and that of their families.

"We did so because you good folk returned the favor. The efforts of five Falhorne alone saved ten times their number of homes in the slums."

Nicco paused, looking into each and every face of the council before continuing.

"Nor can I forget how the Agoge helped during the Black Pox five years ago when the prince quarantined the slums and left the people to die. Only you 'demon worshippers' defied royal authority, even coming yourselves and risking death because you cared. You went from demons to divine spirits of mercy in many eyes. The Church can spit and yowl all its wants about blood sacrifices and Gormani's flames, they know who their real friends are, and I hope you lot do too. The Association itself might be only three years old, but our memories go back a lot further. That's why my boys put our lives on the line yesterday and will be proud to do so again."

He paused again, taking a very audible deep breath.

"Therefore, it is my duty to inform you of this. My spotter Bella watched the zealots from where she was laboring for a seller of fruits across the square. There was someone guiding them and commanding their every move. Everything they did was with his blessing. Riding a horse, he was, and, unlike the priests, he wore bronze armor over his white robe and golden mask over his face. He gave the order for Mia to be killed and oversaw what was done to her body."

Clodius's soot-stained hand began to tremble on the tabletop, while Nestor's face was the color of old porridge. Even Corvus kept his face stubbornly angled toward the floor.

"Inquisitor."

Tagus exhaled the dreadful word in a flat, heavy voice choked by an awful recognition.

His thoughts returned to the battle ten years prior. Of the awful magic, the agonizing pain, the masked white-robed figure with its arms upraised, and Piso's sacrifice. There could be no doubt. The faces that fearfully raised their eyes toward him now resembled the tormented ones writhing in Tylo's nethermost halls in Gormani after the Eternal Judge had weighed their souls and found them wanting.

"Most certainly."

Callidus spoke for the first time since his ill-received greeting, confirming everyone's worst fears.

"And, again, you said the guards stood by, brother Nicco?"

"Yes, as if they would impede such a powerful envoy of Father Church. The wretches had no intention of ending up on a torture rack."

Callidus stepped forward, shifting his tall frame to the middle of the room.

"Councilwoman, I ask your permission to speak."

"Granted, Falhorne."

Tagus clenched his teeth, a turncoat like Callidus did not deserve such an honorable title, nor the right to speak.

The rogue Falhorne began speaking in a loud and authoritative voice, like a captain addressing his troops before battle.

"Brothers and sisters, I come to you from Trastamere. Some would say I come to you from the depths of Gormani itself, and they would not be far wrong. I came to the land beyond the River Tamus ten years ago, and I have seen the truth of how simple plants can become man-eaters. For satincane is a true predator, more vicious than any wolf or lion, and with a far greater appetite for flesh and blood."

Callidus paused, as if to prepare his listeners for what was to come.

"I have seen it devour whole villages, empty hamlets and reduce thriving towns to ghostly shells as the plantation fields hungrily advance. Once peaceful villages are now slave barracks, or entirely levelled so that new villas can be built for those who feed and draw profits from this ravening beast. With every boatload of the precious man-eating plant and its extract that is shipped to the swelling markets of Torio, Avram, Tarn and Fiore itself, more chattel are fed into the plantations. More people are kidnapped from their homes by slavers. More souls are worked to death on stolen land. And more rural folk are uprooted and cast into the shanties and slums. And so, good councillors, I greet you as a damned soul from the pit."

He flashed a grim smile, letting the words hang in the air as he took a long drink from his waterskin.

"But while I have seen proud farmers driven off their land by mercenary gangs, their daughters sold into brothels, their sons begging on the streets, while slaves tramp their former fields under the overseer's lash, I have also seen the rage. I have seen the downtrodden fight. I have let their fury become my own. I became part of a growing mass who refuse to be broken by the planter aristocracy, the death merchants and their priestly allies. In struggle, I have seen slaves become masters, peasants become lords, beggars become gods, and whores turn into goddesses. Perhaps this comes as blasphemy to your ears...."

Callidus half-turned his head, sharp eyes focused on where Tagus stood rigid and unmoving.

"But the godliest of all are the hillmen, Black Vinosians all. 'Dark ones', who would rather die than live in chains. I can only take offense at this council's misguided words to my brother here. For I have nothing but respect for those who fight for liberation. It is what I, as a Falhorne, fight for. It is what the Black King created us for. Did we not defy the great Empire for seven hundred years? Did we not celebrate when it fell at last, saving our people from the fires of the Inquisition?

"Cosimo the Betrayer thought so little of us that he believed he could destroy us in a single day; a single massacre of every Falhorne and every ally they had in Fiore. Failing that, Prince Cosimo thought he could destroy us at Cera Pelleus. After its walls fell but not the Order, he again convinced himself that we were finished when he cornered us at the Battle of Valia. But my father survived that day and thus I was born in Torio."

He paused, taking a deep intake of breath and exhaling before continuing.

"I refused to abide by the false Treaty. It was folly to place our trust in the royal house of Vinos. They are killing you now, just as they killed us then..."

Callidus's fist came down like a hammer on the council table.

"Chero is following in his grandfather's footsteps. Just look at the pacts he forges with the Church. Now the Inquisition has returned to your city. As soon as he deems it expedient to assault those faithful to the gods in the interest of aligning with the Church and the Blessed Realm of the Hierophant in Karados, he will not hesitate."

He paused, letting the shaken councillors catch their breaths.

Tagus felt his teeth clench.

"Brave inhabitants of the Asylum, recognize the trap that this monster has laid for you. Just as his grandfather did for Grandmaster Vannan and my own father. Many died in their beds fifty years ago, slaughtered by a coward's blade. And I refuse to see history repeat itself. I have consulted with my brother Nicco and insist that the entire population of the Asylum be evacuated. The Association has the resources to convey you all safely to the southern hills where you will find safety among my men. I implore you to remember the true friends of our people. We stand among the outcasts, the peasants, the slumdwellers, the slaves, not with the princes. Remaining in the city is suicide, friends."

Callidus's words fell away, but his fierce expression never did. He was serious. He wanted the people of the Asylum to flee with him. Tagus felt his hands clenching along with his teeth, and realized that his hand had moved to the hilt of his sword.

In a heartbeat they were facing each other. Tagus with a hand to his sword, enraged that this rogue would have the nerve to propose that the faithful tear up everything that had been won since Fallonier Fields. He would not stand for it, not after all he had faced.

"I would silence your viper's tongue, traitor!" He roared.

"No!"

Jesta's voice rang out from the high roof, freezing Tagus in the act of drawing his blade. The headwoman's voice was paralyzing. He found that he could not move a muscle, nor turn his head, as the black fire burned in those eyes.

"There will be no violence in this chamber. No bloodshed among brethren."

The paralysis began to loosen, but he was still painfully stiff.

"Sheath your sword."

Tagus did so, his muscles screaming with the effort.

"By all the gods…" Nestor gasped.

Clodius sat rigid in fear, while Corvus was as white as a sheet. Jesta stood between them, appearing twice her height, every inch of her slender form radiating raw power.

"I believe that I can speak for the council," her voice boomed.

The towering figure turned to Callidus, whose olive features appeared equally ghostly. Nicco was cowering behind the tall man.

"Your warning is appreciated, Falhorne, but Brother Tagus's rage is more than understandable in light of your words. Fiore is the city of the Fire Lord. Here the faithful of the gods have always endured, always kept His eternal flame burning in its rightful place. Even in the darkest days of the Devouring, when the imperial governors repeatedly claimed that the holy city of our ancestors was "free of disbelievers", our endurance in the hidden places proved their words were lies."

The headwoman's eyes were a dark inferno.

"The Agoge is the pillar of our community; the scaffolding, the roofbeams, the stonework of a living citadel. We are an eternal fortress that will never shift or crumble while the gods will it to stand firm. This is our city, and no corrupt son of the Betrayer shall drive us from it. We shall stay here. We shall always be here."

The grey light from the rafters now resembled a lone candle amid subterranean blackness.

"It is our divinely appointed task to be the voice of the gods in the mortal realm and neither the Great Betrayal of Callus Invictas, nor the Betrayal of Cosimo Julianus-Agricola can change that which is eternal. Let the white-robes know that Cera Infernus lives within us all. Their cowardly efforts are vain. The people of the gods outlasted the Empire, survived the Inquisition, saw the Day of Reckoning and will continue to survive as long as the sun burns in Sol's sky. We will outlast Prince

Chero as well. No, Brother Callidus, Fiore is where we shall make our stand."

Silence.

The power in the air, the power that had been rattling the skylights and making the roofbeams sag under its weight, suddenly dissipated. Jesta stood there, the thin dark-haired woman she had always been, the black fire gone from her eyes, which had lost none of their determination.

Callidus, still pale, meekly bowed his head.

"Now, brethren, we must decide what must be done."

Chapter 6 – Unforgiven

"This is an outrage!"

Commodus Resti looked as though he might have an apoplexy. The bailiff's prominent nose burned bright red. His formerly sneering confidence replaced with indignant rage as he stamped his foot on the cobblestones beneath the Silo Street Gate. The same place where he had humbled the Falhorne the day before. The petty official had clearly not expected the tables to be turned so quickly.

"By the divinely sanctioned will and decree of the august Grand Prince, I demand that you disperse immediately!"

Tagus again stood with his brethren in an unbroken black line barring the way to the Agoge chambers. But this time the Falhorne and the members of the Watch did not stand alone. The faithful now stood with their protectors, summoned to action by their council. Women had abandoned their garden plots. Men had returned from the docks early in defiance of their boss's threats. They were tired and clad in sweat-sodden linen shirts, but their eyes burned with a pride that could not be matched. Even children had ceased their games to stand with their elders in denying the bailiff access to what was theirs by the right of the gods and the Treaty.

The entire Agoge stood between Tagus and Tarquinus, and even the formerly chastened Nestor and Clodius wore looks of defiance as they stared down the oppressors of their people. Corvus had joined them after seeing Nicco away to safety. Even the distraught Secunda had returned.

They had gone from house to house, gathering the people, with Clodius risking getting shot by the marines to round up the dockworkers at the riverport. Some two hundred people now stood together in the street. Even Callidus had chosen to remain when Nicco retreated. He stood slightly apart from the other Falhorne, arms akimbo, his pistols on prominent display.

"And this is how you repay my leniency..."

Resti had obviously grown cocky. His retinue was smaller than it had been the previous day, consisting of a potbellied sergeant with a bristly moustache and seven other guardsmen wearing cheaply made cast-iron field plate under their liveries and pot helmets. The scrawny figure of the bailiff, grim-faced beneath a broad-brimmed black leather hat, had looked more like a determined conqueror entering foreign lands than a municipal official when he had arrived minutes earlier. Now he looked more like a spoiled child.

He shot a furious glance at the sergeant, who shouted at the assemblage in a deep guttural voice that was no doubt used to cowing others into hasty obedience.

"By His Majesty's decree the public display of arms by irregulars is banned! Drop your weapons and surrender to royal justice," he paused and his lips formed a wicked grin as his broadsword hissed from its sheath, "Or I'll take it out of your worthless hides!"

The guardsmen began to advance, their cocky, sneering faces fixed on the Falhorne band, confident in their superiority in armor and weaponry, in spite of the numbers they faced. After their seemingly total victory the previous day, they must have thought the Asylum utterly defenseless.

"So, these are the mighty Falhorne," the sergeant scoffed, "More like lazy guttersnipes who don't know their place…"

His armor clattered as he angled his blade toward Tagus's chest, just as his men began to lower their pikes. Onlookers on Silo Street gasped and bystanders backed away from the impending violence. Tagus saw some of the faithful flinch, stepping backward behind others, or gathering protectively around their children. But the overwhelming majority stood firm, and this clearly had an effect on the guardsmen, whose confident features appeared more and more shaky as they drew nearer, as if they were walking into a trap.

Tagus set his hand to his sword. Jesta had instructed them to refrain from violence unless absolutely necessary. But he now agreed with what Skarlos had said the day before. He wished to all the gods that he was back at Fallonier Fields with his enemies before him in a real battle rather than this honourless street fight against self-important lawmen.

Still, this was a chance to redeem himself for his previous failures. This time he would not surrender his weapon so easily.

But the clash never came. In a split second, both the sergeant and his men were frozen in their stride, as the renegade Callidus shouted at the approaching guardsmen in a thunderous voice that was both authoritative and uncompromising. Like a magistrate reading out an accusation to a man who has already condemned himself by his own actions.

"By the terms of the Treaty of Trastamere, signed into the highest law of the land by the royal hand of Prince Chero Invictus I of the House of Julianus Agricola, and by the grace of the gods, the right of the Eternal Order of the Falhorne and those who bear arms in defense of those faithful to the Gods of the Celestial Court, is guaranteed in perpetuity until the end of time as stated in stipulation five, line thirty-seven. Such is our sovereign right, that which can never be foresworn nor suspended by any decree, edict, or overturned by any law as is stated clearly the terms of the aforementioned Treaty section fifteen, line forty-five. The *Decree Maximus* is therefore in violation of the supreme law of the land and thereby unenforceable. Any charges brought against the defenders of those faithful to the Gods of the Celestial Court is thereby inadmissible in a court of law."

Callidus stepped forward, until he stood face to face with the sergeant, who had fallen silent.

"Stand down guardsman. Is that clear?"

His hands were on his pistols.

The sergeant looked utterly bewildered. His haughty air of authority drained away like the blood from his face.

"Bailiff, are we done here?"

Callidus did not aim his wheel-lock at Commodus Resti, whose face now wore a shocked expression of equal parts anger and fear, but merely cradled the drawn pistol in his hands. The eagle-beaked official backed away from the Falhorne like he was retreating from some frightful apparition, the onlookers hastily making way for him.

The sergeant hurriedly sheathed his sword. Tagus quickly lost sight of him as he melted back into the crowd on Silo Street, followed closely by his lackeys. Their formerly sneering faces now pale in the face of armed men secure in their own right.

Tagus could only stare at Callidus, who was calmly sliding his pistol back into place as the assembled Old Believers erupted into cheers of triumph. He had acted out of turn, perhaps placing the lives of everyone in jeopardy, but no one seemed to care in the slightest. The bailiff had fled. They had won.

It was a small victory, but, in the midst of a sea of humiliation and betrayal, it felt like the sweetest thing on earth. No one's door had been kicked in nor had any hovel been torn apart in a search for weapons or contraband goods. No one had been arrested or harmed. Parents embraced their children, laughter and smiles split the formerly dour faces of downtrodden souls. It was like Fire Day all over again. Although it could not return Mia to life.

The cacophony only ceased when Jesta held up her hand for silence.

"Brothers and sisters! Hear me!"

The headwoman's words were tinged with a burning passion that Tagus had not seen in the proceedings of the Agoge. But the same black fire blazed in her eyes and he felt its power.

"It has been ten years since the signing of the Treaty. Ten years since The Crown promised us the right to govern ourselves. We were promised freedom, the right to live under our own laws and honor the true gods, to live as we choose and earn an honest living as we saw fit. We were promised that the days of our ancestor's suffering were over, that the Devouring would never return. But they lied. They betrayed us when they barred us from the guilds, when they barred us from the markets, when they allowed the Church to attack us, and when they stole our Mia from this world."

There was roar of concordance from the crowd along with looks of sorrow and anger as the name of the slain girl sounded on the breeze.

"Her soul will guide us on the morrow when all of us shall march upon the guildhall to demand justice in her name and in the name of the gods! At sunup all work will cease and we shall go forth beneath Sol's sky with the blessing of our Lord of Flames within His eternal city! Our eternal city! For we shall rise with His fire! Cera Infernus!"

Cheers and shouts of devotion echoed the headwoman's words of prayer, seeming to breach the clouds above, which had torn asunder to reveal a clear blue sky. But amid all the euphoria and collective spirit, even when displayed by his own brothers in arms, Tagus felt no sense of triumph.

He could see the royal palace now, looming in the distance atop its hill, looking down over the slums like some uncaring god staring with disdain upon their creation. There would be retaliation. It became difficult to separate the cheers and happy people around him from the screams and bloodshed of his memories. Again, he pictured that burning village in the desolation of the Braxian winter, remembered that helplessly wailing child, and felt it merge with the terrifying images in his dreams. But what snapped him out of it was something that only made his teeth clench and the hot blood rise to his head.

"You see, brother?"

Callidus's expression was cool as he firmly laid a hand on Tagus's shoulder.

"I may not agree with the law, but I make it my business to know it. The same goes for your precious Treaty."

He drew his hand back and nodded, a slight smile forming on his lips.

"I bear you no ill will. Regardless of what your praetor may think of me. I'm more than willing to put aside old quarrels. I hope the same can be said of you."

He turned away and was lost in the throng.

****

"I have no answers, Tagus. It is not for me to know the meaning of another's dreams. Antillia's garden is deep and rich and we do not know what bounty she will dispense in our sleep. But sometimes the gods slip messages into her harvest, messages they charge her with delivering to the chosen. Perhaps Ishan is trying to tell you something. If that is the case, it would do you well to listen."

His wife's words died away. Tagus did not reply, looking down at the scarred table top as her hand pressed against his shoulder.

It was evening, and they were sitting in the common room of the Black Horseman, now illuminated by candles whose ruddy glow sent shadows dancing on the walls.

It was also supper time and the handful of denizens in the dimly-lit room were silently devouring the meagre repast of dried meat, crusty yellow cheese, boiled leaks, rough unleavened black bread and weak ale. A few of the tables were now propped up with empty beer barrels after having suffered particular damage during the day's rampage. The food was a gift from the community foot stores, and the meal had begun appropriately with a prayer of thanks. The badly preserved meat in particular was as precious as vintage Samosian wine.

The Falhorne had succeeded in partially restoring the inn's interior after the bailiff's men had torn it to pieces in their search for contraband. The front door had been repaired, although it still sagged inward on its hinges. The smashed tankards and crockery had been cleared away, while some of the broken chairs had been mended with assorted scraps of wood.

Of the eight people present, four were lodgers, all seated together with Callidus at the largest intact table. Tagus was not among them, sitting together with Corrie at a second table alongside Corvus, the burly red-bearded councillor, who had insisted on returning with them after consulting with his colleagues.

It was a remarkable spectacle, rough looking men with grizzled faces, who would have looked more at home in one of Avram City's notorious bar brawls, were eating their dinner with all the quiet dignity of Karadosian monks in a monastery refectory. Tarquinus, Valens, Skarlos, and Remus looked almost serene. Even Callidus seemed to be fitting in and taking his repast silently with the others. Of course, Tagus had made a point of refusing to sit with him; taking the furthest seat he could away from the rogue Falhorne. He had hoped to never see him again, but now he was here and trampling over everything sacred. All the while painting himself a hero.

The bland food provided no respite. Tagus had tried to forget his anger by finally confiding to his wife about the nightmare dream he had had two nights prior. But her response offered little reassurance and he had quickly dropped the subject. Now he was focusing on the conversation between his wife and the councillor, who had completely removed the mask he had worn in the Agoge and was openly speaking as a representative of the Association.

"Sister, you must be patient. Nicco is likely on his way to Meno right now. If our brother alchemist has found anything, he will not hesitate to bring you word."

Corvus's red beard was greasy from the thin soup and his eyes appeared exhausted in the candle light, bloodshot and with drooping eyelids.

"Patience is a virtue none of us can afford, Councillor."

Corrie's voice sounded tired, but her brown eyes were as sharp as ever.

"The fear of this killer is becoming as dangerous as the killer themselves. There have already been several incidents of folk killing or maiming one another, thinking they were about to be attacked by the Low-town Monster. Patience only means more bodies and I already have too many restless souls on my conscience to contend with. How are the brothers coping with this?"

Corvus gave a deep sigh, rubbing his face with his hands.

"Oh, we've tried to reassure folk; but try telling a country boy, never meant for city life, to keep his head on straight when he sees an odd shadow after sundown. The superstitious among the Braxians are saying it's the work of the 'horned ones', emerging from inner earth to punish the sinful and unworthy. The Samosians are whispering about slithering 'dracons' and the Church keeps sending in frantic white-robes to tell the great unwashed to kneel and repent. As if the folk around here don't do enough penance day in and day out.

"Every wretch in the slums, man or gnome, knows the guards don't give a rat's ass for their lives, so why should any god or gods? Migrants are easily replaced and the powers that be want non-humans gone anyway. We've posted sentries of our own outside some of the tenements. Nicco's even thrown together some patrols that will be making the rounds starting tonight, but that's the best we can do with what we've got."

Corvus made an exasperated gesture, raising both hands from the tabletop as Corrie gave her sharp reply.

"I don't doubt your sincerity, Councillor, but I doubt your patrols will catch whatever's doing this. I was with Nicco off Candle Way the other night. I only caught the faintest trace of the thing. But enough to tell me that it knows how to hide its tracks and is as cunning as it is hungry. It's definitely no man. You'll need more than a band of street toughs to bring it down."

The red-bearded man stared down at the torn remnants of the bread on his plate.

"Again, it's the best we can do. We're just a whole lot of wretches trying to survive in a world that hates us and doesn't give a copper if we die. The best we can do is stick together. Do you know how long it took me to convince the Agoge of that truth? The Association's been standing by the folk of the Asylum for years, and this is the first time I managed to smuggle Nicco into a council meeting. To Gormani's flames with tradition is what I say. Take allies where you can find them."

Corrie's expression had changed to a wry smile by the time Corvus had stopped talking.

"Good, then you won't mind this particular heretic tagging along with your patrols tonight than."

Tagus's eyes immediately shot over in his wife's direction. He was about to voice his concern when the inn door crashed open, instantly drawing the attention of everyone in the room. Eight faces looked in the direction of the black cloaked figure in the doorway, immediately followed by a second who closed the door behind them.

As the figure came forward into the dim firelight, the hood fell back from a bald head bearing a perfect circle of scars, revealing the wizened features of an old soldier. Vitus simply nodded his head at the little assembly and strode over to the blazing logs of the common room's fireplace.

Tagus half-rose, instinctively wanting to run to his mentor and report the day's events, but it took one glance from those cold blue eyes to lower him back into his seat. The old praetor had not made an appearance at the Black Horseman in weeks. Only young Callus, as nervous as ever, was at his side. The boy was quickly shooed away and made to sit at a spot by the bar.

All eyes on him in undivided attention, the old man produced a book from the folds of his cloak. It was featureless and bound in leather as black as his robes. The sacred Book of Damas, the law and word of the gods. It opened, exposing its yellowed pages to the flickering light.

When Vitus finally spoke, it was in a deep slow voice, heavy with the distinctive guttural dialect that betrayed him as a native of the Braxian lands of the north-east. A voice which spoke of arcane truths and ages long forgotten by men who had not made it their business to remember the true names of real heroes.

"The Black King is the Watcher in the Dark. The beginning and the end. The Champion of the Four Winds. The Servitor of Earth and Fire. He is the relentless Hammer of the Waves, and the Eternal Guardian of the Gates of Barbarus. By his hand was the Betrayer struck down. By his hand did the gods show their will. By his hand, we were born as divine weapons for the vanquishing of evil. For us Barbarus is core and we greet the world beyond death with open arms; embracing the fate which mortals flee. For we are dead men walking by the will of the gods. We know no fear, for the dead know no fear. We know no mercy, for the dead know no mercy. We are the *Damas,* the Dark Blade in His hands. We are the Falhorne."

Tagus could feel the power of his mentor's words, the words of the *Ascension of Ishan*, the sacred tale of the founder himself. He no longer ate, but listened in silence with the others. He remembered the rule that the Order had observed in the mess halls of Cera Pelleus, and which Vitus had always insisted on maintaining: talking was forbidden at meal times, for they were a time of reflection rather than celebration. And from the days of the Order's birth, that reflection had been focused upon the life and example of one man whose mighty deeds and still mightier sacrifices had brought about his ascension to the Celestial Court.

"Ishan was once a man. The ancient blood of the kings of Karados flowed in his veins and, in the tradition of his ancestors, he bore the Judge's Mark upon his right forearm; the Mark of the Divine Instrument, to be played in the service of the gods from the moment that he was born into this world. As a child, his body walked with the stride of a man and his mind with the stride of a scholar. A priest of the gods at twelve winters and holy guardian of Cera Infernus at fourteen, he served the Lord of Flames, a warrior born from a rocky womb under a blazing sky.

"He strode the roads of the Five Kingdoms like a colossus, the greatest of beasts and the proudest of men cowering before him, for they knew that the power of the Celestial Court marched at his side and coursed through his royal blood. In Vinos he broke the necks of the Seven Bandit Kings; in Tarquin he tore the throat from the Beast of Borgos and avenged the souls of its one thousand victims; in Samos he felled the Giants of Nossos; in Braxus he defeated the Orus Invasion; and in Karados, he avenged his father by exposing the traitor Menes."

Tagus saw Callus in the shadows by the bar, his youthful eyes growing wider and wider with excitement as the great deeds of the Order's founder were read out like a tournament list. The aspiring dragon slayer was excited beyond reason just to listen to such tales and to be in the presence of these warriors of the gods.

Callidus was looking on with an expression that was hard to read. A shiver ran up Tagus's spine as he realized what was likely to happen when the old man noticed the rogue Falhorne. He prayed that the holy words would hold his mentor in their embrace for as long as possible.

"But it was in his mortal ending that his service to the gods was greatest. For his own royal brother, blinded by his own power and corrupted by the whisperings of deceivers, had been seduced by the Betrayer, He Whose Name Shall Go Unspoken. In his madness, the King of Karados would bring fire and sword to the Five Kingdoms and defilement to the halls of the gods – leaving Ishan broken amid the blackened shell of Cera Infernus."

The praetor halted, briefly letting the weight of his words sink into the hearts of everyone.

"But our lord still breathed. And his body, by the grace of the Celestial Court, grew strong again. Wandering the lands, he called upon the faithful, gathered those whose endurance was like the bones of the earth, and whose determination was as hard as Sol's lightning. Them he would instruct in the ways of war, teaching them to be a guard unto their fellows; sentinels against the Betrayer."

Another pause, impregnated by the ghosts of centuries.

"Thus were the Falhorne born from the ashes, new sparks cast from the ancient fires of Lord Fiore. But now Ishan faced his greatest test. His brother had proclaimed himself emperor, subjecting the peoples of the Five Kingdoms, plundering the land and defying the gods in the name of the Betrayer's lies. Fashioning his life into a divine weapon, Ishan showed the young Falhorne the way: ending his brother's life in the tyrant's own throne room, his holy *damas* smashing falsehoods as well as bone. Thus did he cast the traitor from his pinnacle."

Tagus could not resist a slight smile as he looked once more into Callus's shining eyes. Fighting to remember what it was like to be so young, so easily inspired, so on fire with the passion of life.

Callidus was smiling too, but it was a different smile, as though he was struggling between feelings of reverence and skepticism. Tagus's own smile sank into a frown as his animosity returned.

"His task completed, he was pierced by a hundred lances, his mortal form torn to pieces, his severed head crowned with a halo of hot coals on the gates of Moradaleum. But atop sacred Mount Barbarus, the Eternal Judge of all things did witness Ishan's sacrifice and did issue His decree; calling this noble hero to His side. By the will of the Celestial Court was Ishan crowned in the ashes of Cera Infernus – our Black King."

Everyone in the room had ceased to eat by the time Vitus's final words faded away against the cold stone walls. Corrie too sat in complete silence. Callus's soul, and perhaps those of others less youthful, had been born aloft into the realms of gods, heroes, and untold glory. Tagus could see the glittering bronze gates of Antillia's Garden flung wide to the boy's imagination; his mind walking amid the splendor of Lady Inspiration herself, oblivious to the drab bulk of the older men who immediately returned to their meals without allowing themselves to be entranced by the beauty of life and legend. The door was closed. The older one became; the more distant the Lady's garden became until it was lost forever from view as Barbarus beckoned.

Tagus found he could not return easily to his food, his eyes fixed on the old man, so dear to him, as he closed the book and turned once more to his little audience. When he spoke, the realm and gods and heroes suddenly collapsed into reality.

"Hear me, brothers. I am sure that all of you have heard the news by now. But you must calm yourselves. Overreacting is something we can ill afford. The Church is pushing its claims, but not everyone is happy with this. If the lord chamberlain does not admit me into His Majesty's presence tomorrow, there are others who will. The Hierophant is not their liege and they have no desire to be ruled again from Hipireus."

Tagus listened. He wanted to believe his mentor's words. But the thought that the Falhorne had friends in high places seemed absurd. He wondered if Vitus would be using such language if he had been there yesterday; if he had seen the Templars, murder in their eyes, in the midst of them drawing their weapons at the behest of the bishop. Or if he had seen Bailiff Resti's cloying apologies to the Blessed Realm's chief clergyman in Vinos. But also flowing through his mind were the tales of what all Falhorne simply called the Betrayal.

"What if Chero becomes his grandfather, Praetor?" Tagus rose from his seat as he spoke.

"What will we do then?"

Tagus had been astonished on the day he had stood alongside Vitus in Castle Trastamere, bearing witness as the prince put his signature on a treaty that his forebears would have deemed unthinkable. The Treaty of Trastamere had been signed forty years to the day that Cera Pelleus had fallen, extinguishing the Eternal Order of the Falhorne as it had existed for the previous two centuries.

Cosimo, Grand Prince of Vinos, had been the Order's firm ally until an alliance with the Church and its Blessed Realm had beckoned him to turn on one of his closest friends: Grand Master Vannan of the Falhorne. The prince's troops, backed by the Templars and the forces of the Church, had laid every stronghold of the Order to waste, driving the surviving Falhorne into hiding. Cosimo, in a final act of betrayal, had sold his former friend to the Inquisition who had proceeded to burn the grandmaster over a slow fire.

Tagus had not been alive in those dark days, but Vitus had been there; fleeing west to Tarquin and only returning after Cosimo's death in battle outside the walls of Formoros had seen his more tolerant son come to the throne. After all of his stories, all the tales of the Betrayer and his foul deeds, Tagus could understand why some Falhorne thought Vitus mad for signing such a document with Vino's royal house. He had no desire to see their suspicions confirmed.

Vitus gazed at his apprentice. His deep-set eyes showing both amusement and sadness as he slowly shook his head, and Tagus at once regretted his question.

"You are beginning to sound like someone I refuse to name, Tagus. Someone who felt all treaties are betrayals in waiting. That all promises are made to be broken. I understand your fears. I fully understood them then. Because I shared them myself. But clearly you did not understand why I signed that day. I signed because the grandmaster was dead. I signed because the Order was no more. I signed because we needed allies and our people needed peace. For all these years I secured those things for them; those who keep faith in the rightful gods of this land. For that I am justly proud. I have done my sworn duty as a Falhorne."

"Vitus…brother, I am…"

"And you stood at my side, young lion, doing your sworn duty even as others turned away."

Tagus saw the power that remained in his commander's elderly frame, saw the power behind the simple black robe, identical to his own. It had once split the skull of the Templar Master Claudius at the Battle of the Tio, an act which had finally broken the bloody stalemate, forcing the Blessed Realm troops to withdraw in disgrace at the height of the Skaros Schism. He felt that strength, the strength that had turned the tide in favor of his people.

The praetor approached, placing his hand on his apprentice's shoulder, like a father to a son.

"Do not apologize, brother. Never apologize for standing true in the eyes of the Great Judge, whose infinite wisdom will see you attain your rightful place at the Black King's side."

Tagus dropped his gaze in shame at his cowardice and sat down.

Vitus raised his eyes and immediately noticed Callidus sitting with the others.

Tagus's breath caught in his throat as he saw the old man's face flush red, the signs of anger spreading out across a wrinkled map of lines and creases as grey stubble turned into hot coals. Every movement spoke of rage barely contained as the praetor removed his hand from Tagus's shoulder and turned to face the wayward Falhorne of Trastamere.

"The lost one returns. Did you finally decide to listen, churl? Have you now ears for the truth of the gods?"

Vitus's voice was low and growling, and Tagus knew what that meant. It was the same voice that had preceded Rigo's dreadful flogging on the Allia campaign, and the hard slap with the flat of a sword that had left his younger self seeing stars in the practice yard of Castle Firente when he had dared to defy his mentor's precise instructions during blade training. It was a look of violent anger and it only seemed to build as his mentor took a step toward the table where Callidus sat, the younger man's long face unmoving and expressionless.

"You dare to come into my presence again, after all you have done…after you dared to turn away from your brothers!"

A deathly silence had fallen over the room like a shroud on a corpse. Tagus watched, frozen in place where he sat. Part of him pleaded for him to get up and reason with his mentor, that the pitiful remnants of their once proud Order could not afford to fight amongst themselves. But another part wished to see Callidus torn to shreds by his betters, while yet another was terrified of becoming the next target of the old soldier's wrath.

Callidus slowly rose from the humble stool upon which he sat, his tall lithe form still as a statue as he watched Vitus take another aggressive step toward him. When he spoke, it was calm yet serious, and, in spite of his reservations and hostility, Tagus could tell that the rogue meant every word.

"I returned at the Agoge's express request and command, good Praetor. And I bear nothing but respect for my former teacher…"

"Shut up!"

Vitus's roar tore through the still air and surely would have rattled the panes of the front window, had they not been broken and boarded up. Those ice blue eyes flashing like lightning.

"You will speak only when I command you, soldier! Right now, you have no tongue. No voice. No lying words. Only knees with which to bend and submit."

He stepped forward a third time, his words a deathly hiss.

"Then I might give you back your tongue so you can beg forgiveness. Kneel!"

There was silence. Callidus looked at the praetor, his face as unmoving as stone.

"Now!"

"No!"

The refusal was forceful, as defiant as his words before the bailiff.

Vitus's face now burned like the infernos of Gormani.

"Traitorous scum!"

He rushed forward in a blind rage, fists upraised to beat his will into this upstart, to finally break the apprentice who had dared defy him all those years ago. But his blow never landed.

"No…"

This time Callidus's refusal was softly spoken as his long arms reached out and caught the old man by the shoulders, stopping him in his tracks like a furious bull against a stone wall.

"I said that I respect my former teacher. But now the people of Trastamere are my mentors and I bend knee to no one but them. I hope that I have made myself clear, Brother Vitus."

Tagus's urge to protect his mentor suddenly overwhelmed all mental opposition and he sprung to his feet, rushing to Vitus and gripping his shoulders from behind as Callidus's arms fell back.

The praetor's eyes were still alight as he let himself be drawn away from the confrontation.

"Disobedient, treasonous…bastard…whelp!"

The insults continued to erupt from the cracked lips as Tagus pulled him away.

"Whelp…whelp…wh…"

Vitus's words slurred, his arms dropped, and Tagus felt the body of his mentor go limp in his arms.

"Praetor!"

Tarquinus sprung to his feet, while Skarlos, although still recovering from his own injuries, was by Tagus's side in a second, his strong hands gripping Vitus and preventing him from falling. The old man had gone silent, apart from a sickly gurgle in his throat as his mouth hung open and his eyes swam in dizzy circles.

Tagus continued to grip his mentor's shoulders, a look of shock on his face, words faltering in his throat, as the horror coursed through him. What was happening? Was the man who had been his only real father going die?

"Stand aside!"

The slender Corrie practically shoved past Skarlos's burly shoulder, causing his eyes to bulge in surprise.

"Lay him down."

Tagus could only do as he was told, joining Skarlos in slowly lowering the praetor to the rough floorboards, and then looking on in a daze as his wife knelt down beside him. Narrow hands felt around the wrinkled throat, before forcibly tearing open the black robe and exposing muscular chest beneath. He could not tear his eyes away from the horrible spasms that seemed to dance and ripple across it like a stone tossed into water. But his wife's face was purposeful, her hands moving with expert grace as they traced a line across the quivering flesh and pressed down firmly, whilst holding the purplish leaves of a plant he did not recognize.

Tagus heard her whisper something. Perhaps a curse, or a muffled prayer. Suddenly the heavy silence seemed to break. The atmosphere in the room lifted and the spasms faded into heavy, regular breaths as Vitus's chest rose and fell as it was meant to.

Tagus let a long shuddering sigh escape his lips. She had done it. He did not know how. But she had saved his teacher.

"Let's get him home at once. He needs to rest."

Corrie too was breathing heavily and he noticed the redness in her eyes. Callus's frightened face could be seen over her shoulder. Tagus looked at Tarquinus, who was slowly nodding and Callidus who stood stock still. The rogue Falhorne's arms fell and he looked away.

****

"This way, quickly!"

Silo Street was dark as they struggled along beneath a twilight sky. Tagus and Callus steadying the ailing Vitus, who had insisted on walking. His voice had returned in a stilted halting way. His head seemed unsteady on his shoulders, occasionally rolling left or right.

Corrie walked beside them, never taking her eyes off of her latest patient. It was a quiet night, and few people passed by them as they proceeded. The slums and their dark alleyways yawned to the right as the street skirted along beneath the former city wall that now shielded the Asylum on the riverbank. Its ramparts were unpatrolled and its turrets, standing out starkly against the darkening sky, were clearly in a poor state of repair, oddly mirroring the patched and leaky roofs of the tenement houses.

They walked in silence, until they saw the guard patrol advancing out of the shadows ahead. There appeared to be at least a dozen of them, all armed with bills and pole-axes, and they were headed straight toward them. Soon they could be heard hawking and spitting.

"Into the alley," Corrie whispered, "There's no telling what they might do if they see us in a weakened state like this."

"Do you know where it leads?"

Tagus's eyes were still on the guards, but he had no desire to enter the maze-like warrens of the Ox Guts after dark.

"I do," his wife hissed back, "A few blocks and we'll be out on Candle Way, practically under the arches of the aqueduct. Now let's go before those clots see us."

Tagus nodded to the wide-eyed Callus and they followed her lead, helping Vitus along as they entered into the darkness of the alleyway, which ran beneath the eaves of two five-story tenements that were placed so close together that they might as well have been entering a tunnel. The smell of excrement mixed with rotting wood immediately

133

assailed his nostrils as the night sky and its stars all but vanished overhead.

As his eyes adjusted to the gloom, the sights and sounds of the Ox Guts flooded in: people shouting, children crying, arguments and curses barely muffled by thin walls of half-rotten boards. Here and there a stray dog could be heard barking down one of the many side paths that twisted away from the main alley at crazy angles, or a screeching night walking cat's voice rang out distorted and frightening among the closely packed buildings.

Here and there people could be seen, lying propped up against old barrels or on a bed of discarded sackcloth, their clothes nothing more than a mass of tatters as they snored. Some bore the strong scent of raw alcohol, while others made no sound at all, making Tagus wonder if they still breathed. These were souls that not even the filthiest, most vermin-ridden flophouse would take in. The sickly-sweet smell of fireweed hung in the stale air.

Tagus soon lost all bearings. The buildings and alleys blended together until everything looked the same, but Corrie, who was striding confidently ahead of them, seemed to know the way. He smiled. It was like she was the master of her own domain.

But then she stopped suddenly, forcing Tagus and the others to a rough halt at a shadowy junction between the tenements, narrow lanes branching out in four directions.

"This way," she finally whispered, after some moments of deliberation. Before leading them down another alley between two looming three-story buildings that appeared to be derelict. The sounds of the slums now seemed muffled and distant, and the tall structures obscured the light of the moon.

His soldier's sense of self-preservation kicked in as soon as they had passed beneath the eaves of the building on the left. But he was not quick enough. He turned his body, only to find a ragged figure standing directly before him and a long knife pointed at his throat, its slightly curved blade shining ghostly in the low light.

"Mind yer tongue, gnowt."

The voice came in a dry rasp, as though the speaker had a sore throat. Tagus could see more dark figures emerging from the doors and windows of the derelict building, surrounding the little party. Their clothes were nothing but tattered rags, but their blades and cudgels looked deadly enough. There were at least as many of them as there had been guards on Silo Street, and these cutthroats looked like they could be counted on to take more than money…

He clenched the hilt of his sword, but knew that he had no time to draw it. The hooded footpad in front of him was short, his frame almost childlike, but likely skilled enough to drive a blade into his mark's throat in double-quick time. Tagus realized just how out of his depth he was. Having to hold up Vitus only disarmed him further…but what would they do to Corrie? He was sweating now, fearing for his wife but not daring to take his eyes off the blade. He could hear Callus whimper.

"Hand it all over, gnowt, or yer dead."

The command was still raspy, but beneath it he could sense the voice of a youth not yet a man. The desperate cruelty of a beggar-boy taken to mugging and violence to fill his hungry belly, and perhaps that of others. Other voices could be heard now, the lions share of them clearly directed at his wife.

"Look's like a fine set o' tits we got ere', boys…"

"Heh, a street hen for the pluckin' I say…"

"More like a mouse that's lost its way…"

"C'mon, show us somethin' dearie…"

The jeers continued, it sounded like four or five of the footpads were closing in on her, just as the point of the knife was drawing closer to Tagus's own throat.

He let go of his sword.

"Yer dead…"

The knife flashed, but Tagus's fist was quicker. It helped that the youth's hand got tangled in his own ragged cloak, slowing the slashing blade to the point where it only grazed Tagus's shoulder. At the same instant, his fist drove into the darkness of the hood and connected with a distinctly boyish jaw. There was a short crack, a muffled yelp, and the young cutthroat went down like a stone.

Tagus spun around, but the jeering had already exploded into screams and childlike cries of shock and dismay.

When he finally got a look at the footpads surrounding Corrie on three sides, he saw that they were not advancing. Instead, they were cowering in fear, their knives and cudgels having fallen into the mud of the darkened lane. They were backing away from the silhouetted form of his wife, who stood unmoving at the center of the alleyway, her long hair flitting in the night breeze like a wavering shadow cast by an invisible fire.

Even though her back was to him, Tagus still felt the bizarre urge to cower himself, and found that his back was pressed against Vitus's heaving chest. His heart was pounding and he felt fear, a fear so much stronger than what he had felt when the knife was at his throat. He clenched his teeth against it as he heard Callus wail behind him, keeping his eyes on the dark woman, who seemed to be glancing at each thug in turn.

"Begone!"

The sudden command, rising like a wailing storm wind from her throat, shattered the fetid air of the alley. Almost at once every one of the cowering footpads was on their feet, fleeing through the darkness, screaming as though all the demons of Gormani were on their heels. As they scurried away, the aura of fear began to dissolve.

Tagus's heart stopped pounding as the air cleared. He turned his head, only to find that the young knife whom he had knocked over moments before was still there, pulling himself away at a crawl but not taking his wide eyes off of his former targets.

The youth's hood had fallen back, and Tagus was astonished to find that it was a face he knew, olive skin looking glossy in the poor light as it stretched tight across the hairless jaw that the boy was clutching at with bony fingers. It was old Arbaces's grandson. Tagus did not remember the lad's name. But he was among the faithful, a follower of the gods. His former smugness was gone. He was a frightened child in sweat-sodden rags.

"Gormani take ya, demon…"

The boy cursed, spitting blood into the dirt as he fled.

Tagus glanced away, only to see his wife slowly turning her body toward him. He stared in awe as she spoke.

"Come, let's get out of here."

Chapter 7 – Words in the Dark

They reached the house on Mercer Lane without further incident, guided by the light of the privileged districts with their street lamps upon leaving the shadowed maze of the slums. Vitus vanished upstairs as soon as the front door was opened, refusing further ministrations and turning a deaf ear to Corrie's protests that he should rest.

Callus disappeared into his room in the downstairs back hallway, clearly traumatized by the near mugging they had experienced. The former beggar-boy was certainly no stranger to such conditions and Tagus could only imagine what memories their ordeal had dredged up in the lad.

Tagus and Corrie stood alone in the doorway.

"Will you not stay?"

"I can't."

His wife's voice was normal again, no longer the awesome fear-inspiring cry he had heard in the alleyway.

"The Association will be out tonight, looking for the murderer. I owe it to Ella and all the others to be there with them."

"But you are exhausted…"

"Darling, please, don't worry about me," she smiled in that same old way, "You would do the same in my place."

They shared a quick kiss before she faded into the night. Tagus had not had the courage, nor the words to ask the questions he wanted to ask. What had she even done in that alleyway? Or, for that matter, what had Jesta done at the meeting to terrify Callidus into silence? What other secrets were being kept from him? There were no answers. And he shoved the matter aside as he stumbled his aching legs up the stairs in pursuit of his miraculously restored mentor.

The praetor was at his desk when his apprentice entered the study. The first thing that stood out, shouting that something was awry, was the lack of clutter. All the papers that Tagus had seen covering the desk the day before – all the decrees, statements and official correspondence – had been swept violently to the floor and lay in scattered heaps throughout the room. The top of the desk was bare wood, as black and varnished as a starless sky. The only thing that sat upon it was an old map, worm eaten and corroded by age, showing the vague and faded outlines of the original Five Kingdoms before the rise of the Empire.

Vitus was slumped in the high-backed chair, a large leather-bound book opened in his hands, his wrinkled face partially hidden behind its stained and ancient pages. Tagus recognized the tome immediately, the gilded figure of the chained bear on its spine was unmistakable. It was the *Wermut*, the epic of his mentor's native Braxus and a legendary story that he had first shared with his apprentice years before.

Brilliantly illuminated pages told the story of the hero Emda, as he dared to confront, challenge and slay the king of the giants before fighting to free his homeland from the tyranny of the gnomes who had raised him after he was stolen from his family at birth. Betrayed in the midst of battle by an allied tribe, the badly wounded Emda was saved from certain death by the "horned one" Omon, a terrible earth spirit who vengefully dragged the chieftain of the traitorous clan into the underworld for torment. Thus did Emda survive to lead his people to freedom as their rightful king, only to be viciously dismembered by the jealous god of war. All of this was said to have taken place thousands of years in the past, long before even Lothar Blackshield founded Braxus as a kingdom. Although the long extinct ruling house of that northern land had always looked to Emda as its ancestral founder.

The icy eyes crept into view above the yellowed pages. The gaze that met Tagus as he burst through the door was like a pane of broken glass held together in fragments as the large old book fell forward, thumping on the desk and kicking up tiny plumes of dust. Vitus looked exhausted and ill. Even the firm round jaw and weathered cheeks appeared gaunt and sallow, the stubble clinging to them like growths on an ancient tree. He sullenly stared at his apprentice with drooping lips, a frown that resembled a wilting flower.

"Callidus…the ungrateful brat…" Vitus whispered, taking his eyes off Tagus and letting them wander as he continued to mutter.

"That he would dare to show his face to me…to ME…after all this time. An insubordinate scoundrel to refuse my summons…to disobey my express command in Trastamere. The bastard child…Tarn has ruined him…"

The rasping voice faded and, just as suddenly, the sharpness returned to those wandering eyes, which fixed themselves on Tagus with a startled sense of alarm.

"Young lion! I…Please, come here…"

"Brother…"

Tagus hesitated as he approached the desk. He was standing over Vitus, close enough to see the patchwork of veins spreading out from the blue center of the praetor's eyes like crimson tendrils.

"Brother, are you well? Do you remember what happened?"

Familiar lightning flashed across Vitus's gaze as his voice erupted.

"Damn it all, Tagus! Do I look well? Use your mind, boy! Gods know, I spent enough hours trying to get you to use it. I am far from well, but I am no halfwit if that is what you are thinking…"

He looked down at the book spread before him and shook his head, before slamming his fist on the desk hard enough to make it tremble.

"A praetor collapsing like a diseased mule in front of his men, and after losing his temper…By Ishan, they should not have seen me like that!"

"The men's opinion of you has not changed, brother, they simply fear for your life."

Tagus was trying to be sympathetic, but knew he was walking on nails by saying such things. He knew the old man's temper and now his pride was wounded.

"My life is worthless now."

The fist that had been so tightly clenched, having been slammed on the tabletop, suddenly unfurled and splayed flat like a banner fallen on a battlefield's bloodstained grass. The outstretched fingers trembled.

"I am sorry that the council was harsh on you, young lion, for this was my failure. Do not blame yourself."

"Councillor Corvus said that everything happened on his initiative. Mia and the others went to work for the Avram merchant under Association protection. He did not involve the Falhorne at all. Although truly we did fail in our duty to the gods and the faithful by not intervening. I accept the criticism of the Agoge."

Tagus was trying to sound certain. In truth, he desperately wanted Vitus to validate his actions before the council; to explicitly tell him that he was not failure, nor had he betrayed the sacred vows of the Order in any way.

But Vitus only nodded his scarred head knowingly, without looking up.

"I have never seen Commodus Resti return in a greater rage than when he returned from the Asylum this evening," he said. "The Old Believers were 'defiant', 'insolent', and 'disruptive of the Royal Peace'. I can only assume that you will explain to me why the heat of the Lord of Flames himself appeared ready to consume this august official in His Majesty's government."

Tagus related his experiences at the Agoge to the best of his ability. Vitus listened unperturbed as he described the confrontation with the bailiff. Remaining calm, even when the dreaded word "Inquisitor" passed his apprentice's lips. Nor did news of Callidus's rash deeds provoke a response.

Only after Tagus had finished the exhausting and emotionally draining tale did Vitus raise his head, his aged face haggard in the candle light.

"You accepted the criticism of the Agoge. You embraced that criticism by agreeing to march with the faithful on the morrow. And you made the right decision. We must rebuild their trust. It is all we have in these dark times; our lapse was disgraceful and must be corrected. But recognizing our failings will not lessen the tragedy of an innocent girl's murder, and that the sovereign powers in this land would let such a thing happen."

It was Vitus's turn to relate the day's events. Tagus listened, feeling his heart tremble, as the praetor related his experiences at the royal court: how he had been alerted to Mia's murder by a messenger only to be spurned by the lord chamberlain when he had tried to bring her case before the prince. And the bitter frustration showed in his voice.

"It was for nought. I could not even get close to the throne. I met with Agelaus of the Royal Gendarmerie and he told me that Bishop Theophilus now has the prince's ear from sunup to sundown. The Templars were openly gloating about the slaying of 'that witch' in the marketplace. He said he and others like him within the prince's guard were trying to counteract the Church's influence, but thus far their efforts have achieved little."

Vitus slumped against the desk, his head in his hands.

"Chero is convinced that an alliance with the Blessed Realm and its Hierophant is the best path for the security of the principality. He increasing views those who stand against Church power as obstacles to his own. To think that I once signed a treaty with this man, who now returns to the ways of his grandfather out of expediency. These murders and decrees are how he repays my measured entreaties about something as precious as peace. The Treaty was meant to ensure that none of this happened again..."

He continued stare at the desk's dark polished surface.

"When I heard young Mia had been murdered, I foolishly presumed that something could be done; that the prince we once fought for would hear me and punish those responsible. He is ripping apart everything we have won since Fallonier Fields, and now he has gone one step further, for this is far beyond what he did to our Brother Porus. He knows full well how few friends we have left. For all his pledges of support, Agelaus' power at court is nothing compared to what moves against us: our greatest enemies have royal protection, and the greatest among them has royal blood."

Tagus did not bother to hide the look of horror on his face. He had heard these words before, or words so much like them that they blurred together like heat haze in the southlands. Callidus had spoken them. He had railed against the Treaty, insisting that it had all been in vain, and Tagus had very nearly drawn his sword in anger against such blasphemy. But now it was coming from his own teacher and whatever anger he had felt before now faded into a dull grey lump in the pit of his stomach, a heavy stone weighing him down.

"Again, I do not blame you for being at a loss for words before the council, young lion. We have failed them. Nor can we deny our present weakness. I apologize that I did not inform you…"

Tagus froze as his mentor's body was shaken by a fit of violent coughing. The sinking feeling in his stomach was quickly replaced by surging panic and he hastened to Vitus's side, only to be waved away by an angry trembling hand.

"No!"

Vitus ceased his coughing and looked up with a pained expression on his face, the shadows gathering in the lines and creases of his cheeks.

"Lion, tell me, what do you know of my past? How did I come to enter the service of Our-King-In-Barbarus?"

"You have told me many times, brother," Tagus replied, confused by the abruptness of the question and terrified for the old man's health.

He began stating what he knew as if he were reciting a history lesson.

"You were the born the youngest son of a noble family of Braxus. Unwilling to see your elder brother claim everything of your father's estate, you left to seek your fortune in the battle-torn borderlands of Karados. As a mercenary cavalryman, you joined the army of Prince Leonidas of Deimos in the war against Tartosa. You participated in the sack of Brisi and witnessed the burning of the inhabitants of the low-town at the behest of the Inquisitor Gratiano. On that day, you first met the young woman you called Julia. Moved by the suffering of her and others among the faithful, you concealed her from sight and helped her to safety. Deserting the prince's army, you escaped west with her and a band of survivors to the Order's citadel of Cera Damas, where her brother, one of the Falhorne, welcomed you. There you became a warrior of the gods, accepting the mark of the *Ash Crown* upon initiation, and forsaking your previous life to serve the Black King as we all have sworn to do."

Tagus paused and stared with worried expectancy at Vitus, who was staring right back at him – his deep-set eyes joined with a melancholy smile that spoke of painful truths unsaid.

"After all these years, young lion, all these years and you still are capable of falling for a bald-faced lie."

The old man reached out and grabbed Tagus's shoulder with a hand that had lost none of the strength that had repeatedly knocked his apprentice into the dust of the training ground.

"Do not look so surprised, brother. During the days of the Empire, when the Betrayer's forces held sway over Moradaleum under the false name of Hipireus, we Falhorne lived by deception. Now it seems that we must once again cloak our words and deeds before the spreading power of the foe. But I cannot excuse this lie, for it only serves to hide an old man's frailty and weakness…"

Tagus stood in stunned silence at these words, his mentor's hand heavy on his shoulder, barely comprehending what he was hearing: was Vitus saying that he had lied about himself for the past twenty years? Did he not trust his own brothers-in-arms?

"I am sorry my brother, my lion, my son of two score years. But every child must realize the truth that his father is only mortal flesh, blood, and bone – and that these things are weak."

The grip on Tagus's shoulder tightened and he was silent as his praetor began a tale that, even before the first words had entered the dusty air of the study, felt like a blade sinking into flesh.

"I was my father's eldest, heir of all he possessed, and raised from birth in the tradition of the barons of my homeland. I was born to be the master of House Bastarnae and to let none question it. When I was but a lad of ten winters, I remember beating my younger brother bloody one day because he would not bow his head low enough for my refined taste. It was a beating that my father added to and instructed my brother to bear with all the stoicism of a loyal vassal to his liege lord."

There was a strange light in Vitus's eyes as the old man went on.

"As I grew in body and strength, servants feared the back of my hand and my tutors were terrified of boring me, knowing this offense could mean a flogging or the inside of a dungeon cell. Nor did my father chide or discipline me for my growing brutality. For he was shaping me in his image and that of his peers. Oh, how proud he was of his 'little lion'. Proud when at age fifteen, I lost my temper and mortally wounded the old soldier charged with my instruction in the ways of war. I remember father placing a firm hand of congratulations on my shoulder, even as the man's blood drained into the earth of the courtyard, making no move to save the life of the petty commoner who had aroused the wrath of his noble son.

"He was prouder still when my youthful sword-arm cut down a certain insignificant peasant on the high road outside Tema. An insolent fellow who had been too slow in moving his hay wagon from the chosen path of his betters. No doubt he would have been equally proud of the action that would serve to tear me away from him forever, if only I had remained discreet about it, and if only he had been less heavy-handed in instilling the virtue of loyalty in his son and heir."

Vitus's voice was trembling now, and he began coughing violently, his right hand clumsily reaching for his apprentice's opposite shoulder.

"Steady me brother, for none of this fills me with pride. I am crossing swords with a foe that is within me. One that I have long sought to submerge in Mora's depths. But the earth goddess has not been kind."

Tagus silently gripped his mentor by the arms, and felt the truth that his mentor's strength was not what it had been. He was looking not at the indefatigable warrior, his fearless leader in a hundred battles, but at an infirm elder whose demons had finally caught up with him.

"I was taught, as were all the scions of the great Braxian noble houses, that my sovereign right extended to everything within my domain. That so long as my actions did not dishonor the name of my family, I could demand anything of my subjects. At sixteen years of age and a full man, I was the lord and master. My desire was law to anyone of lesser station. And as a virile youth, my cock was beginning to demand satisfaction.

"Just as I had demanded that my brothers bow to me and my tutors amuse me, I had always demanded that the servants submit to my every whim as they would the will of the Most High. So when my manhood craved the body of a certain maidservant among the kitchen staff, I took what I believed was mine by right. She did not resist. For she knew better than to challenge a noble's son, whom the heavens had smiled upon. I took her whenever I desired her. Whenever we were safe from prying eyes, I made her perform her womanly duty to me. A young despot forcing himself upon his inferiors who were but objects for his hands to grasp. May the Great Judge forgive my arrogance."

Tagus could see tears pricking the edges of his mentor's eyes now, as an evident source of deep sorrow threatened to consume him. He could recall only one time that he had witnessed the stoical Vitus overcome with such emotion. It had been when they had stood together on the Fallonier Fields, the sun setting on that bloody day, and overseen last rites for the fallen brethren. The praetor's face had been all stone, until the body of Brother Piso had come before him on the funeral pyre; broken and pierced by no less than seven spear-points. Vitus's face had cracked – tears rolling from his eyes as he buried his head in his hands, hiding his sorrow from the sight of his men. Upon regaining his composure, he had carried on with the rites, saying nothing to Tagus or anyone else.

"Of course, we were discovered. It was not the servants. They had never spoken of our affair, for they knew the consequences if they dared speak ill of their lord. No, it was my own mother who caught us in one of the kitchen stores as she made one of her impromptu inspections, in which she would coldly apply the back of her hand to any servant that had overlooked some minor detail in her ever-changing list of rules, or had failed to clean some insignificant patch of dust on the edge of a table. A high-born woman, viciously protective of the noble seed that she had bore, she was absolutely livid, and would have most certainly beaten the girl to death if I had not stopped her; dishonoring my blood with this 'filthy seductress peasant whore' in her words. I might have saved her life that day, but I could not save her from being whipped and confined to a dungeon cell.

"I was taken before my father. While my mother was present, he was stern and coldly warned me to never again dishonor the family name or stain the glory of my house. But when we were alone in his study he grinned and congratulated me on my 'conquest'; praising me for so boldly taking what was rightfully mine to enjoy. He only warned me to be more discreet about it.

"They let her go, but in the weeks that followed it was clear that the effects of my dalliances could not be hidden, for her belly grew.

145

Everyone knew it was my child. Ashamed for once in my life, and fearful of the consequences of fathering a bastard, I stopped seeing her, avoiding the kitchens and removing myself from the presence of the servants as best as I was able. But she did not intend to let me escape responsibility.

"She found me one day, in spite of all of my cowardly efforts. Clothes disheveled and tears streaming down her face, she demanded that I marry her. The child within had granted her the courage to demand the unthinkable. There was no deference in her voice, no fear of her betters, only the fury of an abandoned mother, the lioness that defends her offspring to the death.

"'This is your seed,' she screamed at me, 'you have sown it in my bosom. Great Sun burn you if you do not give me water!' She was but an illiterate milkmaid from some rustic backwater, but she knew her fables and how the Great Sun, the name the ignorant Braxian peasantry have given to the Betrayer whom they worship in the same manner as their ancient sun god, withers the hearts of men who abandon their children."

A long and painful sigh sounded as the praetor slumped further into Tagus's arms.

"I could have struck her and commanded her to be silent. I could have threatened her with death if she dared to speak further. I could have reproached her to my father, who could have made her vanish, or to my mother, who would have sealed her lips with lethal blows, so that she could never tarnish our family name again. That would have been fully within my rights. Yet I did none of those things. For my father had taught me loyalty: loyalty to house, loyalty to kin, loyalty to one's liege, and it was loyalty I had never questioned. In that moment of confusion, fear, rage, and perhaps something that could be called compassion, it was loyalty that won out; loyalty to that which I saw as my own, my seed.

"There was a part of me inside this 'peasant whore'. A part of me that I could not take back. Against all my instincts and breeding, I took her hand in mine and swore upon everything I held dear to protect her and my child. I spoke the fatal words, the words that would ultimately cast me from my pinnacle and drain the noble blood from my veins. I swore that I would marry her."

His tears had stopped, but Vitus was staring at the floor, clearly not wanting his apprentice to see his pain; just as he had not wanted his men to see the reality of their commander's illness at Black Horseman. At last, he raised his head, and Tagus could see a weak half-smile form upon the praetor's guilt-wracked face.

"Noble ideals have no place in a noble court, young lion, remember that well. I was to learn this truth in the harshest possible way a few days later when my father found out what I had done. This time there was no manly talk of sport and conquest, only a savage blow to the face that knocked me clean to the ground. He no doubt would have taken his boot to me had I been anything less than his son and heir. He condemned me as no better than a traitor; a disgrace to House Bastarnae and all my illustrious ancestors.

"His curses stung worse than the blow. All my life I had obeyed and emulated him. Now I was being punished for showing a loyalty greater than anything he had ever shown to anyone. Perhaps it was youthful hotheadedness, perhaps it was foolish defiance, or perhaps it was simply because I had been trained from such a young age to let no blow go unanswered, but I did the unthinkable. I struck the very man whom I had always wanted to be, my own father."

The weak smile widened. Behind the tears, Tagus caught a fleeting yet intense glimpse of pride.

"The blow that I struck was neither weak nor half-hearted. I was sixteen. I had trained for years in the use of weapons and had even killed men that had aroused my wrath. The blow that struck my father that day shattered his nose and very nearly broke his neck as well. The look that he gave me, lying on the floor and looking up at his eldest son and heir, blood dripping from his ruined face, was nothing short of murderous – the kind of look that a lord gives to a rebellious peasant who is about to go to the gallows.

"While I did not hang, he disowned me, casting me out of the castle gates with nothing more than the clothes on my back. Saying he would kill me if I did not leave the family's domains at once. For I was no longer kin, no longer my father's son, only a common outlaw. I fled not only my father's estates, but my homeland, leaving Braxus behind and going south to the Karados borderlands. I entered the only trade open to me besides begging, mercenary work.

"I do not care to know what my parents did to the 'filthy seductress peasant whore' who dared to steal away their first-born son. I never saw her again."

Vitus again paused, his tears dried, his expression serious as he stared Tagus full in the face.

"Do you still think me so praiseworthy, young lion?"

Words eluded Tagus, his mind swimming in the stream of revelations pouring from his mentor's cracked lips. He struggled to make sense of it all, the horrible complexities of this man whom he had for song admired unquestioningly as a hero.

"What of the sack of Brisi?" he found himself asking, struggling to keep his faith while straddling yawning abysses of doubt.

His mentor sighed, what was left of his wry half-smile vanishing.

"Once more I must beg for your forgiveness, my son. Again, I have allowed my own cowardice to distort the truth of things. I did join Prince Leonida's army against Tartosa, fought under his flaming star banner at Banos when I rode in the vanguard of the cavalry charge that broke the back of the upstart King Aristos's defenses. I likewise proved myself at Terenntus and in many skirmishes before our host descended on Aristos's capital at Brisi.

"By that time, I had drowned my pain in blood and fire: relishing the deaths of each enemy just as I had relished the death of my former arms instructor, all thought of my lost patrimony vanishing with their last breaths. I drowned out the echo of my betrothed's angry words every time that I indulged myself in one of the cheap whores that besieged our camp each night or forced myself upon a miller's daughter in the ruins of some nameless village. I was at the forefront of the battalion that first stormed through Brisi's shattered gates; ready to indulge myself in the twin pleasures that kept the memories of my disownment at bay."

Vitus shook his head sadly before continuing.

"I still remember the dreadful scenes as the city burned around me: the scent of blazing homes mingled with the stench of blood, and the screams of women. Everything being smashed and overturned in the mad search for hidden gold and treasure. Nor was I a mere witness, young lion, for I participated in all those things as I played my part in destroying the greatest and most prosperous community of the faithful east of Vinos…a far cry from the soulless city that Baron Martino was to make his capital years later.

"I still remember the pleading eyes of the tanner that I personally decapitated after he denied having hidden his money. I remember the unarmed weaver we flayed alive in front of his children. I remember the inquisitors, white-robed and golden masked, riding through the terror in search of the heretics Aristos was notorious for harboring. Some of them leading great chains of shackled captives in their wake. And I remember Julia, the pretty young heretic whom I pulled from the sewers as my rightful prize."

Vitus looked deep into Tagus's shocked eyes.

"She was not alone. Her brother tried to protect her from me, unarmed, and in spite of his sister's screams telling him to save himself. I easily knocked the boy to the ground and proceeded to beat him bloody until my boredom caused me to finally run him through. Then I collected my prize, driving off those soldiers who tried to take her from me. Heretic or no, she belonged to me and not to the pyres of the Inquisition that burned all through the night with the fat of countless damned souls."

He suddenly pulled away, stumbling over crumpled papers to the desk amid a renewed fit of coughing. Before wrenching open one of the drawers and gently lifting something out, something he cradled delicately in both hands. He returned and pressed the object into Tagus's palm.

"Look," he commanded.

Tagus beheld a small talisman, expertly fashioned from silver. It had been worked into the form of a mountain. A seven-spoked wheel at its heart embodied the seven blessings of the earth mother, Mora, mistress of the root of the world. It was aged and battered, its upper-right corner partially melted, but the beauty of its workmanship remained. On its reverse side was etched a simple "J".

"Julia's ward," Vitus whispered through clenched teeth, "Perhaps it saved her from the fires that night, although it could not save her from me and my lust. I brought her back to camp. She did not try to resist further, after her initial struggles were met with heavy blows. She knew from the hungry eyes gazing from every direction that to flee would only mean bondage to another or worse. Many others had taken captives in the city, but most were taken straight to the slavers that hovered on the edge of camp like circling vultures. That was smart, given that the Inquisition was burning every woman they could lay their hands on, whether they were among the faithful or not. Most of the mercenaries had already satisfied their lusts in the city and were not willing to risk the wrath of the Church for hiding witches in their beds. I was a bold one not to sell her when I had the chance."

Vitus paused again, evidently collecting his troubled thoughts.

"Back in my tent…I am not sure if it was boredom, or genuine curiosity at having a follower of the Old Gods in my possession, but after indulging my manly passions one night, I ordered her to tell me a story.

"'What would you hear about?' she asked, her former terror replaced with cold stone.

"'You heretics have heroes, do you not?' I casually responded. She nodded silently. 'Tell me of them,' I gestured lazily, like the little despot who had once demanded amusement from his tutors.

"'I will tell you of the greatest hero of them all.' She paused and looked at me with piercing dark eyes without blinking once, 'his name is Ishan'."

Vitus paused, nodding slowly at his apprentice, noting the startled recognition in Tagus's eyes.

"From her I learned of our Lord in Barbarus, and for the first time the Falhorne became more than a silly dark legend that I had heard from the lips of teachers desperate to entertain me. Just as they had once entertained me with the tales from the *Wermut*, finally convincing me that I should learn to read so I could better follow Emda's heroic adventures. Julia gave me a far better education than any of them. For her fear of death had given way to pride in who she was; pride in being among the faithful.

"From her I learned the sacred names of the Celestial Court: Fiore, Lord of Flames; Mora, the Earth Mother; Viro, Mistress of the Waters; Sol, the Sky Lord; and the Eternal Judge who reigns over the souls of men. Over the course of three nights, she told me of the ancient days of the Five Kingdoms, of the rise of the Betrayer, of the sacking of Cera Infernus, of the emergence of the Order, of the Devouring, and of the ongoing struggle of her people to survive against the Inquisition. But of all these things, it was the legend of the Black King that loomed largest in my mind; that greatest of heroes who had challenged an emperor and sacrificed all for his people."

He closed his eyes, remembering.

"When Sol's tears descend on Mora's face, the mountains walk in silence. And in Viro's watery embrace, shall Fiore's flame strike violence. Upon red moon and sundered stars, raise the pinnacle of Barbarus.

"I remember that she spoke those words from the Book of Damas, words she knew by heart. There was something about that story that called to me, summoned me to once more do the unthinkable. Perhaps because Ishan had been a fallen nobleman like myself. Perhaps it was because my soul longed for something greater, and she was showing me the way."

Vitus was leaning heavily against the desk.

"But she was taken from me, of course. I could not hide her forever. Her beauty had caught the lusty eyes of many, and so I should not have been surprised when a certain mercenary captain strode into my tent and tried to take her in my absence. She struggled, and I heard her screams only to find the brute half-naked and standing over her battered corpse. He said that it was his right. He said that he outranked me. He said that he would flay me alive if I touched him. He was saying that even as I cleaved his head from his shoulders."

The praetor coughed again violently, and Tagus saw blood on his mentor's tongue.

"What more is there to say? History repeats itself for the fool. I was a marked man and I fled the camp as a fugitive. Julia had told me of Cera Damas and where it stood on the Vinos frontier, and so I made for it, eluding my pursuers until I reached the Order's domains. Fortunate was I that they were in desperate need of men, besieged and beset by multiple foes. I doubt Praetor Pallas would have accepted dishonored mercenary scum under better circumstances."

The faint smile slowly returned, like a light in the depths of black pit.

"I left my entire life behind when I became Falhorne. Even you shall never know the name that I was given at birth. I have invoked the Lord of Flames to reduce my former life to ashes. Gladly undergoing the agony of the *Ash Crown* at Cera Pelleus, in the presence of Grandmaster Vannan himself, to purge away my sins.

"But I will tell you of my name as you know it. A name that I heard Julia scream on that evil night when Brisi burned. I chose to take the name of her brother. The boy I killed so cruelly. The boy who defended his sister to the death, though he was unarmed. That boy now surely stands by the Black King's side on Barbarus. By taking his name, I hoped that one day I would be worthy of joining him there…"

The choked voice trailed into another fit of coughing. Tagus had to hold his mentor upright as flecks of blood stained the floor, spattering on discarded parchment. His stunned silence in the face of endless bitter revelations was broken by the urgency of now and he found himself screaming.

"Brother! Praetor! Vitus!"

In response to Tagus's frantic cries, and by the bloody coughing echoing through the house, young Callus soon arrived, dishevelled and in his night clothes.

Wordlessly they helped the aged Falhorne into his bed, that same simple cot in the corner behind the desk. Callus gathered some medicine that he said would stop the coughing and allow him to sleep. The medicine was administered, and the coughing seemed to subside.

Soon it was only Tagus who sat by his mentor's bed, keeping silent vigil in the dark as his heart hammered in fear.

"Young lion," a weak, exhausted voice said through the shadows, "You know I would never abandon you…I would never leave my brothers…my sons…"

Tagus could feel tears pricking his eyes. His nerves were shattered from everything Vitus had told him. He had tried to listen. But all he heard were the screams of dying men, drowning bodies beneath the Allia Bridge; an endless parade of carnage from over twenty years of war. The very idea that this man, this great man, who had been among the last to wear the *Ash Crown* and bear the Order's mark, could be anything less than the hero he was filled his former apprentice with a terrified indignation. It was as though the world were coming apart.

"If I truly can be said to have the spirit of a lion," he finally said, "Then you, brother, have the spirit of a lion as great as Sol's sky. Because I am your son. It was you who gave this broken young boy without a mother, without a father, and without words, something to live for; a cause to fight for. You gave me the eyes to read the words of our founder. Regardless of how you once lived, you are Falhorne now, and so I am. To me you are the Black King."

It was true. There was only silence in the darkened room. He sat there by the bedside all night, revolving countless memories, turning Julia's silver amulet over and over in his hands as he maintained his vigil. Until the first rays of dawn crept through the small barred window of the chamber that now felt like a prison cell.

The western horizon was finally brightening the jagged line of rooftops, throwing a dull light across broken tiles and crumbling chimneys, some of which had probably not felt a workman's hand since the days of the Empire. But in the dead end of the alleyway, amid the garbage and stink of human excrement, nothing but cold lamplight pierced the shadows.

Corrie had tasted blood on her tongue over a block away before her escort finally held a light over the shredded corpse, its arms splayed outward and laying on a bed of dead rats. One of the Association men accompanying her, a muscle-bound former enforcer for "The Family", had doubled over, vomiting up the contents of his stomach at the awful sight.

"All Mother protect us."

Corrie's prayer stifled the scream waiting on her tongue. Again, she had to fight to center herself. Fight to remember who she was and her role alongside the visibly terrified men around her. She was their only hope. Their only light in the darkness of a living nightmare. And so, she played her part.

This time Nicco was not there. But she saved some of the youth's blood in a vial all the same before passing it to one of the Association men. The same stocky Samosian that had stood with her over Ella's mangled remains.

This time the Monster's victim was a boy, black-haired, olive-skinned and waifish thin. He could not have been more than fourteen years old, his ragged grime-encrusted cloak speaking of an existence huddling in doorways and begging on the streets. This cloak now lay in shreds on the ground.

Like Ella, the youth's ribcage had been brutally cracked open, his chest reduced to nothing but a mass of bloody gristle and smashed bone. Above this terrible red hollow, his throat had been torn. Corrie could see the teeth marks. One leg had been ripped from its socket and lay nearby, dried blood coagulating around the stump. The rats that lay in a pile beneath the corpse had likewise been torn limb from limb, as though something had tried to build an altar to an insane god. But the worst thing was the eyes. They had been torn completely from their sockets, leaving the boy's face hanging in a blind open-mouthed scream toward the heavens.

Again, the Stream of Life entered the corpse only to return with nothing but a grotesque tableau of ravenous hunger and bloodlust. But then she saw the birthmark on the boy's wrist, and his identity screamed at her.

"Otho…"

She said the name out loud, not caring what the others thought. The shock driving the leaden weariness from her bones.

She remembered the boy. The pox had nearly claimed him when it had ravaged the Asylum years before, taking the lives of his parents and leaving him with no one but old Arbaces. But even in those dark days, when death had drawn close enough to grip his heart, the light of life had never left those boyish eyes. Now they were gone. The boy, among the first that she had delivered into this world, had been left in darkness.

"You knew this one too, eh?"

It was the Samosian talking. Corrie had learned his name was Gorgo.

"Yes. His name is Otho. He was from the Asylum, and he was among the gang that attacked me and my husband."

"He was from the Camp? And a thug?"

He sounded genuinely surprised, using the refugee's common slang term for the Asylum. "The Camp" was short for "Prison Camp", and everyone in the slums knew that boys from the inside didn't run with local gangs. They did whatever heretics did behind their walls. But this kid was obviously an exception.

Corrie could already feel Jesta's outrage. Unlike the Ox Guts, the poor yet defiant Asylum looked after its people. Even a forsaken beggar boy who moonlighted as a thug in the slums would not be overlooked. It was a foreign concept to the refugees who had lost everything in the wars that had shattered their homelands: family, security, tradition, culture, and any hope for a future that did not even belong to them.

She stood up, extending her focus into the stale air until the life in the men around her, their fearful beating hearts pounding in their ears, appeared as a single current of pale green light. The Stream of Life appeared weak and sickly, for its bed ran alongside a power that flowed deeper and stronger in the dark alleys. A power that quickly turned its attention to her.

A flash of deep purple crossed her vision and she felt terror worm its way inside of her like a cold chill shadow. It was death. Not the simple residue that life leaves behind as it re-enters the cycle of being, but the raw power of the nether realms. That which has no natural place in the world of the living.

But its power in the alleyway was old and frail. Corrie let her spirit push back against its cold tendrils and they lazily flowed away. She saw the truth. Jesta had to be warned.

"Take the samples to the Companions at once. We have to go. Now."

****

No guards patrolled beneath the great stone archway when she entered the Asylum. The Association boys had almost died laughing when she'd told them about the bailiff, making all sorts of wisecracks about Resti losing all control of his bowels during his humiliating retreat and making the palace smell like an "old shithouse". But Corrie knew better.

It did not take long to find Jesta. The tall woman, clad in the same black mourning garments she had worn on the Day of Blood, was in the street making preparations for the march. Many Old Believers were already outdoors, although the sun had not yet fully risen and the horizon was a mass of grey haze. All of the early risers were women, so used to taking charge of family affairs while their husbands toiled on the docks.

Corrie felt her former teacher's every move as she moved purposefully among them. From the tips of her nerves to the depths of her soul, she felt the concentration of raw power within this woman. Power held firmly and consciously in check; strength and certainty mixed with delicacy and care. There was love in her fierce glances, a

156

glimpse of feelings that she could not show and truths that she could not reveal, even to those she had dedicated her life to protecting.

Jesta did not belong to herself, but to a destiny and a power that was beyond even her vast knowledge and understanding. Something she had been humble enough to admit before her chosen students as part of their bond within the Craft. Corrie could not help but admire her sheer conviction, even as she sensed that the events of the past two days were tearing her teacher apart. And now her former student was bringing more bad news.

"Move your group over there Octavia, that's right. The rest of you get alongside her in a line. Fill the whole street. Make room for the others…"

Jesta was calling out instructions, even as Corrie drew her aside into a quiet muddy lane that ran between empty back gardens. The light of alarm flashed through her bold black eyes as Corrie placed both hands on her sister's arms and pressed her up against a fencepost beside a ramshackle shed. All the while nervously glancing over her shoulder to make sure no one was looking.

"What tidings, sister? Why have you come at such an early hour?".

Corrie felt her heart beating faster as she described the state of young Otho's corpse. Jesta's face grew cold.

"It was different this time. I must have reached him faster than I reached Ella. The killer left a much stronger trace. Not enough to discern its nature. But The Stream laid bare the contrast. I felt the alien presence from the nether realms flowing in a dark river into the void. It is necromancy we are facing, Soyga."

She was trying to keep her voice low, but it was impossible to stop the fear. She spoke Jesta's secret name with an urgency on the verge of panic. It was something that should not have been possible, something only the legends spoke of.

Jesta's voice was heavy as she replied.

"I sensed you last night, sister, were you attacked?"

"Yes. It was the same gang that Otho was part of. It was he who attacked my husband. I was forced to use the Presence."

Jesta nodded. Her face remained cold and she did not ask Corrie to calm herself. She knew better than that.

Corrie was hardly surprised that Jesta had felt her use of the power, she had been two streets away from the Agoge chambers at Octavia's front door when she had felt her former teacher use the Presence on the previous afternoon. Surely Jesta had her own legitimate reasons for taking such a risk. The powers of the Craft were not to be revealed among the uninitiated unless absolutely necessary.

"I know you handled it as you saw fit," she said. "I trust your judgment on such matters, sister. Did you sense anything during the attack?"

"No. The Stream of Life flowed uninterrupted. Those boys certainly had no power to displace it. The All Mother does not discriminate."

Jesta still had her back pressed against the fencepost as Corrie continued to grip her shoulders. Her teacher's eyes as black and hard as the expression on her face. So much burdened her now, but she remained patient with her one-time apprentice.

"How many have been taken now?"

"Seventeen this month. Perhaps one hundred over the past six. Not even the Association can precisely say when the first killing took place. Not in a place as teeming as the Ox Guts."

Corrie heard Jesta curse under her breath.

"What is it, Soyga? Do you possess any further insights, my teacher?"

The black eyes sank toward the earth and she could tell that her normally unflappable mentor was fending off despair.

"I do, young Sibylline. But All Mother protect us if what you say is true. The Enemy has returned."

It was not often, even in the secret places, that Jesta used her student's secret name. The name that she had given Corrie upon her initiation into the inner workings of the Craft. But "The Enemy" was not a name that her teacher had uttered once since their lessons had concluded nine years before.

The Enemy was something everyone who studied the Craft knew and feared. It had not raised its wicked face in a thousand years, yet its nightmare shadow lingered and hovered menacingly at the edges of their communal vision.

Few beyond the Sisterhood remembered them now. Few remembered the dark days when the powers of the nether had come to earth and the dead legions had marched across the land, tainting it and poisoning the All Mother with their encroaching presence that was anathema to all life. Even the Stream had ceased to flow by the time The Thirsting had been cast down by the Sisterhood and its allies, who had been mighty in those ancient days, and banished into the southern deserts. But the Enemy had not been destroyed. Corrie had felt their taint and it had felt her. She desperately needed answers.

"Where did they come from, Soyga?"

"I do not know."

Jesta was staring at the ground by her feet.

"I do not know how they could have gotten here, or why. Only that the Sisterhood dictates we remain vigilant. Do you know the present whereabouts of our sister, Hecate? Has she returned to Vinos?"

"I have received no word," Corrie replied.

"Then I shall join you personally as you accompany the Association on their nightly patrols. If the Enemy is here, their power is not yet strong. We must strike at them while we may. I pray to the All Mother that this is but an isolated case. Otho will be honored before the gods and I shall send word to Arbaces. But now I have the greater affairs of my people to attend to…"

She turned her stoic face toward the street where more of the Asylum folk were now gathering, pushing against Corrie's arms as she made to leave. But Corrie continued to hold her. Even though she strove to hide it, even though her face remained calm, she could sense the rage in Jesta's soul, see it burn deep in her black eyes, like the great flaming sea that burned at the root of the world and encased it in its fiery embrace. She had already revealed her powers out of anger; Corrie could not let her go.

"You will not be going to the marketplace, Soyga. You will stay here and see to those that remain behind."

The fire that Corrie had seen in the depths of Jesta's eyes flared, rushing to the surface and flashing with almost volcanic intensity.

"Have you lost your senses? Unhand me, child! I will go with my people!"

"No."

Corrie emphasized this word with the Craft, letting the force of the Stream push Jesta back against the fencepost. A look of stunned disbelief split her formerly calm and collected expression.

"I am sorry, sister. But I cannot let you go. I sensed your use of the Presence before the Agoge. And I know my teacher too well. The guild expelled you from your rightful place. By the All Mother your rage was justified, righteous in the face of such a crime against nature. But I know what you will do if you see De Tolley, if you see any of their faces this day. You will again expose the Craft out of anger. And this will only serve to put your people and the Sisterhood in greater danger. Let me go in your place, for I have suffered no personal wrong at the hands of these men."

Jesta stared back at her. The fury in her eyes had subsided, but still boiled deep within.

"I cannot forsake them. This day could witness the cycle overturned. De Tolley and the guilds be damned, this is a matter of duty! I must be with them! It is my place, not yours, Sibylline!"

"I mean you no offense, honored teacher. You have been a mother to all who dwell within these walls, guided them through hardship, healed their wounds, and nurtured their lives as you once nurtured me. You have done all that the All Mother commanded and so much more. I love you, elder sister. Your soul is an unquenchable fire, giving light to the people. You love them. You want to protect them. And that is why you must let me go in your stead. This is my task, my burden, and I shall bear it in your name and theirs."

"It is not your burden, child. I am the guardian here. All such burdens fall to me."

Corrie clenched her teeth in frustration. Sometimes Jesta could be so stubborn.

"None of the Craft share their burdens alone. Guardian or no, you are of the Sisterhood."

The older woman looked down, clearly ashamed at being reminded of such things by her former apprentice. But, for all her conviction and sense of duty, Corrie knew that her teacher also knew herself all too well.

"Then go," Jesta said softly, "I shall maintain my watch here. All Mother protect you, young sister."

"May She watch over us all."

The kiss they shared was full of the fears and urgency of the moment. The heated action of their lips impregnated with the passion of two lives entwined across time, just as Korva the heavenly Red Serpent eternally reflected the twisting course of the Stream of Life among the stars. It was an intimacy that the uninitiated would never understand.

Corrie only became conscious of the weariness in her flesh as their lips parted and she finally removed her grip on her teacher's shoulders. She wanted to laugh bitterly as they left the shadow of that deserted lane to return to the others. She was just as stubborn, just as annoyingly headstrong. Living in the Ox Guts had only taught her to hide it better.

It was only then that her thoughts turned to Tagus.

She had long sensed the power in her husband; a massive concentration of the energies of the Stream, lying untapped at the core of his being. And yet she had never told him of it. Like all those touched by the Craft, he would have to find it for himself if he was to realize the power within. Now she was unsure if her beloved would ever get the chance.

****

"Come along! Come along! Assemble!"

Tagus stood before the little group of Falhorne and Asylum watchmen, his barked order fading into the dawn sky as he struggled to remember the lines and proper pacing of the ritual.

He could not help but allow his mind to be consumed by the awe-inspiring figure that his mentor had been, standing strong before his men at Fallonier Fields.

Vitus's voice had been as grim as the slate colored clouds, his eyes alive with bright flame. The praetor had let his hood slip, exposing the true mark of his authority that was the *Ash Crown.* The ritual he performed that day had not been performed since the Order's fall, and among the assembled warriors it was the aging Vitus alone who bore full knowledge of it. What was half-legend to others had been the praetor's own lived experience. He had never let the discipline of the old days die.

Slowly and with deliberate reverence, Tagus grasped the haft of the great halberd and raised it aloft before the small band of men, the same majestic weapon Vitus had raised skyward before twenty seasoned Falhorne. Its blade was curved, honed to a wicked edge, and completely jet black in color. The dull murmur of voices died out at the sight of it. For it was *damas,* a weapon of the original rebellion against the Empire when the Falhorne had first risen against the usurper.

The acting praetor began to speak. Trying to capture the loud clear voice that had struck like a thunderbolt into the heart of each and every Falhorne at Fallonier Fields.

"Brothers! In the days of the Order, the masters of the Falhorne would choose The Hundred on the night before battle; one hundred proven warriors who would form the vanguard the next day. Today we honor this noble tradition. Today one hundred brave men stand before me. We stand in the vanguard; chosen by the Black King to bear his blessing into battle as we fight for our people and our gods. I expect you to be worthy of this honor."

His voice raised to a roar as he gripped the *damas* in both hands, raising it to the heavens and catching the sunlight on its obsidian edge.

"Brothers! Never forget that we are a weapon! Together we are the arm of the Black King, descended from Barbarus to crush the servants of the Betrayer! Remember that we are the Falhorne, the blade that shall pierce his cloak of lies! Just as the blade of mighty Sol pierced the evil form of Tylo in the Godtime, so it shall be this day!"

The words echoed in the dawn air. No cheers followed the short speech. Valens shuffled nervously, while his brother looked confused. Only Tarquinus smiled in recognition.

Tagus slowly lowered the holy weapon, bowed his head, and began to pray.

"Lords of the Court, hear me, for I am Tagus, your knight, your weapon, your steel in the lands of mortals, and in me earth and sky are one. O Black King, Ishan, Guardian of the heights of Barbarus, be my strength! O Fiore, Burning Lord, Scourge of the Red Plain, be my wrath! O Red Lady, Mistral, Chooser of the Slain, be my courage! For today I offer my life. Today death is my battle companion. Today my soul joins with yours!"

Reaching down he picked up a jet-black shield in the shape of a kite and crashed it against the blade of the *damas*, making a bell-like din of metal on metal that echoed down the lanes of the Asylum as it had once echoed across the plain at Fallonier. Then it had almost immediately been drowned out by the sound of two score voices raised in a deafening roar that burst the clouds before finally dissipating into the ether, beseeching the attention of Mistral, Goddess of Courage.

Tagus remembered the elation of his voice joining with his brethren, all the air exiting his lungs, rising to the ears of the gods above, heralding the arrival of their warrior souls into Barbarus. Let the enemy hear their cries, and fear them, he had thought proudly. For the Falhorne were honor bound to make their enemies join them in death. But today there were only two voices, and they did little beyond startling a few stray cats.

In his warrior aspect, the Lord of Flames embodied a burning rage that fired the warrior's soul in battle. Thus, the chant of his chosen warriors rose like a blazing inferno, that was amplified to a deep crescendo by the reverberation of their shields. The Warrior's Prayer had first been spoken one thousand years ago among the martial lodges of the Chosen of Fiore. Tagus could only grit his teeth at his lacklustre performance.

Still, he pressed ahead. Following in the steps of his mentor, he began moving among the warriors, going from man to man and presenting to them the haft of the black halberd.

Tarquinus was first to grasp it. Bowing his head, the veteran Falhorne repeated the sacred vow before the gods: "Today my soul joins with yours."

As Valens, Remus and Skarlos awkwardly followed suite, Tagus remembered how the same ritual had progressed toward him ten years before. Piso had been the first on that day, then Demos, Menos, Kyros, and finally Tagus himself grasped the haft of the *damas* and swore the oath, inwardly terrified of making the slightest misstep with the holy words. One misworded oath, one mispronounced prayer in the elder tongue, any mistake brought with it the cruelest punishment: the thought that he was unworthy of his mentor and the gods. Now as then, he felt relief when it was over.

The Chain of Brotherhood had been formed and there remained one thing left to do.

"Brothers let us say farewell," Vitus had spoken those words before turning his attention to Piso. "Piso, my brother, may your death march be steady, I shall see you in Barbarus."

Piso had bowed his red fringed head in recognition before solemnly addressing the same words to Demos on his right; his usual jollity shrouded by the grim acceptance of his own mortality.

Now Tagus repeated the cycle with Tarquinus and the slightly bewildered watchmen. At the conclusion of the Warrior's Prayer, the warriors accepted the deaths of their comrades one-by-one before the battle had even begun, each man turning to his neighbor and repeating the same words with only the names being different. A warrior who had failed to accept and embrace death had no place on the battlefield. And death always came first for those in the vanguard.

Ten years ago, Tagus had accepted the death vow of Kyros, the Samosian exile's rough features shrouded by a mane of black hair. He remembered how his heart had skipped a beat upon meeting the severe gaze of his mentor, standing expectantly before him.

"Vitus, my brother, may your death march be steady. I shall see you in Barbarus."

Vitus's eyes had bored into his apprentice for the briefest of moments, before the old soldier nodded and turned away.

For all the oaths of farewell, the commending of their warrior souls to death's embrace, and the denying of one's ties to the mortal world in preparation for the ascent into Barbarus, there was still one life that Tagus could not bring himself to let go of, and that life was not his own. Tagus knew that his mentor was still striving, after all these years, to be everything that the fallen Order had taught him to be, even as the Falhorne suffered merciless setbacks and as times changed beyond recognition.

Perhaps it was true what his mother, in her faded Reshian accent that spoke of desert sands and jeweled oases, had once told him: "With the breath of the teacher does the earth overtake the heavens". He now understood exactly what she meant.

"It is the fate of the warrior to become a corpse," Tagus addressed the now oath-bound warriors in the street before him. "And thus, we face death as corpses, embracing our fate and calling our enemy to Barbarus. This is our farewell."

****

It did not take long for the warriors of the Black Horseman to get underway after that. Tagus had related the wishes of the bedridden Vitus, and they had rapidly reached a consensus on the necessary course of action. Even before he had left his mentor's bedside, he had dispatched young Callus with a message to Jesta and the council stating that the faithful were to assemble that morning in full confidence that they would be protected by their sworn defenders. Together they would uphold the terms of the Treaty, whether the city officials consented to it or not.

Callidus was coming with them. All of Tagus's attempts to bar his presence having been overruled.

So it was that six men, three Falhorne and three of the Watch, made their way through the shadowed lanes of the Asylum as the sun beat down. Simply by wearing their heavy leather jerkins they were in violation of every decree that the prince had passed and enforced over the past year. To say nothing of the blasphemy of publicly bearing arms as an "irregular" armed group, punishable as treason under the terms of the *Decree Maximus*. But they did not care. The Treaty of Trastamere was clear on their right to bear arms in the defense of the faithful.

They bore their weapons proudly and openly as they marched to the Silo Street Gate, swords unsheathed and dangling naked from their belts alongside axes and daggers.

Remus carried an entire bandolier of narrow blades slung across his chest, blades which he was fully capable of throwing with deadly accuracy – having demonstrated this to many unlucky opponents during his time as a mercenary in Samos. His brother Valens bore across his back the crossbow he had once carried into battle alongside his sibling, with which he was a crack shot. Skarlos bore two full-sized battle-axes, both of which he was able to wield one-handed in a whirlwind of cold steel. Tarquinius carried another massive two-handed sword of the same kind he had once wielded at Fallonier Fields, with which the deceptively lanky native of the western coastlands had hewn a bloody path through the enemy's ranks.

Callidus stood apart from the rest, as did his choice of weapons. Alongside his sword and dagger at his side hung the trademark twin pistols with which he had threatened the bailiff the previous morning. Both appeared to be well used when illuminated by the rays of the rising sun.

Tagus was weary from lack of sleep, the weight of his mentor's revelations still pressing down upon his mind, but it was an altogether greater imperative that kept him focused on what was demanded of him and of his brothers that day. Vitus's wishes would be honored, even as they left a sick old man alone in his bed, coughing as he dismissed all protestations by his former apprentice, commanding him to go forth in his stead.

As acting praetor, embodiment of the Black King's spirit on earth, Tagus now bore the weapon that he had stood in awe of ten years ago when he saw his teacher wield its burnished jet-black blade and shout out the words that seemed to echo to the heavens. The *damas* was in his hands now, the masterfully-wrought halberd feeling near weightless after twenty years of training and struggle. But Tagus knew that he was unworthy of the singular honor of wielding this sacred and beautiful relic of the Order's glory days. Nor was he worthy of the finely wrought breastplate, fluted and fringed with archaic chainmail, that he wore over his black robes. The same armor that Vitus had worn throughout the battles of the Skaros Schism.

Like the *damas,* the praetor's armor had sat unused for years, hidden away in the basement on Mercer Lane. Although Callus had occasionally been given the task of cleaning and maintaining it. Tagus had been more than surprised when he had discovered just how well it fit his shorter and more stocky body, as though it had been made for him.

Now, striding forth with his brothers like an avatar of the Black King in full battle array, the weight of its responsibility hung on his shoulders. Today there would be no more hiding, the warriors of the Celestial Court would stand proud for all to see as they fulfilled their divine mandate to guard the faithful. Tagus fought back all feelings of inadequacy and unworthiness; all was now in the hands of the gods.

The faithful were waiting for the Falhorne when they reached the gate. The people of the Asylum had been good on their word. They had come. Boys dressed in tunics that were little more than rags, discolored and filthy from what might have been years of unbroken use, sweat, and toil. Girls whose grey skirts were torn and patched with dirty pieces of cloth scavenged from the refuse piles behind the dockside warehouses. Few among them could have been beyond sixteen years, although there were many adults there too, faces grimy and hair greasy from lives spent cleaning chimney pots, emptying refuse, and gathering the disgusting raw materials demanded by the tanners and saltpetre men. The dockworkers, their backs permanently bent from carrying loads of satincane, stood there in open defiance of their bosses at the riverport.

It was a haggard crowd of downtrodden people, downtrodden yet unbroken. Yesterday one of their number had been killed, while others had arms in splints. They had had enough. Justice would be theirs; they would see to it.

Standing between the faithful and the two-dozen royal guardsmen, drawn up outside the gateway on Silo Street, was a line of men dressed in common clothes. Their faces were obscured by crude masks, little more than leather or burlap bags with eye and mouth holes cut in the front. Most bore wooden cudgels or daggers in their belts. Corvus's allies in the Association had followed through on their promises too, although some of them were obviously jittery about the whole thing.

The whole line shrank back from Tagus's hooded armored form as he strode to the front of the mass, even as a ragged cheer rose up from the faithful. Some of the masked men even made the sign of the Almighty Sun across their chests, mirroring the gestures of the guardsmen who had not expected such a show of force.

Tagus gave a silent prayer of thanks to the gods that none of them were capable of seeing beyond his iron-clad façade. It had been years since he had worn any armor that was even close to this in weight. Even the short walk between the Black Horseman and the gate had caused his leg to act up, his old injury straining under the weight of the heavy greaves. While his left arm was already bearing almost the full weight of the *damas* after his arthritic right had begun to protest. It would be a long walk to the marketplace.

Behind the Association men, the entire Agoge of Fiore stood at the head of their constituents: Corvus, burly and red-haired, appeared nervous; old Nestor wore a sour look, as did Secunda who shot an unfriendly glare at Tagus and the Falhorne, while Clodius appeared fatalistically defiant. But Jesta was nowhere to be seen. Corrie was standing where she should have been. He pulled back his hood and was met by her smile. Some of the pain in his limbs subsided.

"Brothers and sisters, we go!"

There were no great speeches before the procession began. No defiant words or sworn oaths. Everyone knew why they were marching and needed no reminders. The atrocity was fresh in their collective memory as they went forth, summoned into motion by Corvus's shouted command. The guardsmen made no attempt to stop them, parting before them like a double-doored gate as the faithful boiled onto Silo Street in their hundreds.

The mid-autumn sun blazed down as they spread out in a living river between the old city wall and the Ox Guts tenements. Families marched together, fathers carrying little ones on their shoulders, their innocent faces staring uncomprehendingly at the purposeful mass of people streaming by. It appeared as though the entire Asylum was there, having emerged like a waking dragon from its cave.

Although the hood shrouded his vision, Tagus was able to capture the sheer scale of what was happening. It was breathtaking to behold. The faithful were marching behind their Agoge. As they passed beneath the gallows and Porus's hanging body, he noticed Thea and Anna, the two daughters of Octavia whom he had met at the council the previous day, grimly marching alongside a tall thin man, his blond hair betraying his Braxian origin, who must have been their father – one of the many dockworkers who had dared defy their riverport bosses to defend their community, family and faith. He wondered what young Mia would have thought of all this. It was all for her. What would brave Porus have thought…and Piso…

The singing began, rising above the collective rhythm of marching feet. It was not the councillors who began the song. The ancient anthem of the Old Gods arose from somewhere deep within the heart of the people like a primal force of nature that spread outward, voice after voice joining in, until the morning air shook and vibrated with words that would have seen a man burned alive for blasphemy in the old Empire or in the Church lands of the Blessed Realm. A defiant song from defiant throats, praising the gods of the Celestial Court and the legendary heroes of the Book of Damas. It was ancient, born in the days before the sack of Cera Infernus, when the city of Fiore kept the holy fire of the Lord of Flames.

The melody arose from the throats of men, women and children. The youngest of them having been told of the ancient days and songs by their elders, beside whom they marched in that great stream of life.

At the head of the vast column were the Falhorne of Vinos and their watchmen allies. Unlike the singing masses of Old Believers, they said nothing as they advanced together, apart and ahead of the Association men who had by now spread out, screening the side of the crowd as it passed the slums. Tagus and his brothers formed a silent vanguard, slicing like an arrowhead through the streets that were bustling with a cacophony of vendors, housewives, beggars and day-jobbers; shocked bystanders making way for these grim figures.

To these onlookers, Tagus appeared as the incarnation of a dark god, the only thing undermining that image being the presence of the scrawny dark-haired youth at his side. Tagus had let Callus walk with him, even though he had made the boy promise to return to Vitus's bedside as soon as they reached Thresher Street.

The rickety tenements were giving way to fine three-story wooden houses with overhanging gables and slate roofs as the aqueduct's skeletal bulk rose before the crowd. The muddy spaces between the cobblestones were growing fewer as the street broadened.

Passersby had gone from ragged figures in drab and dirty cloth to merchants and well-to-do townsfolk in brightly colored garments. Ramshackle taverns and barroom brawls had given way to high-class alehouses with their own private security. Eyes followed Tagus as he went. Hard eyes. Not the kind of eyes, embittered by poverty and fear, that had trailed him in the slums the day before, but the proud eyes of the "respectable ones" who viewed the great unwashed presence on "their" streets as insulting as well as terrifying.

But rich or poor, respectable or no, they had all heard the stories and displayed only dread and fear as the Falhorne passed by. Panicked housewives snatched their children indoors. Dark lines deepened on elders' stony faces staring down from upper story windows. Street vendors looked on in wide-eyed fear and even beggars melted into dark alleys. Some held up pendants of Solar Dominatus and made the sign of the Almighty Sun across their chests, uttering oaths and muttering prayers as though the end of the world had come.

Chapter 9 – Blood on the Cobblestones

They were halfway to Thresher Street by the time the Church made its presence felt.

At the very edge of the Ox Guts, where the hard-packed dirt of a shadowed lane merged with the cobblestones, Tagus could see more royal guardsmen, pikes at the ready, standing around what at first appeared to be a merchant stall. It was set up outside the time-eroded brick walls of a three-story tenement with sagging eaves that might have once been an affluent townhouse. A long line of people, mostly women in tattered skirts and faded dresses, some clutching sickly-looking children to them, stood before a fat moon-faced man in a finely worked leather jerkin flanked by two linen-shirted assistants.

Between these hard-faced men and the pitiful line of slumdwellers before them was a chest-high wooden partition. Behind them was a cart piled high with fruit, bread, salted fish, and all manner of other foodstuffs. From his place at the head of the march, he could see their harsh gestures of denial as desperate folk tried to haggle with them over prices raised beyond their means. Grimly handing over food only to those who paid the inflated prices with what little they had left.

A second stall stood on the far side of the intersection. Behind it, Tagus could just make out the thin finely-dressed figure of a man flanked by guardsmen and standing behind another partition. A moneylender, one among the many royally sanctioned scavengers preying upon those without the means to pay. Indeed, the prince's golden lion was emblazoned on the partitions themselves, alongside another symbol that Tagus could not make out at this distance. Likely the device of some opportunistic merchant cartel that had gained official favor from devouring people and their livelihoods.

But these were not the only predators stalking the impoverished inhabitants of the low town.

"Save yourselves from darkness!"

"Embrace His holy light!"

"Kneel and repent your sins, for the Most High absolves and cleanses the impure flesh!"

A chorus of impassioned cries, accompanied by deep menacing voices raised in a furious hymn that promised death to all disbelievers. Bedecked in their white robes, their shaven features shadowed by hoods, the clerics of the Holy Church of Solar Dominatus, the so-called Blessed Realm, harangued the wretched masses queuing for their daily bread. Seeking to harvest more souls from the "scum" of the Ox Guts…the place so often compared to the underworld of Gormani.

Tagus gritted his teeth beneath the shadow of his black hood. It came as no surprise. The Church was a key arm of the state in all the impoverished districts of Fiore, dispensing alms to control the restive poor. Corrie had told him how they had expanded their charitable activities and fiery preaching since the "Monster" had begun claiming victims. The inhuman killer in their midst whom the priests told them was divine punishment for their sins.

Tagus knew that charity toward the destitute was viewed as a divine obligation by the cult of Solar Dominatus. However, only believers could receive alms. Part of the efforts of the preachers, who often stood outside the gates of the Asylum, was to convince the impoverished "heretics" within to bend knee to the Church in exchange for relief. They had done this for years. But, thanks to the efforts of the Agoge, few had been ensnared by their lies.

Tagus almost wanted to laugh as he saw their faces turn toward him; the nightmares of these predators coming true as the despised heretics of the Asylum, defiantly singing their blasphemous songs, marched down Silo Street toward them – spearheaded by a black-armored warrior that resembled the demons from their holy books.

Behind the white-robes, the soaring spire of the still unfinished Cathedral of Solar Dominatus pierced the sky over the tenements. It had begun its rise seven years ago as part of royal efforts to "reconcile" with the Blessed Realm in the wake of the crushing of the Skaros Schism and the overthrow of the Church's chosen champion.

The faithful had protested its construction right the start, knowing exactly what it meant and signified. Now the prince appeared on the verge of betraying his own loyal Old Believer subjects for the sake of pleasing the Hierophant. Its hateful edifice, visible from all over the city, added gravitas to the wicked combination of guards, moneylenders and preachers.

Looking at them now, it was difficult for Tagus to tell the difference: merchants, moneylenders, and frenzied priests forming a poisonous triangle around the people, as if draining their blood, while the menacing figures of the city guard in their blue and gold livery stood behind all three points of this unholy trinity.

The Blessed Realm was in the heart of Fiore City with the full assent and protection of Prince Chero himself. The same prince who had once sworn to rid them from his lands and enlisted the support of the Falhorne "Heretic Guard" to do so. Now the fanatics were openly killing people accused of heresy. This was the world that Octavia's child, who had only received the Blessing of Damas the day before, had been born into.

The churchmen did not run as Tagus and the others approached. Even as the guards began to back away into the mouth of the alley and the moneylenders rapidly moved to dismantle and move their stand before it fell beneath the marching feet of the heretic mob. Most of their "flock" had scattered, but the white-robed stalwarts stood their ground, showing that their fervor rested upon more than charitable handouts.

"Cease your unholy progress blasphemers and kneel in the name of the Most High!"

Tagus looked in the direction of this furious shout and spied their leader standing in the mud of the lane, arms raised toward the band of Falhorne as if he were trying to ward off an impending landslide with his bare hands. The priest of Solar Dominatus had his hood down and a shaven head fringed with golden hair crowned a narrow, wolfish face contorted in righteous indignation at the armed heretics before him.

"Return to the shadows infidels! Hide your unclean faces from the light of the Almighty Sun and bow down in repentance! For His holiness illuminates the tainted and burns the impious!"

Tagus struggled to keep his face impassive, but inside his spirit seethed as he recalled Theophilus's deeds on the Day of Blood. The man's high-pitched tirade cutting into him like a razor's edge. He was glad his face was shrouded, for he had no desire to betray his emotions before this servant of the Betrayer. He forced himself to keep walking as he kept his temper in check. Vitus would excuse no needless fights.

"Return to Gormani's pits, damned creatures!"

"The Most High rules over the heathen!"

Holy condemnations filled the air as the priest's assortment of lay hangers on followed their leader's example. Only to have their words drowned out by the defiant singing of the faithful as the main body of the march swept past them. The part of the moneylender's stall that had not been evacuated in time was shunted aside and knocked down in a clattering heap of boards and shelving, dumping an assortment of scrolls and ledgers into the mud.

The members of the unholy trinity could only watch impotently as the column marched determinedly on, filling the air with heretical songs and the tramp of hundreds of feet. It did not take long for the righteous rage on their faces to be replaced by looks of fear. For they were not the ones in control. None of them attempted to get past the line of Association men who stood between them and the marchers.

Tagus could only wonder whether the priest felt as the false prophet Marcomanni had, when the righteous clergy of the Lord of Flames expelled him from Cera Infernus more than a thousand years ago. This man, who would go on to found the first church to the Betrayer, had been a tiny insect in the face of the true gods and their might. He drew some small satisfaction from the truth that the Betrayer's servants could still be rendered helpless by the power of the faithful.

They were in the privileged districts now. Where Thresher and Silo Streets crossed beneath the high arches of the aqueduct.

Turning onto Silo Street was a procession of finely dressed retainers in brightly colored tunics, bearing the golden eagle and crossed spears livery of one of the city's aristocratic masters. A palanquin approached the Falhorne, its occupant invisible behind curtained windows, but it was born aloft by six silent men whose station in life was plain to see. Their thin tunics of black linen failing to conceal the scars that marked the flesh of their backs, visible through the coating of olive oil spread over their straining muscles in an attempt to make their servitude more pleasing to the eye.

Did I say you had a tongue!

Tagus could almost feel the sting of the lash, hear Ranald's hateful words ringing in his ears. He could not hide his feelings of utter disgust and horror, as the procession, seeing the legion of people advancing toward it, hastily turned down a side street and disappeared.

They passed onto the broad way of Thresher Street, the open expanse of Fiore's main marketplace coming into view through the teeming crowds, in the shadow of the guildhall's pyramid-shaped clocktower. This area was heavily patrolled, but the numerous city guards appeared as shocked and fearful as the other bystanders and city folk. They made no effort to bar their progress.

The column carried on, oblivious to the blank looks of shock on the faces of the myriad journeymen on their way to work, apprentices running errands for their masters, day laborers in search of a paying job, and dealers and whores in search of customers. Even the most miserable among them had no desire to be associated with heretics on top of their misery.

Tagus could find no friendly faces among the ranks of alternating blank stares, fear, and looks of knowing hatred. An extravagantly dressed young man in an exceedingly well tailored blue doublet, flanked by two armed guards in finely worked leather jerkins bearing the silver-etched insignia of some noble house, casually spat at Tagus's feet as he passed them by, his white polished teeth flashing above cruelly sneering lips.

Thresher Street was a place of highborn shadows. They walked beneath the great snaking form of the aqueduct, a legacy of the Empire of Five Seals and its cruel masters. In the distance, the crenellated towers of the royal palace reached upward, symbolizing House Julianus-Agricola's bid to claim the legacy of the emperors. The great spire of the cathedral could still be seen as well, a dagger pointed at the sky. While the guildhall, its rectangular bulk drawing ever closer beneath its soaring clocktower, was flanked by the smoke rising from the chimneys of the prince's new cannon foundry, a mark of his power and military prestige.

Chero had taken great pains to improve the quality of the Royal Army since the Skaros Schism. Creating formalized "companies of ordinance" out of the confused array of mercenary bands that had haphazardly won him the victory over Martino. Castle destroying artillery, forged with the help of Tarnish gunners, was but the latest expression of his independence from the great noble houses that had rebelled against him on behalf of the Church. Vitus had been following such developments for years, with no shortage of alarm.

Ringed by these symbols of power, Tagus expected to find soldiers drawn up behind barricades and cannon primed to fire on the crowd as it approached the marketplace. He expected it to resemble a besieged town. But, cresting the rise and beginning the descent to where the market sprawled along the banks of the Tio, he saw neither guards nor obstacles apart from the throngs of people milling about the countless stalls and vendors which dotted the great expanse of cobblestones between the guildhall and the riverport. The merchants and guilders had either been caught by surprise or had no desire to diminish their profits in the wake of a Church holy day.

The market day crowds scattered before the Falhorne as they entered the square. Men and women, some gaudily dressed in satins and velvets, others sporting only coarse cloth, dashed out of the way of this otherworldly band of black-clad men and the ragged masses that followed them.

The sun now burned high in the sky. Encased in the inferno of his mentor's armor, Tagus struggled to maintain his pace in the vanguard.

"Form the chain!"

Exhausted, sweat dripping into his eyes, he barely even registered the shouted command from Corvus that sent the hooded men of the Association scurrying to the front of the column and linking arms to form a long chain that wrapped around it on three sides like a great shield.

It did not take Tagus long to see the purpose of this maneuver. The crowds of market-goers had parted, revealing that they had indeed been expected by the powers that be. Pike-wielding guardsmen, clad not in the prince's blue, but in the green and yellow of the guildmaster who employed them, stood between the Asylum folk and the maze of stalls. Past the unbroken line of plate-armored soldiers, their weapons shining in the sun, Tagus could see the vendors and tradesmen going about their business as though nothing were amiss.

The gaudy blue and red flags of the Tarnish merchants in particular were impossible to miss down by the docks on the far end of the square. Everything was revolving around them: local traders haggling over prices, journeymen bargaining over wages, market slaves rushing about at their masters' beck and call, and customers thronging around cartloads of foreign goods freshly unloaded from boats hailing from the Tarnish dominated port of Torio at the Tio's mouth.

Tagus was aware that even the great stone fort on the island of Gladio, where the Tio split in two beyond the riverport, was partly garrisoned by Tarnish marines manning Tarnish cannon. He also knew the bitter truth of how slaves passed through those warehouses and wharfs on the way to Trastamere, where the plantation owners waited with ready ducats. Even now, out of sight of the main market, down along the stagnant waters, chained feet were dragging through the slime toward the barges that would bear them into servitude in scorching fields of satincane.

In the midst of it all, above the crowds and the din of a thousand voices, was the circular patch of ground where a hateful structure stood out, in stark and brutal contrast, above the throngs of buyers and sellers. The wicked silhouette of the gallows and the dangling remains of three dismembered corpses swaying in the breeze.

It lay in the blade-like shadow of the guildhall's steeple. Unlike the other grand buildings in the city, its commanding brick and marble façade was not a relic of the days of the emperors. Vitus had explained that the grandiose building was less than fifty years old. It had arisen in the wake of Prince Cosimo's betrayal of the Falhorne, its construction fueled by the southern satincane boom.

The guildhall also housed the Council of Peers. Five of its twelve members were chosen by the guilds, while others were hereditary and passed down from father to son in seven prominent patrician families, aligned to the prince and personally ennobled by him. All of them, if Vitus was to be believed, owed their titles to the loyal financial support they had offered the crown during the Skaros Schism and beyond. The present guildmaster was himself a "new man", and a foreigner to boot.

The procession finally halted beneath the clocktower, the faithful fanning out to fill the space cleared for them by the Association men, who, still locked in the "chain", stood face to face with the guardsmen blocking their path to the guildmaster's seat of power. There must have been at least fifty liveried men-at-arms facing them now.

The singing that had united them in their trek from the Asylum had died away. The councillors were shouting instructions, making room for everyone in the corner of the square as stragglers continued to join the crowd.

Tagus finally threw back his hood, blinking through the sea of sweat that obscured his vision as he forced his breath out in long ragged gasps. Pain shot through his leg, nearly causing it to buckle beneath him, and he had to use the sacred *damas* like a staff to prop himself up.

"Soon you'll be havin' a peg leg if ya keep that up, master!"

Tagus had completely forgotten that Callus was still there. He could not hide his look of surprise as he turned, panting, to see the boy smiling back it him with lively dark eyes. You would think the lad was headed to the summer garland festival in Torio rather than a battlefield.

"And you will be feeling the back of my hand if you keep talking like that," he snapped. "Why are you still here? I told you to go home!"

The former guttersnipe was not the least bit phased. He shrugged his shoulders, not losing that cheeky smile.

"No harm done, master. Just lookin' out for yez, that's all."

"Brother, Nestor's calling us to the front. Come on."

Tarquinus gripped his shoulder, but Tagus did not take his eyes off Callus. He found that he could not keep the half-smile from his lips as he looked down at the silly boy.

"Well cub, Vitus needs looking out for more than I do. Get back and see to him. You know what he is like when he gets irritable, even if he is bedridden. Go on now!"

The boy's eyes shone with triumph, just as they had when he had cracked his teacher over the head on Fire Day.

"I be goin' then. Don't forget to keep yer 'ead master Tagus!"

The twinkling eyes turned away and were lost in the crowd.

"Come on, brother…"

Tagus tried to conceal the limp in his stride as he let Tarquinus lead him to where the councillors stood at the front of the crowd, clenching his teeth from the pain but thanking the gods for Callus. He liked having the boy around, as annoying as he could be at times. At least some of the pent-up emotion he was feeling had bled away through his youthful antics. But now the real trial was at hand.

The confrontation had already begun by the time Tagus reached them.

The grimy faced Clodius was practically indistinguishable from the young boys at his side who might have been his sons, save for a foot or so of extra height. Yet he stood mountainlike between them and the menacing pikemen.

Old Nestor was wearing a faded blue garment, lined with tattered fur, that might have once been a fine guilder's robe. As it happened it only made him look like a luckless moneylender who had fallen into a dusty midden heap. Unlike Clodius, he was being anything but stoical, furiously shouting at the impassive guardsmen, his wrinkled face flushed crimson and contorted with rage.

"Give me back my grand-daughter you monsters! Have you not one shred of decency in your hearts? One filthy rag of humanity! Is this what you call law and order? Letting an innocent girl fall to a howling pack of bloody murderers! Give her back to me!"

Secunda was there alongside Nestor. She was wearing the same black dress that she had worn at the council, her furious gaze fixed on the line of guardsmen that stood between her and the dismembered body of her grand-niece.

Corrie stood beside Secunda, her arm around the older woman as if comforting her. The same woman that had called her a "whore" for marrying a "resh" like Tagus. She looked as exhausted as he felt, her dark eyes bloodshot, and yet she stood as unyieldingly as Clodius.

The arrival of the Falhorne alongside the Agoge sent a murmur through the crowd. Tagus could see looks of relief as the faithful remembered they too had armed men on their side. The formerly impassive wall of guardsmen seemed to collectively flinch as the acting praetor and his five comrades stepped between them and the mass of Old Believers, joining forces with the Association men.

Nestor ceased his bitter tirade as Tagus, who had again pulled up his hood, drew alongside him.

"Well met, Falhorne," Nestor said breathlessly, the flush slightly subsiding from his face, "As you can see these clots don't take kindly to our presence here. Even though we are only trying to reclaim the earthly remains of one of our own…what animal would refuse us that?"

"They will not harm you. Is there anything you request of us?"

Tagus was still uncomfortable standing in his mentor's rightful place. Unlike Vitus, he was no diplomat and had no idea how to handle himself if it all came down to negotiations with some self-important civic official.

"I am trying to get the pompous self-absorbed rogues of the guildhall to show themselves and hear our plea," Nestor continued, "but instead they only send their most expensive thugs to menace us. Maybe with you and your weapons, they'll listen to reason."

The old councillor eyed the polished blade of the *damas*. The Association might have the numbers, but the Falhorne had cold steel and tradition on their side.

"That has certainly been my experience with officialdom, Brother Councillor."

Callidus stepped between the two men before the tired Tagus could respond.

"Like I said, Councillor, I come from Trastamere. You learn much when debt-ridden peasants beseech you to save their families from a grasping baron. Or when you're forced to stand up against the gang of hired thugs sent to drive them off their land."

Nestor did not respond, instead glancing uncertainly at Tagus as the rogue Falhorne drew a long scroll of parchment from beneath his heavy leather jacket.

"This has protected me from more than one sword thrust. Please, where are the guild representatives you spoke of?"

Nestor was staring at a commotion among the guardsmen before them. The back ranks seemed to be parting, as though they were opening the way for someone important.

"See for yourself, it seems they would rather come and greet us at long last."

A finely dressed trio, flanked by mercenaries clad from head to foot in full plate armor, came into view from the direction of the guildhall.

"I shall handle this, brothers," Callidus intoned quietly, "Even though you know my feelings about it, the Treaty still trumps all of their petty privileges."

Tagus thought of interrupting Callidus and telling him to know his place. But he knew he had no skills that would be of value against the city's powerbrokers. Ceding authority to a rogue was distasteful, but he saw no alternative and Vitus had long ago taught him that on the battlefield only practical concerns mattered. So, he held his tongue, remaining steadfast by Nestor's side.

The lead figure strode forth imperiously, stopping several feet in front of Callidus and Nestor, who had themselves stepped forward from the crowd. Tagus could hear some of the faithful cursing under their breaths as the man – tall, thin and bedecked in lavish blue and green silk robes trimmed with gold – haughtily placed his hands on his hips. He wore the long chain of golden discs and a guildmaster's blue silk hat, his dignified poise concealing an inherent capacity for cruelty that went hand in glove with his position of power. He cast a glance at the hired muscle ringing him and his associates on three sides before making a great show of scanning the crowd and flashing a contemptuous, patronizing smile at the two men facing him across the narrow stretch of cobblestones.

"I am Maxim de Tolley, master of the merchant's guild, Alderman of Fiore, and protector of commerce and exchange by royal charter of His Majesty's government."

His voice was firm and commanding, lightly accented, and completely confident in its superior power and privilege.

"And you are trespassing on guild property, for which I trust you have good reason."

He once again glanced at the menacing armored figures around him.

"I take a dim view of unlawful gatherings. I possess the sovereign right to remove you by force, but I will allow you to explain yourselves. Why are you here?"

The sour look on Nestor's wrinkled face spoke of a long history of disdain as he eyed the gaudily dressed man before him. His lips twisted into a wry and bitter smile as he replied.

"Well Max, it's good to see you're moving up in the world."

The haughty features wore a momentary look of confusion, disturbed by such a casual address. But they just as quickly hardened as Nestor slid down the worn sleeve of his faded garment, revealing a tattoo of a shield and a pair of scales.

"Remember me, brother guilder?" The old man's face was one of bitter triumph.

"Nestor," De Tolley sniffed, making a face as if he were about to spit.

"You have the gall to crawl away from your shithole and show your face here? Faithless dog. It was you who abandoned your brethren to sleep among the dregs…"

"Dregs? They were once your people too, brother! Have you forgotten? Has senility set in early, oh noble Guildmaster?"

Nestor's eyes flashed with fury as he interrupted the man, pointing at the ragged crowd of Old Believers.

"They are still your people! And don't you dare call me faithless, when you turned your back on them in the name of gold! I chose to stand by them, when the guild gave us the choice between betrayal and expulsion…and, unlike you Max, I stand with them still. You may have all the riches of the Tarnish cartels and a seat on the Council of Peers licking the prince's boots, but at least I can face the Great Judge with a clear conscience when I die."

He spat a gob of saliva into the no-mans-land between them.

"Although it is comforting to know that the Betrayer's lackeys are so tolerant to the foreign-born and the outsider when he has the money bags to prove his loyalty before god and Church. How many plantations do you own again Max? How many slaves toil in your fields so you can buy the favor of those highborn souls who matter more than your own people? More than the honest brother tradesmen you heartlessly drove into poverty and misery? More than the life of my innocent granddaughter?"

Nestor shot a jagged finger at the dangling remains on the distant gallows.

"Is this what your lady mother wanted when she pulled her son out of the burning remains of Sarkal at the height of the northern wars and sent him south to make her proud? Did the guilders who embraced you, a Soldevian, as a brother when you came to this city deserve your knife in their backs so you could feather your own nest? You are a disgrace to all you claim to stand for."

A roar of agreement came from the crowd as they voiced their support for their councillor.

The guildmaster's eyes narrowed further at the noise and he hissed his reply through clenched teeth.

"Had this been another day, you would be in chains for your insolence, you disgusting old man…"

"I know more than a few honest guilders who'd say the same about you, pig!"

Secunda's accusing voice rose to a near shriek.

"Did you blue blooded lot even think to say one word to us weavers before you deigned to throw me and my sisters into the gutter? Expelled from the trades of our great-grandmothers? Not a single representative from our guild taken on by the council in twelve years and you still cut our membership in half by the stroke of a pen! Council of Peers, more like his majesty's sty boys! Three years ago, you took our livelihoods, gobbling up our shops for yourselves like mangy dogs. Now you take our lives. Did you have fun cleaning my grandniece's blood from your doorstep?"

She roughly pulled back her sleeve, like Nestor, exposing the old guild tattoo on her forearm.

Maxim de Tolley did not reply. He did not even look at her, keeping his hate-filled eyes on his former guild brother.

"I am a god-fearing man, Nestor. I do not negotiate with heretics. You chose your own path."

He shot a glance at the black-armored form of Tagus, as rigid as a statue.

"That the thrice accursed Falhorne would dare send a missive to me yesterday is an insult to the Council and in defiance of royal and guild law. Of course, I had my assistant burn it at once."

Shouts of anger and groans of disapproval echoed from the crowd, as Tagus tightened his grip on the *damas*.

"As for the girl, you know well that by royal decree those that blaspheme against the One True God are banned from all commerce within the jurisdiction of the Council of Peers. This includes employment by foreign interests. I mourn your loss Nestor, but take no responsibility for the misguided actions of a lawbreaker or the repercussions that she brought upon herself."

The crowd erupted. Multiple shouts of "murderer" filled the air. Nestor looked like he was ready to tear the guildmaster limb from limb. But it was Corvus who spoke, his barrel-chest shaking as he bellowed.

"Guildmaster," he roared as the shouting died down, scarlet burning through his grizzled cheeks, "Or should I say 'monster'? A child has been murdered on your watch, in the shadow of your guildhall. And I see you tore our Mia to shreds just like all the other poor souls you cornered in the Ox Guts for the past three months. Now I see the truth. Are you proud of your handiwork, butcher?"

The cries of "murderer", now joined with accusing shouts of "monster", continued as the expression on De Tolley's face went from smug pride to unreasoning rage. And the rage only mounted as Nestor spoke again.

"You dare to speak of 'guild law', Max? I remember a time when not even Prince Cosimo's persecutions and massacres were enough to cause the guilds of Fiore to abandon their members. I was but a child when my father's brother leatherworkers gave my family shelter until Cosimo lost his worthless head at the siege of Formoros. That is guild law. Brother tradesmen protecting and safeguarding one another, regardless of faith. Where is this loyalty now? You have sold your soul, Max, just as you sold your brothers down the river three years ago. If you still had a soul, I would still have my trade, and my granddaughter would still have her life."

Shouts of agreement followed, including scattered cries of "brotherhood" and "guilders return".

It was then that Callidus stepped forward, faced the enraged guildmaster with a face as hard as stone, and pointed an accusing finger at the mutilated remains on the scaffold.

"Alderman, you are hereby in violation of the Treaty of Trastamere, whose first stipulation clearly states that the facilitation, either directly or indirectly, of injury, despoliation, or death against a follower of the Old Ways is a crime, a breach of the peace, and blasphemy against the sacred principles of justice established in this land from the days of the Five Kingdoms."

He then paused, and briefly stared into his opponent's hate-filled eyes.

"Furthermore," he continued, "In accordance with stipulation two of the above-mentioned Treaty, the Eternal Order of the Falhorne is granted full authority to guarantee the security and protection of all followers of the Old Ways in the face of all criminal acts perpetrated against the sanctity of life and limb. Thus, our people stand before you in accordance with our sovereign rights as subjects of this principality and citizens of Fiore."

The Alderman's features were now clenching and unclenching like a fist, as rage gave way to shock then back to rage.

"In addition, in accordance with stipulation twelve, we Falhorne, the rightful sovereign guardians of the followers of the Old Ways, have come to take possession of the cadaver of one among the faithful for the administration of last rites to be performed under the watchful eye of the gods of the Celestial Court in due accordance with the faith of the woman in question."

Callidus once again stared into the eyes of the guildmaster, which were now trembling like twin wagon wheels jostling along a rutted and potholed city street.

"We expect full cooperation."

All this time, as this wayward Falhorne stated the terms of the Treaty as though he were reading them directly from a codex of laws, Tagus watched the imperious guildmaster struggle to maintain control of himself. His fury sent tremors through his attendants and henchmen, and armor plates clattered as the grim-faced mercenaries at his side edged closer to their master, tightening their grip on their wicked-looking poleaxes.

One of the hangers-on, a tall lanky fellow in a blue robe, went deathly pale. Some of the guardsmen lowered their weapons in anger, while others backed away in confusion, almost losing their grip on their pike shafts.

None of the crowd of faithful seemed to breathe. Even the interlocked hands of some of the Association men could be seen trembling. Clodius stood silently, protective arms clasping the two frightened children, whose whimpers resembled the squeaking of mice in the presence of predators. It was as though everyone was waiting for a smoking volcano to erupt.

But it was not the Alderman who spoke, but one of the finely dressed attendants, a short, rough looking man, whose bristled beard hid his expression as he leaned close and whispered something into his master's ear. And ever so briefly, Tagus caught a glimpse of something emblazoned on the crimson sleeve of the man's silken shirt. It was a symbol, an odd heraldic device showing three black pyramids against a looming white disk that looked like a full moon. It was surrounded by a circle of writing he did not recognize in the few seconds that he saw it, but which nevertheless seemed eerily familiar. Whatever merchant cartel this man belonged to, it clearly had influence.

The Alderman's features softened, his boiling rage gradually replaced by a half-smile, although he was still clearly struggling to keep a straight face. He spread his hands before him in a half-hearted gesture of goodwill.

"Very well, we would not dare to contravene or infringe upon royal authority in this matter. It is clear that there has been a great injustice. You must forgive our ignorance."

He motioned toward the hanging corpse.

"You may claim what is yours by right."

Nestor, who had been completely silent during Callidus's proclamation, could be heard to chuckle with a bitter sense of irony.

"Oh, so it's to be generosity now, eh Max? Giving my granddaughter's body back out of the goodness of your heart…does that explain why you let a screaming mob into the sacred heart of the guild's property to tear her limb from limb? Did you just happen to be feeling generous to them too, or do these armored hirelings of yours faint at the sight of white robes?"

The Alderman looked as though he might erupt again, yet somehow maintained that strained half-smile as he held out his hands to his former colleague.

"Nestor, you know as well as anyone that I am not a public official. Just a humble man of business. Business that I regret to say was disrupted by the same fanatics that caused this outrage."

His eyes again narrowed.

"Surely you are aware, my former brother, that we guilders do not command the guards here. I suggest you inquire at the palace about such matters."

He pointed away down Thresher Street, at the grey stone towers of the royal palace looming in the distance.

"Oh, spare me your platitudes Max!"

Nestor again looked like he wanted to spit.

"Do you think I haven't kept abreast of guild matters during my forced absence? You yourself led the re-negotiation of our charter last year. Now practically every ignorant peasant in Vinos knows full well that Fiore's grand market is patrolled by guards hired from the guild's own coffers…"

"And they know this because they must pay a toll to the guild in addition to their taxes to His Majesty for the privilege of entering this great city."

Callidus's interruption was so smooth that it sounded like Nestor's voice had merely declined in age and become more youthful, albeit no less harsh.

"Now Alderman, explain why your men stood idle while a young girl was being murdered? We expect reparations as well as a body. Her life was not worthless."

The familiar scarlet sheen was beginning to creep back over the guildmaster's features, indignant at being contradicted, yet again, by a lowly soldier who did not know his place. But Tagus saw the bristly bearded man tap the Alderman's shoulder and his expression mellowed once more, as though this nameless attendant possessed a soothing power in his finger tips.

"Quite right warrior," Maxim de Tolley said to Callidus through tight lips, "but you should remember where you stand. I am generously allowing you to collect the body of one of your own. But my patience is beginning to wear thin…and this square remains guild property."

He almost hissed these last words, gesturing not so subtly at the armed men at this side. The guards had regained their composure and more of them had levelled their weapons.

It was then that Tagus saw the hot blood rise to Callidus's face, which had hitherto been as cold as a mountainside. The rogue Falhorne's voice came forth in a low growl of righteous fury.

"How could you do this to your own countrymen?"

The guildmaster's smile appeared genuine as the façade of his formerly impassive interrogator crumbled. He made no response.

This was all too much. The acting praetor finally decided to intervene, and Callidus's body tensed in shock as heavy gauntleted hands grasped him by the shoulder. For the first time Tagus spoke to the imperious Alderman, letting his hood slip back.

"Very well, Guildmaster, we accept your offer, but we will be maintaining our watch here. There will be no more crimes against our people."

Callidus stepped back, shaking off Tagus's grip as he did so, fury still burning hot in his cheeks.

The guildmaster sneered as Tagus's black skin came into view.

"I should have known there'd be an insolent Resh under there."

He chuckled as Tagus fought to keep his anger in check, before casually snapping his fingers, the guildmaster's whole entourage following him in a brightly colored cascade of silken finery. Only the bristly bearded man glanced back, before turning and hurrying away. Soon they were all out of sight among the stalls.

The crowd fell silent as the councillors exchanged uncertain glances and looks of suspicion. But there was nothing to be done, except see to the grisly task at hand.

The market guards had finally pulled back from the line of Association men and now flanked the path over which Tagus, Corrie, Secunda, Nestor, and Clodius passed, glowering at the five of them as they advanced toward the gallows, as if wishing the same fate upon these unwelcome interlopers and heretics.

The crowd watched their leaders' progress with bated breath as they passed beyond the wall of pikes. Nestor walked tall and dignified in his faded guilder robes, but Tagus could see the anguish in his eyes, anguish he was desperately trying to conceal from the guards as the hanging body of his own grandchild drew closer and closer. Only they had been allowed to proceed, the guards forcing the rest to remain at the juncture of Thresher Street where Tarquinus had temporarily taken command and where Corvus had stayed to coordinate the Association men, broken their chain of interlocking arms to let the five representatives through. The indignant Callidus had also remained behind.

Corrie had quietly slipped her arm around Tagus, as she had on the day of their wedding, by the time they came to the top of the raised area of ground where the gallows stood. Surrounded by a miasma of buzzing flies as the harsh midday sun shone upon the three corpses.

Nestor stifled a sob and Tagus felt his own heart tremble. Mia's body had been cut into thirds – legs, torso, and arms – yet they had been tied together and were dangling on one rope, suspended by her two strong hands. Her head was gone.

The old man could not even look into his granddaughter's face. Secunda had begun to weep uncontrollably. Soon her wails could be heard above the din of the surrounding and uncaring marketplace that had not slowed its operations since the confrontation began. Tagus struggled in vain to forget the dancing and how that girl had put her arms around him on Fire Day, moving to the rhythm of ancient songs before the sacred flames. How could the gods be so cruel?

But Mia was not alone. Flanking her horribly dismembered form were two intact bodies swaying in the rising wind, their identity clearly displayed in the torn garments that they wore – the green tunics of guild journeymen. The boys couldn't have been more than sixteen, their youthful faces frozen in suffocation above their broken, twisted necks.

Clodius shook his head, firmly gripping Nestor by the shoulder.

"So this is what happened to them," the grimy faced councillor said, "I heard from the lads on the docks that two journeymen had been arrested for arguing with the masters and threatening to join the Association if the businesses they worked for weren't protected from slave labor and cheap Tarnish imports. I suppose we should be happy we're not the only ones getting lynched around here…"

He spat on the wood of the scaffold and cursed, never lifting his hand from the shoulder of his fellow councillor as he did so.

Nestor's tears were also flowing freely. Tagus nervously, tentatively, as if he were about to touch an open flame, joined Clodius in resting a hand on the old man's trembling shoulder. While Corrie held the trembling form of Secunda in her arms.

"You are coming home now, Mia," Nestor shuddered between sobs, "It is time to return to Viro's waters, child…forgive me…"

Clodius softly intoned the words of the Prayer of the Dead to the Lady of Waters from the Book of Damas as he and Tagus held the sobbing elder.

Into my arms flow the agony of man.

Unburning in the peace of cool waters.

Once more the guards parted with menacing glares to let them pass. Nestor bearing in his arms a reeking bundle shrouded in a tattered silken sheet. The crowd was silent, all heads bowed in unison. Above them the bell of the guildhall's clock tower tolled midday, mournful as a young soul passed to the side of the Great Judge who would decide her place in the heavens.

But the tolling could not drown out a new sound. A sound that arose like seething thunder on the breeze, coming like a rumble or a cacophony boiling down Thresher Street. Mourning faces looked up in terror beneath the hard sun beating down on their heads.

Now Tagus could hear the impassioned cries, the furious shouts, all bound up in the slow rolling thunder of priestly chanting as it echoed through the streets; prayers spoken in Imperial High Ceremus. He could only recognize one name, one name spoken again and again with fanatical devotion:

Solar Dominatus.

Beneath that name, the shouts were getting nearer and angrier, cutting the air in their hate, as they rose above the solemn chanting like animal shrieks and howls:

"Get the dogs! Strike the mongrels! Bash them!"

Now the throng was coming into view, a cold grey mass dotted with white robes, coming up behind the crowd of Old Believers like an onrushing tide.

Tagus left his wife's embrace and ran toward Tarquinus. The guards that had formerly surrounded them had backed off, and their place had been taken by a crowd of green-clad journeymen, shouting and jeering at the faithful, some of them brandishing clubs improvised from chair legs and wooden planks. They were coming from the direction of the guildhall, like a pack of unleashed hounds, with the hooded men of the Association struggling to reform the human chain to block their advance.

He could see faces young and old consumed by fear all around as the people of the Asylum realized they were surrounded. He knew the thoughts that were going through their minds: the history, the memories, the legends, from the fall of Cera Infernus to the sack of Brisi. Clodius rushed to comfort one young boy, surely no more than ten years old, who had burst into tears.

But, amid the chaos, Tagus felt some of his old confidence return, something of the feeling he had known at Fallonier Fields. There was no more confusion. No more ambiguity. The enemy had shown himself, and now he must be defeated.

"Brothers, draw your weapons!"

Tagus bellowed the command, struggling to be heard over the fury of the oncoming mob as he staggered up to Tarquinus, who had already unlimbered the greatsword from his back. Callidus had unholstered his pistols, while the uninitiated watchmen gripped axe hafts and sword hilts.

The first volley of stones struck the crowd and the first screams of pain cut the air. Pandemonium ensued. The apprentices had brought piles of rocks with them and were ripping up the cobblestones in order to get more missiles with which to hurl at those unclean souls who did not matter…or who could be counted on to sell their labor a little more cheaply out of desperation. They had their status to maintain in the face of these unwelcome outsiders, and that was enough.

Stones were falling thick and fast now, like a cruel rain, the Association's "chain" being powerless to stop the barrage. The Falhorne and watchmen joined the adults in shielding the panicking children from the downpour, but there were only six of them attempting to protect hundreds.

Struggling to shield the others with his armored body, Tagus saw Nestor rush to the side of a young girl who had fallen to the cobblestones, blood trickling down her face. Like a father rushing to the side of his injured child, his worn hat tumbling to the ground beside her.

Running his hand through her hair, he stared down at the motionless face and unblinking eyes, a tear of crimson descending one ruddy cheek. Stones clattering to earth all around him, the old man looked up with fury at the rock throwing apprentice boys. His aging face seemed consumed by fire as he rose to his feet and pointed an accusing finger. Standing over the girl's body, his thunderous shouts could be heard above the din of insults and obscenities.

"Scum! You have killed her! You have killed a child! Did your masters not teach…"

He said no more. The piece of broken flagstone striking the exposed crown of his bald head with a sickening crack against the bone. Time seemed to slow as the outstretched arms dropped, the once fine guilder robe fluttering helplessly in faded shades of blue, as the old guilder himself toppled to the ground alongside the girl he had been trying to shield.

Tagus heard the screams behind him, but they seemed distant, faraway. He could barely hear the furious shouts as Tarquinus tried to stop an enraged Clodius from running to the side of his fellow councillor amid the storm of projectiles. He could not take his eyes from the spectacle before him, the grisly scene whose very horror eclipsed everything else, as if vision alone could blot out the sounds of suffering and bloody-minded savagery. The dead bodies of two people. Two corpses – one young, one old – just lying there. The faded blue robe of one partly shielding the frozen youthful form of the other. Lying in a deathly embrace on the bloody cobblestones.

Chapter 10 – Crowns of Wind and Water

Agelaus stood by the bubbling fountain, watching as the ripples spread, lapping gently at the stone walls that kept the crystal-clear waters tame and controlled. Small shapes darted to-and-fro in momentary flashes of color, revealing the prince's prized collection of exotic southland fish. It was only the final flourish in a garden designed to imitate the glory of the emperors and the splendor of the imperial court in Hipireus as it had been before the fall. The fountain and its clear pool stood in the center of a broad and perfectly square courtyard. Straight paths, paved with bricks, crossed one another at right angles between the regimented hedgerows. Exotic shrubs and beds of brightly colored rare flowers perfumed the warm air beneath the olive trees and cypresses.

All was in its right place, wild nature strictly managed. Overseen by a commanding marble effigy of Emperor Domitian of Commus; native of Vinos and the scourge of Tarn and the northlands. A beautiful mosaic of a golden sun spread out across the ground in all directions from the outer wall of the fountain where Domitian's inert form stood, stylized rays of semi-precious stone lapping at the flowerbeds. It was as if the artist had wanted to create the impression that the long dead emperor was radiating some sort of light.

Agelaus grimaced as he returned to pacing anxiously up and down. As far as the prince was concerned, the brute might as well have been a hometown hero. Fortunately, he and some of his subordinates were educated enough to know the true history, and the truth was a far cry from the deceptive peace of a pleasure garden. To him it all looked like an oil painting anyway, the wound he had received at Fallonier Fields having long since removed his depth perception along with his right eye.

The royal chapel, like the garden itself, stood out in stark contrast to the stone towers of the palace's inner walls. Though it appeared just as flat and rigid to Agelaus's single eye. As the imperial governor's former fortress, lording over what had been a conquered and restive city, its builders had not had beauty in mind when its titanic keep was raised over the blackened remains of heretical Cera Infernus. The grey stone forming a dark cloud over the chapel's immaculate white marble.

Its eaves of painted pottery were etched in gold trim and decorated with images of the three divine messengers that had approached Marcomanni in the desert. A great bronze frieze, covering almost half of the chapel's façade, showed the legion of the Heavenly Host, countless divine warriors radiating outward from the Almighty Sun of the Most High. They were descending to aid the soldiers of the first emperor, Callus Invictas, as he marched on the Gormani-spawned heathens of Fiore. At the center of the frieze was a great glass window, allowing the light of the midday sun, now faltering amid sombre grey clouds, to strike the holy altar of Solar Dominatus within. Little "holy light" could be counted on to enter the building from its narrow side windows, shielded as they were by disciplined ranks of poplars.

Agelaus kicked a small stone toward the fountain with his polished riding boots, watching as it struck the low wall at its base and bounced off. He had been waiting for almost an hour now, and was sweating freely inside his finely tailored doublet; the urgency of his message setting his every nerve on edge as he endured the torture.

But the two guards, loyal Gendarmes both, standing rigidly outside the chapel's bronze doors, were admitting no one until His Majesty had finished midmorning prayers. His status as their superior officer had not been enough to shake them from this stance. As professional soldiers, they were under royal authority and acting on the prince's personal instructions.

Agelaus sighed, running a despairing hand across his bald scalp as he glanced once more at the gates of the inner courtyard, and his heavy heart finally gave a leap when he saw Arnim approaching. The captain of the royal cavalry wore his breastplate over a quilted jacket, simple black breeches merging almost seamlessly with his high boots. He wore no helmet, his closely cropped blond hair complimenting his pale skin and sharp blue eyes.

If not for the ugly scar stretching from his right ear almost to the left corner of his chin, the thirty-seven-year-old career soldier might have passed for one of those unspoiled northern youths celebrated in the

Braxian sagas. As it stood, it looked as though the man's face had been cut in half. Nor did his jacket hide the mechanical iron appendage that he wore in the place of his left hand and forearm. It dispelled any fantasies about the true nature of this hardened veteran of the Grimagen imperial officer corps and the bloody wars between his sprawling former homeland and their Tarnish neighbors. The men had not given him the nickname "Grim" for nothing.

His sense of discipline was impeccably "Grimag" as well. Precisely five paces from where Agelaus stood, he stopped, stood ramrod straight, and saluted with all the pomp and circumstance of a parade ground; raising his right hand to his temple.

"Captain Agelaus."

Arnim's voice was as formal as he looked, so much so that Agelaus felt like the rough mercenary he had once been as he reflexively returned the salute. He was a Gendarme now, and his oath to the prince had likewise pledged him to endless rounds of disciplined formalities. But those formalities died as his hand dropped from his brow.

When Agelaus spoke, his voice was far from calm and his frustration showed through every word, in spite of his efforts as a military man to keep a stiff upper lip.

"Captain Arnim. Do you have any further news? Has Theophilus begun to move his people?"

Arnim's scarred face was serious as he nodded, giving Agelaus the reply that he dreaded.

"Yes, Captain. My agents have informed me that the mob has left the Temple District; they will have reached Thresher Street by now."

"Numbers?"

"All the churches have let out their congregations early from High Sun prayers. Bishop Theophilus has one thousand of his flock by his side, perhaps more."

"Damn it! And what of the Old Believers?"

"The crowd remains in the marketplace. Guildmaster De Tolley has detained them in negotiations over the body of an accused witch."

"Any violence?"

"Not as of yet."

Agelaus's olive features twisted in anger as he shot a glance at the guards and the chapel doors that had still not opened.

"By the Sun, Arnim! I won't stand idle while a massacre ensues. Are those your boys over there? Tell them to stand aside. The chaplain can shove Almighty Sanctity up his ass. His Majesty will know of this!"

Arnim followed closely as Agelaus led the way to the chapel door where the two sentries stood unmoving, both of them in full plate armor and bearing pole-axes in their gauntleted hands. But no sooner had he stepped before them, "Grim" barked out his orders in a voice that could have been heard across a battlefield.

"Gendarmes, you stand relieved! Return to barracks!"

One of the startled soldiers instantly responded to the command, snapping his body to the side and shouldering his weapon. The other had more nerve, standing his ground and replying brusquely to his superior's order.

"Sir, His Majesty himself commanded…"

"Silence! We shall handle the matter from here, soldier! Go before I give you time in the stocks!"

Responding to Arnim's command, the chastened young soldier likewise turned, shouldered his weapon and marched toward the gate.

Agelaus promptly shoved open the heavy bronze door, letting light spill into the darkness of the chapel. He was met by the sound of voices raised in prayer. It was pointless to hesitate now. The prince would be angry and a demotion might even be in the cards, but the gravity of the situation was such that he did not care. Chero routinely missed dawn prayers dallying with his mistress before overcompensating in his devotions at midday. It was an open secret at the palace but he would not see people die because of it.

Thy Light guide our path,
Triumphant in our faith.
Unworthy in our flesh,
Clad in Thy Divine Mercy.

The melodious strains of the Hymn of High Sun filled the air, along with the fragrance of incense burning within the censers held by the swaying forms of the white-robed clerics beneath the high altar. Its great raised disc of pure gold illuminated by the rays of the ascending midday sun.

The Royal Chaplain, Pupienus, stood in his mitred robes at the center of the small throng, his ethereal voice adding an otherworldly aspect to the scene. The heads of a handful of richly dressed noblemen and members of the royal household turned to look at the two soldiers as they purposefully strode down the aisle between the polished wooden benches, making for where the prince sat alone in the place of honor before the singing clerics.

Standing against the white marble wall of the chapel, was what looked like a massive leaning shadow blotting out the pale light from the nearest of the side windows. As Agelaus and Arnim approached the prince, the shadow suddenly stirred to life and the titanic bulk of a man, his face as black as cold iron from a smith's forge, strode into the light of the candles. Swiftly setting himself between the two officers and the royal person like an unyielding wall.

Secure in Thee,
For You banish all shadows…
The hymn went on as the two of them abruptly stopped and saluted the mighty man, for he was a fellow Gendarme and the prince's own bodyguard. Although his status was far from ordinary, even in a force consisting largely of ex-mercenaries with colorful backgrounds. "The Gladiator" as he was known, was the prince's personal slave, purchased directly from the killing arenas of Viropolis in the deep south of Samos. His real name was unknown to them and perhaps to anyone other than himself and his royal master.

The Gladiator, a head taller than either of them, grinned as he saluted back, revealing rows of ivory white teeth. The air of the chapel was stuffy and hot, but he wore his suit of full plate armor without complaint, his gauntleted hand gripping the hilt of a sword that even Titus, the tallest Gendarme in the force, would have been hard pressed to wield. His grin, accompanied by twinkling dark eyes, shone through the raised visor of his great helm, itself wrought in bronze and bearing the features of one of the Heavenly Host, as though the prince viewed his mightiest household slave as a talisman of divine protection. Certainly, the former pit fighter was almost never allowed to leave his side.

Aware of the disruption they were causing, Agelaus leaned in to speak in the ear of the mighty bodyguard, only to stop when an abrupt snapping of fingers pierced the incense-laden air. It was followed by a handclap, just as authoritative, that echoed from the vaulted ceiling and sounded over the singing, that rapidly faded to nothing, like well-drilled soldiers coming to an abrupt halt at a single order.

"That will be quite enough, good Pupienus, thank you."

The white-robed chaplain stood frozen at the sound of the prince's distinctly nasal voice, both arms raised in almost perfect imitation of the bronze statue of Marcomanni upon the altar. Agelaus's flat vision and the general gloom made it difficult to be certain, but it looked like the priest was about to burst into tears. As a man of the Church he was obviously enraged at having his service interrupted, but as a loyal lackey of his sovereign, he meekly bowed his shaven head and briskly snapped his own fingers at the members of the choir who loyally followed him out through the side-door.

"Good lords and ladies, accept my humblest apologies, but I must confer with my soldiers in private. Leave us."

Agelaus's ears made up for his vision, and he overheard the murmured curses and expressions of disgust from the highborn throats behind him. Gendarme or no, he was still a rough-born commoner, and commoners never interrupted the prayers of their betters without risking a flogging or the hangman's noose. But Agelaus knew full well that he could expect neither. For his prince rewarded loyalty above privilege.

The Gladiator remained grinning as he stood aside, amid the chorus of closing doors that echoed in the smoky fragrant air. As his massive frame shifted, the face and figure of Chero I of Julianus-Agricola, Grand Prince of Vinos, came into view, the sunlight from the chapel windows causing the golden diadem on his forehead to flash and shimmer. Its halo hiding the prince's balding head and turning the onlooker's gaze away from the less than flattering assembly of chins beneath his fat cleanshaven face.

But Chero's hazel eyes were sharp. Agelaus could even spy some relief in them. His prized Gendarme "war dogs", as he was fond of calling his elite guardsmen, had rescued him from further boredom. It was a good sign. At that moment, a sharp gust of wind suddenly arose outside, rattling the chapel windows and whistling over the roof tiles.

Chero smiled through thick lips, and Agelaus could not help but notice the contrast between his sovereign's paunchy figure and the muscular warrior prince who had stood before his men at Fallonier Fields. But the haughty self-confidence had never left his voice.

"My dogs come to me like a bull at a gate," His Majesty exclaimed with a chuckle, "what tidings could they possibly bring to their master?"

Like good soldiers, Agelaus and Arnim bowed their heads before their liege lord and commander in chief, before solemnly taking the knee. As they had done in the main square of Brisi after Fallonier Fields. Chero triumphantly reviewing his soldiers in the ruins of his rival's capital.

"Oh, stop it, mongrels! You may rise!"

Both of them did as they were told.

"Now speak."

Agelaus did as his master commanded and related the information that had been very nearly bursting from his chest for the past hour. His nerves were wholly on edge, but he managed to deliver it with the bearing expected of a royal soldier.

"Most august liege, I must report on the grave situation in the streets of the capital. The inhabitants of the Asylum are en masse before the guildhall, protesting the murder of one of their own. Even as we speak, His Holiness the Bishop Theophilus is leading a pious procession from the Temple District to confront the Old Believers. I fear that slaughter and chaos will erupt if the Gendarmerie does not intervene immediately to keep the crowds apart. I…"

"Very good, Captain," the prince interrupted, "But I did not ask for your opinion."

He turned his gaze to Arnim, who stood rigidly at attention.

"Captain Arnim, is this true?"

"It is, my Prince."

Arnim's terse response was met by cackling high-pitched laughter, as the sovereign of Vinos threw his head back, jowls quivering.

"Oh, how my dogs are merciful! So much concerned with the lives of the humble. You shall be donning white robes and joining the Brothers of Benevolent Dawn handing out charity to the guttersnipes at this rate!"

Agelaus felt his jaw clench. It was no laughing matter.

"Highness, this is an extraordinary threat to public safety. The whole of Fiore could be plunged into violence. Your subjects must be protected."

"Oh, shut up, Agelaus!" The prince snapped, dismissively waving his bejeweled fingers.

"You're a fine soldier, but you bark too much for your own good. I know the situation. I know the city. And I know the temperament of my subjects. I have already spoken with Brother Varus of the Templars of the Host; the matter has been dealt with."

Shock passed through Agelaus's body at these words. The prince had spoken to the soldiers of the Church before his own men? Feelings of insult and disgust boiled within as he struggled to keep a straight face. Though Arnim appeared as impassive as ever, he could tell that the battle-hardened officer was seething beneath his well-practiced façade of perfect obedience.

Theophilus's lackeys were out of control. Did they really think they could stage a religious massacre in the market square, plunge the beating heart of Vinos into carnage, and get away with it? This was madness.

Agelaus struggled to reply, but he nearly lost what little composure he had left when a new voice sounded behind him: deep, serene but commanding, and lightly accented in the tongue of the foreign lands to the north-west. The voice swept past him to the ears of the prince as effortlessly as a fast-flowing stream over time-eroded rocks.

"Royal Highness, I hear talk of unrest, of bloodshed, of disruption of trade and commerce. It sounds most unwelcome."

The bulk of the Tarnish Ambassador swept past Agelaus and reached his master's side in a matter of heartbeats. His Excellency Owain Trevelyan, representative of the Republic of Tarn and its Lord Protector, wore his ermine-trimmed robe effortlessly in the stuffy hot air. His golden chain of office bearing the ship and sea-dragon emblem of his great sea-faring nation. The fine high-collared silken shirt that showed beneath was likewise a deep ocean blue and contrasted immaculately with the finely trimmed red beard that flowed from the ambassador's square jaw. His deep, sea-blue eyes bore a look of concern, but also certainty that the concern would be promptly addressed.

"Your Excellency."

The prince bowed his head in greeting, his face now solemn and serious. Far from berating the ambassador for remaining in the chapel after he had just ordered everyone to leave, he appeared almost as meek before the representative of mighty Tarn as his chaplain had been. Owain, for his part, seamlessly continued.

"I assume that Your Majesty has the interests of our great merchant houses in mind this day. As you know, your noble city is of great importance to us. We would not see it come to harm. Nor would we wish to see threatened our recent pact to supply cannons to the royal army in exchange for a guaranteed increase in the outflow of satincane to our mills. Destabilization is in no one's interest here; would you not agree?"

The ambassador's voice was soft, but the power and influence of his words were palpable. Agelaus had to stop himself from smiling. If there was one thing that could get the prince to rein in Theophilus it was gold, specifically Tarnish gold, and the fear that it would be diverted elsewhere. Chero was certainly not slow in responding.

"I assure Your Excellency that you need not worry. The Grand Principality of Vinos always upholds its obligations. All pacts shall be honored and all threats to their sanctity dealt with. Law and order shall be upheld to the satisfaction of the honorable merchants of our great ally, of that you can be sure."

"Good. Remember our prior arrangement. Adieu, Your Majesty."

The ambassador bowed his head and was gone. The prince stood alone before his "war dogs", his broad face flushed red.

"My liege, your orders?"

Arnim spoke at last. Not leaving the ramrod straight posture he had been holding since they had first presented themselves before their sovereign. If he had been at all disturbed by the sudden intervention of a representative of his former battlefield adversary in the Tarn-Grimagen wars he did not show it. But the prince's irritation showed in spades.

"Get on with you!" He snapped, eyes burning like hot coals, "Take two companies and restore order. I want the streets cleared. Any riots broken up."

"Sire, what of Theophilus?"

Agelaus wanted the prince to make his position absolutely clear on this. The bishop would surely have armed Templars at his side, along with his other sycophants.

"Tell him to come to me at once. His followers are to disperse peacefully. The plan is to proceed accordingly and I need no further complications from him or his mob…"

"Sire?"

"Just go!"

They bowed and saluted before turning on their heels, only to find yet another supplicant standing by the chapel doors. He wore robes of snow white. A gold mask obscured his face with the features of the Heavenly Host. He made no move as they walked past him and as the doors to the chapel closed behind.

Outside, where the rising wind was hissing in the olive trees, Agelaus looked up to the chapel roof to see a falcon perched above the bronze frieze of Solar Dominatus, tearing apart the bloody carcass of a pigeon. He quickened his pace, his heart thumping, hoping that young Callus remained at the gatehouse. Vitus and his people had to be warned.

Chapter 11 – Murderers

Seconds bled into eternities, as Tagus gazed at the awful sight before him; the onrushing white and grey tide of churchmen and zealots surging down Thresher Street toward his people. Their wicked chants and shouts of hate assailing the sky over Nestor's fallen body. They had already surged through the Asylum on the Day of the Almighty Sun, leaving a trail of destruction in their wake, now it was clear that they had far worse intentions.

He struggled to tear his eyes away as the stones continued to fall in a pattering hail from the direction of the apprentice boys, plunging down on the chaos of bodies and calling forth screams from the injured and dying. He remembered the stories Vitus had told him of the brutal massacres in Fiore that had preceded the Order's Betrayal fifty years ago. History was repeating.

"Falhorne! By all the gods!"

Clodius stood before him, blood trickling down an ashen face that was also streaked with tears.

"Fight them! Keep them back while we get our folk to safety!"

Tagus forced his aching, sweating body into motion as the councillor ran off into the crowd. He had to protect the faithful. He had to get them out of here. This was a battle, he had to act now. Surrounded, they needed an escape route, but they also needed time. He could not see Corrie in the mass people, and he had to fight down the panic rising in his chest.

Stones bounced ineffectually off his armor, making a sound like little bells, as he moved to where Corvus was rallying the men of the Association. The big red-bearded man now wore a steel skullcap and bore in his hands a square-headed iron mace with which he directed his commands.

"We're going to rush them! It's the only way!" He bellowed when Tagus questioned him. "We'll see how well the guildmaster pays his lackeys!"

"Then face the apprentices. We shall handle the zealots! We have to buy time!"

"Good luck, Falhorne!"

Some of the stronger men of the Asylum, including Thea's father, were lining up behind the Association men, all of whom bore truncheons in their hands. Some had blood pouring down their faces from the falling stones, but they stood firm. Other men were attempting to gather the wounded, bearing them toward the women, children and elderly whom the councillors were frantically trying to get out of harms way.

Finding his voice again, Tagus shouted for his comrades. Within moments they were about him, hearing the call of their acting praetor amid the pandemonium. Wordlessly, he gestured a gauntleted hand toward the mouth of Thresher Street, and his brothers followed him through the rain of stones toward the surging mob.

All had their weapons drawn. Valens had his crossbow leveled at the oncoming zealots with a bolt in the firing position. Remus had drawn one of his throwing knives. Skarlos had a lethal gaze in his eye as he hefted his axes, moving forward in a half-crouch.

Tarquinus moved more cautiously, his greatsword held against the shoulder of his leather jerkin, but he still bore the look of a soldier about to enter a bloody melee. Tagus raised the blade of the *damas* to head height, keeping the weight concentrated on his non-arthritic left arm.

Amid the chaos, he did not notice Callidus's absence until the gunshot came like a thunderclap, echoing through the city streets and drowning out the din with brute force. He turned his head, and saw the men of the Association surging forward as the barrage of stones slackened and then abruptly ceased.

A second report tore through the noon air, and, as the smell of gunpower met his nostrils, Tagus saw Callidus standing calmly behind the advancing line of hooded journeymen, smoking pistol raised in the air. Even though the bullet must have traveled high over their heads, it had achieved the desired effect; the apprentices were running, looks of terror on their faces as they scurried away toward the guildhall.

Corvus was struggling to rein in the more hotheaded Association men who wanted to pursue them back to the doors of their masters, brandishing their truncheons and calling out taunts as the apprentices fled before them. Callidus's eyes were narrow, like a huntsman, as he lowered his weapon, calmly twisted the arcane wheel-lock mechanism and methodically began to re-load.

As the stones ceased to fall, Tagus turned his gaze to the crowd of faithful, who were in no mood to celebrate this victory. Adults clutched at bruises and cuts while children sobbed over bleeding wounds or simply cried from the trauma of what they were seeing with their young eyes. A small crowd had gathered around the bodies of Nestor and the girl. He could see Secunda among them.

Clodius was running frantically back and forth, getting the people to fall back into the marketplace's south-east corner, where a handful of small side streets branched off between the high-faced shops. Corrie burst out from one of these retreating groups, and Tagus saw her run toward the cluster of people standing over Nestor, shouting that they needed to flee. Clodius had just hauled an injured boy to his feet, and was trying to comfort the crying child as he kept walking, calling for the people to get out while they still could, the councillor's grimy, bloody face full of pain and exhaustion as he shouted and gestured for the others to follow him. Slowly, the crowd of desperate people moved in the direction of the narrow street.

But it was too late.

Corvus had been trying to get the Association to reform their ranks to block off Thresher Street. But before the masked journeymen could even form the "chain", the zealots were upon them.

Screams of "Solar Dominatus!" and "Death to heretics!" tore through the air as the mob's vanguard crashed down, hundreds of feet clattering like a cavalry charge across the cobblestones. The chants of the priests further back being drowned out as street fighting began and a massive brawl erupted beneath the aqueduct's arches. At least two hundred screaming faces, full of hate and righteous fury, bowled through the few dozen journeymen and Tagus could catch further snippets of their frenzied cries as he struggled through the confusion alongside his comrades.

"Death to the disbelievers!"

"Burn the black dog filth!"

Their hatred seemed to tear at the sky itself, and behind it all was the chanting. The same low chant he had heard droning beyond the screams of the dying at Fallonier Fields. He saw the white robes. He saw the weapons. The enemy had swept past the Association men and were running full tilt toward the Falhorne. He would have to fight them.

But…should he kill them? However brutish and violent these men were, they were not soldiers. They were not Templars. Once again, he wished Vitus were here. The exhaustion, the heat of his armor, the chaos…everything was making his head swim. Thoughts of entering the Mortis state, of attaining perfect focus, entered his mind, with all his brethren together it might do something, but there was no time, nor was he in any condition to try.

"Brothers! Stand your ground!" It was the only command he felt sure in giving.

It was Remus who made the decision for him. The former mercenary was the first to move, his catlike reflexes the telltale sign of years of training and harsh experience. The time that it took for his dagger to travel from the bandolier on his chest to its target was barely the time it took to draw in two breaths.

Tagus saw a fair-haired young man, his youthful face contorted in sneering contempt as he prepared to throw a stone that he had just torn free from the ground. But the sneer turned into a look of panicked shock as the dagger hit home with masterful accuracy, pinning the youth's sleeve to the wooden post of a market stall and forcing his slightly raised arm to drop the stone as he struggled to free himself.

Remus allowed himself a grin of satisfaction before letting loose again, aiming at another zealot rushing forward to help the first. The man fell flat on his face, his pants pinned to the same stall. There was no blood. Tagus could see with his own eyes now why this native-born son of Fiore had been told that he belonged in a circus and not the army.

His one-eyed brother had not been idle either. His weapon looked like it belonged on a hunting estate rather than a battlefield, its simple wooden construction appearing light and maneuverable. It was remarkable to see the man load the bolt, pull back the string, drop to one knee and fire in the space that it would take an average soldier to simply load such a weapon.

Scarcely a heartbeat after the bolt took flight came a scream of pain, and Tagus could see another grey-clad man, face twisted in agony as he tugged helplessly to free his hand, which was now impaled on a post, neatly bisected by Valen's bolt. The archer gave a cold shrug in response.

But, unlike the apprentice boys, the zealots did not retreat before this show of force. Nor did they fall back when a deafening report from one of Callidus's pistols sounded above their heads.

Tagus's command was hardly necessary, for Tarquinus and the others had already prepared to receive the charge. It came not in a disciplined line, but in a pell-mell rush of bodies, brandishing clubs, knives, hatchets, and staves. He looked into those faces, felt the sweat drip down his own, and his aching shoulders screamed as he raised the *damas* to strike.

Beneath his weariness and pain there was only anger and fear, any sense of mercy having been drowned. He thought of Porus's hanging corpse, Mia's mutilated and desecrated body, and Nestor and the little girl side-by-side on the cobblestones beneath the guildhall. The memories merged and the rage took hold.

The first to reach them, a wiry man wielding an iron-tipped club, appeared to hesitate for the briefest of moments, eyes wide, as if realizing for the first time that he was face to face with heavily armed soldiers. But this consideration of his own mortality was dashed as he was shoved forward by the zealots behind him, men who were clearly too caught up in their holy fury to realistically consider their chances against Tarquinus's mighty sword or Skarlos' axes. Skarlos, to his credit, showed restraint by merely knocking him to the cobblestones with the flat of his blade.

Tarquinus likewise struck a man to the ground with the pommel of his weapon, when he easily could have swung the two-handed blade like a reaper mowing through a wheat field. Remus drove his elbow into the stomach of another fanatic, who collapsed along with his broken-nosed colleague. A staff-wielding man didn't last much longer as Valens struck him in the face with the butt of his sword. But, just as before, this did nothing to keep the mob at bay, and the fallen men simply vanished amid the press as more of them surged forward.

In scant seconds Tagus was all but surrounded by robed men, baying for the blood of the faithful, as they threw themselves at him.

He could see the zealot's snarling face, round and crudely shaven, bearing the remnants of a yellow beard. He could taste the sour breath that reeked of onions and cheap ale, as he swung the hatchet. He felt the ring, the metallic twang as the crude axe head struck the *damas's* polished black haft, the force of the blow sinking into his arms and chest, flowing through him like his own blood in his veins. Just as the force was about to dissipate, he threw it back at his assailant. The snarl became a perfect "o" of surprise, hatchet flying from the man's grasp to clatter to the ground as his body hurtled backwards. Tagus's mora stance was perfect.

He found himself laughing, roaring in mirth at the man's crazed stupidity in taking on a fully armored warrior of the gods. Contempt filled his mind as he watched them keep coming. A kennel of mindless dogs herded forward by their masters, whose unholy chants he could still hear above the sounds of struggle.

"Die heretic!"

Tagus brought the *damas* up just in time to deflect the club aimed at his head, just as another zealot slammed into him from the right. He did not even turn his head as he seized the man in a "bear trap" with an arm around his neck, throwing the second attacker to the ground even as he shoved the club wielding fanatic aside.

But they kept coming. A staff caught him a glancing but painful blow across the shoulder, and he had to fight to keep himself in mora as two more zealots ran at him with short swords. He knocked one blade aside, but the second was coming too fast, and aiming right for his chest just as the staff caught him again in the side, making him stumble on the rough cobblestones.

That was when all hesitation left him. Vengeance surged over his weariness, eclipsing pain with its molten tide.

The *damas* lashed out in a wide arc. The honed blade effortlessly cutting through cloth into naked flesh. The entire world beneath his hood turned red. Only one of his assailants had the chance to choke out a scream before his ribs split apart and his life's blood became a crimson fountain.

"For Ishan!"

Another zealot lost his head, the ancient blade licking out like a swift serpent claiming its prey, before Tagus, his vision still full of blood and rage, felt strong arms seize him from behind, locking painfully around his sword-arm.

"No, brother! No! Get back!"

Tarquinus's horrified voice sounded through a murky haze, just as Vitus's shouts had been distorted by the waters beneath Allia Bridge. Tagus felt himself being dragged backwards; arms clasped around his breastplate. In front of him, through eyes clouded with sweat, he could see three dead bodies and the zealots swarming in terror and confusion.

"Praetor!" Tagus was staring into Remus's youthful face, lined with worry and concern.

"Come on, we have to move!"

The mob was falling back. Skarlos had been grappling with no less than five zealots surrounding him. Blood was dripping down his bald head as he wielded his axes like clubs, striking men to the ground left and right. Valens was likewise holding his own. With no room to swing his weapon, he had seized it by the blade as well as the hilt and was using it like a stave to trip and batter the foe. As the lanky swordsman turned, Tagus saw a long dripping wound winding down his cheek beneath his missing eye.

The men of the Association were falling back as well, and he saw how badly many of them had fared. All appeared badly beaten. Some had their hoods torn away, revealing bloody scalps and head wounds. At least five that he could see could no longer walk, and were being dragged along by their comrades.

Tarquinus had effectively taken command. Corvus stumbled up to him, gripping his limp right-arm with his left, blood dripping into his beard from a gash across his forehead. Tagus could not hear the words they spoke, but Tarquinus, his face drenched with sweat and blood, quickly turned his head and issued the necessary command.

"Back! Fall back! This way!" He called out, gesturing for the Falhorne to pull back in the direction of the side street.

Remus, still gripping Tagus by the shoulders, immediately responded to the order. With Tarquinus, Skarlos and Valens covering the retreat of the Association partisans as they withdrew.

Of Callidus there was no sign.

Exhaustion was now cutting through the adrenaline. Tagus did not turn around until after the first stone had struck his back, ricocheting off the fluting of his armor. Then the familiar shouts and jeers began to assail his ears once more above the fading din of the retreating mob.

At first, he thought the apprentices had regrouped, but it was not an undisciplined gang of stone throwing youths that met his eyes when he turned around, but a disciplined block of thick-set, powerful looking men in green tunics. The stones they were now unleashing came in equally disciplined volleys. But they were not aiming at the Falhorne, no, they were aiming at the still unarmed faithful, a frightened mass of retreating humanity, pushing toward the side street and completely exposed to their hateful missiles.

This time it was a woman. A woman whose age was impossible to tell behind the grimy mask she wore, as thick and dark as Clodius's, speaking of days spent on windswept slate roofs in rain and scorching heat sweeping the ashes from chimney pots, all in the name of a fallen husband's broken neck and the hungry bellies of her children. Struck on the head, this impoverished life crumpled to the cobblestones, its only epitaph a long wailing, inconsolable "aaaaaaaaaaa".

Tagus gazed at the body, then at the crowd of panicking women and children, then back at the whistling, jeering hired thugs with their volleys of stones. And he saw the source of their brutal discipline: Maxim de Tolley himself. The aristocratic guildmaster sat astride a tall grey horse, gazing like a proud monarch over the carnage and mayhem that had consumed this tiny corner of his domain.

His bright blue robe fluttered in the wind, full of life in contrast to the feeble flapping of the fallen woman's faded garments, moving in time with the brightly patterned banners atop the guildhall. As the alderman surveyed the scene, Tagus saw his eyes linger on the abandoned corpse of old Nestor and a disgusting gloating smile form across his lips. He had seen that smile before and he knew what came next. He looked again at the woman, at Nestor, and at the dark line of warehouses looming in the distance over the river wharfs. This was a kingdom with no love for the outcast and the downtrodden. They might as well be cobblestones to be trampled on.

De Tolley scanned the chaos in triumph. The sun seemed to shine upon him and nowhere else. It glinted off of the weapons of his armored bodyguards. Bathed the golden wine cup that he accepted from the hands of the dutiful slave boy at his side. Illuminated the imperious face that had treated Nestor with such contempt prior to his cruel death.

Tagus barely felt Remus grasp his arm. The shout in his ear felt as faraway as the gods themselves. And, in the blackest pit of his heart, he knew he was afraid: alone, besieged on two fronts and not knowing what to do as his broken people fell back under the hail of stones. Vitus was stricken, the wrongheaded Callidus was nowhere to be seen, and the mob of zealots was advancing again; stirred into a fever-pitch by the deaths of their brethren at the hands of a heretic.

He was bewildered. His victims were not enemy soldiers. He was no praetor. He was not Vitus.

Tagus could only wearily nod his head and allow Remus to draw him back from the scene. He could see the others battling to keep the fanatics back as they pressed their renewed attack into the marketplace under the maddening drone of that damnable chant.

Another youth fell to the raining stones with a scream, greasy dark hair soaked in crimson on the ground. Tagus again saw that face, that cruel gloating face, open its mouth in laughter, amused at the sick sport he was urging his followers to partake in, as though he were keeping score of the corpses strewn over his precious "guild property".

De Tolley turned his head slightly, as if to hear something a dismounted advisor was saying. It appeared to only add to his twisted mirth as the guildmaster began bellowing with unconstrained laughter which echoed around the surrounding rooftops, down the streets, and through the dark alleys swarming with fugitives from his little kingdom.

So did the shot that immediately followed, silencing the evil laughter in a clap of thunder.

Once more the world stood still even as the battle continued to rage. The light still shone on that face, now frozen, mouth agape, a thin trickle of blood bubbling over the lips that had once sneered so cruelly at a fallen man. Then it fell back, away, out of the sun and to the earth below.

There came a whinnying shriek from the horse as its rider toppled, and shouts of rage and astonishment from the retainers who had mere seconds before shared in the jests of their master, gloating over the carnage that seemed to touch no one but low-born wretched heretics. Only when the lone dark figure, brandishing twin pistols, emerged from behind an abandoned butcher's stall did they realize their true vulnerability.

Tagus's own mouth hung open in shock as he watched Callidus step into the light. The formerly disciplined thugs were frozen on the spot, before scattering like frightened rabbits, running away as though all of the fiends of Gormani were on their tails. All that remained were the guildmaster's advisors leaning over his dead body, and a dozen mercenary guards with weapons drawn.

"Run brothers! Get out of here!" Callidus shouted, as the guards charged with a great cry at De Tolley's assassin.

The last thing Tagus saw before Remus dragged him into the side street was Callidus drawing his sword against the onrushing mercenaries. He was aiming his second pistol at a white-robed priest screaming encouragement at the pursuing zealots.

They were out of the marketplace.

The Falhorne and the Association men were now the rearguard of the retreating mass of the Asylum folk being channeled through a maze of backstreets and alleyways. The zealots soon gave up the pursuit, now that they could not bring their numbers to bear and risked being cleaved in two by a vengeful blade.

Tagus, several times almost stumbling to the ground from sheer exhaustion, felt relief when the Falhorne finally emerged from an alley onto a broad street that looked familiar. It was Silo Street, and they were barely a block from the Asylum gates. He muttered a prayer to the gods that Clodius knew the city so well.

Yet his relief was short lived.

The normally bustling thoroughfare that they stood on was strangely deserted, impossibly so for an early afternoon. No bystanders, no street vendors hawking their wares, no housewives or playing children, no beggars, nothing. Even the clerics that had screamed curses at the faithful on their way to the marketplace were nowhere to be seen. The sounds of the city seemed far away, as though they were standing at the edge of a wilderness. The feeling was unearthly. Something was very wrong.

The bedraggled crowd pressed on, still shielded by handful of Association men, many of whom had quietly slipped away into the slums. Tagus spied Clodius standing under the eves of a seemingly abandoned tenement house, urging on the faithful as they made their way toward the Asylum gates, where the gallows loomed darkly.

Upon seeing the Falhorne, he beckoned for them to join him and Tagus finally pushed off Remus's shoulder, slumping against the rough wooden wall and pushing back his hood. Dried blood encrusted Clodius's face.

"Mark my words," the councillor spoke gravely, his voice wheezy as though he had just emerged from a coal pit, "We've kicked a nest of vipers, and by the fiends of Gormani they'll be here soon…probably burn the whole Asylum to the ground just to find the scum who killed De Tolley."

He stared directly at Tagus, and the acting praetor could feel the burning desire of a man, a simple man, who simply wanted to protect his people from destruction.

"We need you now," he said at last, "The Watch must come with me. I'll gather the Agoge. I only wish we had time to mourn Nestor and the others."

"We will be there," Tagus swore, breathing heavily but looking with conviction at the faces of his brothers, "no matter what happens. The Falhorne do not abandon those they guard."

Clodius looked downcast, dropping his gaze to the street as his voice filled with grief, "So many left behind. Too many…"

He placed his hand against the wall to steady himself.

"…Damn, that old goat Nestor will surely rise from Mora's realm and haunt my sleep..."

He gave what might have been intended as a chuckle, but it came out as a dry choking cough as he began to walk away. Rivulets of salt water washing furrows in the grimy bloody mask and revealing, for the briefest of seconds, the flesh beneath: the ruddy, brown skin of the southlands.

Fear seized Tagus as the councillor left. Corrie. He had not seen Corrie since the flight began. And what of Vitus? He was a sick man, bedridden, and young Callus was in no position to defend him…if they came. What if they had come to Mercer Lane? He had to do something.

He turned to the others; a small group gathered in the abandoned street. There was not much left to be said, but he was determined to redeem himself after his loss of control at the marketplace, even though his nerves were shattered.

"Brother watchmen, you must get the Asylum ready for defense. I want all of you to report to the Agoge and await their instructions. I will not be joining you. I must find our praetor and get him to safety. You will obey Brother Tarquinus's commands until I return."

Tagus's voice trailed off as a familiar figure emerged from the shadows of the alleyway across the street, the blood-spattered face giving him the look of a wounded soldier coming in from the battlefield.

"I am sorry to be late, brothers," Callidus muttered breathlessly.

In spite of his obvious injuries, he managed to sound like a young nobleman casually returning from a particularly hard-fought tourney, a rough and tumble sporting event, rather than a life and death struggle.

Tagus could see the irritation this brought to more than once face in the little band of men who had only just fought their way clear of a near massacre.

This time it was Tarquinus who spoke, the fury in his voice evident and rising.

"What in Fiore's flames were you thinking, brother? You just shot a city alderman! Are you trying to call down Gormani on these innocent people?"

"I gave these innocent people their revenge, brother," Callidus responded coldly, "that self-righteous murderer is no longer breathing, and you can be sure that I gave his guards a taste of steel as well."

"It wasn't your place!" Tarquinius shouted these words, his face a blazing red. They echoed down the empty street.

"And who are you to tell me what my place is, brother?"

"A man who defends his people, not a reckless assassin!"

"Is it recklessness to strike down monsters?"

"Enough!" shouted Tagus, there was no time, "What is done is done. We need to move. Valens, help me take off this armor!"

The watchman quickly moved to help him remove the heavy breastplate and greaves. Tagus felt relief as its weight was lifted from his aching limbs.

"Take it to the Black Horseman and secure it, go!"

Skarlos and Remus followed their comrade as he headed off in the direction of the Asylum.

Tagus, now wearing only his sweat-sodden black robes, turned his attention to the two Falhorne before him, who were still looking at each other with angry faces.

"Tarquinus, return to the Agoge and lead the defense. Callidus, you must leave. You have done enough and the other Falhorne of Vinos have to be warned."

Callidus nodded, taking no apparent offense at the rebuke.

"It is all I can do, Praetor. I am a marked man," he cast a sharp glance at Tarquinus, "And I will not risk bringing harm to any of my people here. I will return to Trastamere. You can be sure that the brethren there will be ready. Should you ever need to find me, pass by the castle town and find an inn called *The Prince's Respite*. I will be there. Farewell brothers."

Turning away, he began walking with quick strides, making it halfway across the street before Tagus stopped him, determined to have the final word.

"Brother," he said, causing Callidus to pause and turn his head, "see you in Barbarus".

It was the proper farewell of a Falhorne. Perhaps the reckless bastard did not deserve it, but it was proper nonetheless.

Callidus smiled in reply before disappearing down the alley.

"The same goes for you, brother," Tagus said, returning to Tarquinus. "Make the Black King proud."

The tall Black Vinosian smiled coolly, but his eyes were full of sorrow.

"It's all in His hands."

****

The backstreets were even more eerie as he re-traced his steps. Here and there a shutter creaked in the wind or muffled voices could be heard behind the closed door of a house or shop. The folk inhabiting the narrow streets around the marketplace seemed to be in hiding. No doubt the riot had driven them to ground, but no one was emerging now that the zealots were gone. Now rid of the stifling claustrophobia of Vitus's plate armor, Tagus strained his senses for any sign of life, but could hear little above the clamor that was growing in the distance with every step he took.

Shouts, screams, and cries of defiance were mixed with the whinnying of horses and the clatter of hoofs on cobblestones as it boiled over the rooftops. He began running.

The marketplace was all but deserted when he reached it. Broken stalls and overturned carts attested to the ferocity of the riot. The guildhall loomed like an uncaring giant against the grey cloudy sky as its bell tolled ominously, a single note sounding one in the afternoon. The colorful banners of the Tarnish merchants flapped in the rising wind, although they themselves were nowhere to be seen. Nestor's body and the remains of the others still lay on the bloodied cobblestones as Tagus pressed on, not daring to look at them, making his way toward the furious sounds emanating from the beneath the aqueduct's arches.

He saw that the riot had not ended. Although its participants had shifted, as had its epicenter. The junction of Thresher Street where it met the marketplace had been cleared, and in the distance, near where Silo Street met the course of the aqueduct, Tagus beheld the source of the noise.

Some two dozen armored cavalrymen had formed a cordon across the street, their barded steeds driving forward as the tips of their lances flashed in the momentary shafts of the light that penetrated the thick blanket of clouds. The prince's Gendarmerie had arrived and were forcing the zealots back in the direction of the Temple District. Evidently there had been a struggle, the shopfronts between the marketplace and the beginning of Mercer Lane were in shambles, with broken planks and smashed barrels scattered about in the dust.

For a moment, Tagus allowed himself to believe that the prince had at last decided to fulfill his obligations. That the out-of-control mob of Church fanatics had finally convinced him of the vital need to uphold the Treaty.

That was before he noticed the expanding column of black smoke boiling over the top of the aqueduct.

Mercer Lane was empty and silent. But the telltale signs of struggle and desolation could still be seen outside one house and one house only.

Vitus's house was on fire.

Tagus slowed his steps and gripped his weapon with renewed conviction as he approached, taking in the destruction. The garden gate had been torn from its hinges and lay in the middle of street. The front door had been kicked in and the ground floor and second story windows smashed. Orange flames licked out of the second-floor window of Vitus's study, trailing black smoke into the grim sky. The scent of burning wood filled his nostrils as he beheld the sign of Solar

Dominatus, the four-pointed sun, scrawled in black tar against the brickwork beside the front door.

Above this hateful symbol, the sign of the sackers of Brisi and long ago Cera Infernus, hung a body. Tagus could smell the newly spilt blood. As fresh as it might be on the blade of an assassin. It was all Tagus could do to keep his grip on the *damas*. An icy claw gripped his heart.

"By Fiore's sacred flame…"

He was hanging from the window of the study. As prominently displayed as Mia's mutilated remains had been on the gallows. The rest of the world faded when he saw that swaying form, thumping and bumping in a sickening rhythm against the walls. Blood trickled down the stonework to the street below, running through gaps in the flagstones at the threshold of the kicked in front door.

The body, though brutally slashed open and mutilated, was only too recognizable; completely naked, stripped of all its coverings and left lifeless, helpless, and in shame. Vitus had been strung up by the ankles, upside down like a pig in an abattoir. Tagus could not count the cuts, slashes, and stab wounds, all of which drained great quantities of blood onto the flagstoned walk, where the flies had begun to buzz. The face was so caked in gore as to be unrecognizable to anyone who did not know the aging Falhorne as well as his apprentice. Tagus saw the old scars, the old marks, the signs of a warrior of sixty winters. But the bright blue eyes were gone, blood trickling from empty sockets.

I am your son…To me you are the Black King.

Now his father was no more.

His racing mind stopped. Unable to process the sheer scale of the feelings that were crashing over him in a great wave. He found himself staggering forward, eyes fixed on the hanging body. Stumbling forward, arms outstretched, as if to embrace that beloved face.

It was not rage that led him to face the hooded figure in the doorway, his mentor's *damas* leveled toward the man's throat. Human emotions had left him far behind. He was deep in the trance of living death now, walking in Barbarus, his rage held down as under a weight of ice, yet it permeated every move he made and filled every purposeful step he took.

These cowards who dragged old men from their sick beds. These butchers, these "righteous" souls in white robes and their lackeys who razed Brisi, burned homes, raped women, stole children, and publicly dismembered the charred bodies of their fathers as an offering to their debased god. They would die. They would all die, tasting the wrath of Barbarus and the Black King's chosen executioner.

Remember that we are the Falhorne, the blade that shall pierce his cloak of lies!

By the time the crossbow-wielding assassin had emerged from behind the rose bush next to the front door, Tagus was already moving at a full sprint. The priest of Solar Dominatus shouted something, but it came too late for the man. Tagus only recognized the golden lion of the royal guard after he had rammed the spike head of the *damas* through the assassin's chest, punching through plate metal like it was a weathered strip of cow-hide.

He was at Fallonier Fields again, feeling nothing but the lethal cold precision he had felt as the Templars bore down on him. He did not even hear the white-robe's scream as he pivoted, wrenching the *damas* free and swinging it in a perfect arc. Watching impassively as the priest's body flopped to the ground in two halves, ribs smashed like rotten timbers.

He did not remember the next few moments. He barely recalled cutting down the blue-coated figures that attempted to pass through the door. Of striding into the front hall over their poleaxed bodies. Or hunting down the last of them, a sniveling coward hiding in the downstairs pantry, and gutting him like a snared fish.

He remembered nothing, before the cold precision of the Mortis state finally left him, and he tumbled to the kitchen floor. All discipline, all focus leaving his body as the world was broken.

His body was wracked by uncontrollable sobbing as sorrow, guilt and rage poured out of him like it was his life's blood.

He could not tell how long he laid there, beating on the floorboards with his fists until they were red and sore. Finally, he lay on his back, staring through the smoky air at the familiar ceiling beams like a child looks for faces in the clouds. But there was no innocence here. One word was thundering into his shattered consciousness. The Asylum, he needed to get to the Asylum, he needed to help his brothers and Corrie…but what of Callus?

Tagus searched the ground floor, unable to reach the second story now that the fire had spread to the stairs. He could find no trace of the boy, before the gathering smoke forced him outside, where he stood again under Vitus's hanging body. He only hoped that Callus had made it out and was smart enough to make his way to the Asylum or the Association.

He looked at the dead bodies of the guardsmen, of the priest, the servants of Church and state who had done this to a sickly old man. Like Callidus, he was a marked man now. He silently begged forgiveness, gazing up into those hollow eyes. For he could not give the old warrior the honorable last rites that he deserved. He could only pray that his noble spirit would find Barbarus.

Gods be merciful to the soul in death dishonored.

He choked on the words as he tried to speak them, and nothing passed his cracked dry lips. What would he tell Tarquinus? How could he explain what had happened?

Tagus tore his eyes away and ran down the empty street, senses screaming with blood and fire as he fought back the tears.

He first heard the sounds as he hurried up the deserted potholed lane toward Silo Street, his bad leg reducing him to an awkward, limping gait. The piercing sound cut the wind and it did not take long for it to be joined by the sickly scent of something burning accompanied by shouts and the sound of marching feet coming from somewhere over the rooftops, joined in turn by a low rumble of hoofs and cartwheels moving over cobblestones.

The entire Asylum was now cloaked in a dark pall of sooty bad-smelling smoke. Obscuring from the eyes of the gods the evil deeds being done below. The smell of burning thatch, wood and tar carried on the breeze.

Chapter 12 – The Face of the Enemy

"No, it cannot be. Swear before the gods that you are telling the truth, child!"

Jesta felt her temper flare as she stared across the table at the callow youth, the praetor's messenger boy. After reading the contents of the hastily written note, she could feel her insides turn to water, but she refused to let him see that. She was trying vainly to convince herself that this was some sick boyish prank for which she could take a rod to his backside.

"Swear!"

"I swear, mistress! By all the gods, it's true! Sirrah Agelaus heard it from the prince himself!"

Callus appeared terrified, his dark eyes resembling twin gaping pits. The boy's fear stemmed from more than the anger of a member of the council.

Cursing her temper, she let the energies of the Craft subside, drawing her raging aura back into herself so it would continue to burn unseen within her soul.

She let out a sigh, her stern expression vanishing as she returned her gaze to the neat, flowing writing on the crumpled page before her.

"I believe you."

She wanted to tear the letter to shreds in despair. But her sense of duty as the elected matriarch of her people, forced calm and certainty into her voice as she rose from her chair in the Agoge chamber, empty apart from her and the young messenger.

"What of the praetor?"

"He's sick in bed, mistress. He told me to go to the palace right when I got back from the marketplace. Them Templars gave me a rough time, told me they'd have me flogged, but the gendarmerie told em' to shove off and I got in. Sirrah Agelaus told me to come right away with this."

"Then you had best remain here for now," Jesta said as she crossed to the front door, "I must…"

Suddenly there was a clatter of heavy boots on the steps outside and the heavy wooden door burst open to reveal a short and stocky man in a mud-spattered cloak. He pulled back his hood to reveal a broad tawny face and balding head soaked in sweat.

He faced Jesta and his breath came out in choked gasps as he spoke.

"Mistress Jesta…I come on behalf of the Association."

Jesta stopped and looked at the man, whom she had seen speaking to Corvus the week before. His name was Gorgo, a Samosian and former dock worker…although his reputation as a convicted thief and former denizen of the royal dungeons superseded his more honest titles. At least now he appeared sincere.

"Speak. Do you bring word from the marketplace?"

"Yes," he gasped out, leaning his body heavily against the doorframe, "I bring word from Councillor Corvus. A riot's started. Theophilus sent a mob of his fanatics at us and we were attacked by the apprentice boys. They killed Councillor Nestor. We're trying to get the people to safety. Several of my fellows were beaten up pretty bad by the time I left…I've never seen it get like this."

Jesta could see the trembling in the man's exhausted eyes and she felt her heart sink. It was confirmation. She knew what was coming. It had already begun.

"Thank you, Gorgo," she managed to reply, although her face felt numb, "You have done well. As have you, Callus."

She turned to face the boy, who continued to stand nervously by the table in the center of the room, as though he were a young soldier awaiting orders. She provided them.

"I would ask both of you to go about the Asylum. Knock on all the doors, gather all the people who remain and tell them to come here. I will meet them on the front steps. Go with all haste!"

Corrie had told her once that she could be as cold as ice one moment and hot as fire the next. Her words to the two messengers came out as hard as frozen water in a mountain lake as she let the Craft impregnate her words.

Callus abruptly scurried from the room. Even the exhausted Gorgo, wheezing and gasping from his previous ordeal, made no complaint as he hastened to do her bidding.

She hated to use such methods. Her grandmother had taught her mother as a child that a true practitioner of the Craft honored the All Mother and used her gifts only in the direst of situations. Her grandmother had died at Brisi, burned alive atop a pyre as tall as a house. Such was the example that the Inquisition desired to make of this "devil woman" and "demon-inspired witch". Jesta had never known her except through her mother's stories of a peaceful life turned to ashes.

Jesta followed the messengers out onto the front steps.

She focused, shutting her eyes, drawing the energies of the Craft to her and invoking the twisting contours of the Stream of Life. Her mind coursing along it as she sought out her former apprentice.

She knew the warning she must give, and its dire intensity boiled the spectral waters as it raced on, only to strike something and stop dead.

A burst of energy sent her stumbling backward, her eyes flying open as her back was pressed against the worn brick wall. She sensed the power, the alien will that had dared to obstruct the energies of life itself. She recognized it only too well.

Standing alone on the steps, she surveyed the grim horizon. Wondering if today it would be her turn to burn.

****

Clodius was sprinting down Silo Street, lungs burning in his haste to reach the Asylum ahead of the others. Corvus had already sent people back, but Clodius could hardly say that he trusted some of their characters and was determined to take matters into his own hands.

He arrived at the gateway only to find the great arch partially blocked by an overturned cart. Sweat-sodden and shirtless, Gorgo, the Association man, looked like he was about to keel over with fatigue, as he worked alongside five elderly men, who did not seem to require his help in the slightest as they laid down a makeshift barrier using old barrels. Clodius recognized Arbaces right away, and the sight of the white-haired former soldier, clad in the dented ancient breastplate he had not worn in twenty years, nearly stopped him in his tracks.

"Welcome back, Councillor," Arbaces' grey eyes had the look of sharp iron as he set down the barrel he had been holding. "Good to see you didn't want to miss the celebrations."

He did not wait for Clodius's reply, spitting a wad of saliva into the dirt before returning to his task.

He was just about to slip around the half-finished barricade in search of Jesta when the exhausted Gorgo stumbled up to him.

"Wait! She knows, Councillor," the man gasped, looking like a dockworker coming off of a double-shift of loading satincane. "I gave her the message."

"What's going on?"

"What does it look like?" Arbaces spoke without invitation and without turning his head.

"This is a military matter now, Councillor. If the enemy's coming, we'd damn well better have the place ready for defense. Put your back into it, we could use more hands!"

The survivors of the riot were trickling back into the Asylum by the time he had broken away and found Jesta. Clodius could not help but feel a small swell of confidence, despite the bleak situation, as he watched her standing in the middle of the street, directing the efforts of the people just as she had done that morning before the march.

Arbaces might have likened her to his old commander from his mercenary days. Clodius just saw her as a more attractive version of his former boss on the docks, although at least the headwoman had a heart as well as a commanding tongue that could stop a horned one in its tracks with fear. In spite of the world coming down around him, the twinge of nervousness was still there as he approached her in the shadow of the old port authority building.

"Councillor…" He began.

"Clodius," she responded, cutting him off, "How do our people fare? Is everyone back safely?"

"Forgive me, Jesta," he paused, she never failed to surprise him, even now, "They are returning, but, by the gods, we lost…"

"Nestor, yes, Gorgo told me of his death. Name the others."

Clodius's mind was reeling at the businesslike tenor of the headwoman's voice. He managed to relay the shameful list through trembling lips, his heart sinking deeper with every name.

"Little Sabine, Priscilla's girl, died first, from a stone to the head. Nestor tried to save her before he was hit. Sybll was next, also a stone to the head. I don't think she had any next of kin left. Terrence from the docks had his skull smashed by a club when the churchmen attacked us. The brave man stayed to fight alongside the Association folk. Now his family has lost its breadwinner. His boy Commus also fell to a hurled flagstone. We couldn't take their bodies with us. There were so many injured, Corrie is seeing to them now…"

"Thank you, Councillor," Jesta again cut him off before he could say another word, "I shall notify the families. They will be remembered."

Clodius exhaled a long, gasping sigh. It felt like a boulder was on his back. The only relief came from the knowledge that his wife and children had remained in the Asylum that morning. To think that his Marcus could have shared the fate of young Commus, his little skull broken on the cobblestones...

Outside the Agoge, he could see a gang of old women laboriously hefting a ramshackle assortment of barrels, crates, and large stones into place, struggling to block the narrow road. The Asylum was being prepared for a siege. He wanted to ask Jesta about the preparations, about the barricades. Was an attack truly imminent? Had she received a warning? But his questions answered themselves before he could even speak.

He recognized Praetor Vitus's messenger boy as the dark-haired youth careened out from one of the muddy lanes, his leather doublet caked with dirt and sweat. Callus dashed up to Jesta and spoke, his voice wheezing with fatigue yet overflowing with dread and alarm.

"Mistress, they've blocked the Rivergate! The Tarnish gunners, they're all outside, five ranks of em'!"

"Have they entered the Asylum?" Even the unflappable headwoman sounded shaken.

"No…they're just standin' out there, like they don't want anyone to leave."

"I see. Go back and help with the barricades. Return at once to me if anything changes."

No sooner had Callus dashed back the way he had come, Gorgo appeared out of the swelling crowd.

He approached them, stumbling like a drunken man, and the look he bore on his sweat-covered face was one of stark terror.

"Councillors…they're coming! From the slums, down Silo Street!"

Clodius felt his heart hammering in his chest as he watched Jesta bow her head, give a knowing nod, and say nothing.

"What are you talking about, man? Who is coming?"

He shouted these words, the fear in his own voice stinging his ears. But Gorgo's reply was enough to send the urine he had been holding since the riot trickling down his leg.

"Templars…"

****

Corrie heard the shouting as she was in the midst of bandaging Thea's head. The young girl was still whimpering in pain from the stone, thrown by the arm of a coward. But the sudden screams of terror that followed drowned out the child's sobs.

They had taken over the yards of two hovels, a safe distance from the Silo Street gateway, to form the makeshift hospital. And there were many who sought treatment. Too many people with bloody faces and broken bones. Too many eyes.

She had seen painfilled eyes before: the eyes of plague victims, of people burned in tenement fires, of violated women and beaten men. But this was different. These eyes were the eyes of a people, an entire community, an entire nation, gripped, not only by the pain of their injuries, but the fear of what was to come. In all the years she had spent in Fiore, in all the years she had spent at Jesta's side, she had not seen anything like this. It was like everyone was holding their breath.

Jesta had only stayed long enough to see their makeshift clinic completed, having offered up her own and Secunda's dwellings for the purpose. She had said little, but the look in her dark eyes and the subtle expressions of the Craft that Corrie had been trained to recognize gave everything away. She knew what was coming. And she knew that she had to safeguard her people at any cost.

Councillor Secunda was helping her, as were several of the other Asylum women who knew something of medicine. The old woman said nothing as she moved from one patient to the next, bandaging wounds and applying herbal ointments.

Only Corrie was entrusted with the many broken limbs, quietly making use of the Craft to speed the healing process in the full knowledge that there was no time. She focused on the task at hand, trying hard not think of Tagus or worry where he might be amidst all this.

Thea's head injury was easy to treat and the child's sobs soon ceased. But the pain in those youthful eyes quickly turned to fear when the screams began.

It was Octavia, Thea's mother, who burst into the yard. Her skirts in disarray and her eyes bulging in terror as she clutched her wailing baby to her breast.

"Templars! At the gate! Hundreds of them!"

All eyes turned to the terrified young mother and her terror became theirs. Something had awakened in their minds, a collective memory, a shared nightmare that now stalked them in broad daylight.

Corrie took Thea's hand and they ran to her. She did not interrogate the sobbing woman. She did not speak at all as she put her arms around Octa's shoulders.

It was in that moment that she sensed the call and turned her gaze to where Jesta stood in the middle of the street. She was not looking at Corrie, but up the hill toward the barricade, where many of the Asylum's menfolk had gathered. Everyone else had gone into hiding and the street was nearly empty.

Without turning, Jesta spoke to her. There was no sound. Her lips did not move. The message passed along the hidden corridors of the Craft, passing from the mind of one adherent to another, like two streams meeting and merging in a riverbed.

Take the route that Nicco showed us. Get my people out of here. Farewell sister.

The communication ceased. Jesta strode toward the barricade, a black shadow in her mourning dress.

****

Corvus looked out at the white figures approaching down the street. The Asylum gate throwing himself and his companions into shadow as the wind whistled eerily beneath the archway. His shattered arm was numb where the fanatic's iron-tipped club had struck him. The bone having snapped midway through his bicep, rendering the entire limb useless. Now it lay bound in a sling of dirty cloth. There had been no time for anything else, apart from raising the barricade. His good left arm burned from the one-handed effort of hauling empty barrels and crates for the others to stack up inside the gateway in a jagged line.

Too many of the survivors bore similar injuries, and he refused to let them bear burdens that were his to share. Luckily, they were nearly all dockworkers, and the added incentive of defending their own homes and families had sent them into a frenzy of motion. Out of the more than two dozen Association men who had accompanied the march that morning, only two remained. Gorgo likely because he was too exhausted to make it anywhere else.

Corvus did not blame them. All came from the Ox Guts and most had their own families to look out for. He knew for a fact that Gorgo didn't. Nor did Sev after he had lost his wife and child in the fire that had burned down the Malt Lane tenements last year. Now, like Corvus, he was a doomed man.

"You think they deserve some final words?"

Old Arbaces stood beside him in his aged breastplate, an equally antiquated sword held in his still muscular right arm. White-haired and grey-eyed, his broad shoulders crowning the remnants of the soldier's body he had gained from his mercenary days. He was another doomed man, his grandson the latest victim of the Lowtown Monster, his only daughter dead from childbirth. He had no more ties to an earthly existence.

"I guess I'll give them a few, if they're polite enough to ask."

Corvus forced a wry smile as he heard Arbaces' grim chuckle. None of the other men said anything. They stood behind the barricade, trembling hands gripping whatever weapons they had gotten hold of. Mostly large hammers and wood axes, tools that would accomplish little against the heavily armored foes approaching with their long lances and broadswords.

Gorgo and Sev still held the square-headed iron maces they had wielded in the riot, as did Corvus, who clutched the weapon awkwardly in his off-hand. Arbaces' ancient sword was the only real military weapon they had. He still did not know how the old soldier had kept it out of Resti's hands.

Arbaces was also the only one with any real military training. Tagus had not returned and the Watch had been sent to guard the barricade at the Rivergate where the Tarnish marines were threatening.

The Templars of the Host advanced, five abreast, their white mantles emblazoned with the four-pointed golden sun of Solar Dominatus. Their polished plate armor did not shine, but appeared a dull grey beneath the sky and its racing clouds. The visors of their great helms, wrought in bronze in the image of the Divine Messengers, were closed, and they advanced with disciplined precision as though they were moving across a battlefield.

Corvus could see seven ranks of them drawn up. From his position behind the barricade, he could see a dark, boxlike form emerge from the shadow of the tenements accompanied by the ominous rumbling of heavy wheels. Apart from this and the sound of marching feet, the Ox Guts appeared dead. As though the whole slum were in hiding.

The front rank was only fifteen feet away, when the whole body suddenly stopped. The line of armored figures parted, and a white-robed man, wearing the golden amulet of the priesthood of the Almighty Sun, stepped forward. He appeared young, but it was hard to tell given that much of his face was lost in the shadow of his hood. In his hands he bore a scroll with purple wax seals dangling from it, which he proceeded to unroll before speaking in a loud, clear voice that had every intention and expectation of being obeyed immediately.

"By the divine authority vested in His Holiness Bishop Theophilus by the divine light of the Most High and by His Exalted Holiness Hierophant Invictas XVII, this area and all within are declared *malus civitis.* All heretics are directed to submit peacefully and to accept the cleansing of their immortal souls in accordance with their perpetrated sins. The Most High is merciful. His Holy Light all-embracing. Submit to His divine benevolence or we who are His chosen weapons shall be left with no choice but to compel your submission as demanded by His commandments. Which path do you choose?"

Corvus felt his hand trembling, his knees felt weak, and he nearly dropped his weapon. But it was not only fear that possessed him, but rage, hard-driven burning rage.

He had been three years old, little more than an infant when the Templars had come to Brisi. He remembered little, apart from the terror in his mother's face, a terror his young mind could not understand. Then he was running, Secunda gripping him by the hand. He remembered the fire and the screaming. He did not let go of her, his protector, the daughter of their neighbors, who had run as fast as her sixteen-year-old legs could carry her to get him to safety. Adopting him as her own son when they had reached Fiore and Nestor's father had taken them in.

He had never seen his parents or older brother again after that night. All these years, fifty now, he had carried on in the knowledge that he had lived while the rest of his family had died. Now they had come for him. He could join his parents and brother in the afterlife if the Great Judge willed it. But he would not go quietly.

The defiant words rose up in him like a storm splitting the sky. "Gormani's pits take your lies, Priest! Remember Brisi!"

He roared it to the racing grey clouds, roared it to the gods of the Court as he spat in the direction of the white-robed cleric.

"Remember Brisi!"

Trembling hands gripped their poor weapons more tightly, lips sealed by fear parted and joined the call.

"Remember Brisi!"

It rose from the dry throats of fifty men, echoing over the home that was theirs by right, and that of their fathers and their grandfathers before them, all the way back to when Cera Infernus still loomed over the sacred city of the Fire Lord. As Jesta had said in the Agoge chamber, the faithful would always be here.

"Remember Brisi!"

The white-robed messenger gave an irritated glance at the defiant heretics behind the barricade and turned away. His proud form vanishing from view as the ranks closed behind him and one hundred lances were lowered in the direction of the gateway.

"Remember Brisi!"

"Sol Invictas!"

The battle cry drowned out the shouts of the defenders.

Then came the charge.

Corvus watched them come, muscles straining as he struggled to raise his weapon against the Church's chosen killers. He saw the bronze mask thundering toward him, standing his ground with the wry smile that he forced himself to wear on his lips.

Perhaps some could flee, as he had done fifty years before. Perhaps, by his sacrifice, some young people could get away and keep the memories alive.

He heard Arbaces bellowing at the others to stand their ground, the old soldier standing at the very front of the group, as immovable as a mountain.

He saw him strike back at them, the old soldier bellowing in fury as he was pierced by three lances simultaneously and fell.

It came too quickly to dodge. Two feet of burnished steel impaling Corvus through the chest as he swung his weapon. In his last moments of consciousness, he felt it weakly strike and bounce off the flaming sun symbol in the center of his enemy's chest.

It was the closest he had ever come to the beasts that had taken his family. He had struck the bastards, and they had felt it. The smile that he wore as the world faded to black was genuine in every way.

Tarquinus was bleeding badly by the time Callus received the order to run back down the Strand to the Agoge in search of aid. The Falhorne had been holding his guts in with his hand, slumped against the remains of the Rivergate barricade beside the body of the armored thug who had given him his wound, and who now wore Remus's last throwing knife as a throat ornament. To Callus it had looked like the bloody "Gormani smiles" that the gangs in the Ox Guts used to give to turncoats and others who crossed them.

"Find Tagus."

The words had been sickly, a near gurgle, as blood dripped from the black moustache.

Remus and Valens were dead. The latter having downed one the of the mercenaries with a crossbow bolt before flinging his weapon aside and engaging the foes swarming the barricade with sword and dagger.

Callus had been knocked to the ground, a massive snarling man in chainmail looming over him with a battle-axe. In that moment, as his blood turned to water, he remembered what Tagus had said before…not every blow was lethal.

Callus had stabbed the man with the short sword Remus had given him, striking at the mercenary's face as he tried to scale the crates and barrels of the barricade, and he had got him…right on the chin. The blood had soaked into the grizzled beard and the man had roared like a dragon in the tales when the hero's blade met its great throat and the beast began lashing out in its death spasm. But this was no tale.

Valens had intervened and cut down the man from behind, before he could land the killing blow on the young scamp who had tried to cut his throat. Callus had looked up at his savior, only to hear the crack of a musket and see the watchman topple.

Then Callidus had arrived.

For an instant, Callus had almost allowed himself to believe that the outsider had treacherously shot Valens in the back. Master Vitus had said that Callidus was not a real Falhorne and a "traitor". Shooting a comrade in the back was something traitors did.

But those thoughts died when the tall man from Trastamere fired both his pistols into the mercenaries before the barricade, dropping two of them before throwing himself to the melee, sword in hand. Drawing stunned expressions from both Remus and Skarlos even as they fought for their own lives…Remus being run through seconds later.

Somehow, they beat them back. The armored men that had stormed through the Rivergate, passing freely through the lines of Tarnish marines with their uniform blue and white jackets, had worn no livery of any kind. But their intentions had been all too clear as they advanced against the barricade and its meager number of defenders.

Apart from Tarquinus and the three watchmen, the hastily-built barricade had been manned by dockworkers and old men, many of them armed with nothing more than staves. Most had fled by the time the mercenaries retreated. A few lay dead where they had fallen. Only two stubborn old men remained, awkwardly holding swords they had taken from their dead attackers.

Skarlos, the hulking ex-mercenary who used to hold Callus spellbound with his tales of fighting Orcs in the distant Red Marches and serving under the legendary Captain "Two-Cuts" Zorba at Fallonier Fields, was standing over the bodies of five men he had killed single-handedly. The big Samosian was covered in blood, but, unlike Tarquinus, whose mighty sword had cut down the same number of foes, he was still on his feet.

He and Callidus were now effectively the only thing standing between the enemy and the Asylum. His brutal show of strength and furious bellows of defiance driving the mercenaries to retreat.

But they would be back. Callus could see them regrouping under the arches of the Rivergate as he ran up the street. Just as the barricade passed out of sight behind walls and fences, he saw Skarlos turn to face them, twin axes raised.

Callidus turned his long face toward Callus, who was still looking back toward the barricade as he climbed the low hill in the direction of the Agoge. One of the tall man's cheeks was dripping with blood, and his russet hair was matted from where a glancing blow had caught him in the head. Yet he smiled, eyes twinkling strangely through the pain, as he waved, motioning for him to keep running.

"Bite the tusk of the boar!"

No sooner had Callus turned his head away, the old battle cry of the Red Boars rose into the sky like the bellow of a wounded animal as Skarlos roared his defiance at the next wave of attackers.

In that moment, the last of Callus's heroic fantasies, dreams that had once warmed his shivering body in dark alleyways and made him forget the painful rumbles of his hungry belly, died and sank beneath the ground.

He tried to be strong as he ran along the Strand, past the blackened hovels burnt on the Day of Blood. Tagus had told him to be strong. But Tagus was probably dead, and he couldn't hold back the fear, just like when he had crossed "Half-Ear" Mar and his gang. They had chased him, threatening to hang his guts from the rafters after they'd had their fun with his mother. Tagus had saved him then. But now he was gone.

Nevertheless, even as his heart threatened to explode from his chest, he almost allowed himself to believe that there was a way out of this nightmare as he reached the T-junction by the Silo Street Gate and saw the dark figure of Jesta pass before him.

He called out to her. But the headwoman of the Asylum did not respond. She was staring straight ahead, slowly walking toward the gateway.

When Callus turned to follow her gaze, he froze instantly in fear.

The barricade lay in shambles. The barrels and crates had been scattered and only the overturned cart remained in place. Dozens of men-at-arms in white coats were shoving their way through the debris. They were Templars of the Church. He recognized them from the palace, the soldiers in the frightening masks who had tried to keep him from reaching Agelaus.

At their feet he saw the bodies, the bloodied remains of those men of the Asylum who had stood their ground. He thought he could make out Corvus's red beard resting next to one of the Templar's iron-shod feet.

Jesta continued walking calmly and slowly toward them, like one of the dark shades Callus had read about, vengeful ghosts kept from the afterlife for lack of proper funeral rites. The Templars were facing her with their blank and emotionless masks as the flames suddenly arose beneath their feet and the bloody dirt and cobblestones about them began to blaze like kindling in the dry season.

The scattered barrels and the cart were set alight as the fire rising from the ground became a raging inferno in the same strong wind that sent Jesta's dress billowing like the black smoke pouring into the sky all around. Callus could hear the screams of pain and suffering from men being burned alive in their armor, their writhing forms appearing as silhouettes against this wall of fire that now barred the way to the Asylum's streets.

He stood rooted to the spot. The wind singing all around him. He could smell the smoke as his eyes remained fixed on Jesta, who stood motionless in the middle of the deserted street with her arms upraised toward the heavens. All the stories he had been told of witches, evil women who trafficked with Gormani's demons, flooded his mind as the magical fire continued to burn, consuming the dead and the living alike with relentless orange and yellow tendrils.

Suddenly he was on the ground, like a giant hand had smashed him headfirst into the dirt. Dazed, his head spinning, he lifted his eyes to the street. The fire was gone. The air was cool, far cooler than it had been mere seconds before. Even the wind had stopped. Ash and blackened timbers choked the now empty gateway, while Jesta lay sprawled on her back in the middle of the road, as unmoving as a corpse.

A lone rider appeared beneath the archway, mounted on a grey horse and robed in white. An expressionless golden mask gazed down at the fallen body of the councilwoman, before slowly shifting its focus to the petrified young boy crouching in the dirt.

****

The flames were spreading now. Amid the roar of the fires, spreading trails of orange and sickly yellow from Silo Street down to the Tio,

Tagus could hear the sound of men groaning, children crying, women screaming. But these were not the noises of war.

He had heard the screams of the dying on the battlefield, heard the cries of wounded souls waiting for their release into death, but this was different. They were the sounds of a particular kind of suffering and despair, a deep collective wail of agony. Anguished rage welled up inside him as he recognized it for what it was – a dark echo from the past ringing in his ears. He could not see, but he could feel the chains being fastened to helpless hands. It was the sound of captive souls being taken into bondage.

Tagus's heart was hammering in his chest. It all made sense now. Through the smoke, a ghastly and all too familiar shape came into view, a dark box-like silhouette resembling a moving cage on wheels, and surrounded by long lines of shadows. They were enslaving his people. Taking them away. And there was no one there to stop them. At least no one still living.

He struggled to shove the images of lifeless comrades from his mind. Picturing Remus's dead eyes staring up from the bloody cobblestones, then Skarlos, then Valens…then the image of Vitus's lifeless dangling body passed before his mind's eye and he had to fight the urge to once more break down in sobs.

Now he heard the sounds that he dreaded: the clatter of chains, the scrape of naked feet on stone, and then the voice, the cruel shouting voice that finally maddened him beyond all reason:

"Move slave! Move!"

The harsh words were instantly followed by the crack of a whip and a muffled cry from what sounded like a little boy. A little boy with dark features and deep-set brown eyes, wide with terror and overflowing with the shock of betrayal.

All concentration was now broken, all dispassionate focus shattered. His rage boiled black within his mind as he limped the last few steps toward the gateway.

The sight that met his eyes, as he drew nearer to the smoky shapes and menacing silhouettes, was one of blood, chains, tears, and downcast faces, amid stinging whips and brutal shouts. Arranged single-file into three long lines outside the Asylum gate, bound by iron manacles that clanged and clattered in a gruesome din of metal on metal as they gripped wrists and ankles, each person's ankles bound by chains to the wrists of those behind and forcing them to walk in slow shuffling gait, the folk of the Asylum were being loaded into the barred wagons.

Pitiful sobs came from the throats of the children, bound and chained just like their elders; their mothers unable to do anything but look on with ashen tortured faces. The men were trying in vain to remain stoical, the proud protectors of their families, if only for one last time. However, most could not hide their fear of the monsters that stalked around them with whips in hand.

There were at least ten slavers, but they were accompanied by perhaps forty soldiers armed with pikes and bills. Even through the choking smoke that filled the stagnant and oppressive air the prince's lion roared aloud on every blue-clad breast.

The slavers themselves wore plain white tunics and iron breastplates bearing neither design nor heraldry, their heads crowned with bronze helmets that shadowed their faces so only their white teeth flashed as their hateful orders spat into the close muggy air.

"March! Move your worthless hides!"

One column was shuffling forward, the people in it being slowly swallowed up, one by one, into the darkness of the wagon. The sound of their chains, their groans, their sobs, muffled and then silenced altogether as they vanished into that black hole. One man hesitated, clearly terrified, only to cry out when the slaver's whip cut his back.

"Move or bleed, slave!" Shouted another slaver somewhere on the opposite side of the column.

He saw a third slaver take the back of his hand to a tiny black-haired girl sobbing at the back of the second column that had yet to move.

"No!"

Her mother, a thin older woman in a ragged green skirt hysterically screamed something Tagus could not make out over the clattering chains and dragging feet, before falling silent as a guardsman struck her from behind with a mailed fist, causing her to crumple limply to the ground. Her chained limbs splayed out crazily like some oversized puppet. They did not yet know the most brutal of lessons, that a slave's tongue was his master's, not his own.

Tagus had no master then but his rage. He recognized a child in the line of shuffling bodies. Small bare feet dragging, sliding over cobblestones, struggling to keep up with the others as they headed toward that evil wagon. He was a little red-headed boy, the same boy whose playful, careless words had so chilled him just two days before.

Black dog, blunt sword, run, run, run!

The nearest guard did not have time to react before Tagus was on top of him. Blood fountained as the bluecoat's shoulder was cleaved from his body. But even with the piercing scream that burst from the man's lips, his neighbor had no time to level his pike before he too was furiously eviscerated on the blood-stained tip of the *damas* and cast aside.

Tagus was sweating heavily now, his black hooded robe feeling closer to cast iron field plate against his tired muscles. Somewhere in the back of his mind a desperate small voice was whispering the bitter truth, that this was a hopeless battle. But his rage ran roughshod over it.

An entire street full of soldiers were now levelling their weapons at him and crying out in shock and anger. Downcast heads and reddened eyes turned upwards at the black-clad warrior before them. For just the briefest of moments, a flicker of hope passed through them.

"Falhorne!"

An old man cried out from the front of the line, face lined with anguish, desperately trying to extend a manacled hand toward the source of his fleeting hope. The slaver closest to Tagus punched the man full in the face with almost casual disdain, as if he were swatting a fly. The bloodied features of the man falling away amidst an obscene jangling of chains as the slaver turned to face him.

He could see the cruel grin in the shadow of the bronze helmet, hearing the proud self-confidence in the man's voice as he called out to the soldiers:

"At ease guardsmen! The black dog is mine!"

Tagus's furious arcing blow, bearing the full force of the *damas'* blade, was parried with almost contemptuous ease. The slaver's short sword appearing in his hand as if from nowhere and executing a swift counter-attack that the former barely had time to dodge. This was no mere thug, but a seasoned warrior.

He lowered the *damas* for a thrust, but his opponent darted aside. This time Tagus could not evade the riposte and had to turn his shoulder to deflect the well-aimed blow, only to feel the blade tear through the fabric and cut into his flesh. Blood soaked his shoulder as pain shot through his arm.

He dropped back into mora stance and struck out again with a sideways slash, aiming the cut at the left side of the slaver's rib cage. But another rapid parry knocked his weapon upwards and it did nothing but tear a small hole in the white tunic.

The tunic fell open at the shoulder, and in that instant a small gilded insignia fell from its folds and came to full view: a four-pointed sun with an expressionless face, the sign of the Betrayer. The slaver was a Templar. The white-clad fanatics he had faced at Fallonier Fields were here in the heart of the capital, and carrying out the same atrocities as they had at Brisi.

The two battling warriors were surrounded now. Some of the guardsmen still had pikes lowered in Tagus's direction. Furious, hate-filled looks on their fire-lit faces. But others appeared jubilant, leaning casually on their pikestaffs like they were watching some kind of deranged sport. The prisoners stood immobile in their lines. Even the cracking of the whips had ceased as the slavers silently watched the spectacle unfold, hands on their blades. Children barely daring to breathe as the men exchanged blows.

A Falhorne and a Templar, their guardian versus their enslaver, the gods versus the Betrayer, the Black King versus the First Emperor. History and myth were given new life by the bladesong. The clatter of approaching horses' hooves was drowned out as a shimmering figure rode into the small crowded square, white robes billowing behind them, their face concealed behind a golden mask as impassive as the one engraved on the Templar's insignia.

Tagus felt as though a hundred pounds of lead covered his bones. His muscles were straining with every strike and parry until the *damas,* which he had so proudly accepted from the hands of his fallen mentor, felt like a boulder in his arms. His foe was quick. Even his swiftest blows seemed to slice past the Templar's tunic and hit nothing but air. Quick thrusts from his opponent had penetrated both his guard and his robes, and it was only by twisting his body that he had managed to deflect them.

The pain in his bleeding shoulder increased and he cursed himself for having discarded Vitus's armor. He was looking for an opening, anything that he could exploit, any weakness at all, but there was nothing. This was not a melee, but a duel, and he knew he was outmatched. He had no comrades here. None who could reach him. He was all alone. And he was so fixated upon the movement of his foe that he did not see the white-robed rider, or hear the low droning chant which carried over the apocalyptic scene of chained bodies, blazing pyres, and tortured souls.

Suddenly his body froze.

In the midst of drawing his weapon back for another thrust and stepping back into Mora, Tagus found that he simply could not move. His joints ached while his exhausted muscles kept straining at nothing.

His mind spun in dizzy panicked circles. He was helpless. Utterly helpless. Like a cornered animal fatally wounded by a spear and about to be finished off by a hunter's crossbow.

His foe stopped, lowering his blade as he turned his head toward something which Tagus could not see. Then came a voice, proud and imperious; a master surveying his barbaric realm of slaves and overseers.

"Disarm the dark one, Brother Varus. The Most High will decide his fate, but before that he may have his uses."

The Templar's cruel grin returned, and his reply was as harsh as the crack of his whip.

"As you wish, Brother Inquisitor, may this dog prove a worthy pet."

He casually reached out and pulled the *damas* from Tagus's paralyzed hands. He ran his hands over its ancient matchless edge and smirked before casting it to the ground and turning away.

It was only then that Tagus noticed the gallows, its skeletal arms embracing the demonic scene, nooses hovering over the heads of the condemned. Porus's rotting body had been joined by another. Tall, thin and bloody, moustache drooping below blind eyes. Tarquinus had joined his brother in Barbarus. His hands were unchained. The gods could still be merciful.

There came a rumbling of wheels as the wagon passed in front of him, bearing away its human cargo. In the jolting, stifling darkness, inside a cage of iron bars and metal plating, crouched a familiar young figure, gripping the bars with the frantic desperation of a trapped animal. Tagus could just barely recognize the battered, terror-stricken face between the welts on his cheeks, his clothes torn apart in ragged lines, exposing the skin beneath.

It was Callus. But it also was another boy. In another time. In another cage. It was him, watching all he knew recede away into the darkness of oblivion. The last thing he saw with any clarity was the sign emblazoned on the wagon below Callus's hanging hopeless face: three black pyramids against a looming white circle.

A thousand blows struck at Tagus's frozen body, an unearthly force which slammed into him from all directions, knocking the wind from his lungs as it pumped the life out of him. He tried to cry out, but his jaw was locked firmly in place. He was spinning now, falling, the faces of his people, enslaved, manacled, swirling around him as the sky crashed down on the cruel world. He hit the ground like a millstone and blacked out.

Chapter 13: In Darkness

Tagus awoke to the sound of dripping water, and the touch of cold wet stone against his face. He strained his eyes in the musty darkness, his head feeling like the well-used anvil of a particularly efficient blacksmith, pounding in the wake of hard hammer blows on hot iron.

But the blackness was impenetrable. When he tried to lift his face, his vision swam. His wet cheeks sank to the floor as he tried to force his mind to cut through the pain, in a vain attempt to determine where he was. Was there truly no light, or had his captors plucked the eyes from his head?

I must keep fighting…

I must…

Pain flooded through him as he slowly regained feeling in his arms and legs. The numbness retreating into white hot agony, making his body twist and spasm on the rough stone.

But that was not the worst of it. Not by far. It was the noise. That murderous, horrendous noise of iron chains as they rattled against each other, the clatter of metal on stone, and its dull thud against raw flesh.

His dry throat spasmed into a scream that died before reaching his lips. The silent scream of a man who knows he is in bondage. His limbs weighed down by chains on the floor of a dungeon cell he could not see, but which every other sense confirmed was real.

In was then that most evil, most terrifying, and most humiliating of words filled his mind like a choking cloud of smoke:

Slave.

Thrashing his arms and legs did nothing to free them from the heavy manacles. Nothing to loosen the grip of iron, as thick as a man's fist, that joined his ankles and wrists to the scarred and filthy walls.

After a useless revolt of struggling he collapsed, the dripping expanse of the ceiling falling on him and rushing at his face as he again sank into darkness.

Slave. Slave.

The terrible word kept thundering in his ears, a distant thunder from high above or far below, he could not tell.

"Get up worm!"

The blackness receded as his stomach seemed to explode, throwing his vision into blazing whiteness, before fading, not into the shadows of a dungeon cell but into the pale blue sky of a hot summer's day. Burning rays of sunlight plunged at him like spears through the swaying boughs oak trees in a familiar forest glade.

His gut felt like a boiling pot of tar as he tried to move, only to be roughly seized by the throat, a big choking hand squeezing into the soft flesh followed by a cruel whisper:

"Does the bastard want to play…fetch?"

No.

He desperately flailed within his mind.

No, no!

Whack!

The rough bark of the tree branch cracked across his ribs, once again blinding him with pain. Yet he did not cry out. He could not. He would not show it.

The hateful face of his legitimate half-brother loomed above him. A lock of dirty blond hair falling across those sadistic hazel eyes. He had always been bigger, but now he was a giant. Impossibly large, as tall as the trees themselves in that evil clearing of green grass.

Victor sneered. He was a squire now. Fourteen years old. Almost a knight. Almost the heir his father had dreamed of having. Almost the master he dreamed of becoming.

"Remember, mongrel" rasped the booming voice from above, "Whatever my father may call you, whatever my father may call your bitch of a mother, you will always be the son of a slave, you will always be a slave, you will always belong to me. If you forget that, I will kill you…now fetch, dog! Fetch!"

The stick flew over his head, impossibly high, impossibly far, and his body, his ten-year-old body, so tiny, so boyish, so weak, cringed as he prepared for another blow.

"Come on dog! Fetch! Move! Move slave! Move! Move slave!"

The world spun, the glade a whirlwind of color, and the blackness returned.

Where was he now?

Fear gripped him. Somewhere in the darkness he heard the screech of rusty hinges. Faraway, yet the sound ripped right through him. Then came the ear-splitting clang of a metal door being slammed shut somewhere nearby. The earth began to move beneath him, and he could hear a rumbling sound like millstones turning.

Suddenly the darkness exploded into columns of light and he saw the bars before him. He gripped them with his hands. His tiny hands. He was just a boy. A tiny, frightened, helpless boy in a cage.

Outside the bars was the familiar road, the flagstones, the high hedges lining its sides, the gabled rooftop of the manor, its hard stone cold and dark. It was his home. This boy's home.

But he was not going home.

The rumbling continued, the mad sound pulling him, pulling him away. He could feel it disappearing. The fading memories of a lost world filling his mind like bubbles bursting inside his mother's tub of water; her dark hands smoothing over the garments she was washing. While her voice, deep and melodic, carried visions of the southlands, of baking desert sands, jeweled oases, mighty cities, and gods and heroes whose names Tagus could no longer remember…they were all gone.

They were all gone. Marcia the kind lady in waiting, who never hit him or called him names like his father's wife and the other highborn ladies did. Alexandros the cook, a gruff but soft-hearted fellow who always snuck him a little something, even on those days when his lord father ordered his bastard starved because he had been too slow bringing the wine or sweeping out the firepit of a great hall's chimney. Nayla, the slave girl from Tarquin, who would always play tag with him, running giggling through the orchards like carefree sparrows.

But now it was all over. The slaver's wagon was drawing further and further away from the only home that he had ever known.

Two shadowy forms stood in the gateway, appearing smaller and smaller as the manor fell away in the distance.

Tagus seized the bars, tried to scream, tried to call to anyone who could save him. But no sound left his lips. There was silence. Even the terrible rumbling had stopped.

Then the shadowy forms came close, so very close, and he saw they were his parents.

His father, Sir Leandro, the lord of Pennemont Manor and master of all it possessed. His dark beard framed a narrow pale face and hard green eyes behind which burned the pride of his ancient family name.

His mother, broken and sobbing, her simple black dress of coarse cloth in stark contrast with his father's fine robes of blue and red silk. Her ebony skin appearing to merge with her clothes like a weeping shadow, her head buried in her hands, her body wracked with sobs. Tagus could not even remember her name.

"Spare him, my lord. Please, spare your son…"

His father's expression remained proud and ambivalent.

"You really are a stupid boy," he said, without even looking at his bastard son through the bars, "Why do I keep you?"

On the ground, Tagus could see the wine spreading at his father's feet, blood red, from a smashed earthenware jar. A jar that Tagus had dropped in his haste to clear the dinner table.

"So clumsy," his father said contemptuously, "so useless. Why do I keep you?"

"Spare him my lord. He is your son. Please, spare him…" Came the sobbing pleas of a simple serving woman. He would not even look at her.

"Why do I keep you?"

Then he turned, and the full bore of those hard eyes burned into his son.

"Would you rather be sent away, stupid boy?"

No. No. He did not. He did not want to be sent away. No. *Please father. Please.*

Nothing but silence. The darkness returned. His father's cold stare vanishing into the shadows behind the wagon as it gained in speed.

Tagus knew he wasn't going home. He had been sold.

"Did I say you could speak, mongrel!"

The whistle of oiled leather through air, a sickening smack, and all was red.

"Did I say you had a tongue!"

Red became white, as the dreadful whistling came again, the impact tearing into his torn and ravaged flesh. Flesh that was fourteen years old, but just as weak and useless.

The whip came down again as agonizing white faded into pitch black. Before an explosion of blinding stars as Tagus's jaw cracked audibly.

"I never told you to sleep, worm!"

Overseer Ranald pulled up the bloodied boy with the smashed face by the hair, bringing the pathetic sunken eyes on level with his own. The boy trembling before this giant, towering figure of tanned skin and hardened leather.

"Slack again at the brick kiln and I'll feed your worthless heathen hide to the fire, boy…" the overseer snarled in his heavy Tarquin accent, which made his booming voice almost a growl.

Pulling the broken face close he whispered menacingly, "You've got the darkness of the southlands in your flesh. And I'll be charring it a little blacker if you step out of line again. Understand?"

He casually dropped the boy to floor of the small filthy cell and called out to a frightened looking old man in a beige tunic.

"Slave, take this pathetic creature to the Laetitsa and get him patched up. Snap his jaw back in, but remind him he'll be losing his tongue if I catch him so much as opening his mouth again in my presence."

"Oh yes," he continued, turning back to the boy's crumpled, bleeding form, "you can sleep now."

A savage kick to the side of the head brought darkness once again.

Now he was drowning. The darkness around him was the shadowy green and black of murky water. Tagus could see others in the water around him. Other men, their limbs flailing, helplessly slipping downwards into the abyss below. Above there was light, but it seemed impossibly faraway.

He was at the Allia Bridge again, struggling through the gorge's dark waters after the entire central span had given way in the midst of the battle against Lord Sempronius and his bannermen. Plunging men and horses alike into the raging torrent. But there was no splashing, no sound at all.

Suddenly there was a face above him, and his heart leapt as he recognized Vitus's weathered features, those deep blue eyes cutting through the murk and confusion. Strong hands reached down to grasp him, to save him from the arms of death that were pulling him down and down.

He reached upwards toward the light, toward that dear face, toward salvation. But his hands touched nothing. Those strong hands withered away to lifeless hanging tendrils, and the face became the bloody, twisted face of a hanged man, slipping away as he was dragged deeper. His mentor was gone.

As the abyss claimed him, a single terrible word thundered through Tagus's shattered mind:

Unworthy.

The world was again on fire.

Again, the awesome figure of the Black King loomed over the burning city. In His majesty, He gazed down on the pathetic, unworthy, dark figure that ran through its streets, powerless to stop the inferno consuming everything it held dear.

****

Callus awoke. Immediately the bars of the compound screamed at him as he felt the terrible weight of iron chains pressing down on his wrists. As consciousness returned, so did the burning in his limbs, along with the overpowering smell of sweat, shit and urine that struck him in the face like a fist.

All around him the shadows moved. In the dim silver light that showed through the bars of a tiny window, he could make out the silhouettes of people. But they were faceless and ghostly. For an instant, he thought that he was back in the orphanage. The air was stifling, hot, and closed-in.

Callus felt the sweat caking his own body as he breathed faster. Moans of pain, sobs and whimpers of fear could be heard all around.

Was he in Gormani? Had he died and faced the Great Judge only to be deemed unworthy? Was the underworld not a fiery pit but rather a dark prison for tainted souls in which he would remain trapped until his penance was done? That was not how Tagus had described it. And why was he still breathing? Why was his heart beating so fast if he was dead? How could he still feel pain and fear?

"Are ya awake now, boy?"

The deep labored voice was familiar. It came from right next to him, from what appeared as a great looming shadow crouched against the wall. There was a clatter of chains and the dragging of leathery flesh through the dust as the dark mass slowly transformed into the figure of a large heavy-set man. He was so close, his sleeve touching Callus's shoulder, that he could make out the remains of a shredded jacket of black leather, the faint moonlight picking out patches of dried blood on cracked olive skin.

Skarlos' great round face looked down at him from the gloom, unshaven and grizzled, and so swollen with bruises that his normally wide and jovial smile appeared choked and strangled. But he was still smiling.

Callus gasped. He was amazed the big watchman was alive. The last he had seen of him, Skarlos and Callidus had been defending the Rivergate barricade almost single-handedly against a wave of onrushing mercenaries. How had he allowed himself to be taken alive?

Callus felt his sense of relief crumble as a far more pressing question cried out within him.

"Where are we?"

Callus's frightened whisper barely got beyond his lips. The Asylum had been under attack. He remembered strong arms grabbing him, chains being placed around his limbs, the rows of people, the wagons. He did not remember when he had passed out or how long he had been in this place. It felt like a nightmare. Yet he knew he was awake.

"All I know is this ain't no dungeon, lad," came the hoarse reply. "It's a slaver compound. Could be anywhere north of Trastamere, if that's where they're taking us."

Slavers. Trastamere. Those words sent chills through Callus's body as he looked around the cramped low-ceilinged chamber. His eyes had adjusted to the darkness, and he could see the moonlight glinting off the chains.

There must have been thirty people in the room with them. Stone walls surrounded them on three sides, the fourth consisting of stout iron bars, beyond which could be seen the glint of torches and the pacing outlines of armed guards. The window, perched high in one of the walls, was also barred.

The fear built inside of him as the memories grew sharper and he remembered the cracking of whips and the screams. And he remembered what Tagus had told him about Brisi.

"Are we slaves now?"

The great head stared down at him and there was a defiant fire in those dark eyes as they looked upon the frightened boy.

"No, son. We are not. We will never be. No child of the Lord of Flames can ever be caged. No Falhorne lets his people fall into the hands of the enemy. Mark my words, boy, they'll come for us, even if they have to chew the guts of every single bastard out there. Our Tagus is still alive and free, and so are the Falhorne of Vinos, so I don't want you getting all afraid on me now. These people here need you to be strong for them, understand?"

Callus was shaking, the metallic jingling of his chains ringing in his ears like evil music.

Skarlos's voice, that deep voice had told him so many heroic tales, from Emda in the Wermut to Zorba in the Red Marches; tales that had filled him with awe at the bravery within men's hearts. There was something in that voice that gradually made his pulse beat slower and his breath cease coming out in panicked gasps.

Tagus. Tagus was free. He could save them. The Falhorne could save them all. He just had to be strong, strong like those heroes in the tales. Strong like Master Tagus would want him to be.

"Yes…"

He forced his lips into a weak smile, forcing his mind to dwell on those ancient champions and their victories over monsters. He wondered if those great men had ever been so afraid.

****

Tagus was unconscious when they dragged him from the cell. He awoke to the impact of the jailer's fist as it met his jaw.

The darkness exploded in a clashing red and yellow haze out of which slowly formed the image of a brutish face, unshaven and as grimy as the bare stone walls that expanded around the man's thickset body. The jailer was clad in a rough leather tunic, a tarred and greasy black, his bare arms swollen with muscle. A malevolent smile exposed a gap-toothed maw of yellowed teeth and bright eyes twisted in delighted anticipation of having yet another worthless life to torment.

"Are ye awake now, black dog?"

Tagus felt the left side of his torso burst in agony as the jailer drove his fist into his kidneys. He could feel the blood trickling down his chin and wondered if his jaw was broken. He could not move his lips.

Through the pain, the walls screeched at him, but by now his senses had returned enough for him to tell that it was not the walls themselves that were screaming but others like himself, prisoners alone and helpless inside this dark dungeon, at the mercy of their tormentors. Somewhere in the distance he could hear the cracking of a whip, and a scream, followed by cruel laughter.

His captor snickered, and he knew he was not dreaming. This was no nightmare. Nor was it Gormani, as much as this sadistic jailer might fancy himself a pretender to Tylo's throne of blood and bone.

"Ah, ye still breathin, eh? Luck of yer gods be with ye..."

This time the blow came directly at his nose. Tagus only became conscious of the heavy wooden frame, holding his entire body in a vice-like grip, when he instinctively tried to turn his head, only to have it remain immobile and his vision explode in a red cloud and bright stars as the ceiling seemed to cave in.

But the darkness did not return. There was only the steady sticky stream of warm blood running from his shattered nose and down his face. Only then did he see the shimmering white robes emerge from the shadows and hear a voice he recognized.

"That will do, sergeant," said the voice, calm, as cold as iron, and merciless as hard stone, "there is no need to cause further damage to our honored guest. An esteemed knight of the Eternal Order of the Falhorne deserves our most polite hospitality. For who can say? By the grace of the Most High, whose Eternal Truth illuminates the most clouded of minds, this sinner may indeed repent."

Tagus felt gloved hands on his scarred cheeks, and through the one eye that was not blinded by his own blood he saw that he was staring into a golden mask. The flickering torches on the walls of the torture chamber made the inquisitor's false features dusk and glint, but within the mask's empty eye sockets he could feel a powerful will and an ice-cold intelligence examining him.

He could feel it prying at his body and mind, looking for secret doors, passages, and openings into the innermost depths of his soul. And he could feel his own nakedness before its power. His naked body was once more the heavily muscled form of an aging warrior, but it was just as weak and helpless as the boy in his dreams had been. Now his mind felt just as bare, exposed and vulnerable to attack.

The voice came again. The same voice he had heard amid the chains and fire on that dark street. The same voice that had commanded Brother Varus of the Templars to spare his life…so it could be put to use.

"Tagus," it said, "Tagus, bastard child of the noble Sirrah Leandro Pennemont and a Reshian slave girl. Sold into servitude by his own father so that his tainted offspring might do penance for his filth encrusted soul. And what a filthy soul you had…"

Tagus felt the grip tighten on his bloodied cheeks, the gloved hands drawing together like a vice.

"Five masters in five years. Five years spent toiling in the plantations of Trastamere, the orchards of Samos and the salt mines of Braxus. Five years of insubordination and rebellion. You were a stubborn boy. So very stubborn."

The grip was crushing him.

"You had to be punished, and punished you were. The lash being an effective cure for sickly souls…"

The vice grip just as suddenly became a slap. A backhanded blow that would have knocked his head back had it not been tightly secured with iron bolts. All he felt was the bitter sting and flash of yellow light across his flickering vision, which was once again filled by that hateful golden mask.

"But not yours. For you are a special kind of heretic," the inquisitor continued, his voice dropping an octave into a menacing snarl which stood in stark contrast with his previously polite and civilized tones.

"You would not be corrected. You refused salvation when it was offered to you. When the Most High extended His Divine Hand in forgiveness you spat upon it!"

Tagus felt hands close around his throat, tightening, squeezing, crushing the life from his lungs.

"Instead of embracing His Holy Light, you plunged deeper and deeper into the shadows of sin. Through your blind and foolish eyes, you beheld the debauched Vitus Bastaernae. You saw him as your savior and guide. And you followed his treacherous path to the downfall of your immortal soul…did you really think that you could escape judgment?"

The hands around his throat now felt like hands around his mind.

"Stupid boy. Did you really think that your mentor's unclean ways ended with his ascension into your inglorious Order? Do you know what disgusting deeds this honorable man has done to the bodies of innocent souls? What unholy violations he has performed…"

The voice faded into a torturous hiss that stabbed needles into his consciousness.

"I can see her now. Her beautiful, pretty young face, twisted in terror, clothes torn and stained with her virgin's blood. The farmer's daughter who came to sell her family's meagre produce at the army's camp, only to be accosted and deflowered by a howling savage who could not control his lust."

The needles widened into knives.

"He flung himself upon her like a wild animal. I can see those blue eyes now. The perverse desire consuming them. Consuming your noble commander outside of Lomos, on your first campaign by his side…oh how you looked up to him, you silly, stupid boy…"

The hands tightened further and pain burst upon him from every direction as his body and mind were strangled…burning daggers thrusting at his very soul.

"You do not believe the truth? The Most High reveals all. He is the Eternal Truth. You cannot escape His Judgement. What of the pretty young mill-hand your noble mentor violated at the feet of her own father, while you were on the march through the Arcades of Samos in your third winter as Falhorne. Your late Brother Tarquinus restrained and beat the sobbing miller while your false savior delivered his own sick benevolence upon a god-fearing man's only daughter."

The voice was thunder in his ears.

"What about the time when you and your brethren made your heretical stand at Fallonier Fields, defying the chosen warriors of the Most High Himself? Tarquinus again played the enforcer that day, silencing the screams of his master's latest victim. Holding her down as she struggled to break free. Did you really think that he tarried so long in the village for the sake of buying provisions? Such a weak, disgusting man, his life of sin dragging him into the depths of depravity and vice. And with you alongside him, believing all his wicked lies…"

The strangulation was agonizing now.

"His lies…"

The inquisitor's voice was like a dragon's roar in his mind. A dragon salivating over the human feast that lay before its great jaws.

"His lies…you believed his wicked lies! His evil lies! You are tainted by his sin! Your own sin!"

The roar felt as though it came from within his very soul. A beast trying to claw its way out from the depths of his being.

"Lies…you believed the lies of the heretical Falhorne! You believed you were protecting your people. But who killed the followers of the rightful Church in Fiore's marketplace? Who provoked the wrath of the One True God and drew the ire of the Most High down upon those he sought to defend? Upon whose hands does the blood of Vitus Bastarnae truly lie? You betrayed them. In your foolishness you betrayed them all: Nestor, Jesta, Mia, even Cornelia, the very wife you cherish. Through your selfishness, you have condemned them! Now they must be cleansed in fire. You have denied them salvation!"

A ring of dragons surrounded Tagus's mind and roared, "Salvation! Salvation! Salvation is in the light of the Most High! Bow before His Eternal Mercy! Save your polluted soul! Save yourself! Save those you love! Lay their souls upon His merciful altar! They burn because of you! Give them peace! Name them! They burn in Gormani's flames because of you! Give them peace! Name them all! Show them mercy! NAME THEM!"

Tagus's mind felt like flayed skin, stripped from bones in a madman's abattoir. Voices, the voices, all he could hear were the voices tearing at him, surrounding him, pulling him apart. His soul was shredded, everything withering, polluted, damned…damned…damned…until there was something.

The flaying voices clawing at him in that torture chamber struck against something that would not yield. Something that burned black in the rubble of sacked temples and amidst the ash of burning hovels. Lightning flashing through its twisting morass like the agonized screams of murdered souls…calling from the root of the world and surging toward the upper air in a furious wave of untrammelled anger.

The eruption burst from the rock, splitting mountains asunder and levelling city walls, an apocalypse burst upon a guilty world.

But all the inquisitor heard before a power beyond anything that he had ever felt or known banished him from the formerly helpless mind of his victim was a scream. A furious scream of primal pain and rage that issued from Tagus's throat and dislocated jaw, echoing through the very bowels of the dungeon until it seemed its stones would crack and its foundations split apart. A wave of raw power that drove this hard enforcer of dogma, burner of men and flayer of souls to his knees.

A guttural, frenzied "Aaaaaaaaa!!!!"

The dungeon cell had become his tomb. Tagus did not know how long he had been there. His sense of time had been reduced to waiting in the shadows for rations of foul-tasting water and bug-tainted mush, which he could only eat by crawling to where it had been thrust under the door. His chained hands useless, he would bury his face in the mush and consume it without pausing to think. Like an animal he would rip the maggots in half, chewing and swallowing the bitter flesh rather than spitting it out in disgust. He did not know why they were keeping him alive, but his survival amid this filth was the one victory he could claim. Even if it made him a beast and a madman, he would endure against the monsters that had taken everything else.

The cell was never lit, apart from a tiny ray of light which shone under the heavy door of wood and iron, cast by a lantern in the passage outside and sending sickly yellow beams stabbing into the tiny space, where he was kept, naked, amid his own piss. But it was enough for him to see the chains that bound him to the wall and shackled his arms and legs. As though his captors sought to remind him of his powerlessness, cruelly teasing him with the forlorn hope of seeing the outside world again.

Beyond the black door of this tomb, the torture chamber was the only "outside world" he had been permitted to see. The bloodied bandages his tormentors had wrapped him in, tightly and painfully bound over his many wounds, attested to that. His growing list of injuries proving to be the only sure way of marking the passage of time between the horrifying moments when the cell door would fly open and a sack shoved over his head before he was dragged into the presence of the prince's jailer.

The method of torment was always crude: fists, whips, and cudgels, in addition to the unending torrent of abuse from a man who loved his job.

"How's my mongrel this fine day?" The jailer's first remark always followed by the back of his hand. "Yeez such a naughty dog…"

How long the torment lasted depended on the sort of mood he was in. But, however many bruises, welts, and cuts he laid on, he never let Tagus die. Oh no, this "pet" of his was going to last him awhile before he finally decided to break it. An assistant would always patch up whatever wounds his master had inflicted on his "naughty dog" before he was thrown back in his cell and once again bound with heavy manacles, his body numb from repeated blows and lacerations.

A familiar figure stood next to the jailer one day. Familiar green eyes shone above a vengeful and entitled smile of satisfaction. The lace-edged doublet, decorated in the same ivy-like patterns of white and green, appearing completely out of place amidst the gloom and stench.

But Cosimo Gratano's marble-white cheeks appeared corpse-like enough to belong in that bloody chamber. The young noble's chance to witness the torment of the "boy" who had publicly humiliated his dignitas in broad daylight must have driven him to hold his nose against the filth. At least that was how Tagus consoled himself while the jailer administered the worst beating yet, for the benefit of his distinguished guest.

"Give the filthy Resh more."

The command came again and again. And each time the blows rained down harder, while that cruel smile grew wider. At last blacking out, he had awoken, swathed in yet more bloody bandages, on the floor of his cell.

It was all for sport now. They had given up on getting him to talk. The inquisitor never returned. Never again tried to break him. Tagus did not know what he had done or how he had resisted the awful magic that had very nearly torn his mind apart, but he had.

Somehow, he had won. Somehow, he had defeated the might of the Church itself. It was some consolation at least, something he could be proud to take to the grave with him. Even if he was going to die alone as some torturer's plaything.

But if the gods had preserved him in the face of torture, he did not know to what end. It was all over. He knew it. He was empty: no purpose, no reason, nothing but a stubborn animal refusing to be broken. It was only a matter of time before his captors grew tired of this game and ended his miserable existence. He had failed. He had failed Vitus. He had failed everyone.

Tagus sometimes entertained himself with thoughts of what his death would look like: the door opening as he slept, a noose falling about his neck, silently garrotting him in the subterranean darkness; or some gruesome public spectacle where he would be hanged and gutted in front of a frenzied mob of human creatures, baying for the blood of heretics…or simply looking on, his death an entertaining diversion from a day of drudgery and thankless toil. Some months ago, he had heard that the faithful laboring on the riverport's quays had been given an hour's rest by the bosses so they could watch the hanging of a disobedient journeyman…of course, there probably weren't any faithful left alive in the city to claim an hour's respite in his death throes.

He knew their fate. He had seen the bodies of the disobedient hanging alongside Mia's dismembered remains in the shadow of the guildhall. Perhaps he was the lucky one. At least no overseer would find him here. He would not die as anyone's beast of burden in the stifling depths of a salt mine or in a plantation field under the scorching sun.

Slack again at the brick kiln and I'll feed your worthless heathen hide to the fire, boy.

Tagus wanted to laugh like a madman when he remembered Ranald's words. They were so ridiculous now…he couldn't get him anymore, he couldn't make him work, he couldn't make him do anything.

Sometimes he thought of Vitus. He didn't think of the revelations. He did not think of how "Vitus" was not his mentor's real name, only a mark of shame taken from an innocent boy that a certain dispossessed aristocrat had so brutally killed in front of his violated sister. No.

His mentor was not some highborn debaucher. Anyone who said so was lying. Even as a mercenary captain he had kept his men disciplined and they had been forbidden from gambling, ransacking captured towns, or getting drunk. Among the rough bands of soldiers crawling the Thousand Cities in search of plunder, the Falhorne under the praetor's command had been paragons of virtue. He was a knight, an honorable guardian of sacred traditions that the white-robed monsters wanted forgotten. But they would never be forgotten. Vitus was a mountain of stone, constant and unyielding. Even the greatest of earthquakes would never change that.

No, it was he himself who was unworthy. He who had lost the arms and armor of his mentor; he who had allowed the holy relics of Cera Peleus and the Eternal Order of Falhorne to fall into enemy hands. He who had let the closest thing he had ever had to a real father die a dishonorable death. He had failed to protect him, just as he had failed in his sworn duty to protect his people.

He pictured Tarquinus's body, hanging alongside Porus, and he envied him. His brother Falhorne had surely taken many of the attacking scum with him before being strung up. Surely, he had died a worthy death; going down fighting alongside the members of the Watch. Or the Templars would not have made such an example of his body. Furthermore, Tarquinus had not been forced to endure the sight of what had become of their commander. His brother had died with a clear conscience, whilst his own was as murky as swamp water.

Sometimes he fought maddening battles in his head. Sometimes he caught himself believing the lies of the inquisitor, and blaming himself for the pogrom. Sometimes he broke down in sobs, letting out moans of anguish at the thought of those people, his people, being dragged away in bondage. And when he remembered Callus's frightened eyes, he openly wished for death.

But his thoughts of Corrie were the most painful. Thoughts of his wife's beautiful face and raven-dark hair. He had to clench his eyes shut and press his fist to his forehead to drive away the memories that he knew would destroy him. He would never see her again. Their love, their marriage, their struggle to stay together in a cruel world, none of it mattered anymore. That cruel world had won.

Sometimes he dared to think of the gods. The true gods that Vitus had taught him about in their long-ago lessons at the castle. The gods honored by the faithful. He thought of the Celestial Court and being called before the Great Judge to answer for his sins after death had finally claimed him. For surely it would not be long now. He remembered all the prayers that his mentor had taught to him, and how empty they seemed now. Even the furious clarion of the Chosen of the

Lord of Flames – *Blessed be the warrior that dwells in fire* – seemed utterly dead within this black hole.

If this was the palace dungeons, he was in the very foundations of Cera Infernus, the holy of holies where Ishan himself had once walked before the Betrayal. He tried to believe, to keep faith, but the more the dim light illuminated the filth and stench of his surroundings, the surer he became that the gods had abandoned this place. They would not hear him. What was once sacred was now lost.

He remembered how his mentor had tried to teach him, an untutored outsider, about the ways of the faithful. He even remembered some of the cryptic words that he had never truly grasped no matter how hard he had tried: *When Sol's tears descend on Mora's face, the mountains walk in silence. And in Viro's watery embrace, shall Fiore's flame strike violence. Upon red moon and sundered stars, raise the pinnacle of Barbarus.*

He remembered those words, and almost laughed at his ignorance. They were from the Ascension of Ishan, one of the key texts within the Book of Damas, but neither he nor Vitus, who had taught him what he knew from that sacred tome of the gods, had the faintest idea of their meaning. Tradition was more important than understanding, and he knew now that he would never get a chance to understand. It was just another reflection of his own weakness.

Sometimes he remembered Fallonier Fields, the great battle that had brought an end to the Skaros Schism and cemented the Treaty of Trastamere with Falhorne blood. He pictured Vitus, standing proud and strong before his brethren. A true son of Ishan, a true knight of the Falhorne Order and guardian of Cera Peleus, arrayed in the armor of his ancestors and brandishing the *damas*…the same *damas* that Tagus had shamefully lost.

Brothers! Do not forget that we are a weapon! We are the Falhorne, the blade that shall pierce his cloak of lies!

He remembered those words. That rousing speech. His mighty oath sworn before the gods.

Vitus, my brother, may your death march be steady. I shall see you in Barbarus.

And then that hanging face. That body, once strong and fine, now shattered, twisted, and made hideous by pain, dangling there outside the house that the prince himself had given him as a place of safety.

It is the fate of the warrior to become a corpse. And thus, we face death as corpses, embracing our fate and calling our enemy to Barbarus. This is our farewell.

He remembered Piso. The brave Falhorne who could stare into the face of death itself and laugh, hum a tune whilst looking into oblivion, crack a joke when his own doom was scarcely moments away, and then have the nerve to tell his brethren not to take it all too seriously.

Tears wet Tagus's face as he recalled that smiling face, surmounted by a crown of fiery red hair. The man was crazy and yet he would have the proudest death of all: no lynchings, no dark dungeons, only a glorious end on the field of battle and a glorious ascension unto Barbarus. Piso had killed an inquisitor, sacrificing himself to bring down the greatest of his people's enemies. Tagus only wished that he had been so lucky back then, if luck it was.

Either way, it was over now.

There was nothing left to do but wait. To wait for the evil noise of approaching footsteps, of rough leather on dirty stone followed by the scrapping of bolts, the sound that would surely bring on the end, even if it was still many torturous days away. It would come. It would come, and the Great Judge would call him to atone before his final journey to Barbarus to stand alongside the Black King until the final battle against the underworld that would seal the fate of creation. Such was the fate of a Falhorne. Whatever he had been guilty of in life, he would gladly do penance in Gormani's flames before ascending to join Vitus, Tarquinus, and others more worthy than himself.

He shut his eyes in anticipation, but it was a very different noise that came to echo through the corridors of his mind. He finally had to open his eyes just to be sure that he was not dreaming. The scarred walls of his cell screamed in his face, but there it was, sounding softly somewhere nearby. The unmistakable tapping of hands against stone.

Perhaps it was the strangeness, the very novelty of the sound, too heavy to be the scurrying of rats, that gave Tagus the strength to pull himself into a crouch, his chains clattering together as he trembled from the cold. He looked up at the low ceiling of the cell, barely illuminated by the weak lantern light coming under the door.

The tapping was closer now and growing in its intensity. It was regular too, not like some animal scrabbling in the darkness for its food, but the slow and purposeful sounds of a person testing for weak points in a surface they were unsure of.

As a slave he had known a man of the far north. A great yellow bearded man with a name he could neither remember nor pronounce. He had spoken of his home in the snow-bound regions of perpetual cold, where it was not uncommon for hunters to carry a stout staff of pine wood with them to test the thickness of the ice on the frozen lakes and rivers that crisscrossed that distant land…if only to spare themselves from a freezing death. It was as if this person, if person they were, was doing the same to hard stone – patiently testing its thickness to see if it would crack or give way. He wondered who would waste their time doing something so stupid.

Now the tapping was coming from directly above him, a small echo bouncing off the tomb-like walls. Then it stopped. *Tap. Tap. Tap.* The noise staying in the exact same place overhead above the ceiling. *Tap. Tap. Tap.* Persistently striking the cold stone. *Tap. Tap. Tap.*

What was going on? *What manner of creature crawls above ceilings in the dark?* Tagus thought to himself. He was not afraid. He was almost amused. Had fate decided on a more creative end for him? Was he about to provide a meal for the ever-hungry dead things that his mother had tried to scare him with as a child? Things which supposedly stalked the cursed oasis towns of Reshi, devouring man and beast alike? Or had one of the fabled "serpent men" of the southlands decided to slither into his tomb to end his torment?

He actually grinned as he recalled the silly stories that Skarlos used to tell of his time as a mercenary hired on by an expedition to the remote southern jungles the Arcadian Empire was bent on colonizing. Since then, the big watchman had been afraid of practically every scaly-skinned beast that ever walked or crawled, no matter how tiny.

"Look!" Remus had once said, amidst a particularly dull moment one night at the Black Horseman, shooting to his feet and pointing at a small lizard scurrying across an empty table on the far side of the room, "A dragon!"

Skarlos had knocked the entire bench over in his haste to get to his feet, glancing all around as his comrades roared with laughter.

Now Tagus couldn't keep himself from laughing. For a moment the tapping stopped, before abruptly resuming with renewed vigor.

Come on beast...come and get me.

His chains jangled as he bent over in cackling madness. If the thing in the ceiling didn't get him, his tormentors eventually would.

The tapping was getting louder. Resonant thuds could be heard on the stone overhead. Tagus stopped laughing as he heard a sharp crack and handful of dust fell to the floor scarcely inches from him.

He quickly glanced upwards to see that the stone slab above him had not been broken, it had completely vanished. Looking down at him from the shadows, faintly illuminated in a spectral white light was the face of a woman.

He could not make out anything but her face amid the enveloping shadows, but that face seemed to almost glow. Her skin was very pale, more so than Corrie, to the extent it reminded Tagus of the moon waxed full on a starry night. Indeed, her fine features had the appearance of having been chiseled from fine marble, even more exquisitely than Sir Cosimo. For a split second he wondered whether the Eternal Judge had dispatched one of the *Druchii*, His otherworldly servants, to claim his soul. But the woman's eyes were mortal, cat-like orbs darting about nervously as single lock of midnight black hair fell across her statuesque face.

"Falhorne," A whispered voice, soft as shadow, yet also firm and purposeful, called down to him, "I have come to get you out of here. We must make haste. Take hold of this."

Her accent was not one that Tagus recognized. Austellian perhaps? A dialect of Tarnish? It was certainly foreign. But then again, this whole situation was itself foreign and bizarre. Who was this woman? And how had she found him?

Like a long black serpent, a rope slithered down from the shadows and fell within Tagus's reach on the floor.

The woman seemed to lean down, peering closer at him from above, and he heard something that might have been a muffled curse.

"You are chained," she muttered.

The face abruptly vanished, and Tagus could hear the muted sound of hands scuffling on stone. He only noticed the dark form sliding silently down the rope when it had practically reached the floor of the cell.

"Do not move," came the whisper, this time from directly beside him.

What a silly request, thought Tagus. What would be the point in moving? He was completely at this woman's mercy. If she was a ravening serpent monster in disguise it wouldn't be hard for her to make a meal out of a chained and beaten man.

He did not turn his head as the dark figure reached for something behind him. Suddenly he felt a great weight give way. His leg shackles fell away to the floor with the barest of clinks, releasing the lower half of his body. But when he tried to move, a dreadful stiffness overwhelmed him and he had to shut his eyes to keep from crying out.

When he opened them again, his hands had also been freed, and the woman's face was once more staring down at him from the ceiling.

Still wincing in pain as feeling returned to his legs and arms, he could not help but stare at her in awe. Not only had his chains been broken, but his shackles had been completely removed and were lying on the floor beside him. He held his unbound hands up to the pale light in amazement, red and raw from where the metal had dug into his wrists.

Tagus worked his bruised and battered jaws. He had not spoken in days. When his voice came, it was weak and wheezy, like that of an ancient beggar crouched at the corner of a crowded street in the slums.

"Who – who are you?"

"There is no time," came the terse reply, "I have released you, take hold of the rope."

Tagus's mind flailed about like a gutted fish. He did not trust her. He did not trust this woman, if that was what she truly was, with her foreign accent and stealthy movements in the dark. Surely, she was some mad witch, an agent of Gormani, crawling around the bowels of this forsaken dungeon in search of lost souls to snare, and all the while claiming to be his savior. But what did that matter? It was over. He had failed. He didn't even deserve to live, let alone be rescued. If this woman sought his death, or outright damnation, it would be his just punishment. In any case, it would grant him merciful release, whatever the afterlife might hold in store.

For a moment he could only stare up at those dark eyes in confusion, no longer shifting nervously but locked onto him with unblinking conviction. They were as dark as Corrie's and yet there was something about them that shone like beacons, reminding him of another pair of eyes…bright blue eyes that had years ago stared at him through murky water, followed by firm hands.

Tagus painfully shifted his weight, the bloodied bandages across his chest tugging as he began to crawl across the filthy floor, his tortured muscles screaming. He grabbed at the rope and held it with what little strength he had left in his reddened hands…and suddenly he was rising, rising off of the slimy stone of the cell, pulled by a force of immense strength. The light from the door and the false hope it had tormented him with fell away amid shadows, and all he could see were those cat-like eyes, unwavering, as he came closer and closer. His whole-body straining, he held on until a pale hand extended from the darkness above and grasped his own.

"I've got you," whispered the voice.

He had never felt such strength, as his battered body was lifted effortlessly through that hole in the ceiling and into the blackness beyond.

Behind him he could hear the grinding sound of a stone slab being slid back into place.

Darkness. Tagus could once again feel damp stone against his bare legs, while his nostrils inhaled the smell of dank stale air in a space that was barely large enough to crouch in. He could not see the face of his rescuer, only feel something moving off to his left before a dim yellow light flared, illuminating the low tunnel and casting pale watery shadows on the slimy walls.

The place looked like a drainage sump, and smelled like it too. In the poor light he was finally able to make out the form of the mysterious woman, crouching barely inches from him in the low tunnel. Her pale face was now a sickly yellow, her dark eyes casting about nervously as though seeking out hidden dangers in every mould-filled crevice.

She was dressed in a tight-fitting black hooded garment, the details of which he could not discern, for it seemed to merge with the shadows around her. She said nothing, merely putting a finger to her thin lips before beckoning for him to follow as she began to swiftly crawl away.

Confused, pained by his injuries, and bewildered by the pace of events which had broken his terrible ordeal below, Tagus followed her agile movements. His bandaged legs and feet sliding clumsily forward through the fetid darkness.

The light his mysterious companion was carrying neither flickered or wavered as they pressed on. He could not even see its source. Not that it mattered under the circumstances as the animal instinct of survival took over. He did not know whether life or death awaited, wherever she was taking him, he just wanted to leave his cell and the torture chamber far behind, so he crawled in silence through the stinking sludge that by now coated his hands and shins.

Hope was not a luxury that he could afford to enjoy, but at least he would not die completely helpless, even if this woman meant to deliver him to a worse fate than he could imagine. At least his unchained body could fight back now, and meet something approaching a warrior's death. Either way, he would keep going.

She continued to say nothing to him as they moved together through the low stone cut tunnel. It was becoming apparent that it was only one of many, perhaps hundreds. A labyrinth of twists, turns, junctions, and openings. Some tunnels were blocked off by debris, choked with dirt, or flooded with foul-smelling water. They must be somewhere in the palace's drains, he concluded, although the tunnels appeared disused and incredibly old.

He could even see carvings, badly eroded armored figures crossing swords with each other, and what looked like writing cut into some of the walls, although it had been made unrecognizable by age. Everything seemed worn, dirty, and crumbling, and he did not like thinking about the immense weight of ancient stonework poised above his head. Even the slightest cave-in down here would mean a ready-made grave. Was he crawling through the remains of Cera Infernus itself?

For what seemed like a very long time, there was no light at all apart from that carried by his companion, but as they progressed onward through the endless maze, he began to notice small openings and metal grills at intervals in the walls and ceiling. Sometimes the flickering light of a torch or the weak glow of a lantern would even make its way down from what must have been the palace's upper floors.

Sometimes he made out distant sounds, people talking, the gruff voices of guards or the mutterings of servants and slaves as they went about their duties, unaware of the two fugitives moving unseen beneath their feet. Tagus was seized by the sudden worry that one of the castle staff might decide to dump something appropriately filthy on his head, but nothing happened, and the voices never seemed to stray too close to the drains.

He almost chuckled to himself, remembering how filthy he was already and trying to remember how long it had been since he had last washed. A week perhaps? Two weeks? He wondered if the prince's jailer, who had taken such a liking to him, had ever bathed in his life. The bastard's stink had been torture enough.

He continued to entertain himself with these idle thoughts, trying to escape the horrible pain in his limbs, as the twists and turns continued. Gradually the way grew drier, the tunnel sloping gradually upwards and the shafts in the ceiling disappearing.

After what seemed like hours of crawling naked like a worm, his whole-body aching and raw to the point of collapse, he heard something that made him freeze. Suddenly, from somewhere nearby, he heard a voice that he recognized. It was a deep voice, calm and brutally precise, a precision that instinctively made Tagus cringe in anticipation of renewed agony.

"It is as Your Majesty wishes. Their penance is being carried out. These heretics were born for slavery."

It was the inquisitor.

His guide also froze ahead of him, the dim light suddenly going out. The whole tunnel was plunged into darkness, except for the faint light showing through the small grate in the left-hand wall. Faint flickering firelight made its way in and made small dancing shadows on the low curving roof. Now he could hear the murmur of multiple voices somewhere below.

He squinted as his eyes adjusted, and he saw the woman slowly turn her head to peer through the grate. Without turning, a pale hand extended from the shadows and beckoned at him with thin fingers, motioning for him to crawl forward and see for himself. Against his better judgement, he did, edging to the small firelit grill and looking out into the room beyond.

Tagus was looking down into a vast chamber that must have been all or partially below ground. A great flagstoned hall, lit all around with flickering lamps in alcoves and a large blazing fireplace. The grate was positioned high up in the wall and barely illuminated by the dancing flames below.

A large round wooden table was positioned in the center of the room and seated around it in high-backed chairs that largely obscured them from sight, sat five shadowed figures. From this distance, he could just make out the gestures of their hands in the firelight and wine glasses silhouetted before them. The men were speaking clandestinely in low voices, but one of their number would occasionally raise his voice as he made a particular point to the others, making it easy to hear in the echoing recesses of the high-ceilinged hall.

"And what of the Falhorne? Have your useless efforts finally served to loosen those canine lips?"

The voice was nasal, aged, but with the undeniable authority of a man used to being obeyed. If anything, it was a royal voice.

If anyone responded to the man's question, he could not hear it, but the man's own reply was nothing short of deafening.

"Save your platitudes! I am surrounded by idiots! If the Resh dog is of no use, I want him dead. That half-breed Vask is having too much fun kicking around the mangy animal as it is. It's time that we put this worthless creature out of its misery."

Put him out of his misery. Clearly, they had not yet checked his cell, otherwise the place would be swarming with guards and alarm bells would be sounding everywhere.

It was the inquisitor who spoke next, as usual with calm measured precision: "Justly spoken, Your Majesty, a heretic must have a heretic's fate. An example must be made of this Falhorne. We must publicly cleanse his filthy form by holy fire so that the other blasphemers might know and repent, knowing full well the ordeal that awaits them should they fail to submit."

The chill in the inquisitor's voice penetrated Tagus's weary bones. It was a visceral and unmistakable hatred, for him and all his kind. And this fanatic had the ear of the prince himself.

"Need I remind you of the outrage suffered by the merchant's guild, its master shot by a heretic's bullet in broad daylight, no man of coin can rest easy in this city until an example is made. This blasphemy could have been avoided entirely had the Gendarmerie not been unleashed upon the followers of His Holiness. The arrival of the royal guard was a signal to these heretics that their sinful gathering had official protection. The same mistake must never be made again..."

"I beg your pardon Your Majesty, but I must urge caution."

It was a new voice that spoke, thin and reedy, yet clearly possessed by a man of age and some experience.

"As Your Grace knows, the crown has many enemies, and there are many Falhorne sympathizers among the lower orders. The Association's tendrils continue to spread among the foreign riffraff in the slums. A public execution of this criminal might arouse their passions and drive them to all manner of mischief. Nor would Ambassador Trevelyan approve of further unrest. I understand the just and righteous sentiments of the merchants, it was a cowardly criminal deed, but we do not want to create martyrs. Better to make him disappear, seal his lips in the dark. He is at Your Majesty's mercy, simply end his miserable existence and cast his corpse into a midden. It is the sympathizers we should be concerned with, but my spies are already on their trail."

Tagus could not tell which voice was more menacing.

"Ha! Such bloody-minded advisors I have!"

The prince clapped his hands.

"Owain can rot in Gormani for all I care. I will not see him crowned the next Prince of Skaros, the hounds of Tarn splitting my lands asunder. I answer to no one but the Most High and I am happy that the Blessed Church at last understands this."

There was a heavy pause.

"Master Inquisitor, remember we have the matter of their bitch of a leader to handle as well. She would make a far better example, her womanly screams rising above the flames and all. She might even dance for us. This far better suits your purposes, I am sure."

The prince dismissively waved his hand.

"And you can throw the black dog in the midden Marcus. Vask is probably tired of his latest toy by now anyway, he'll be only too willing to wring his neck. Both of you have leave to hunt the other heretics as you see fit. I unleash my hounds on them across my city and my lands. And I don't need to remind you to be appropriately creative with our fugitive dark-horse when you find him. We cannot afford to disappoint the illustrious men of business, surely? By royal decree, the guilders will have the blood they crave and I'm sure that you shall have a grand time out hunting such an exotic animal."

There was a throaty chuckle from below.

"Be sure to bring its skin back, Marcus, it will look nice on the wall at least, even if it's not worth much. Better here than Castle Trastamere, Sandro hardly deserves it given the piss poor job the old man's done tracking the fellow. But enough of this. What of the guaranteed profits you promised me for the others, Representative Drachosius?"

"Do not fear, Your Majesty. Everything is well at hand."

This voice was strange, dry, rasping and heavily accented in another tongue that Tagus did not recognize and wholly different from the others in every respect.

"The transaction is already underway. The masters have agreed to the terms of our arrangement. Your profit is assured. Further examples need not be made, we shall quietly handle any further heretics that you wish to dispose of at the agreed upon price."

Of all the menacing voices below, this one was truly terrifying.

"Good. And I trust that the Ambassador shall remain safely ignorant of this. Tarn's cartels must be excluded. Has compensation for Lord Gratano in this matter been arranged? His son…"

"Be still, my lords!" Suddenly the voices fell silent, and he could hear the inquisitor speak again, "I sense a presence. Prying eyes…"

"Where!" Came the alarmed cry of the prince, and there was a flurry of activity below as Tagus instinctively pulled his face back from the grating, like he was avoiding an axe-stroke aimed at his head.

Now he could feel his companion's powerful hand on his shoulder, and in scant seconds they were scurrying away down the tunnel like rats away from some predator. Not stopping until the grate was far behind and they were once again lost in the labyrinth of drainage tunnels.

By the time they had slowed down, Tagus could go no further, slumping to the rough stone. With the same terribly strong arms, she began dragging him.

Gradually the tunnel widened, the bare walls giving way to dust and crushed cobwebs as the dim light came closer. The stale air was broken by a slight breeze, like shallow gasping breaths, until they finally emerged from the stifling darkness into a small deserted room, with dusty stone walls and a timber roof. A lone lantern with a glass enclosed flame burned atop a barrel, casting a dim glow over sacks of oats and bales of straw.

The woman's figure grew a little clearer in this steady light, although her black outfit, which now appeared to be made of close-fitting leather, still appeared to blend with the shadows as she flitted over to the lone wooden door in the opposite wall.

Tagus lay on the floor where she had left him, gasping, his lungs burning along with his filth encrusted limbs. Looking behind, he could see that the semi-circular tunnel entrance, little more than a large drain with no protective grating, had been hidden behind several barrels, all of which had been roughly shoved aside. Clearly someone had put a lot of effort into getting inside the palace drains. But how had this woman found him in such a maze? And how had she been able to pinpoint the very roof of his cell? It made no sense.

Nor was she communicative, once again turning to him and raising a pale finger to her lips before peering through a crack in the door.

For a moment she was silent and unmoving, and Tagus dared not even breathe. Was she really here to save him after all? Why? Who was she and why would she go to such trouble? What about the Inquisition? Were they hunting her too? Surely, they would soon be after him…

His companion finally turned away from the door, seemingly satisfied that the coast was clear.

He saw her kneel beside a sack of oats, and pull some kind of bundle out before throwing it to him.

"Here, put this on." She commanded.

Tagus self-consciously looked down at his naked, filthy, bandaged body, before gazing helplessly at the dark rough spun cloak she had tossed to him. He had not the strength to put it on.

Shaking her head, a momentary look of frustration flickering across her face, she retrieved something from her belt and knelt down beside him. Pressing a vial of foul-smelling liquid to his cracked and swollen lips.

"Drink."

Tagus coughed and wretched as the thick liquid burned down his throat, doubling over on his side and clutching his gut before the fit finally passed.

He lay there on the cool stone, breathing heavily.

"Now get up."

The pain in his limbs had lessened. Hesitantly, he tried to rise to his feet and found that, although aching painfully, his limbs had somehow gained the strength to move. He snatched up the cloak, covering his nakedness. His mind was hazy. What drug had she given him?

He stumbled forward as the door eased open, and Tagus saw that they were in what looked like a vast stable. Moonlight spilled through narrow windows spaced at regular intervals through the long empty room and numerous iron rings were fastened to the bare stone walls. No horses could be seen, and the place seemed deserted. Yet they stayed close to the wall as she led him to a small door nearby.

This time she knocked slowly, once, twice, three times until a dull metallic thud sounded beyond, followed by the sound of a latch being thrown.

Tagus froze at the sight that greeted him the tiny courtyard beyond. On a patch of grass, gleaming ghostly in the moonlight, stood a tall figure in full plate armor. Tagus flinched, and instinctively reached for a nonexistent sword. The stranger was even wearing the golden lion of the prince, emblazoned on the fine blue tabard which covered his polished steel breastplate.

Tagus's clouded mind raced with memories and contradictory emotions. This was a Gendarme, one of the prince's personal guards, dressed exactly as he had seen them in full battle array at Fallonier Fields. The knight stood next to a small iron door at the base of a high stone wall shadowed by battlements. Had this been a trap all along?

The woman said nothing, but simply nodded at the Gendarme, before anxiously looking back at Tagus and gripping his shoulder to urge him forward. The silent warrior did not move until the entrance to the stables swung closed and the tiny courtyard was once again in isolation.

"Do not fear, Falhorne," came a slow voice, low and muffled by the great helm that obscured the man's features. He raised a gauntleted hand in salute to Tagus's cloaked and haggard form.

"Some of us still remember Fallonier. Always walk in strength, my brother."

The lone Gendarme nodded to Tagus's companion and swung open the metal door below the battlements, beckoning them through. And then he was gone. Tagus, his head spinning, fell into unconsciousness beneath a blanket of stars.

Chapter 15 – Companions

This time his slumber was mercifully dreamless. Tagus awoke to someone insistently dashing water across his face. The cold making his eyes sting, like pins and needles against his skin.

"Well, my darling, it seems our friend here is a tough bastard and a half. Especially after what you dragged him through. I'm surprised the quickleaf mixture worked on him at all, what with a cramped cell, a river of filth, and multiple rounds in the torture chamber. One of nature's mysteries I guess…"

Tagus found himself squinting into the broad, round face of a gnome. With ruddy cheeks, wide grinning lips, and an even wider moustache that looked more like a small silver-grey boat with a high prow and stern. The top of the ball-shaped head was crowned in a green skullcap. Wide curious brown eyes watched his every move.

The room around him was slowly coming into focus. It was small with grey stone walls, a stone floor, and a timber roof of split logs. Sunlight streamed in from two tiny narrow windows with iron bars on the outside. Both were spaced close to the ceiling, illuminating his spartan surroundings.

The air of the room was cool, perhaps he was in a cellar. The bed he was lying on was the only item of furniture in the room apart from a wooden bench set against the far wall and a small table nearby on which an assortment of metal tools, which looked like medical instruments, lay amid a jumble of beakers and flasks holding multi-colored liquids. Tagus was briefly reminded of the improvised field hospitals he had seen while on campaign as a mercenary. But at least here there were no horribly mutilated men screaming while some saw-bone amateurishly carved off an arm or leg. Not to mention the tools seemed clean.

The gnome, who was clad in a badly stained pale green apron which matched his skullcap, had just been handed a tankard of water from a tall graceful figure that Tagus recognized instantly.

It was the woman who had rescued him from his cell. She wore high leather boots, a loose-fitting green shirt and tight beige leggings which made her look like a huntswoman returned from the chase. Her black hair was neatly tied back in a bun.

Her pale impassive face glanced at him, dark eyes as intense as Jesta's momentarily looking him up and down, before turning away, nodding to the gnome as she walked toward the room's only visible door. Her footfalls barely audible on the flagstoned floor.

Tagus tried to move his limbs, and winced in pain as his flesh seemed to catch fire.

"Easy now, Falhorne" the gnome said softly, resting a reassuring hand on his naked shoulder. "The prince's jailer is one piss poor physician. It speaks more to the bastard's sadism than his medical training that he bound you up in shit-stained rags. But Vask was always a blockhead."

He shook his round head slowly back and forth before continuing.

"I've spent two days cleaning you up. Thank the Most High, or whatever gods you Falhorne pray to, that you didn't get blood poisoning or some other appropriately lethal infection. I'll give you credit for stamina, that's for damn sure!"

The gnome laughed, the jolly sound booming against the walls.

Tagus found himself glancing wildly around the room. Who in Gormani's flames were these people and where had they taken him?

"Who are you?" He gasped through clenched teeth, not bothering to hide the obvious suspicion in his voice.

His jaws felt as though they had not been opened in weeks.

The gnome grinned, his head bobbing from side to side as if to emphasize his happiness that his patient was finally talking.

"Oh, pardon my manners, it's been awhile since they've counted for much! The name's Meno Farkin Vesalias, third of his name, last of a long line of bloody inquisitive gnomes that can't get enough of sticking their noses into other people's business. Oh yes, and a recovering academic, graduate of the Academy of Alchemical Sciences and Sorcerous Sundries in great Arcadius, with distinction I might add, doctor of medicine, man of letters, and sometime court alchemist of the

Grand Principality of Vinos…until his royal highness saw fit to fire me that is…"

The grin faded slightly, yet stubbornly persisted.

"Don't worry, I've got plenty more equally meaningless titles that I'll gladly share with you later. As for herself," he nodded in the direction of the door where the woman had just disappeared, "she'll introduce herself when she's good and ready. Right now, you need to rest and stop squirming. By all that's holy, which admittedly doesn't amount to much, you're among friends!"

Tagus did not know whether he should laugh or threaten this bizarre gnome with violence. Not that he could follow through on such a threat in his current state. His arms felt like blocks of stone and he could not even feel his legs and feet. Head swimming, he remained silent.

Meno soon departed, still grinning. It wasn't long before sleep returned.

The next few days were hazy. Tagus didn't leave his bed. Sometimes he woke up to find Meno sitting there next to him, but the gnome said little, merely nodding over his patient and muttering the occasional comforting phrase like "easy now," and "all is well". Sometimes his wounds burned and his skin itched maddeningly, his moans prompting his doctor to give him some dark liquid out of a small vial. It was horribly bitter, but it eased the pain.

Sometimes he woke up to find no one in the room, only a small bowl of gruel or porridge and a tankard of water sitting on a tray by the bed. It was difficult to eat at first, but gradually his sense of taste began to return along with some of his former strength.

He did not know what medicine Meno was giving to him, but he blessed the purported alchemist in the name of Mistral, lady of courage, that it kept the nightmares at bay. Whenever he awoke, he could remember nothing of his slumber. Sometimes in his waking moments, he was seized by the fear that the jailer, or even the inquisitor, would suddenly walk through the door, ready to subject him to new torments.

But these panic attacks never lasted long in the face of the drug's calming effects.

He did not see the strange woman again.

It was only after several days in that tiny chamber that Tagus slowly got to his feet, half expecting to discover leather straps under the blankets binding him to the bed. His wounds were dressed in fresh bandages, his strange host must have been changing them regularly. As he moved, the bandages pulled and his disused muscles ached, but the pain was too dull to stop him.

The stone floor was cold beneath his feet and he took three steps before stumbling, bracing himself against the wall to keep from falling. His body felt so heavy. Only as he stood there, breathing heavily as he leaned his weight upon the smooth stone, did he sense another presence in the room. He turned his head to see the pallid woman standing there, clad in same hunting garments.

"Good. You are walking," she said in a calm, businesslike voice.

It was only then that Tagus realized he was naked and his confused mind raced into something close to panic…what would his lord father think? His stupid half-breed son disgracing him like this, he would be sent away for sure this time. And would his wife ever forgive him for exposing himself before another woman? But the pale face, framed by a dark halo of midnight locks, betrayed no awkwardness, no silly ladylike blush or faint-hearted attempt to avert her eyes.

There was no expression on those red lips, no emotion at all in her voice as she continued.

"I am Aileanor, and with all respect Falhorne, that is all you need know for now. That and I am on your side. Put these on."

Tagus had barely even noticed the neatly folded clothes she had been carrying before she carefully laid them out on a bench against the far wall.

Tagus could barely stammer a "thank you", the first thing he'd brought himself to say since Meno had revealed his identity. He sounded so weak and pathetic, he thought. Before a more rational inner voice intervened and sternly stated that he was lucky to be alive.

Something like a faint smile formed on the woman's lips.

"You are welcome," she said. "But now there are urgent matters to attend to, if you have not forgotten. I am sure you still want to save your people."

She gestured to the door, "Come to the end of the hall when you are ready. I shall let Meno do the rest of the talking. He enjoys such things."

Just as before her feet made almost no sound as she turned and left, shutting the door behind her.

Tagus leaned his back against the wall, watching her go, a part of him admiring the uncannily graceful motion of her hips. She sounded so much more formal now than she had during their escape. In his confused mind, it reminded him a little of Marcia, his father's overly friendly lady in waiting, and how she could freely swap between being a bawdy, loud-mouthed peasant wench among the servants to being the most decorous, polite, model of a high-born lady in the drawing room. Such a strange woman.

A few minutes later, Tagus, now wearing a simple linen shirt and a rather tight pair of trousers, was walking down the short passageway outside, limping from the well-stitched up wounds in his legs.

He was definitely underground, likely in the basement of a large house. It even reminded him of Vitus's cellar on Mercer Lane. Massive wooden floor beams hung over his head and a few of the several doors he passed were half-open, revealing a pair of well-stocked store rooms containing various foodstuffs.

The unlocked iron-reinforced door at the end of the corridor opened into a large and very comfortably furnished room, although to call it crowded would have been a serious understatement. The walls were lined with shelves overflowing with books, scrolls, manuscripts, and loose leaves of parchment. With piles more stacked on the floor so that it was impossible to make out the design on the rich, but evidently aging blue and yellow carpet. In one corner of the room was a desk, its surface likewise invisible under piles of books and papers.

Beside the desk was another table, this one lined with a crazy assortment of glass tubes, beakers, bowls, and jugs. These contained a kaleidoscope of multi-colored liquids, some of which bubbled and shifted about in their containers as though they possessed some mild awareness of the chaotic mess around them. The walls were covered with illustrated charts showing various species of herbs and flowering plants, maps showing the entirety of western Titanus, the Great Continent, and a great deal beyond it too, as well as several anatomical drawings of lizards and insects.

The whole space was lit by a strange ball of golden light which appeared to float in the air above the desk, bathing the room in a soft glow which somehow extended to its furthest corners. It was bright enough to force Tagus to squint as he glanced around the place. Two other doors exited the room at opposite ends.

In the middle of the room was a large wooden couch laden with red cushions and before it sat two other comfortable looking cushioned chairs. Meno was sitting on the couch, clad in a fine blue silk robe, absent-mindedly drawing a thick liquid that looked like mulled wine from a large oak barrel placed conveniently next to it. Far from the surgeon in the stained green apron, anxiously poring over the frightful wounds of a fallen soldier, he now looked more like an eccentric, and perhaps slightly tipsy, scholar surrounded by his collection of oddities.

The gnome looked up with a slightly startled look on his ruddy features as he heard the door open. Of the woman who had introduced herself as Aileanor, there was no sign.

"Oh," Meno exclaimed, shutting off the barrel's spigot and gulping down a mouthful of wine before leaning forward on the couch.

"My apologies, Falhorne, please sit down."

Tagus stood in the doorway. He had mostly regained his senses now, and the horrible memories of the pogrom and his imprisonment were slowly falling into place as he took in his new surroundings. So many things, so many people, so many voices. He had to fight down rising panic as he became conscious of how vulnerable he now was. He certainly didn't feel like sitting down or relaxing. This strange gnome had better start making sense.

"Where am I?" He said gruffly, "Who in Gormani's flames are you people, and what am I doing here?"

The formerly flustered gnome grinned and chuckled, his wide moustache bouncing along with his lips as his bright eyes lit up.

"Right to the point, eh? Like a typical warrior, always asking what's going on and who's the next person I'm supposed to kill. Well, fortunately I don't fit into the latter category. You have plenty of enemies and you're lucky I got to you before they did. Short answer, you're in a safe house, a nice underground bolt-hole protected by some very reliable friends of mine. The powers that be are turning the city upside down looking for you. Every street and alley crawling with guards, and whatever other lackeys that the Inquisition has poking under doors and down drain pipes. They're going door to door, and I've heard them rummaging upstairs a few times, but they haven't found what they're looking for…and I intend to keep it that way."

"Am I your prisoner now?" Tagus replied, the snarl not leaving his voice.

"Ha! Hardly," the gnome laughed, "You could leave, if you felt like hanging or being burnt alive. And I am Meno, in case you have forgotten, alchemist and hoarder of scientific curiosities."

He gestured grandly around the room.

"And just like you and your kind, I'm a marked man. I'm sure his majesty Prince Chero would just love to flay me alive, very, very slowly, if he found out I was giving shelter to the last Falhorne in Fiore. Don't vex yourself. My fate is your fate either way. I got you out of that hole, and now we live or die together…oh, and what is your name by the way?"

Tagus's suspicions began to subside, but not entirely. Still, it was no good trying to remain anonymous before one's savior, however dubious they might be.

"I am Tagus. Are you with the Association? To whom do you owe allegiance?"

Again, the gnome's eyes lit up.

"Tagus…Tagus, yes! Now I recognize you. My brother Nicco spoke highly of you, said you were quite an upstanding fellow. And, may I say, your wife is a most stunning criminal investigator! But I digress…"

"You know my wife? Where is she? Is she safe?"

"Corrie, of course! Best midwife and healer in the slums, finest collaborator the Association's ever had…and, yes, I do in fact owe my allegiance to that most worthy cause. Although I try to keep my head down these days. Unlike my brother, I wasn't an obscure tradesman in the past. But, yes, your wife is fine. I will take you to her when you are sufficiently recovered. She is rather busy right now."

Tagus's mind burned with questions. How did the gnome know all this? Corrie had never told him of these gnomes before. Nicco never had a brother, as far as he knew. But then again, he knew so little about the former owner of the Black Horseman, who had apparently been living clandestinely in Fiore for the past three years. Although it made some sense that the Association would want to spring him from jail, why take such a risk for one man? Especially if the situation in the city was as bad as Meno made it out to be. But one question stood before all others.

"What happened to the folk of the Asylum? Where were the Old Believers taken?"

Meno's grin disappeared, and a look of deadly seriousness crossed his broad face. When he at last spoke after a notable pause, his voice had lost its jovial aspect.

"The brethren helped as many as we could, your wife among them. But the slavers got their hands on far more. We think we know where most of them were taken, but, before you ask anymore about my motives, I'll tell you exactly what this gnome wants, Falhorne. I want justice."

Tagus found himself walking forward toward the center of the room. Something about the gnome's intensity drawing him in. He walked five paces and then froze; it was like he was talking to Vitus.

"What do you mean?"

"I want the same thing you do, Falhorne. You lost your friends, your people, your life, and you're not the only one. Corvus, Nestor, Jesta, even that crotchety Clodius were my friends too, and I've helped them in more ways than you know."

"Then why have I never heard of you?"

"Because you didn't need to," Meno frowned at the interruption. "And before you ask, I'm not helping you because I lost my job. Trust me, there are plenty more inbred little princes in this land looking to hire a talented alchemist if it keeps their sorry flesh alive a little longer. If I wanted to work for any of them, I would have left this shit-heap of a city behind long ago. I stayed because this isn't about me. It isn't even about Nicco and us non-humans…not entirely anyway."

He looked Tagus up and down, his wide lips stern and severe.

"Your kind has a reputation, Falhorne. From what my contacts tell me, the people can't decide whether to talk about the Asylum burning down, its people being led away in chains, or the way that fellow Callidus sent a bullet straight down Guildmaster Max's hole. Now let me tell you something about those guilds that our late alderman presided over in his infinite wisdom."

Meno took a heavy swig of wine, wiping his mouth with the back of his hand.

"Gnomes used to be in them. Quite a few actually. And women too, just ask your Councillor Jesta, if you ever see her again. She inherited the blacksmith trade from her mother, a fine woman. You couldn't have asked for a better smith, not that her daughter had a chance to keep the family business alive for very long after she passed into the ether, but I'll get to that. And, as you know, all ye good old heretics were in there too, quite a good little brood of Old Believers inside one big happy family of honest and not so honest tradesfolk. Not even old Prince Cosimo could change that. Very good while it lasted, most definitely."

He took another long sip of wine before continuing.

"Well, they came for the women first. It didn't matter if they were heretics or not. It didn't matter if they were non-humans or not. They were all forced out seven years ago, even those who had been in their craft for generations. Oh, Jesta pleaded her case before the masters, even threw down the gauntlet and challenged anyone among them to match the quality of her ironwork. They just laughed and dismissed her womanly 'handicrafts'. Of course, what Max and his cronies really wanted was less competition. Especially with those Tarnish merchants coming in and everyone jockeying for a piece of a shrinking pie."

Meno belched and shook his head.

"No one took a stand then. Your dearly departed Nestor might have been a fine man, but he didn't say a damn thing when the women in the leather trades wound up on the docks or in brothels. He even took over the shops of a few of his former colleagues and expanded his business with Max's blessing. Nicco wasn't any better. He was a weaver back then, if you can believe it, not a brewer or anything, and too damn selfish to look out for others of his kind. I was the same. We packed our own sister off to Tarn when she couldn't practice the family trade anymore around here. Fortunately, she's had decent luck up there in Ormoros, which more than can be said for most."

He cast the empty wine cup to the floor, sending it rolling against a bookcase.

"But then they came for the rest of us non-humans. It took them two years, but they came. The Church was coming in all high and mighty by then and Max and his alderman decided to demonstrate their piety. They'd already broken the bank building that wretchedly ugly guild chapel, but that wasn't enough. They expelled every gnome with his manhood still attached. Because it wouldn't do to have such 'impure' beings polluting the trades. Sound familiar?"

Tagus felt his blood begin to boil as the gnome went on.

"I mean, besides giving Theophilus and his boys bragging rights, it was just another monopolist landgrab. Nicco was lucky to have the inn our father left him. Everyone else ended up underground or in exile, especially a few years later when our august sovereign banned us from every honest line of work under the sun. Why do you think so many gnomes ended up in the Association? They were the only ones who would accept us, apart from the smugglers that is. I know more than a few ex-tradesmen who turned their hand to counterfeiting – now that requires genuine skill, artistry really!"

Meno chuckled and stroked his beard thoughtfully, a bitterly ironic smile on his face.

"Most of us well-to-do types wouldn't have been caught dead in such company during our old lives, but that changed pretty quick when we started breathing slum air. Getting stuck in dung-ridden tenements because no one would take our money in the more pristine parts of town.

The Family really starts calling your name in those conditions. You'd think our upstanding human colleagues would have put in a good word for us, but, again, no one took a stand. Nestor just watched us go. He didn't even kick up much of a fuss when my brother lost the inn."

He paused and looked at Tagus, who, try as he might, could not think of anyone apart from the Falhorne who had stepped forward to help Nicco out three years ago.

"Then finally they came for the heretics. That was less than three years ago now. Me and Nicco had gone into hiding by then. I still remember his bitter laughter when he heard about Nestor's impassioned pleas before the aldermen…pleas he never made for gnomes or women, even those who shared his faith. The rest is history, as they say: the whole lot of the 'disbeliever' scum were banished to the Asylum and thence to the slaver wagons."

"What is your point, gnome?" Tagus was getting impatient; the painful memories were growing stronger by the minute.

Meno wiped his brow and shook his head.

"Sad isn't it? The way people don't work together. Even after he was kicked out himself, that stubborn bastard Nestor never trusted old Nicco because he was non-human. I think Corvus and Jesta were the only ones who gave him any respect on his infrequent trips to the Agoge. Even Clodius was hesitant to back the Association because he was worried that non-humans and foreigners would take Old Believer jobs at the riverport."

His hand abruptly slammed down on the table.

"It wasn't until the new laws against non-humans were passed, making that impossible, that he changed his tune. Of course, now the bosses are just buying slaves to do the work, given that the price of human flesh is so low. Everyone is losing their jobs while those poor bastards toil in chains. People let each other suffer. The way survival makes them shrink back so they can hold onto their own for just a little bit longer, until fate finally comes for them too."

"You still have not answered my question…"

The little alchemist stared at the floor, and then back at Tagus, a faint smile on his face.

"We failed back then. Everyone failed everybody else. This time we work together. They've carted your people away in chains. They've driven my people underground. They've made us all suffer, together. And together, we're going to make them pay for their crimes. The prince, the Inquisition, the lot of them. Do you understand me now?"

Tagus stared at Meno, dumbfounded by the gnome's defiant words. He could not shake the paranoid feeling that he was being used, but what greater proof could he expect as to his benefactor's intentions?

He thought of the wagons, of the hanging oppressed faces of the captives, of Callus's dead stare through the bars. He had to protect them. He had to free them. Perhaps he should have died in that cell. But now he had to live, for them.

"I will hold you to words, gnome," he at last said firmly. "And what of yourself? I should like to know more about my supposed savior…you and that woman."

Meno's reply was just as firm, his voice losing none of its determination.

"I've told you, Aileanor will tell you about herself when she's good and ready. As for me, well, you'd most likely be dead if I'd chosen to follow any other trade besides alchemy. Prince Chero hired me right after you and your comrades thrashed the Inquisition and their boy Martino. Back then, I foolishly believed that the Church's failure to split Skaros off from the rest of Vinos would mean a golden age for us small folk. I even saved Chero's royal son from the pox and his daughter from her own anemic blood, not that she ever showed much gratitude. Academy trained physicians are few and far between west of the Noctus. He should have counted his blessings that I happened to be in Fiore at the time."

The gnome let out a low chuckle.

"Well, as his former personal healer, I can tell you that the man has no principles. None. He stabbed many a man in the back before finally getting around to me. He never shut up about his bloody schemes about becoming a real king someday and making Vinos the center of an empire to rival that of Lucius the Proud. Aileanor tells me the two of you were able to listen in on some of his drivel on your way out. As you've probably figured out, your precious Treaty isn't worth the parchment it was scrawled on."

Tagus almost wanted to spit as he recalled that gruff, arrogant voice he'd heard through the grate in the wall.

What of the guaranteed profits you promised me for the others…?

"Of course, the Fiore Asylum was set up to provide a refuge for the long-persecuted…"

"Yes. I was present in the very chamber at Castle Trastamere when the Treaty was signed. Do not mock me, gnome."

Tagus had regained something of his pride since rising from his sickbed. He would not allow this alchemist to talk down to a follower of the gods.

But Meno carried on, ignoring the interruption.

"The Agoge began duly exercising its sovereign authority, but found that royal guarantees only went so far. I was at court then, and remember the endless stream of merchants, the former owners of the old riverport, pouring in to demand compensation. Your esteemed praetor had the royal ear, and Chero brushed them all off, but that didn't stop them from taking legal action."

Monsters. Tagus remembered Vitus privately cursing the slumlords and their endless court cases. But there had been nothing in the Treaty to protect against them; a gaping loophole he had recognized too late.

"Then the first 'purity' laws were passed, first banning Old Believers from government service and escalating until they were banned from all but the lowliest jobs. The glorious Blessed Realm had carved out plenty of space for itself in Vinos by then. But there was no rebellious 'holy league' among the nobility this time, no Templar invasion, everything was by the book. When Theophilus began whispering promises of kingship in the prince's ear, the old man listened. Fallonier was long ago, and he had the interests of his house to uphold. It was all expediency. The Treaty of Trastamere, the alliance with the Inquisition, and now the pogrom against his own subjects. He didn't reach the age of sixty by playing fair."

Meno paused, and Tagus nodded grimly. He could still hear those accursed voices: The prince, the inquisitor, and those others whom he did not recognize.

"I finally realized the truth two years ago when he summoned me into the audience chamber where he was casually sprawled on his great seat, sharpening his great-grand father's gladius as he habitually did even in the midst of council meetings. The slave girls who waited on him that day could not have been more than twelve, although I am quite sure they had all shared his bed more than once. The bishop, all pristine in his white robes, looked down at me like I was a bloody insect.

"Chero gave me a bored glance and snapped his fingers to send the slaves scurrying for cover before staring back into his goblet of wine. Not bothering to look at his little healer. Theophilus on the other hand, never took his damn eyes off me even once.

"'I like you, gnome,' the prince said at last, 'but fate makes for hard choices. What would the other princes think if they saw me surrounded by a rabble of non-humans? What would the Holy Church think? My honor would never survive the scandal, and there's no telling what the blessed executors of the Most High's wishes might do to you if they caught you whispering impure things in my ear one night. No, old boy. It's time for you to leave. For your own safety, you understand'."

Meno again chuckled bitterly, his face oddly illuminated by the strange ball of light hovering above the desk behind him.

"I might as well have been invisible. He never said my name once. I was taken by the guards and thrown outside right then and there without so much as a thank you. I suppose I was lucky. Not long after that the Inquisition carried out its first public execution in decades of a non-human for the crime of blasphemy. Her name was Pema, not that it means anything to anyone now. Another innocent executed as an example to the rest of the impure amongst us. God, I hate them. Those bloody-handed priests…don't think for one second that it was only you heretics who got set on fire at Brisi fifty years ago. Tartosa held the richest communities of gnomes between the Noctus and the Red Cliffs. Now none of them remain. My father was the last survivor of his house when he came here. Believe me when I say that my kind remembers."

We must publicly cleanse his filthy form by holy fire…

Tagus's initial suspicions morphed into indignation. It was true. The alchemist's enemies were his enemies. Now he really did sense a kindred spirit, an ally, someone who could help him get his vengeance on the creatures that had stolen everything from him.

They were silent for a time. Tagus standing. Meno sitting.

"How did you find me?" Tagus finally asked, resting a hand on the back of one of the chairs but not allowing himself to sit down as he beheld his host with a new found respect.

"I still have a friend or two," Meno replied, "Not everyone within those walls is so keen on the degree of power the Church has gained, or the sway the bishop holds over their prince."

Some of us still remember Fallonier. Tagus felt his mind drifting back to the pyre, to the solemn wounded faces, Vitus's clear and steady voice speaking ancient words, and the armored strangers who had come to pay their respects to the fallen alongside a band of heretic outsiders.

"My praetor told me that many in the Gendarmerie opposed the prince's alliance with the Blessed Realm."

"Well, he was right. Not surprising, really, given that the very forces they defeated at Fallonier, now have the run of the capital city and the royal court. If I was a Gendarme, I'd take that as a slap in the face. They warned the Asylum you know. Sent a message even as the riot was raging. Nicco tells me there were barricades up by the time the folk got back from the marketplace, so someone must have received it. And it likely saved your wife too. You have friends, Falhorne, remember that."

It certainly appeared so.

"And what do you plan to do now? Is the Association working with these Gendarmes?"

"There has been, some collaboration," Meno sighed, "Nicco could tell you more. Suffice it to say that the palace is not exactly open to people like us, nor do most self-respecting members of the prince's elite guard spend their days traipsing about the slums. Still, your boy Callus was getting pretty good as a go-between."

The mention of Callus's name caused Tagus to grip the edge of the chair until his knuckles ached, that nightmare image screaming in his mind. The revelation that his apprentice had been secretly in league with the Association this whole time barely registered at all.

But Meno continued without pause.

"The Association was tipped off about the pogrom. There is considerable sympathy for us among the low-level guild members. The guild system isn't very healthy these days. The purges of women, non-humans and heretics becomes more understandable when you realize just how much the market has shrunk. Only the ruthless survive, getting stinking rich while everyone else winds up loading barges with satincane bound for Tarn or laying stonework for that cursed cathedral. Step out of line and you get the noose. Not everyone's happy with that, funnily enough."

Meno slowly got to his feet, his skullcap barely reaching the level of Tagus's throat. He was gazing up at him with those bright big eyes, the anger of a few minutes before having melted back into something approaching cheerfulness.

"So, thank the insiders for your escape, not to mention the five years or so I spent mapping out the palace's foundations. Seek truth from facts as they say. You were crawling through the old chief temple of Fiore you know, or what's left of it anyway…all those carvings of gladiatorial contests and sacrificial bloodletting to the Lord of Flames. I figured that a believer in the old gods would appreciate that. But anyway…"

He turned and walked toward one of the room's two other doors.

"Aileanor will be back soon, and we should really get some food in you. You'll need your strength. And you can trust that I won't be sprinkling essence of nightshade over your sausages. Follow me."

Tagus shook his head and followed the gnome out of the room. His eccentric new ally was full of surprises to put it mildly. He thought of asking more about Corrie, about how Meno knew her, but his mind was too full. Even though he was relieved to hear that she was well, the thought of seeing his wife again was overwhelming. What would he say to her?

Aileanor at last joined them at the dinner table, a small wooden rectangle that stood in the center of the room next to Meno's study. The pale woman said nothing as she hung her dark cloak on a hook and sat down, only briefly nodding her head at Meno who nonetheless gave her a warm welcoming smile.

Tagus's worries all but evaporated at the sight of the hearty meal before him, and he suddenly found that he had a raging appetite. The food was delicious, with Meno rather proudly stating that he had prepared it all himself, perhaps dwelling a little too much on the effort he had put into the stew in particular. Tagus didn't care either way, the former prisoner ate it as ravenously as a hungry soldier at the tail end of a forced march.

He was so engrossed in his food that he didn't notice that Meno and Aileanor had been talking past him for several minutes.

"…And you're sure it's unguarded?" He heard Meno say.

"Yes," Aileanor replied, staring dispassionately at the gnome across the table. "There are no guards to be found at the entrance, and it leads directly into the building's sub-basement."

"Did you see where the guards are stationed?"

"Two at the gate and two inside on the ground floor. The rest are positioned around the slave pen. Twenty in all, that I could see."

"Any indication as to when they're going to move them? Or where?"

"No. I counted three wagons, nowhere near enough to move all of them. They are probably still looking for buyers."

"Or waiting for instructions from certain authorities we could name…"

Tagus knew what they were talking about, and his mind hardened to stone as he recalled more of the vicious words he had overheard. *We have the matter of their bitch of a leader…she would make a far better example…the transaction is already underway…the masters have agreed…*

Jesta.

"We are going to rescue them," he said sharply, drawing surprised looks from both the others, "And I will kill anyone who tries to stop us."

Meno's eyes flared in the glow of the three flickering candles that lit the small room. Aileanor's expression of alarm quickly fading into a jaded mask.

"You'll need that courage, Falhorne" the alchemist finally said, "It seems the heretics of Fiore are awaiting their 'penance' in the compound of the Seven Moons merchant company. You look spry enough to make the trip, so tomorrow I'll introduce you to your other partners in crime."

Chapter 16 – Underground

"He's one of yours, isn't he?"

Corrie's voice sounded hollow, bouncing back at her from the curve of the tunnel roof as though nature itself had rejected the question as obscene.

Nicco did not immediately respond, kneeling in his dirty grey coat beside the stagnant pool. The only saving grace of the reeking mass of slurry being that it mercifully blotted out the stench of death, blood, and slowly rotting internal organs.

"Yes…yes he is…" The reply came in the form of a poorly concealed sob.

The overpowering stench of her surroundings did not stop Corrie from observing the purple miasma of deathly energies that hovered over the half-submerged corpse. Its pale face screaming silently at the ceiling, above where the horns of its cracked open ribs protruded from the putrid water.

She sensed the choking, alien magic, just as she had sensed it in the alleyway days before. It clung to the walls, to the ceiling, to bits of unrecognizable filth floating in the dark pool, just as it clung to the mangled flesh of the young man's body.

It had led them to this forsaken spot beneath Fiore's streets. Corrie had heard its breathless call and had guided the others to the pool of sewage runoff just before the point where the ancient tunnel had collapsed. As though whatever had done this to the poor youth had wanted them to discover its grisly handiwork. It had even left the man's face intact.

Nicco was crying now, his sobs muffled by his hands and wide-brimmed hat, but still perfectly audible in the confines of the tunnel. The armed Association men with him, neither of whom Corrie recognized, stood silent and spectral in the low lantern-light, mourning the death of one of their own.

Corrie herself knelt beside him, one arm around the gnome's shoulder, playing the role that she had played countless times.

"You were a good fella, Dacon, quicker than a rat with its ass on fire," he gave a chuckle that came out as a wet gulping sound, "Guess it didn't help you much in the end. But you tried…it's all a brother can do."

Dacon. They had been searching for the missing messenger for two days. The one the Association had dispatched from the Mill Gate to the Asylum in a bid to warn the Old Believers of the approaching slavers and their wagons. But the message had never arrived. Now they were looking upon the Monster's latest confirmed victim.

****

Tagus barely slept that night. Whatever drug had made his slumber dreamless had worn off. He could not close his eyes without scenes of fire, chains, and suffering faces flooding his vision.

He must have finally nodded off, for he awoke to find a steaming bowl of porridge beside the bed along with a mug of ginger tea. He gratefully ate the simple meal, trying to clear his head, before rising and dressing himself, the pull of his wounds less irritating than they had been the day before. Looking down, he saw that his bandages had again been changed.

Only a faint pale light streamed in from the tiny windows, and, looking out, he saw dark clouds shrouding the sun outside. Fitting, he thought, on a day when he would likely have to sacrifice his life. It was the only redemption he could expect after his previous failings.

No sooner had he finished dressing the knock came at the door, which opened to reveal Aileanor's tall, slender form. Her hair was tied back, her pale face a ghostly mask, and she had swapped her hunting greens for the same tight-fitting black outfit that she had worn when breaking him from his jail cell. She said nothing, beckoning for him to follow her.

When they got to the crazily cluttered room with its charts, books and bizarre floating light source, she gestured toward a black leather jerkin spread out on the couch where Meno had been seated the day before.

"You will need that where we are going", she said.

The strange woman then turned away, heading in the direction of the dining room, her booted footfalls making no sound on the carpeted floor.

At first Tagus just stood there looking at the armor, remembering the last person to give him armor to wear, and what had happened to him. He finally ran his hands over the hard surface, the quilted arms of the jerkin expertly studded with iron rivets.

Beside it lay a polished longsword, its hilt likewise clad in simple black leather with a round brass pommel, while the cross-guard was reinforced with a metal ring to protect the wielder's hand. The blade was fine steel, the work of a master smith. A skillfully crafted scabbard of black leather lay alongside it. In the more than twenty years he had carried a sword he had never set eyes on one so fine. An equally impressive dagger lay next to the wine cask.

Moving hesitantly, he put on the jerkin, which fit perfectly over his shirt. He had just picked up the sword, its weight balanced perfectly in his hand, when he heard a familiar voice behind him.

"My apologies, Falhorne, but we currently aren't stocking any halberds."

Jovial chuckling filled the air, and Tagus instinctively spun round to see Meno standing in the doorway.

"Polearms wouldn't exactly be ideal where we're headed."

The alchemist stepped into the room, the soft glow of the globe of light illuminating what must have been his work clothes. He was wearing a black apron over a brown leather jacket and he also appeared to have leather leggings. A large pair of goggles, bound around his head with a strap, sat atop the gnome's bald head. Meno's broad face looked redder than usual, as one hand played with the handlebar of his outrageous moustache. Tagus could smell the wine on the gnome's breath.

"No doubt things will be getting ugly today, friend. Downright disgusting probably. No telling how high the sewer gas levels will be, it fluctuates by the hour, especially in the old tunnels. Oh well, this is what I get, my old man had to remind me that I was a gnome, not a dwarf, what with all the digging and poking around I used to do. That may be, but if you want the truth you almost always have to dig for it. You can always trust me to dress appropriately…"

"Well, good morning to you too," Tagus said, a wry half-smile on his face. It felt a little odd in light of recent events, but the gnome did look ridiculous.

"Oh yes," Meno chuckled again, "I need to mind my manners. It's been too long since me and Aileanor have had real company down here."

"Of course," Tagus replied, again having no reason to doubt his words, "Are these…"

He gestured at the sword in his hand and then the dagger on the couch.

"Yours," the gnome replied, "A warrior needs his weapons. And those are the work of Jesta's mother. I told you she was the finest smith this side of the Noctus. We did some business back in the day, me and the old dame, and her work has more than stood the test of time, why I'm even wearing some of it myself."

Grinning, Meno pointed at his own leather jacket, which Tagus now noticed was very fine indeed, its workmanship almost putting his new jerkin to shame.

"She even got some orders from the prince back when he was young and appreciated craftsmanship over dogma…but don't get me started."

"Well," Tagus said, trying to take it all in, "I am most thankful. I only hope I am worthy of wielding a blade like this."

"Oh, don't worry," Meno walked briskly to his desk and began rummaging through a pile of books and scrolls, "I'm sure that if a mixture of ferrous metal and carbonate could talk, it would be telling you how gorgeous you look in the mirror."

He laughed as he drew out a large slightly crumpled parchment scroll, "Though it might criticize your exceedingly bad odor after our little sewer crawl…"

"Sewer crawl?"

"Exactly. How else did you expect to get inside this little slave pen? Stride right through the front gate in a locked-down city crawling with guards? As a house guest? Oh, you'd get accommodations alright if you were that stupid!"

Meno spread the parchment scroll across the small table before the couch. It was a map. Tagus could make out the vague outline of the city, but it did not show streets but tunnels. *Fiore Sewer System,* was written in bold black lettering across the top.

"This city is more than two thousand years old, Falhorne. Built layer upon layer. The landscape changes a lot over the years, especially when you build a major metropolis beside a river. Many of these tunnels were once streets. Whole squares, once open to the sky, remain as underground reservoirs for the city's slurry. Go deep enough and you can see the old temples. I'd take you sight seeing if we had the time."

He pointed a fat finger at a certain junction in the middle of the map.

"Aileanor tells me there's a hidden tunnel through a collapsed section here. That'll lead us straight into the Seven Moon's sub-basement. All the really old buildings in town have multiple layers underground, even if the present inhabitants don't know about them. In fact, we're in such a sub-basement right now. I only hope that the Seven Moons are a little more ignorant about their own cellars than my good friend upstairs. With a little luck they'll never see us coming, and we'll be able to deal with the guards and slip your people out below street level. The stench might be bad, but it's better than slavery."

"But what do we even know about this merchant league? I've never once heard of it. I'm assuming you know how many guards we're dealing with here?"

"Right now, less than ten," came the blunt response from another familiar voice.

Aileanor, true to form, had made no noise when she entered the room. Her midnight black hair spilling behind her as she joined them at the table.

"I scouted the area once more," she said, "A whole delegation of merchants just left for the palace along with nearly half of the compound's guards. If we go now and go quickly, we will most likely succeed."

"They enjoy royal favor; I am not surprised. But what are the capabilities of the guards that remain?"

Tagus's military mind was asserting itself.

Aileanor turned to him with those dark eyes that seemed to pierce the soul.

"Mercenaries all of them. The Seven Moons can afford the best, so they will be skillful. But with surprise on our side, we should be able to overwhelm them one by one without raising the alarm."

"Well," Meno responded, "I know that tone in your voice, darling, we'd best get moving. Nicco can tell you more about our merchant friends once we catch up with him, my good Falhorne. Let's be sure to take some provisions, some of those people down there could probably use some nourishment before we move on. How are gas levels?"

"Clear as of an hour ago," came the reply, "But the patrols have moved to the sewers. So far, they have not entered the older tunnels. Gorgo will be taking watch now, making sure that remains so."

"Gorgo? Nicco let him take watch when he only has one eye? Well let's hope his other senses don't fail him, Gio's next shipment is due this evening."

Tagus's head was spinning, "What are you both talking about?"

"Oh," Meno paused, immediately after snatching up the map, "That's right, I forgot to tell you. The folk of the Asylum that the Association managed to save are still in Fiore, or beneath it at any rate. The deep tunnels of the undercity were the only safe place we could find. Nicco, and your wife have been looking after them down there ever since. Don't worry, we'll be going to them first, you'll get to see your Corrie, as I promised. Either way, we need to get the place ready for the additional folks we'll hopefully be liberating this afternoon."

He folded up the map, walked back to the desk and crammed several unmarked vials of liquid into a satchel before heading for the dining room door.

Tagus hurriedly sheathed the sword and dagger, buckling them at his waist, his mind so full of conflicting emotions that he could not think of anything more to say. The thought of his people hiding underground, as they had in the darkest days of the old Empire, when the Inquisition reigned supreme, filled him with rage. But the thought of seeing his wife again, that she was in a safe place, brought forth relief, joy, and apprehension in equal measure. He still did not know what he would say to her, once he could look again into those beautiful dark eyes. Feelings of guilt and shame welled within him, adding to the maelstrom. Part of him still wondered if the strange gnome could be believed, and if this was not just some ploy to sell him to the prince. In the end, it was his desire to free his people, to revenge his mentor, to redeem his failure as a Falhorne, that set his feet in motion.

As he followed the others out the door, he noticed what Meno was carrying, secure in a wide belt behind his apron: two finely-made wheel-lock pistols that would put Callidus to shame, alongside a stout-bladed short sword. This gnome was clearly more than a bookish alchemist.

Everything proceeded briskly. After stopping briefly to get provisions from the safehouse kitchen, which they crammed into a large sack that Meno appeared to carry effortlessly. Aileanor led the trio from the dining room to a narrow stone cut passageway outside which wound around to the right.

The only light came from the dim glow of rows of fluorescent yellow fungi, stretching across the ceiling in a perfect rectangle all the way down the passage, following it as it curved. Tagus raised an eyebrow. It was like an upside-down garden plot. Meno appeared to have some odd hobbies, but this one evidently had its practical uses.

Following the glow of the ceiling fungus farm, they turned the corner and Tagus saw that the passage ended in a stout metal door. It was a simple low square, head-high to Meno, but he and Aileanor would have to go through bent double. As he drew closer, he once more had to raise an eyebrow. The door looked impregnable. It looked like it was made of solid iron etched in brass and with no handle or keyhole that he could see.

Without pausing, Aileanor bent down until she was eye level with the door, placing her hand against its surface and whispering something Tagus could not hear. There was a low rumbling sound, a metallic grinding of gears, and the door horizontally slid open revealing pitch darkness beyond.

Aileanor, bending down, silently slipped through the opening with all the grace of a hunting cat. Seconds later he could see the dim yellowish glow of her strange light outside, just as it had appeared during their escape from the palace. Meno grinned back at Tagus before following her, tucking his chin as he passed through the small portal.

After Tagus had himself passed through the opening, he heard the rumbling again. Turning around, he saw the door close behind him, only it looked completely different, not a metal slab but rough and grey, like an ordinary block of cut stone. A split second later he could not even see the door at all. Even its outline was invisible, as though it had completely merged with the wall, which was dripping moisture and covered in patches of slimy mould.

Now he could smell the decay and rot all around him. They were in the sewers.

The three of them were standing in a square low-ceilinged room, lit only by the glow of Aileanor's light. A tunnel opened in the left-hand wall, while the rubble and debris piled against the opposite wall hinted at the existence of a second passage that was now caved in and blocked. A rusty iron grate lay in the center of the ceiling, and droplets of foul-smelling liquid fell at regular intervals.

"I told you it would be disgusting," Meno whispered with a chuckle, noticing Tagus's contorted face, "Don't worry, you'll get used to it..."

Tagus had to resist the urge to gag as they passed down the low tunnel, which soon joined another, and then another, until he couldn't have found the way back to the tiny door if he had tried. Aileanor, whose stooped figure formed the vanguard of the small party, never wavered however, and moved with all the purpose and certainty of a woman who knew these warrens like the back of her hand. Her extraordinary ability to find a lone prisoner via the palace drainage system became less mystifying as he followed her, shoulders aching and back bent.

For awhile they traveled along a downward sloping tunnel, then took a left, another left, and a right, before emerging into a large tunnel that was half flooded by murky sewer water. In the distance he could see a faint ray of sunlight shining through what must have been a grating in the ceiling.

"Old Thresher Street," Meno remarked softly, turning to Tagus, "Actually back in the Five Kingdoms it was called The Road of Flames, led right up to the Temple of Fiore. It's still the main artery of the undercity…"

He was cut off mid-sentence as Aileanor motioned for him to be silent. She glanced first left and then right down the tunnel, before pausing as if to listen for some distant noise. Tagus froze, and he realized just how out of his depth he was. In all his years as a soldier, he had never traveled underground, let alone fought there. Fear began to creep into his bones.

After what seemed like a long time, she finally signalled for them to move down the tunnel to the right, away from the shaft of light. They wordlessly set off, the only sounds being the dripping of water and the low scrape of their boots on the slimy stone.

They walked along the broad tunnel for what must have been at least a mile. Occasionally a shaft opened in the ceiling, while here and there patches of luminous fungus clung to the damp walls. Aileanor allowed her light to go out in these better lit areas, before letting it shine again as the darkness returned.

The stench of slurry and decay continued unabated, and Tagus eventually had to cast dignity aside and hold his nose against the smell. The others didn't seem to react to the ever-present putrid odor at all. If anything, they looked completely at home, walking briskly amid the subterranean filth as a normal person walks briskly down a city street. This was far from their first such excursion.

As they walked, he heard noises: the unending drip of condensation from the roof, the rush of water through the drains, including little waterfalls which descended into the main stream from stone pipes jutting out from the walls beside the path. Every now and again he heard a plop that might have been a clump of dirt falling into the water, or a small splash that might have been a water creature slithering off an unseen shore into the murky depths.

Here and there they passed the openings of other tunnels, some large, others little more than culverts. None of them appeared to have anything like the dry path on which they walked, and several were completely choked with earth and debris, blocking all access.

At last, they came to a large junction in the tunnels. Here the stream branched in four directions, forming a wide circular pool. A grate in the ceiling sent a beam of light down into the dark water. Faint sounds of city life drifted down into the tunnel. The path branched off in three of the four directions, the left-hand tunnel featuring a wide stream of slurry which seemed to be flowing downward. From that direction Tagus could hear the distant roar of what might have been a waterfall. The path they were on crossed a simple stone slab bridge in front of them, continuing into the darkness, while another path veered off down the right-hand tunnel.

As they approached the junction, Aileanor again motioned for them to stop, immediately extinguishing her light at the same time. For a few seconds Tagus heard nothing, but then over the rush of water and the other sounds of the sewer, he began to hear voices approaching. From the shadows directly in front of them, the light of a single swinging lantern could now be seen, bobbing in the darkness as it came closer. Soon another light came into view, then another.

Tagus felt fear clench at his chest as he began to make out some of the words, but only two truly terrified him, two terrible words that so often stood together that one could be used in place of the other: "fugitive" and "Resh", meaning "dark-skinned runaway". His escape had indeed been discovered. He was being hunted and that hunt had cast its net very wide.

"Like you said, darling, they're sweeping the sewers too," Meno whispered, turning his face toward Aileanor, who had dropped into a crouching stance.

They followed her lead, crouching down and placing their backs against the moist stone of the tunnel wall.

The band of men stopped at the junction's tiny bridge. There were seven in all. The weak light reflecting off their iron pot helmets and mud-splattered livery betraying their identity as royal guardsmen. Down here they carried no pikes or pole-arms, but Tagus assumed they were well-enough armed. All carried lanterns, illuminating their hard, grizzled faces which stood out ghoulishly amid the shadows.

Now there were more voices. This time coming up the right-hand tunnel. Tagus could see the lead lantern of what must have been a second patrol emerge into view.

One of the original group of guardsmen strode forward and the barked order, "report!" sounded down the tunnels. The sergeant, or whoever the patrol leader was, had apparently not gotten used to the underground warrens where such a shout could betray one's presence a full league away.

Tagus felt his back digging into the slimy wall of the tunnel, as if his body was searching in vain for a way out, looking for a crack or hole to slide into and disappear like an insect. Facing perhaps fourteen men-at-arms, there was no chance of fighting their way out. He only hoped that his new companions had a contingency plan. If they sought to betray him, this would be the time. He had nowhere to go.

Both patrols had paused at the junction, the men conversing in hushed voices, when Aileanor turned to him, her face a hard circle of alabaster, and silently motioned for him to begin falling back in the direction they had just come. Not daring to breathe, Tagus forced his feet, clad in the scuffed brown leather boots Meno had given him, to slide backward on the wet stones, trying desperately to be silent. Slowly, Meno followed, with Aileanor herself bringing up the rear, her eyes fixed on the guardsmen as the three of them crept back down the tunnel.

Tagus only hoped that the guardsman's "report" was a long one, and that the half-glimpsed movements of sewer snakes or water rats would lead the soldiers down the wrong path until they were irrecoverably lost in the stinking morass. That is when he heard the sound of marching feet above water. They were crossing the bridge.

In that terrible moment, he tried to remember Vitus's words on the castle's training ground, his shouted commands before battle, his brave example in both settings. It was all he could do to keep himself from running.

The alien environment of the sewers was playing games with his mind. As he crept backwards, the approaching footfalls echoed all around him. Gritting his teeth and closing his eyes, his bandages pulling painfully against his flesh, Tagus forced himself to keep steady, gripping his leather scabbard like a vice lest his sword drag on the floor and give him away.

The heavy boots came closer, now joined by muttered curses and loud hawking and spitting. They had backed around a sweeping curve of the tunnel, meaning that the guardsmen were no longer in view. But when Tagus finally found to courage to open his eyes, he saw nowhere to hide.

Heart thumping, visions of dungeon cells and torture chambers stabbing through his mind, he turned to look at Aileanor, just in time to see her signal a stop. Was she insane? Stopping in plain view with a dozen of the prince's men on their tail. It was suicide. But Meno stopped, and, like an obedient soldier who has been ordered into a hopeless battle, Tagus stopped too, trying in vain to halt his heavy breathing.

Then he heard it.

From somewhere close by, barely audible above the threatening clatter of approaching boots, came a low whistle.

Glancing around like a trapped animal, he noticed an alcove in the wall next to them, a jagged crease in the stonework where perhaps a tunnel had once opened. It looked impossible to enter. He had not even noticed it before.

The low whistle sounded again, and slowly a gloved hand emerged from the small opening. It gave a little wave before the fingers abruptly flattened against the wall and withdrew from sight.

Aileanor quickly moved to where the hand had been, stepped forward, and abruptly vanished into the stonework. Taken aback, Tagus looked down at Meno, who merely nodded at the alcove and whispered "go".

Bewildered, Tagus stepped forward into what looked like impassable stone, only to find himself staring into Aileanor's dark eyes down a low narrow tunnel that sloped downward into the earth.

"What's that!"

The shout came from somewhere behind and he instinctively plunged forward after her. When the three of them were halfway down the cramped passageway that reeked of stagnant water, he could hear the crash of hobnail boots rushing away down the main tunnel.

"Well Tagus," whispered Meno, turning to his companion as the shouts and crashing feet faded away, "Looks like we're going to have a slight detour. On the bright side, you'll be seeing some history, so treat this as an educational experience..."

Then, from somewhere just ahead, a new voice chimed in. A rough Samosian accent that spoke of a life spent in overcrowded tenements and thankless menial toil.

"Is that you, Meno? Saved yer arse again, ya crazy old bastard."

****

"How long has she been like this?"

Corrie ran her thin fingers down the infant's bony, yellowed cheeks.

"A day, maybe two…By the Great Judge, how am I supposed to tell in this godsforsaken place?"

Octavia's wail echoed eerily from the arched ceiling and rotted colonnades, until it faded along the dank passages of the undercity.

Corrie turned her concerned gaze to the young mother, who looked little better than her sickly daughter. Octavia had been among the first to follow when Corrie had led the survivors through the riverside sewer entrance, where the men of the Association were waiting to take them to safety. What that "safety" consisted of were the tolerably dry remains of what Nicco described as the ancient baths of Emperor Lucius, the infamous conqueror of the east. Now nothing more than a crumbling dust-filled shell deep beneath the streets of Fiore.

The nearby freshwater spring, that had once fed the baths, was its great advantage, but it was hardly a place meant for human habitation. The dust was the real problem. Even though they had swept the place clean to the best of their ability, the epidemic of coughing and congested lungs had taken hold in many. It did not help that half of the hundred or

305

so folk that she had managed to lead from the Asylum were children, their immature constitutions hardly sturdy by any measure.

"Have you been giving her the medicine, like I told you?"

"Yes, yes. That's not the trouble. Oh, Antillia have mercy, I've stopped giving milk…"

Corrie looked at her, the weight of the awful news sinking in, although it was hardly surprising. The poor health, the despair of losing one's community, the fear of never seeing one's husband, parents, neighbors or children ever again. Nicco said that the Asylum had burned for two whole days, blotting out the sun with black pillars of smoke from which the caravans of the slavers emerged with their human cargo.

She had comforted too many sobbing children, too many despondent women. The few men who had escaped among them had foolishly attempted to keep up a strong façade at first, but they soon cracked and sank deeper than anyone into the despair of having their world shattered. That hopelessness, combined with ill-health, was more than enough to cause a young mother to go dry, leaving her infant stranded and without nourishment. It was just another painful reality. A reality she tried not to think of amid her pressing responsibilities. There was no time for tears.

"Be still, sister," Corrie said, resting her hand on the woman's trembling shoulder, "I'll get you help. I swear it."

Octa only nodded, cradling her silent infant in her lap, crouching atop the poor bedding she had been provided with. The poor woman had lost two of her children to the slavers, along with her husband. The baby was all she had in the world.

Keeping her breathing as regular as she could, Corrie slowly stood and surveyed her surroundings, brushing the dust from her own faded and patched dress. Like the garments of the other survivors, it bore the lingering stink of the sewers even after repeated washing.

For what felt like the millionth time, she took in the absurd spectacle of rough tents and lean-tos that had been raised among the fallen masonry, so far from the elements and the open sky. The air was still smoky from the morning meal. She and the women who helped her with the cooking had tried to use as little fuel as possible to keep from polluting the already foul air. Mealtimes being one of the only indicators of the passage of time beneath the earth. She gave an inward thanks to the Association for supplying oil lamps, torches would have been a nightmare down here.

Fortunately, the area of the baths was spacious, capable of housing twice their number. Fresh water was plentiful, and human waste could easily be carried to the nearby sewers. From where Corrie stood by Octavia's lean-to, she could see a trio of gaunt-faced women coming from the direction of the spring, which bubbled up from the rubble in the heart of the baths, hauling buckets of water as they shuffled along in the semi-darkness, a few of them glancing hurriedly at her as they passed. The Stream of Life flowed pale amid these old ruins.

An explosion of harsh coughing nearby snapped her back into the moment, and she hastened forward across the broken stonework of the floor, her shadow dancing in the wavering lantern-light.

She cursed her circumstances, wishing she could use the Craft to bring on a more reliable light source, but to do so would only reveal herself. And that was forbidden. The same went for using her powers to heal.

As more coughing rang out from all directions, she found herself cursing Meno fiercely under her breath. Where was that bloody gnome and his "scientific" medical talents when she needed them? One of the esteemed "Companions" of the Association, he had promised to be here before breakfast, and he was late again.

The old woman was coughing into a bloody cloth when Corrie found her. She bore the same look as the others who had seen the world fall away in blood and fire. So many survivors had asked her about their lost loved ones – a husband, a child, a parent – and it was rare that she could give them an adequate response. Nicco had told her there was nothing but a sea of ash around the burnt-out shell of the old port authority building. Telling the survivors what had become of their humble yet beloved homes only led to agony.

Corrie saved her own tears for when she was alone in her tent, maintaining the calm façade that concealed her own pain and uncertainty, not to mention her own grief for the beloved man she might never see again. None of the Agoge remained and she was the closest thing they had to a leader down here. They were counting on her, even if she was not truly one of them.

She had just given the woman what little sleeping draught she had left, cradling her wizened body as the old one drifted off into slumber, when a young girl whose mother she had helped the previous day ran over to her, wheezing as she tried to catch her breath.

"Mistress Corrie, you must come! To the entrance!"

She heard a commotion through the doorless opening that led to the former front hall of the baths. Following the girl's lead, she wearily stepped through the portal, expecting to find another poor soul with a worsening condition, but quickened her pace when she saw the small group of silhouetted men and women between the colonnades.

Squinting through the gloom, she could make out the features of Gorgo, the Samosian, his face still heavily bandaged from the wound he had received on the day of the pogrom. Meno, looking utterly ridiculous in his apron and goggles, stood next to him, alongside that strange and silent woman he constantly had around him.

But it was the badly scarred face of the fourth newcomer that turned her quick steps into a run, her heart practically exploding from her chest as she ran to him, flinging her arms around his neck and kissing those beloved lips with all the strength that she could muster after so many days spent caged within this tomb. Her Tagus returned the kiss and, for a beautiful fleeting moment, they both felt alive again.

Chapter 17 – Among the Ruins

Their love-making was too short. The moment of bliss so fleeting. When it had passed, Tagus could remember little from their time spent in the confines of the tiny tent with its walls of yellowed cloth. Corrie's naked body had smelt of dust and sweat, but in that moment of their rejoining it was sweeter than the flowers of Antillia's garden, putting Lady Inspiration herself to shame. His maelstrom of emotions had flowed with those of his wife, merging with an intensity born of desperation and the need to hold onto something beautiful in the face of horrific realities.

But those realities refused to wait for long.

"Mistress Corrie!"

The plaintive voice cut like a knife into their reverie, with the woman called Octavia tapping Tagus's foot by mistake in her haste.

"I am sorry, but you and your husband are needed immediately."

Privacy was out of question in such a place. Corrie sighed a despairing sigh, burying her face momentarily against his naked chest before replying that they were coming. There was no time to talk, no time for intimate conversation, no time to relate the details of their ordeal to one another. Both of them had responsibilities.

The trek down from the site of their narrow escape in the sewers to the ruined Baths of Lucius had been arduous to say the least. They had followed a winding path that snaked through the maze of narrow tunnels. Some were almost completely choked with debris and they had only been able to pass through by pressing their backs against the wall or by crawling forward one-by-one on hands and knees. Other tunnels were bone dry, while still others were entirely flooded, forcing them to wade through ice-cold water which gushed through a grating in the ceiling or from a crack in an ancient wall.

Throughout the ordeal, Tagus had marvelled at the condition of his formerly bad leg. The dull pain that had all but crippled him on the day of the riot and which had tormented him for the past ten years, was gone.

Nor did it return after what felt like hours of trekking through the undercity. Was this Meno's work? If so, it was extraordinary.

Unlike the silent Aileanor, their new guide Gorgo had continued to speak the entire time, going on and on in his low-brow accent. He had been one of the masked journeymen who tried to get between the guards and the crowd of Old Believers during the riot and claimed to have narrowly escaped death on the Asylum's barricades. His jovial smile was cut in half by the bandages that crisscrossed half of his face, an injury he cheerfully explained as being the work of a slaver's sword. He went on to say that he had crawled into the sewers after dispatching his attacker. He was now a marked man who would be hanged if caught, something he seemed rather proud of.

"Ya should've seen the way I capped him, Falhorne! Me face all a bloody mess, but I still caved his ugly 'ead in! Yer Falhorne mate said I'd make a fine addition to yer brotherhood one day! What d'ya think o' that?"

Tagus had not replied. The fellow certainly knew how to make light of dreadful situations. He must have had lots of practice. Part of him thought that Gorgo would have made a good soldier, but he dismissed this thought quickly when he realized how much blood the Association man was likely to lose from repeated floggings before getting a chance of closing with the enemy. He was struggling to keep the fate of Tarquinus and the others from his mind, it was simply too painful.

True to form, Meno had never shut up. The gnome had pointed things out as they progressed, illuminating them in the weird light of a strange lantern that he had removed from his bag: the remnants of a carved stone archway at a tunnel junction, the crumbling face of a demonic bug-eyed monster grinning evilly above an old doorway that led nowhere. In one large chamber the broken remains of statues stood in tall alcoves, and Meno had speculated out loud as to whether they were old gods or the forgotten rulers of ancient kingdoms.

"Oh my…by the ancestors is that king what's his name's arms? Aileanor…darling, help me out, I'm sure I was looking at that exact same crest just the other…"

By the time they had reached the shattered colonnades of the baths, at the edge what had once been a wide-open square, Tagus had been well and truly irritated. The reunion with his wife finally giving him escape from the endless lectures whose only benefit had been to keep his mind away from darker things.

When the two of them left the tent, he walked with Corrie through the rows of crude shelters that the Association had set up to house the survivors. Tagus felt their eyes on him, mostly young mothers with children or elderly women. Some appeared relieved that a Falhorne was walking among them. Others wore looks of suspicion, perhaps thinking him a coward or a turncoat for not fighting and dying alongside his brothers. The same sentiment that had hung in the air of the Agoge chamber when Secunda had condemned him.

They joined the others in a deserted area that resembled a miniature amphitheater: tiered seating leading down to a circular area of worn stone, presumably where jugglers and other performers had once entertained the half-naked bathers in centuries past.

Meno looked as entertaining as ever in his goggles and apron, twirling his outrageous moustache as he stood before the small group, that, apart from Tagus and his wife, consisted of Aileanor and Nicco, who sat in front row seats as though they were about to watch a show.

The alchemist's brother was wearing the same long coat that he had worn at the Agoge, and he had let his once neatly trimmed beard grow into a wild mess. His broad-brimmed hat was gone, and his bald head shone in the light of the lantern that sat nearby, bathing the small congregation in its steady glow.

Corrie did not sit down when Nicco motioned for them to do so, but continued to walk purposefully toward Meno, who quickly turned face her, his merry eyes suddenly serious.

"The infant will be fine, my dear," he said solemnly, "I gave Octa the potion. It should restore her milk in a few days, so long as she receives proper nourishment. In the meantime, two other women have volunteered to nurse the child."

Corrie stood over the gnome, looking like a giant by comparison, in spite of her slight build.

"Thank you, my friend," she said. "But we cannot afford delays with those compounds and herbs you promised us. Lives are at stake."

"As I know only too well, sister. You needn't worry. I'm not the moneygrubber I used to be; lack of coin isn't going to stop me from aiding these good folk."

He spoke with his head bowed in response to Corrie's commanding tone. She calmly nodded and sat down beside Nicco. Tagus, who had been silently watching her exchange with Meno, moved to join her.

By the time he sat down, Meno had already begun to speak.

"Well, my brother, do you plan on filling in our Falhorne friend here about what you've found. I'd hate to see him going blind into the lion's den."

Nicco got to his feet, the folds of his coat making a flapping sound in the stale air. Getting up beside his brother, he gave a loud hacking cough, followed by a short curse.

"First of all, Falhorne," he said gruffly, "welcome to your new life as a tunnel rat. You wouldn't be the first among your kind. Going underground is a proud tradition among those who fought against the powers that be. At least you and your heretics got a few more years than I did in the upper air before having to hide out with us non-humans…"

He paused, again coughing into his gloved hand before staring hard at Tagus.

"Has your wife told you much about the Lowtown Monster?"

Tagus glanced at Corrie, who silently shook her head.

"We have had little time to talk."

"Yes, of course," Nicco sighed, "I keep forgetting how time flies. Five days in his majesty's dungeons for you, then three more in my brother's care. It's been an eventful week. There's still a curfew in place, the slums are crawling with goons, royal proclamations screaming about secret cabals of witches casting evil spells to subvert the prince's peace. They're calling on loyal citizens to report all suspicious activities to the proper authorities. It's given the masters an excuse to clean house, if you get my meaning. Seven journeymen and apprentices have been hanged in the last seven days on the mere suspicion of being a part of the Association.”

He paused and wiped his brow with a heavily calloused hand.

“That’s not even getting into what those churchmen have been up to. The Inquisition has its eyes and ears everywhere now. Naturally they blamed the folk of the Asylum for their own fate: accused them of black magic, treason, murdering the guildmaster, rioting, looting, blasphemy, killing followers of the Most High in cold blood etc. etc. I don’t think I need to elaborate further. To put it bluntly, for the sake of peace and moral righteousness, dozens of innocents needed to die and hundreds more loaded with chains. I’m sure the merchants were checking their ledgers with some satisfaction as they lowered De Tolley into the ground…”

He then produced a large parchment roll from his belt and casually flung it at the Falhorne’s feet.

“You might want to see this…”

When Tagus picked it up and unrolled it, he saw a crude illustration of his own face beneath the word “WANTED”. He did not bother reading the accusations. He already knew he was a marked man.

“Your brother told me that you know who is responsible for this. What is this Seven Moon’s merchant cartel? I have never heard of them before.”

Tagus’s voice was cold as he threw the wanted poster to the floor.

“Meno didn’t say much, eh,” Nicco replied with a grin, “Trying to build suspense, brother? Like the time you tried your hand at being the undisputed king of gnomish fiction?”

He gave his goggle-eyed brother a playful shove before continuing.

“Yes, they call themselves the Seven Moons. And I never heard of them myself until a month ago, but they’ve got big players behind them by the looks of it. They’ve set up shop a block from the palace on Council Street, and, as far as we can tell, they’ve got a monopoly on the sale of the folks taken from the Asylum. How newcomers managed to get that kind of privilege over the heads of Duke Gratano’s pals in the merchant guild, I have no idea. But we’ve kept watch. They started shipping people out of the city three days ago, mostly south, no doubt to the Trastamere plantations. So, we'll need to act fast."

"Then why are we waiting?"

Tagus's fists were clenched. His uncertainty and fears falling away amid his rage. He wanted nothing more than to enter this compound and lay about with a suitably heavy polearm until all that remained of the slavers were dismembered corpses. That would be some justice.

"We've delayed because of what me and your wife have found," Nicco replied, unphased by the Falhorne's anger, "this same cartel might have something to do with the murders in the slums. We've been following the killings since they began, given the authorities don't give a rat's ass. And it's worse than I could have imagined."

It was then that Corrie turned to her husband. Her expression grave, her eyes filled with a sorrow that must have been growing there for days.

"The Association tried to warn the Asylum about the slavers before the pogrom," she said. "The messenger tried to use the sewers to reach the Agoge unseen, but the Monster found him. His body looked just like the others when we found it, but it wasn't the only one. Others were scattered nearby, abandoned in the same condition. I recognized some as people who have been missing from the Ox Guts for weeks. The killer is in the undercity, and we managed to follow their trail."

"That's where you come in, Falhorne," Nicco interrupted, "We tracked them all the way to the old temple of Viro, which is practically beneath the foundations of the Seven Moon's compound. The killer's not human. I've had my boys going around in groups of ten ever since Dacon was found shredded, and we've warned everyone here to stay close. The Inquisition might not know we're here, but the Monster does. If whatever it is has any connection with these shady merchants, well…that's not good."

"You told Gio to watch his back with his next shipment, right?" Meno's voice casually chimed in. "He won't want to risk taking it through the gates this time."

"Yes, yes, damn it," Nicco replied irritably, rounding on his brother. "I let him know my boys will be waiting at that spot by the Rivergate and will escort him and all his latest contraband. I know he's your mate; don't you worry your pretty little bald head."

He turned back to Tagus, hands smoothing out his long coat.

"Look, you'd better get moving if you want to see this through. All I'm saying is be careful. I wish I knew what in the pit's name is going on, but I'm just as stupid as anyone else here."

With that, he began making his way up the steps of the amphitheatre, his coat brushing the floor and kicking up small plumes of dust.

He reached the top before glancing back at Meno.

"I'm going to get the rest of the stuff now. I'll be back in one hour. If you're headed to that viper's nest over there, don't do anything stupid."

Meno laughed out loud, somehow managing to sound jolly in the stagnant dusty air.

"Hey, it's not like your eminently reasonable ideas have worked miracles, brother. Maybe it's time for something a little crazy."

"Have it your way," Nicco replied with an exasperated look, "I'm just trying to keep the people we've already saved alive. If you somehow manage to add to my burden today, I'd be elated."

He looked back one more time at Tagus.

"Oh, and Falhorne, don't believe the bullshit Gorgo tells you about his 'heroic escape'. The Templars swarmed over that barricade like wolves. The fellow only survived because he was left for dead and had the bodies of three men piled on top of him. He made up that story about braining the slaver to take himself feel better, I can't blame the poor bastard really."

Nicco shook his head and walked away, vanishing from view.

"Well, my brother sure is one uplifting little bastard, ain't he?"

Meno's belly was shaking inside his apron, only to tense up and look startled when Aileanor, looking like a long pale-faced black cat in her strange outfit, suddenly spoke up.

"I trust we shall be delaying no longer?"

Her voice was calm, but the undercurrent of impatience was there.

"Indeed, my dear, we'd best be underway," Meno regained his composure and dropped his goggles back into place, "Right after these lovebirds here say their goodbyes and all. Let's leave them to it, shall we?"

Aileanor rose from where she sat with all the liquid ease with which a shadow flits in firelight. Both of them ascended the steps, Meno's stout strutting form following her long fluid strides.

"Find us at the entrance when you're ready," the alchemist called back over his shoulder, "but I don't think I need to remind you that time is money, especially for slavers. We'd better move if we want to keep them from cashing in. And Corrie! A promise is a promise! I'll get you those herbs!"

Tagus and Corrie were alone in the amphitheater.

"Strange company you keep down here, darling," he said after a moment of silence during which he had tried to find the proper words.

Corrie looked at him, a half-smile playing about her lips, but exhaustion had not left her dark eyes.

"Strange times we live in, love," she said. "Smugglers are the only thing keeping us alive down here, same as when they sealed the slums during the pox. When folk think you're scum, dealing with real scum to keep your belly full isn't so peculiar. Nicco's a gangster. I've known that for years. But at least he's a bastard with a conscience."

She spoke in the same matter-of-fact way that Tagus recognized from the very first time they had spoken. That conversation too had been in hard times.

"What about Meno?"

"One of the Companions running the Association. He ran the investigation into the murders. They sent samples to him from all the victims, but I only met him down here. The little fellow was standing by those crumbling pillars at the entrance when we arrived, beaming from ear to ear and holding a bag full of medical instruments and potions. He's as crazy as he looks, but he sure helped a lot of folks that day. We had plenty of injuries, some bad ones, and he took care of everyone. He wouldn't accept payment. Just kept right on smiling, even as people were bawling their eyes out in grief. We've helped each other ever since and I hear he helped you too…"

"That he did."

Tagus told her what had happened. He told her of the riot, of Vitus's death, of his arrival at the Asylum, of his imprisonment and torture, and finally how Aileanor had freed him from the royal dungeon. He was aware of the time it was taking, aware that he had to leave, but he would not go before telling her the truth, even when every word of it hurt.

When he had finished, she held him, taking him in her arms and leaning her head on his shoulder. Strong and comforting. Silently reminding him she was there and would remain, just as their love had endured throughout the chaos of life.

"I wish I could forget sometimes," she said softly, "Everything they've told me about the fate of their neighbors. I only did as Jesta asked. I'm the one in charge now that she and the Agoge are gone. Imagine what old Secunda would think of that…"

Her hoarse laugh ended in a coughing attack and Tagus gently ran his hands down her back in response.

"They fought back, you know," she went on, "Let no one say that the folk of the Asylum meekly submitted to those beasts. No armor, no real weapons, nothing apart from history. If it was going to be another Brisi, they were going to fight to the end, like their ancestors did. A lot of the folks here only made it out because the menfolk chose to stay behind. But the women fought too. Some climbed on top of their own hovels and hurled anything they could carry on the attackers. Callidus managed to rescue a few of them…"

"Callidus?"

Tagus pulled his head back and looked his wife in the face.

"He was here?"

Corrie slowly nodded, her expression taking on a nervous appearance.

"I know your feelings toward him. I didn't want to be the one to tell you, but yes, he was here."

"He was supposed to leave the city, I told him…"

"He was the only defender to make it out. The last inside the sewer entrance when the Asylum fell. Full of holes he was. I've never seen a living man with so many wounds. Meno had quite the time patching..."

"Where is he now?"

Tagus could hardly believe it. A turncoat like Callidus risking his life for the Asylum?

Corrie looked away as she replied.

"He's gone. He left two days ago, as soon as Meno told him he was fit to walk. He said he wanted to stay, even volunteered to help storm the Seven Moons compound with you once you'd recovered. But Nicco insisted that he leave. He said the crackdown could spread and the people in Trastamere needed him more. It didn't stop the people from cheering him when he went. They think he's a hero."

"He is no hero," Tagus scowled, "I do not care what he did or claimed to do. And do not be deceived. That one has much to answer for."

"Look, darling, I know," there was a pleading look in her eyes now. "But a lot of folk wouldn't be alive if not for him. When the slavers tried to land a boat by the Agoge, he fought them off almost single-handedly. I saw it with my own eyes. And then, after he'd taken several wounds, he fought alongside the others at the Rivergate..."

"Stop! I will hear no more!"

"Husband, I can't condemn him. People saw what he did. He was the only light this place had at first. Folk who had lost entire families looked to his example. He only left after pressing Nicco on supplies and making sure everyone was getting what they needed. He left with all our blessings. Whatever he did before, he is your ally now. And we need good folk on our side if we want to live."

Tagus sighed and looked back at her. She was his wife. He trusted her word. Even if it did not erase his misgivings about the rogue Falhorne who had defied his praetor.

"Fine. I wish him a safe return..."

****

For what seemed like hours they ventured through the undercity. It was just the three of them again, with Tagus following the lead of Aileanor and Meno as they tread along the twisting passages that had once been city streets. Sometimes the remains of houses or temples could be seen, most of them unrecognizable apart from a partially collapsed column or the marble face of an emperor sticking out of a pile of rubble. The buried ruins of ancient Fiore were silent and still.

Beyond the occasional patch of dimly glowing algae or fungus, there was nothing but deep blackness all around. Even Aileanor's light appeared insignificant in the face of it, until Meno again lit his lantern. Tagus heard the alchemist speak a handful of muffled words before their surroundings seemed to explode with a bright bluish light. It was bright enough to force him to shield his eyes before they finally adjusted to the weird device, which shone more strongly than any lantern he had ever seen. The gnome smirked at his startled reaction, betraying a strong sense of pride in what must have been his own handiwork.

Their pace was steady, in spite of several detours around collapsed passageways and flooded out tunnels. But, after they had been wandering for some time, Meno suddenly stopped, kneeling down beside the crumbled remains of a doorway. The passage beyond the ancient portal was completely blocked by fallen masonry.

He held out his lantern to illuminate something on the dusty stonework.

"Look at this, Falhorne."

Tagus could hear the splash of falling water somewhere nearby as he approached and knelt to see what the gnome was pointing at. Squinting in the bright blue light, he made out what looked like writing carved into the stonework inside the door. He peered closer, seeing the odd characters with their straight lines and crosses spaced at regular intervals between what must have been word groups. The shock of recognition hit him like a thunderbolt.

"A fine sample of the Ormus tongue," Meno grinned at him, "Can you read it?"

Ormus. Tagus had almost forgotten that word.

He stooped down, tracing the ancient letters with his finger. They had been cut deeply into the soft sandstone and were clearly centuries old. After a few seconds, he had to admit he couldn't read them. But he remembered what Vitus had taught him. Something he had briefly mentioned in one of their history lessons back when Tagus and Piso were staying in the old tower of Castle Firente.

He could recall the drafty round room, the shuttered windows, and the slow pace of his mentor's feet as he walked about on constant patrol. Drumming oral stories of the past into the heads of his two pupils.

It had been a tale of the Falhorne known only as the "Shadowman". His true name was unrecorded, but he had led the resistance against the Empire from the southern reaches of Tarn, supposedly after seducing the Tarnish king's daughter and worming his way to the top of court politics through cunning and intrigue. He thus won royal support for his daring cross-border raids as well as a regular base of supply in the fertile floodplain of the River Orm. That was before the Inquisition had infiltrated its agents into the region, unleashing a reign of terror against the Falhorne, the exiled faithful, and their supporters that would culminate in the Emperor Domitian's brutal invasion of the lands to the north.

In the name of protecting their people and the Order which safeguarded them, the Shadowman had combined his cunning with the knowledge of the scholar Telemachus, a fellow exile and believer in the elder gods, to create a secret language complete with its own alphabet. This was Ormus.

The Shadowman was said to have dressed all in black, dyed his shield black, and even dyed his body a midnight blue before leading his followers on nocturnal raids. Many of his followers began to adopt these methods too, which not only assisted with concealment, but also proved to be useful for intimidating enemies; making them think they were being attacked by a howling pack of netherworld demons.

"Defeat in battle always starts with the eyes," he had supposedly said, and such unconventional tactics only added to the Shadowman's legend, with the Church hierarchy condemning him as a demon-incarnate. He and his men were said to have infiltrated the most heavily guarded and impregnable imperial strongholds, until the emperor himself shivered in his sleep for fear of their coming.

Ormus was how they coordinated these spectacular assaults. With individual Falhorne slipping through the defenses and leaving the coded messages behind for the next wave of infiltrators to read, allowing them to slowly build up their numbers and take up positions for a surprise attack against which there could be no defense.

That was the story anyway. He remembered Vitus dismissively saying that it easily could have been a myth. Ormus more likely evolved over generations among Falhorne struggling to survive in the Tarnish borderlands before gradually spreading to other fugitive bands waging clandestine struggles within the Empire itself. It had never been standardized and had fallen out of favor with the Order once the Empire had collapsed. Tagus could barely remember the handful of characters that his mentor had bothered to teach him, scrawled on the back of a sheet of parchment. Some of the characters carved into this door frame did look familiar, but he couldn't be sure if they were the same as the ones that he and Piso had briefly studied long ago.

There was only one sign that he both recognized and understood. It was the coat of arms of the old Falhorne Order. A sigil he knew from looking at the handful of old books and regalia which Vitus had saved from Cera Pelleus before its fall. It had even been emblazoned on his mentor's armor. But all it told him was that a Falhorne had once been here, and had left his mark.

He finally looked over at Meno's expectant face and shook his head. Piso surely would have remembered more.

"Pity," Meno sighed, "I'd been hoping for a Falhorne who could teach me a little of the old tongue and its secrets, but there's barely any of you left who remember the Order, let alone its language."

"My praetor could have…"

Tagus fell silent. He could not bring himself to speak Vitus's name.

The coat of arms had been a secret sign of the Falhorne when they existed as an underground organization. Consisting of three black spears standing side by side within a dark circlet representing the Ash Crown of the Black King and his martyrdom pierced by a dozen lances.

Meno frowned and got to his feet, but Tagus remained fixated on the faded traces of his heritage.

"Can I expect any more delays?" Aileanor asked softly, making both of them jump as it was the first thing she had said since they had left the baths.

The journey continued, but this time Tagus found himself curiously inspecting his surroundings, peering curiously at broken masonry and the shattered remnants of a bygone age.

Meno kept talking. Talking about the long-lost ruins of Norundin-Watan, the great Gnomish city that once stood on the site of Fiore, until it was destroyed by the conquering armies of Reshi nearly two thousand years ago. He talked about the history of his own ancestors, admitting that much knowledge had been lost with the downfall of the old gnomish kingdom that had stretched across the entire region before the rise of any of the human realms.

"It's all buried now. You'd have to go down much deeper than this to see even the palest slice of it. Not something we have time for today, regretfully."

Tagus was hardly listening. He knew that the followers of the Old Gods had taken refuge in many "hidden places", some of them centuries old and used by generations of heretics hiding from the Inquisition and other imperial authorities. This area, deep beneath the sewers of Fiore, deeper than the Baths of Lucius, had evidently been such place.

He saw artifacts in the dust, abandoned in forgotten corners by generations long gone by. Most were very ordinary household items like earthenware jars, but, in the bizarre light of Meno's lantern, he sometimes caught sight of small clay idols and other things that hinted at the forbidden rites that had persisted in these subterranean depths.

Tagus found his heart beating faster. Before seeing the inscription in the Ormus tongue, he had been following the others numbly, trying to forget his wife and their goodbyes. Now he was actively wondering about this place and the ancient days when it had been part of a bustling city full of people like him. People who venerated the true gods, and offered prayers of thanks into Sol's sky, their feet kissing the contours of Mora's earth while they drank of Viro's water and basked in Fiore's flames. Back when the Agoge had been the Fire Lord's temple court presiding over a proud city and not a council of fugitive tradesmen that could be snuffed out in the space of one day.

What a time it must have been. And even after those days were gone, the Falhorne, the warriors of the Black King of Barbarus, had been there to keep the bright flame burning with the promise to remember and restore that which had been lost. Perhaps the Shadowman, Kurnos the Fox, Tallos the Javelin, and those other heroes Vitus had told him of, had walked these very ways and scratched their words into the walls for their brethren to find as they pursued their hidden war against the Betrayer's servants.

But this renewed sense of pride was fleeting. So much had been lost. He felt as illiterate as the young slave he once been, travelling in darkness and ignorance.

****

The whip cracked again, splitting the air with a sound that made Callus want to dive behind old Secunda's legs, to burrow into the earth, to become a rat in a hole.

There was a terrifying whistle as the guard drew back the length of raw hide for another blow, aimed at the red ruin that was now Skarlos's back. Callus imagined steam rising into the morning air from the watchman's mangled flesh.

The whip struck again. Yet still the big man did not cry out. Although his bald scalp was drenched in sweat. His teeth as well as his eyes were clenched tighter than the clamshells that the masters of the orphanage used to have the children shuck for the Fiore merchants.

Callus remembered those days before he had escaped. Escaped from the endless toil, the foul meals, the religious services, and the back of Brother Sorren's hand. Begging in the slums had felt like freedom after all that, at least there had always been somewhere to run to when dealing

323

with the street toughs. But now it was just as the orphanage had been; nowhere to hide and no mercy.

The priests had told him of divine love, that every child was blessed in the eyes of the Most High. But that light had never penetrated to the warehouse by the fish market, into Brother Sorren's office, or into this dreadful compound with its guards and slavers.

Callus wanted to cry out. He was the one who had shielded Thea from the guard who had tried to hurt her. Trying to be brave like the Falhorne master Tagus had wanted him to be one day. Skarlos had intervened, punching the man full in the face.

The big man had volunteered to take the whipping, and was somehow enduring the thirty lashes, even as the bandages over his battle wounds strained with every stroke. The crowd of assembled slaves, forced to watch the cruel punishment of one of their own, winced at the awful sound. Skarlos was brave, but it was not enough. Nothing was enough. Not here.

Just beyond the whipping post lay the barred wagons, the wagons of the slavers, hovering like chariots to the underworld. Looking at those wagons and at the frightened faces, he was sure that Tagus was dead like all the others. The gods didn't care.

Chapter 18 – Monsters

Tagus did not how long they had been journeying through the desolation of the undercity before the rumbling began in the distance, a sound like a hundred waterfalls as they drew nearer. Passing through another carved stone archway, decorated with what looked like corroded stone dragons spitting fire at nothing, they entered a massive chamber, its vastness faintly lighted by multiple shafts in the high ceiling, although little of it penetrated this far down.

They were standing on a stone platform overlooking a large underground reservoir. Three levels towered above them and two more below, each with multiple stone culverts that gushed water from all six stages into the vast pool, which was bubbling and frothing. Stone walkways could be seen jutting out at every level, but Tagus could see they were mostly ruined, whole sections having fallen away into the churning waters.

The falling water wavered and danced in the spectral light of Meno's lantern as a look of undisguised awe spread across his features. He called out to Tagus over the omnipresent roar, his voice displaying an almost childlike sense of wonder.

"Be on your best behavior, Falhorne! This is the Temple of Viro, the Mistress of Waters herself!"

Tagus looked closer and saw it was true. Much of the decor had crumbled away, but some of the culverts above them still had their spouts carved to look like the mouths of fishes, whales, and the scaled faces of the fabled peoples who dwelt under the waves, whose beautiful music called sailors to their doom. Their eyes were now blind holes, their features eaten away by centuries below ground, yet Viro's servants still kept watch over this sacred place.

Awestruck, Tagus could not keep his mouth from falling open as he stepped toward the platform's edge. Vitus had told him that the temples of old Fiore remained, deep under the foundations of the modern city, but he had never seen them for himself.

325

He was so absorbed in his surroundings that he barely noticed as Meno kept talking.

"A grand sight isn't it? I've been down here three times before and the place never fails to amaze. But I wouldn't want to have been here in its glory days. Viro was a hungry mistress, the annals say, who knows how many poor souls met their end in that pool there. You wouldn't catch me diving down there to count the bones…"

He went on. Describing how human sacrifice, mainly of enemies captured in war, had been a regular feature of public rituals, particularly among the followers of Fiore and Viro, during the increasingly war-torn period of the late Five Kingdoms. The sacrificial rites of the Mistress of Waters usually involved ritual drowning, while those of the Lord of Flames consisted of burning victims alive. Neither had been practiced among the followers of the Celestial Court for many hundreds of years.

Ignoring the gnome and his morbid scholarly musings, Tagus was staring at a large stone-cut frieze in a nearby wall. It was flanked by the rushing waters of two culverts carved to resemble oddly scaled fish heads.

He made out the features of an armored warrior. The face had been worn away into blank nothingness, but the scaled armor, the large round shield bearing the device of three jagged shark's teeth and a trident, and the long spear held in the warrior's right hand were still plain to see after countless generations.

It was one of the Chosen. The military orders of holy warriors that had once guarded the temples of the gods. This man, whoever he was, had been among Viro's champions in the periodic ritualized "holy wars" between the great temples that supposedly mirrored the contests of the gods in heaven. He was thus an ancestor of the Falhorne, whom Ishan had raised from among the surviving Chosen following the sack of Cera Infernus.

Tagus stepped to the very edge of the platform, eyes scanning the vastness of the chamber, trying to picture what it must have looked like thronged with worshippers. Their chants and prayers echoing from every level and carried upward into the open sky from which the Sky Lord's rain cascaded into the Water Mistress's depths, giving life to the numberless creatures of the earth. Who were these people? Vitus had told him of their bravery. Of their faith and devotion unto death.

When the Betrayer first showed himself for what he was, raising an ungodly dominion over the bones of the faithful, the adherents of the Water Mistress had decided death was preferable to submission. Rallied by the High Priestess Arista, the Chosen of the temple had made their final stand on the Red Cliffs of Tarquin, dying to the last man against the imperial legions which had closed in on them from all sides.

But it was not only the warriors who had given their lives that day. Vitus once told him that it had been customary in those days for women, and even children, to accompany the male warriors to battle. While they did not fight, their shouts of encouragement, their prayers, and the simple fact that losing the battle would mean the deaths of their families, often drove the combatants to legendary acts of courage and sacrifice.

The battle on the Red Cliffs would be the last time that this tradition was ever invoked. As the last warrior fell, Arista herself had led the women and children in one final act of self-sacrifice; Viro's faithful joined hands, plunging from the towering cliffs into the waters of the Gulf of Remas. They had never surrendered. And they had been here in this very room once. He tried to see their faces and their dark blue robes. He tried to hear and understand their words, trying in vain to communicate with ages long gone by and people long since dead. But all he could hear was the roar of falling water, drowning out the voices of the past.

It was all too much for him.

As he began to move away, something heavy crashed into him from above.

Tagus stumbled to his knees, crying out as slimy scales wrapped themselves around his shoulders and a terrible hissing filled his ears.

He heard Meno shouting something, but could not make it out as mucky coils, rank with sewer water and smelling of dead fish, closed around his throat. His scream was reduced to sickly gurgle as a sharp pain tore through his thigh and he fell face first to the wet stone, breaking his fall with one arm while the other desperately flailed at the serpentine creature that had just sunk its teeth into him.

He gasped as he felt the coils tighten around his neck, trying in vain to draw air into his lungs which felt as though they were being crushed. His hand closed around the beast's body but only slid across the wet scales, unable to get a grip. The hissing filled his ears again and his vision dimmed as he felt it begin to crawl upwards, a hungry predator getting ready to deal the killing blow by sinking its fangs into his neck.

Just as suddenly it stopped. The hissing ceased, and the disgusting scales loosened their grip before falling away dead.

Tagus lay sprawled on the floor, both hands clutching his slime encrusted throat. Looking up he could see Meno kneeling over him, examining the wound in his leg. Tagus closed his eyes tightly as the stinging pain cut through him.

"Easy, lad!" He said sharply, "Stop your flailing! Sewer snakes have mouths as filthy as a rat's midden soaked in eel piss. If you don't want lockjaw, I suggest you stop moving. Aileanor, put that reptile down and help me hold him!"

He felt powerful arms seize his shoulders, forcing stillness into his trembling muscles. Meno had withdrawn a bottle from his bag and a burning sensation made Tagus grit his teeth as some kind of liquid was poured over the gaping hole in his thigh.

"Steady now. This will take away the pain."

The alchemist's voice was calm again, that same soothing voice he had first heard break through the darkness around him days earlier. The burning abruptly ceased. He felt his body and his breathing begin to relax. For an instant, a bright spark of blue light eclipsed the spectral glow of the lantern. The faint scent of ozone hovered in the moist air, and the pain completely vanished.

He looked down at the wound, but there was no trace of it beyond a telltale gash in his leather leggings. The gentle hands on his shoulders drew him to his feet. But the pain did not return.

"There, Falhorne, it's done." Meno's face appeared tired and pale in the lantern light. "I don't normally use melding for such an injury, but we're in a hurry. See a tailor about those pants when you get the chance."

Breathless with shock, his hand touching the gaping wound that was no longer there, Tagus tore his eyes away from the six-foot-long serpent whose body lay in broken "s" shape next to him on the floor. Its skull crushed.

He hesitantly began walking, expecting the pain to shoot through him again at any second, following the others along the ledge and through another arched door in the far wall of the forsaken temple.

All thoughts of his ancestors, all thoughts of the spirits haunting this ancient place, had vanished from his mind. Instead, he found himself glancing nervously around, eyes searching for whatever other subterranean horrors might be lying in wait.

****

The rusty iron door looked as though it had not been opened in a generation or more, welded shut by its corroded auburn seal. It did not appear to have a keyhole and no handle was visible. But Tagus could see scratches in the rust. Perhaps this desolate place was not as abandoned as he had first thought.

They had finally reached the hidden passage that Aileanor said led into the basement of the Seven Moon's compound. Getting there had been arduous. They had been forced to make several detours because so many of the tunnels beyond the old temple had been flooded. His encounter with the sewer snake still fresh in his mind, Tagus could have sworn that he had heard hissing sounds and splashing echoing from somewhere in the dark waters. He had tightened his grip on his sword in response, taking no chances.

The cramped upward sloping passage had been hidden inside a disused and thoroughly rusted out cistern, a level of security that gave Tagus pause for thought. The faint signs of use in the rusty door at the top confirmed his suspicions.

"This feels like an ambush," he finally said to the others, as they halted outside, "Are you sure this is the right place? Have you checked everything?"

Aileanor's pale face looked wraithlike in the blue light as she turned to him with an uncharacteristically agitated frown.

"Of course," she bluntly stated, "Did you not hear? I scouted the entire area of the compound this very day, above and below."

"This is where the blood trail led us," Meno interjected, "It's definitely the right place, but the situation could have changed since your last scouting run, dear, so we'd best be on our guard."

"I always am," she responded tersely, stepping up to the corroded door, "And this is no barrier."

Now that they were standing right outside the strange iron door, Tagus could see that there were symbols carved into its rusty surface. The ugly glyphs, each consisting of a series of crisscrossed slashes, had been neatly arranged into rows that ran back and forth across the entire door. The strange writing meant nothing to him, and its sinister appearance made him feel sure that it was some sort of warning, or even a curse. Surely the Seven Moons would not leave the lower reaches of their compound unprotected. Still, the door and the message appeared far older than they possibly could have been if this newly established merchant cartel had put them here. Could it be a relic of the distant past that they themselves had overlooked?

Whatever the case, Aileanor seemed to know what she was doing. She had lit her strange light, which appeared to issue forth from her hand itself, and was holding it close to the neatly flowing rows of glyphs. She appeared to be reading them carefully. There was understanding in her dark eyes as she began making a series of rapid hand passes over the middle of the door, her palms moving in a veritable blur as she muttered something unintelligible under her breath.

A black spot gradually became visible through the rust. A keyhole.

There was a faint rustling in the dark folds of her cloak, followed by a low scrape of metal on metal. The door slowly swung inward; the sound of its rusty hinges reduced to a mouse-like squeak as Aileanor carefully eased it open.

Tagus saw Meno pick up his lantern and adjust something. The blue light dimmed until it lit only a narrow space around them, barely penetrating the total darkness beyond the door.

Aileanor led the way, her feet silent on the stone floor.

The small room they entered was bare and empty. Unlike the tunnels below, it was bone dry and a heavy coating of dust covered the floor, to all appearances undisturbed. Perhaps it had once been a storeroom, but now the only thing of interest was the door in the opposite wall, also made of iron.

As they approached, Tagus could see that this inner door was far better preserved. Indeed, on closer inspection it looked new. Its dark surface was free of dents, scratch marks or rust, and even the bolts and nails shone brightly in the faint lantern light. Even if no one in the compound had used the hidden sewer exit in a generation, the basement was evidently far from abandoned.

Still, he could hear nothing but his and Meno's slow footsteps as they crept forward.

This time Tagus was close enough to see the tiny instrument that Aileanor pulled from her cloak and carefully pressed to the stainless lock plate. It appeared to be a piece of wire, bent at one end while the other was serrated at the tip. Her wrist seemed to flicker, blurry and indistinct for the briefest of instants, and the door slowly swung inward. Making no noise at all as Aileanor carefully guided its well-oiled hinges open before quickly stepping through.

He and Meno followed close behind, leaving a clear trail of footprints in the dust.

The other rooms they passed through were much like the first, vacant storage rooms joined together by short stone-cut passages. But unlike the first, they were hardly devoid of life-signs. The floors were not dusty, and appeared to have been swept clean recently. One could make out the faint outlines where shelves had been built into the dark stone walls before being hastily removed. These rooms had been deliberately emptied, although there wasn't the slightest clue as to why.

Maybe the slavers were preparing to abandon their base of operations, Tagus thought. Either way, Meno and Nicco appeared to be dead wrong in their assumption that this place was the source of the Lowtown Monster murders. Someone had obviously been down here, but there was no sign that they had entered the undercity or even passed close to the exit.

It was only after passing through several of these emptied out storerooms that they came to a much larger chamber. To the left, a flight of stone steps led upwards, while to the right a large cellar extended into the darkness. But not total darkness.

Floating in the far reaches of the cellar, which was full of crates, boxes and barrels, there was a very faint pale glow, floating in mid-air like a Willow-the-Wisp. It did not seem to be drawing closer, but it was moving, hovering and occasionally darting from side to side in short bursts, spilling its ghostly light over the tops of barrels. The air in the cellar was cold, so cold that it reminded Tagus of the Braxian mountains in winter.

As the three of them stood in the doorway, a second ghostly form appeared, and then a third. All glowing with that spectral light which never seemed to dim or waver. There was menace in the cold air. A lifeless stinging chill that Tagus had never felt before.

He then noticed Aileanor's face. Her normally calm and impassive features were contorted into a feral snarl, like a wild animal that has been backed into a corner. Her white teeth were bared and her black eyes narrowed to near slits.

Not taking her eyes off the lights, she moved her lips. The whispered voice that came out was a low hiss that reminded him of the serpent that had attacked him.

"Get to the stairway. We have got to get away from here. Do it now!"

Hardly daring to breathe, his blood racing as the unnatural cold seeped into his bones, Tagus did as he was told, following Meno quickly toward the steps and creeping upward to the floor above.

Low, so low he could barely hear it, a voice behind him came through in a hoarse gasp.

"No…"

There was another iron door at the top of the stairs. This time their entrance was far from silent as the visibly disturbed Aileanor fumbled with the lock, causing it to rattle wildly, before flinging the door open so violently that it would have crashed against the wall had Meno not leapt to grab it.

Aileanor did not pause, forcibly shoving her companions into the hallway beyond before rapidly closing the door behind them. It slammed shut with a metallic clatter that rang from the high vaulted ceiling, surely being heard the length and breadth of the building.

All three of them stood still, bathed in the flickering glow of a single red-paneled oil-lamp which dangled on a long chain from the ceiling. Tagus had drawn his sword and was breathing heavily, while Meno had shut off his lantern and pulled the pistol from his belt. Aileanor was leaning against the door, her breath coming out in labored gasps as the snarl slowly left her lips.

But nothing happened. There were no shouts of alarm, no approaching footsteps, no sound at all beyond the collective hammering of their hearts.

After some moments passed with no sign of trouble, Tagus's fear turned to anger as he turned to face his former rescuer, his voice hissing with rage.

"What in Gormani's flames were you playing at? Are you trying to get us all killed?"

Aileanor did not even look at him, her face downcast to the tiled floor, her breath coming out in ragged bursts.

Meno shot him an angry look, "This isn't the time, Falhorne!"

He grabbed his companion's shoulders with frantic intensity.

"Aileanor! You have to look at me!"

The gnome gripped her cheeks, stretching his arms to reach the face of the woman who was over a head taller than himself, before shaking her head violently. Aileanor did not respond. Her pale skin was now tinged blue. Her eyes wide and frantic, like those of a wounded animal about to be finished off by a huntsman.

As Tagus looked at them, a strange sensation washed over him, as though he had been immersed in cool water. The anger left his face, the anxiety draining from his nerves, as he felt his emotions withdraw into darkness and nothingness. His mind was a void, detached from the world and floating in empty space.

His companions appeared distant, Meno's voice muted alongside Aileanor's hoarse breathing. It was as though he were looking at them from afar and they were strangers. Nothing clouded his mind, which hung suspended in a state of total focus. Nothing obscured his memory or prevented him from recognizing the state he was in with anything less than perfect clarity. He had entered *Mortis,* the walking death that was the first step on the path to Barbarus. It was the all-consuming focus that allowed the Falhorne to briefly step into the lands of the dead and become, for the briefest of moments, an incarnation of the Black King himself.

It was something he had not experienced in years, something that could only be entered into through the combined will of multiple Falhorne trained in the ancient ways. Fallonier Fields had been the last time that he or any of the Falhorne of Vinos had entered the lands of the dead, and even the initial step of *Mortis* had been beyond the means of the survivors, apart from himself, Tarquinus and Vitus. And Tagus knew from his long-ago training in the forbidden arts of the old Order that the three of them acting together would have been insufficient to enter even this first stage of the walking death. But he was in it now, and somehow, he had entered it alone.

Then it was gone.

Just as suddenly as it had come, the focus vanished and a storm of emotions flooded his mind.

Tagus reeled backwards against the wall, feeling as though he had been punched in the gut. His vision blurred as he reached out to steady himself. What had just happened?

When he had regained his senses, his head still throbbing, he saw that Meno had thrown down his lantern and was rummaging furiously through his bag, audibly cursing as glass bottles and mental instruments clinked together.

After a few seconds he withdrew a tiny glass vial, unstoppering it before holding it up to Aileanor's face. A tiny bluish cloud of vapor formed around her gasping lips, but Tagus could smell nothing. The steady rasping of her breath collapsed into an explosion of choking coughs and she doubled over, sinking to her knees with Meno's steady hands around her shoulders.

"I am sorry…" Came an exhausted whisper.

Tagus moved unsteadily toward the pair, "What happened? What is wrong with her?"

"Never you mind!" snapped Meno, looking up at him from the floor with a face full of bereaved anger, "She'll be fine. And we're lucky. There must not be any guards inside or they'd have been on us by now. We need to get upstairs. That's where the offices will be."

He slowly stood, easing Aileanor to her feet, holding her around the waist by one arm while poising his pistol in the other.

"Information is what we need right now, Falhorne. Let's dig up whatever secrets they've got. Then we'll figure out how to bust your people out of here."

Tagus, bewildered from his bizarre brush with the Mortis state, meekly nodded. Nothing seemed to make much sense. Then again barely anything had since he had woken up in the company of these two. He tried to steady himself, turning all his thoughts to the people he had come here to save.

The hallway was dark and windowless, apart from the single lantern hanging above the cellar door. They passed several other doors, but all of them were locked, in further confirmation that the place had been closed for the night.

Aileanor was walking without Meno's support. But she remained obviously shaken by whatever madness had afflicted her. She moved with none of her usual fluid grace, stumbling like someone who has had too much to drink.

The stairway at the end of the hall stretched upwards, straight and wide. A carpet of deep crimson covered the steps and the walls to either side were draped with rich wall-hangings. At the top of the stairs, through a long narrow window, its view mostly blocked by twisting tree branches, Tagus could see the last red streaks of sunset.

The stairs, as well as the landing above, were completely deserted. Just as in the downstairs hall, no sound could be heard apart from their own breathing and muffled footfalls on the rich carpeting.

The second-floor hallway of the Seven Moons was wide and straight, ending at another large moonlit glass window in the distance. Two red-paneled oil lamps burned at opposite ends of the hall, which was adorned with luxurious purple wall hangings and rich tapestries. The luxuriant crimson rug flowed along its entire length. The dyes for such decorations alone would have bankrupted the average nobleman several times over, thought Tagus as he surveyed the scene.

Two sturdy wooden doors were visible in the right-hand wall, while to the left, half-way down the hall, stood a single iron door bearing the distinctive crest of seven crescent moons arranged in a perfect circle. There was no sign of life and the macabre silence continued.

"That iron door must be a strong room," Meno whispered, "Their offices must be on the left, I'll deal with the locks."

Aileanor was still limping slightly behind as the alchemist rushed forward, clearly impatient to get the job done.

But Tagus hung back. He had not put away his sword and was scanning his surroundings left and right with wary eyes. Something was wrong. He had been in enough ambushes in the field to recognize that unsettling feeling in his gut. The whole building was too quiet. Too empty. Aileanor had been stricken from nowhere and practically paralyzed. And there was himself and the sudden entry into *Mortis* without warning, which should have been impossible.

He slowly walked forward after the others. There was still no sound. No telltale scrape of boot leather on stone or metal on leather as a blade was drawn from its sheath, nothing that would betray a sneaking assailant.

Traps? It would not be hard to conceal a false floor under that thick carpeting. Or a thread-like trip-wire rigged to send some nasty surprise springing out at them from a hidden panel behind one of those equally extravagant tapestries.

He began to examine the wall hangings more closely and quickly noticed odd things. Rich, expensively dyed silks and satins, the material might have been fit for a king, but the quality of the artwork was just terrible. One scene on a large tapestry next to the strong room's iron door appeared to show a coronation: the new monarch being hailed by his courtiers. But Tagus did not have to know a damn thing about art to see how pathetic the detail was. The poorly drawn king looked like a peasant boy showing off to his friends in a funny hat.

The equally gaudy tapestry that stood between the two office doors seemed to show a hunting scene. But the animal being gored by the lances of two horsemen looked more like a man dressed in deer hide. Everything about this place spoke of riches, from the carpets to the crystalline panels of the oil lamps. Would these fabulously rich merchants really settle for such poor artistry?

He was about to check behind the wall hangings when Meno called out to him. He and Aileanor had opened the first of the two office doors. The gnome brandishing the same lockpick his companion had used in the basement.

"Let's check in here first, it probably belongs to one of the directors. If so, there'll be enough secrets to sink their entire operation."

The alchemist determinedly stepped through the dark doorway, Tagus following cautiously.

The large office had none of the hallway's poor taste. The room's single tapestry covered almost the whole wall opposite the door and was a masterful depiction of what looked to be a great southern city. Perhaps the great metropolitan trade center of Avram or one of the fabled cities of Reshi. Indeed, the multitude of figures that thronged the streets, public squares and vast open-air markets had skin dark as ebony, as dark as Tagus's own.

The walls were expensively decorated with oak paneling and bookshelves lined the room on every side, crammed with volumes, scrolls and ledgers. A large wooden desk stood between two curtained windows at the far end of the room. But Tagus's eyes were drawn to the large painting which hung above it, illuminated in complete detail by Meno's lamp.

The artist had done an exceptional job on the detailed contours of the sharp bristly dark beard, deep-set black eyes and weather-beaten leathery skin. He was even clad in the same rich crimson silk doublet and wearing the same cunningly murderous look of pride on his rough face. The painter had done his best to make his subject's features appear more finely chiseled than they actually were, but there could be no doubt.

It was the mysterious advisor who had stood beside Maxim de Tolley on the day of the pogrom. The same man, resembling a grizzled mercenary in fine robes, who had whispered in the guildmaster's ear before the riots and killings began. The portrait bore no name plate, but he was obviously a high-ranking member of the Seven Moons to afford such an office, perhaps even their master.

In the painting, the man stood before an open window, which overlooked a pastoral landscape of farmland. Peaceful villages stood against a backdrop of gently rolling hills, upon which a grand castle could be seen looming in the distance. A full moon hung in the sunlit sky, directly above the castle's highest tower.

Tagus felt the hot blood rise to his cheeks in the dark room.

Meno, who had placed his lantern on the top of the desk, was already struggling to open one of the drawers with the lockpick. Aileanor rummaged through the nearby shelves, her deft fingers quietly rustling the scrolls. She appeared to have recovered from her earlier trauma.

Tagus, struggling to repress bitter memories, tore his eyes away from the portrait and approached the desk. He hoped to be of at least some use in this search for "secrets".

They were not hard to find. In his haste to open the drawers, Meno had neglected to look at the document laying on the desk itself. As though the shadowy owner of the office had been in the process of reviewing it prior to his departure, not bothering to put it away.

Leaning over the sheet of parchment, Tagus felt his heart skip a beat as he recognized what it was. He still remembered the word emblazoned on the paper that the Samosian noble had been holding, a sick smile on his lips as the overseers dragged his new purchase to the waiting wagon. Tagus's old master had stood next to him, warning that his newly acquired "mule" might give him trouble. Tagus himself had been gagged, bound hand and foot: a troublemaker that his master wanted rid of. Even then, as an illiterate boy, he had still been able to understand the word "sold".

The document was a bill of sale, a slave bill of sale, and the list of names was very long indeed. Thanks to Vitus's tutoring, he could now read the full text. But he would have only had to understand one other word. For there were no names. Only "heretic" and the numbers from one to one hundred and thirty-seven. Next to each number on the list was a price, made out not in bronze ducats but in Vinosian gold regals. The differing figures the only way to tell the anonymous "heretics" apart.

Their names were of no matter now. The Inquisition had seen to that, and the slavers would do the rest. They had become property. Tools. And tools, from the hammer to the scythe to the living tool of the slave, needed no names, unless their master chose to give them a little personality once the deal was done. Numbers and price figures would suffice in the meantime.

Tagus felt his blood, already hot, begin to boil as his mind went step-by-step through the process of their ordeal. Their bodies must have already been examined, the brawny field hands separated from the lanky domestics, the pretty potential concubines separated from the plain kitchen help. He wanted to vomit as he remembered what it was like: poked and prodded like a piece of meat.

The seller was listed as "Seven Moons Merchant League". The buyer was not named. But there could be no doubt that these slaves were his people, the victims of the pogrom that had destroyed their homes and lives.

With one trembling hand, he picked up the document, startled suddenly by the click of the lock and the sliding of wood as Meno finally wrenched open the drawer that he had been working on.

There was a short note at the bottom of the page, made in a flowing elaborate script that was completely unlike the neat secretarial hand that had drawn up the rest of the document. It said only this, Tagus struggling to read the words in the low bluish light:

"The above sale has been concluded to your lordship's specifications and suitable transportation arranged for the aforementioned chattel in

accordance with your lordship's will and preference. The authorities have blessed this enterprise. Your profit is assured. Your obedient servant. M.A."

No less than four coats of arms had been stamped to the bottom of the page in hardened red wax that could not have been more than a day old. He recognized all of them: the prince's lion, the Inquisition's three-lobed eye and sun symbol, the seven moons arranged in a hexagonal pattern, the symbol of the cartel itself. Finally, there was the nameless symbol he had seen through the flames below Callus's tearful face as they took him away, the three black pyramids beneath the pale disk of the full moon. This enterprise had indeed been blessed by the authorities.

"Look at this," he said to Meno, holding out the document when he had regained something of his composure.

The alchemist had been in the process of sorting through a stack of papers that he had taken from the desk drawer when he looked up.

"It is signed by the highest authorities in Vinos."

Meno squinted at the bill of sale in the semi-darkness, and swore under his breath.

"Highest authorities alright…I've never seen such a liberally stamped receipt before. It's hardly surprising though. Maybe they intend on splitting the profits too."

He took the document from Tagus and examined it more closely.

"Bloody mad prices too," he frowned. "This is nearly three times what you'd pay for a slave at the riverport these days. Someone's paying through the nose for these folks. Not even the richest planter lord in Trastamere would pay such prices for ordinary field hands."

"If it was so important, why did they not have it under lock and key?" Tagus asked, "It was right there on the desk."

He found himself scanning his surroundings again, his senses twitching uncontrollably as he held his drawn sword.

"They probably figured no one would get a chance to find it," Meno grunted. "The Seven Moons are secretive enough as it is. Its author must have decided locking his office door was enough."

Tagus's mind was reeling. His people had been sold, but where were these monsters taking them? Who was this "lordship"? The prince? It was all too convenient. They had not been attacked or followed. There seemed to be no protections at all, nothing had been guarding the basement of this secretive merchant organization from intruders. And then this important document had simply been left out for them to find…

"Who is this man?" he said at last, pointing to the painting scowling down at them.

"One ugly bastard, that's for sure," Meno frowned, "I can't say I've had the pleasure though. Nicco might know something. He's obviously some bigwig around here. We should find a name if we keep looking."

He went back to sifting through the papers. Aileanor was still poring over the bookshelves. Tagus returned his gaze to the top of the desk. And then he saw it. Something sitting on its very edge, just outside of the halo of lantern light, its shiny surface glinting slightly. He gasped when he saw what it was. An amulet of Mora, the earth goddess.

Cautiously, he picked it up, turning the image of the mountain and the seven blessings over in his hands until he saw the initials that had been scratched into its metallic surface. The same initials that had glinted in the fire light when it had been given to him by his mentor. It was Julia's amulet. The talisman of the woman who had shown the young Vitus the error of his ways amid the burning streets of Brisi.

Tagus felt his body grow rigid as his heart beat faster. The amulet had been taken from him after he had been struck down and captured. What was it doing here? How had the Seven Moons gotten hold of it? And why? Again, it had been left out in the open, as if someone had wanted him to find it. He closed his hand protectively around it as he slid it into his pocket.

"Aha! I've got it!"

Tagus's heart nearly stopped beating. He looked up with a start and saw Meno brandishing another piece of paper. He had just opened the second drawer.

"What is it?"

He half-stumbled over to the gnome to get a better look.

"A letter in the prince's own handwriting. I was his physician; I'd recognize it anywhere."

His hands dug back in the drawer.

"And here's one from his holiness Bishop Theophilus, one from the most gracious Inquisitor Fortius, oh, and four from our distinguished Guildmaster Maxim de Tolley, two from the lord chamberlain…and look at these, letters from the Gonzagas, Gratanos, and just about every noble family this side of the Noctus, what a correspondence these merchants have been accumulating…"

"The new prime slavers to the nobility, I assume," Tagus muttered, attempting to steady himself while tightening his grip on the hilt.

"Well, there has to be information on where they're taking them…"

"Were you looking for this?"

They had not even heard Aileanor approach. She was holding a broad ledger with a black leather cover, opened to the first page.

"Heretics. One hundred thirty-seven. Trastamere," she mechanically read out, "There are five more shipments planned. Eight hundred and forty in all."

"Damn," Tagus cursed, "Does it say where they are being taken in Trastamere? Which plantations?"

She shook her head.

"Well, that's bloody convenient," Meno grumbled as he looked over the page, "Still no buyer listed. It could be any one of the great houses with cash-crop interests. I still can't think why they'd go for such high prices. Are the Moons trying to pass off enslaved heretics as luxury items or something? We'll have to go south after we free the folks here. Callidus and his people will know more."

Tagus nodded, as distasteful as it was to hear that name again. It was a start at least, even if the thought of entering the southern plantation country caused his hair to stand on end.

As the three of them stood in a triangle around the desk, he held out the bill of sale for a second time, indicating the large "M.A." initials at the bottom of the page.

"Do you recognize these?"

The gnome scratched his head beneath his leather cap and looked the note over before shaking his head.

"No. The Seven Moons are a shy lot. The cartel's members never show their faces, going everywhere in blacked out carriages. From what Nicco tells me even their secretaries go by aliases. Their clients also appreciate discretion, needless to say. These initials could have come from anyone. I would think it's this grim fellow in the painting, but, like I said, I've never seen him before."

"I have," Tagus responded, briefly relating how he had seen the man alongside Maxim de Tolley on the day of the pogrom.

"Well the letters certainly bear that out," Meno said, before quickly glancing at the ones from the guildmaster.

"Damn, they don't give a name either."

"Well, who are these blasted merchants? When did they even appear in the city?"

Frustration was rising in Tagus's voice. He was still nervously glancing into the shadowy corners of the room, even though silence filled the air and they were obviously alone.

Meno sighed.

"This place was vacant when I was kicked out of the palace. It was the former manor of the Montanos in the city before they fell afoul of the prince and lost their holdings. Rumor has it they fell afoul of the Inquisition for keeping non-humans on staff, despite repeated warnings. Our merchant friends must have bought it for a bargain price."

"Is this sigil theirs?"

Tagus pointed to the bizarre moon and pyramid device.

"I sincerely doubt it. I know the symbol. I first saw it only a week before the pogrom on a passing trade wagon, and then suddenly a whole slew of them show up for the big day, right on que. They're probably a partner of the Moons. Maybe some middleman consortium of slavers with a taste for exotic art. Whoever they are, they'll be getting a handsome cut from this sale."

"Well," Tagus seethed, "I hope for all our sakes that you have a proper plan to get my people to safety before this accursed deal goes through. We have wasted enough time here…"

He turned impatiently toward the door, angling his sword toward it like it was an opponent in a duel. In his other hand he held up the bill of sale, the paper slightly crumpled from his rough grip.

But he stopped dead in his tracks when an icy hand gripped his shoulder, and he heard the urgent whisper in his ear.

"Do not move…"

The shadows in the corners of the room seemed to grow darker along with the tension in Aileanor's voice. Even the light of Meno's lamp appeared to deaden and grow fainter.

"There are guards outside," she went on. "At least fifty. They are loading people onto wagons. The whole courtyard is lit with torches."

"What? How did we not hear them?" Tagus whispered back in disbelief.

He got his answer.

Tagus turned his head, only to see the bill of sale that he had been holding directly in front of him neatly bisected by a curved steel blade. So sharp that it cut through the paper like melting butter.

He cried out in alarm, bringing up his sword as the black clad figure before him instantly recovered and sent a second thrust angled directly at his unprotected throat. It easily would have pierced had he not instinctively turned his body.

More than twenty years of muscle-memory surged through him along with adrenaline, but the flurry of blows came so fast that he was straining to mount an effective defense. He was barely able to parry his assailant's third thrust which would have impaled his heart.

He saw that there were more of them. The shadows in the room seemed to have come to life with these dark-robed swordsmen; hooded, their faces hidden behind black featureless masks. They made no noise apart from the hiss of their scimitar blades as they arced through the air, striking out with the speed of viper fangs.

Meno had ducked back against the desk, the tip of his assailant's blade embedded deep in the wood above his head.

Aileanor had drawn a short sword from her cloak. She had clearly recovered her former uncanny strength, as she dextrously parried the blows from yet a third attacker.

The close muggy air of the office had become as ice cold as that of the cellar.

Just inside the office door stood a figure that was neither robed nor masked. The woman's head was defiantly uncovered, showing her finely hewn aristocratic features. As regal as the gaudy leather doublet she wore, its chest quilted and dyed crimson and purple inlaid with serpentine black dragons, while her finely worked black leather leggings conformed fully to her lithe form.

Her blond hair was cut short, in the same manner as the female mercenaries Tagus had served with on occasion, but her piercing hazel eyes were almost amber in color and did not have the jaded look of a woman forced to prove her worth again and again on male-dominated battlefields. They were cruel, commanding and as sneeringly confident as her smile, as if the whole scene existed solely for her entertainment. She had not even bothered to draw the twin short swords resting at her hip, watching as her henchmen lay into him and his companions.

The blows kept coming as Tagus struggled to ward off his mysterious foe. The warrior was fast, inhumanly fast. He barely blocked one thrust and the razor-edge of the scimitar slid down his left arm as he narrowly deflected a slash aimed at the side of his neck. Fortunately, Jesta's mother's armor held.

He gritted his teeth and attempted a riposte aimed at the swordsman's throat, but his blow was easily blocked and the return strike narrowly missed Tagus's jugular.

The movements of his enemy were calm, emotionless, and made with a deadly certainty and focus. It reminded him of a warrior locked in the *Mortis* state in the heat of battle. He had somehow entered the walking death himself downstairs, but now all trace of it was gone. He knew, as the arthritis begin to take hold of his sword arm, that he could not match his opponent.

Whatever he was facing was not of this world.

He was so caught up in fighting for his life that he did not see Aileanor's move. Only a small flash, like the match of a musket, only brighter.

Suddenly one of the cloaked swordsmen toppled backwards, a black viscous substance hissing as it burst forth from the gaping hole in the faceless warrior's chest.

But the body did not strike the floor. Hovering above the carpet, it appeared to disintegrate in mid-air, silently merging with the shadows. In seconds it was gone.

The contemptuous smile on the strange woman's face did not change when she saw this. She nodded in satisfaction, gazing at Aileanor like a master watching over their apprentice.

The warrior facing Tagus suddenly stepped backward, as if it had sensed that the odds were shifting against it.

The swordsman whose blows Meno had been clumsily dodging turned, barely deflecting a slash from the flickering edge of Aileanor's short sword. The blade moved so fast that it was a complete blur.

Her attack was instantly followed by a blinding blue flash. The unearthly warrior pitched over and came apart as bizarrely as the first. Black liquid streamed from its collapsed side and rose into the air as if it had shadows for blood, while the wickedly curved blade disintegrated as quickly as its bearer.

Tagus saw that the alchemist's twitching hands were glowing, held together in front of his chest and encased in a nimbus of crackling static. The sudden healing of the snakebite had aroused his suspicions, but now it was clear that the gnome was a worker of magic.

Again, the strange woman gave a satisfied nod in response.

Tagus struck out at the final swordsman. Bringing his sword from below in an underhanded "Samos Scythe" attack, after his foe had easily blocked an overhand "Avanti" strike steeply angled toward the neck.

The pain in his arthritic hand was burning, shooting down his arm with every movement and forcing him to grit his teeth. But his enemy seemed slower now, as if the evil magic that drove the inhuman warrior were somehow waning.

It barely dodged his attack, and was utterly helpless against Aileanor's onslaught, which in an instant had cut straight through the dark cloak, neatly removing the creature's head. It immediately erupted into a shower of darkness which quickly vanished into the air.

The woman by the door nodded her satisfaction yet a third time, calmly crossing her arms in front of her richly patterned doublet as they all turned to face her. Her otherworldly servants had been defeated, and yet she showed no sign of fear.

Tagus noticed that Aileanor's face was once again contorted by intense emotion as she looked upon the stranger. There was hatred, shock, but also something else, something like familiarity, even kinship.

"Cybelle" she whispered through clenched teeth, her short sword glowing with a cold blue light.

"Aileanor," the woman said, in a voice that was every bit as proud and sneering as her lips, "I see you have not completely lost your edge, girl. Fortius would be so proud."

"Fortius is no longer my master," Aileanor hissed, her body lowered into a combat stance that placed all the weight on her back foot, as if she was preparing to spring at her mysterious foe.

"Nor mine," the woman casually replied, hazel eyes twinkling in amusement, "I serve far worthier masters now. Do not worry, child. I did not come here to fight. Only to give you a little test. You looked so…off-balance before. I had to know for certain that you remembered your training…"

"What do you want?" Aileanor did not shift her stance or lower her blade.

Meno was cowering behind her. His back pressed against the slashed and gouged wood of the desk, as if he sensed something about this stranger that had made him want to be as faraway as possible.

The woman laughed at Aileanor's question in a way that sent Tagus's nerves trembling. He had his own sword angled toward the stranger, but had the unsettling feeling that it was useless. The pain continued to shoot up his arm, and the blade was shaking in his hand.

"You have a new man, it seems. And a Falhorne no less. Such exotic tastes!"

She looked Tagus up and down and smirked.

"What do you want, Cybelle? Why are you here?"

Aileanor's lips were now in a snarl, like they had been in that moment of terrified confusion in the compound's basement.

"I have told you. I came to test you. But be warned, child. Next time it will not be so easy. You and your friends are on a dangerous path. If you continue, those I serve will lose patience very fast. Remember that you can always return…"

"No!" Aileanor shouted furiously, her jaw clenched.

All amusement had left the woman's face. But she did not move or attack. She simply vanished, fading away into the shadows as if she had never been there at all. The three of them were alone in the dark room. The unnatural cold was gone, replaced by closed stuffy heat.

"What were those things?" Tagus breathed, his chest heaving, "And who was that…"

"Wraiths," He was surprised when Aileanor, rather than Meno, responded, "And we are being hunted."

She was looking at him straight in the eye, her dark gaze striking through him as she spoke.

"Well done, Falhorne. Not many humans have stood against a wraith and survived. We walked right into their trap. They could not have done that had I been fully in control of myself…"

Meno, who had been trembling with his back against the desk, finally stepped forward, supportively resting his hand on her shoulder.

"It's alright, love. You saved our skins, that's for damn sure."

The gnome's teeth chattered as he spoke. His eyes were exhausted. And the magic that had played about his fingers was gone.

Tagus stared back at Aileanor, unable to process what she had just told him. His pale-faced companion stood there, as still and enigmatic as ever. The short sword with which she had vanquished their bizarre foes was gone, along with its mysterious blue glow.

"How…how did you do that? I have never seen…"

"Training," Aileanor replied, not waiting for him to finish, "I would explain further, but this place is not safe for us. We must leave."

Tagus's frightened mind was a maelstrom of unanswered questions. But they were all interrupted by the sounds outside: shouted orders, the clattering of chains, and the creak of wagon wheels…and beneath it all, the drag of dozens of pairs of hopeless feet through the dust. They came from the courtyard outside that had, by some awful power, been muffled entirely only moments before.

An anguished scream of pain sent him running to the office's iron-barred window. He threw back the heavy curtain and looked out, gasping as he beheld the terrible scene.

The cobblestoned expanse of the courtyard was surrounded by a high stone wall. It was packed with soldiers, all of them armored and equipped to the same expensive standards as Maxim de Tolley's personal guards had been on the day of the riot, their wicked halberds shining cruelly.

It was also crowded with wagons: the same iron cages on wheels that his people had been herded into in the midst of that burning street. So many of them that they obscured the view of the compound's outbuildings. Blazing torches and lanterns illuminated them in an evil glow, reflecting off the iron bars.

And he saw the people. His people. Once more forced into lines before the black maws of the wagons. Three were being loaded. Five others already had been. And at least nine others stood waiting like hungry beasts for their human cargo. They were shipping them out under cover of night, like cowards, away from prying eyes.

Tagus was too far away to see the faces, the tears, the sullen resignation, the emotionless stoicism held over abysses of fear. But he felt them. He felt those haggard outlines and broken silhouettes of creatures no longer seen as men by the monsters who now held them in their grasp. And he knew he could not get to them. Once again, he was powerless.

He seized the bars on the window in rage and frustration, as if he too were caged and was about to be dragged off into oblivion…just as a certain young boy had been.

"Tagus."

Weeping, tears pouring down his cheeks, he turned his head to see

Meno standing next to him in the stifling shadows.

"We have to go, now," he said, placing his hand on Tagus's shoulder. "Please, we're not abandoning them. We will never abandon them."

"I will not see my people sold as cattle!"

Tagus's fury was drowned out by the rattling of chains and the harsh shouts of the overseers. Tears continued to stream down his cheeks as he looked at those three ragged lines of men, women and children. He saw Callus's fearful face in every one of them.

"You won't be any use to them if you end up dead," Meno's went on. "We know they're headed for Trastamere, and so are we. The Association has contacts there that will be able to help us. Now come on!"

The gnome's grip was solid. Unwavering. Just as Vitus had always been.

Closing his reddened eyes against the terror, his breath hissing through clenched teeth, Tagus nodded and turned around.

Meno gathered up the letters and documents, stooping to pick up the neatly punctured bill of sale, before making for the office door with the others in tow. Tagus willing himself to put one foot in front of the other as they left that nightmarish place.

Outside in the second-story hallway, he again had to fight down the urge to panic and run. The tapestries with their crudely detailed scenes were gone. A blank stone wall met his eye, in the center of which stood an open door leading to a small room. It was completely empty apart from the three naked bodies laid out in a tidy row upon the black shroud that covered the floor. Their broken, lifeless forms arranged in macabre poses that reminded Tagus of giant puppets.

****

There was no time. Corrie's arms felt as fleeting as the words they spoke in the dusty air, outside the ruined Baths of Lucius. Tagus had been unwilling to go inside, unwilling to stand before the survivors of that bloody day and admit his failure to bring back even one soul; even one of their lost relatives. Instead he cried in his wife's arms as he told her farewell.

The Tio was splashed with bright moonlight as they emerged from the low tunnel, having crawled nearly up to their bellies in stinking sewer water for what had felt like miles. Even though Gorgo had insisted that it was only a few hundred yards. Tagus and Aileanor were wet to the waist, while the smaller Meno was thoroughly soaked, barely able to hold his head above the slurry. The gnome was spitting mud from his mouth, having fallen into a pool of stagnant water after being practically spat out of the pipe-like tunnel opening by the current.

The three of them stood together on the riverbank, in the shadow of the city's southern wall. Fiore was quiet as the grave behind its high battlements. The curfew Meno had spoken of evidently remained in full effect. Tagus wondered how much longer Chero intended to keep his capital under lockdown just to catch one man. The merchants would not be pleased with the loss of profits, even if they were still baying for the monarch to avenge their guildmaster.

The mighty water gates for which Fiore's riverport was famed stood closed and barred. The great archway blocked by a massive portcullis of finely wrought steel bars that the prince had purchased five years ago from the manufactories of Tarn. Its frame had supposedly been cast all in one piece via methods Tagus could not even imagine. The river water made a hissing noise as it passed between the bars, forming miniature rapids that resembled boiling cauldrons in midstream.

They were at the edge of a swampy area of wetlands, flanked by the drooping spectral forms of willow trees, one of which sheltered them from view as the long dark shape of a river vessel came into view from downstream. As it approached, they could hear the lapping of its double banks of oars hitting the water in rapid succession. Soon the mouths of the war galley's brass cannon were glinting in the moonlight as the ship and sea-dragon arms of Tarn fluttered in the night breeze from its top mast.

The deck of the ship was bathed in the glow of several lanterns and Tagus could see musket-armed sentries pacing back and forth as the vessel approached the Rivergate and began to turn. One bank of oars being hauled in while the other thrashed madly to bring the ship about. The three of them remained hidden in the shadows as it reversed course and continued its patrol, finally passing from view beyond the trees.

"A fine ship," Meno muttered beside him, still cleaning the mud from his long moustache, "I'm so glad they could join us on our little excursion. Facing down batteries of cannon while filthy and sleep-deprived truly enlivens things. Too bad they're also blind as bats it would seem."

Aileanor rolled her eyes as the alchemist shook out his sodden apron.

Tagus's eyes followed the in the ship's wake. The Tarnish cartel chiefs were clearly doing their part to enforce the prince's decrees.

"Alright," the alchemist huffed, "Stay in the cover of the trees. The village isn't far."

Tagus was exhausted and had to force his legs into motion along the muddy overgrown path that was barely visible in the darkness. Apart from a brief rest outside the old baths, they had been travelling since sunup, mostly in the dank and lightless reaches of the undercity. That he had been able to defend himself at all against the terrifying ambush was surprising. Jabs of pain continued to shoot through his arthritic right hand.

The return journey from the Seven Moon's had been a hard slog, as had the trek through the sewers to what was the Association's secret way in and out of the city. Having just used it for the first time, he couldn't say that he envied those who had to use it on a regular basis to bypass the city's heavily guarded gateways. They might as well have been giant sewer rats to crawl into Fiore that way. He hoped the tiny half-drowned tunnel was not the only way that the survivors were getting their supplies.

Tagus fought to keep his wife's sad face from his mind as he staggered on under the dark trees. She deserved better. Their goodbyes had been so brief. His departure so sudden. Not since his days as a slave had he possessed so little control over his life. Forces so much bigger than himself, forces he did not understand, appeared intent on controlling his every move as he was pulled onwards beyond the streets of a city that was no longer home. Away from the woman he loved.

They were now on their way to Trastamere. Heading for a place that Tagus had begged every god in the firmament to never see again. But he would rescue his people, even if it took him into the pits of Gormani itself. Even if it meant that he would never look into Corrie's lovely eyes again. It was in the gods' hands now. For all he knew, the dark things that he had seen in the merchant's office were still hunting them and they would be dead by morning, their corpses washed up by the river.

The mosquito infested swamp was behind them now. They had reached an area of woodland some distance from the riverbank. Aileanor led the way beneath the swaying shadows, her low light bobbing from her hand ahead of them as they passed through low underbrush that looked as though it had been eaten back by hungry sheep or goats. The lights of a small village soon came into view through the trees. The moonlight falling on the whitewashed mud walls of a cluster of one-story cottages.

Meno drew a finger to his lips as they carefully made their way around the perimeter of the village, well beyond the weak circles of flickering firelight that spilled from the small glassless windows.

When they were behind a particular cottage on the far side of the tiny settlement, a cottage every bit as nondescript as its neighbors, the alchemist brought both hands to his lips and blew through them in a low whistle.

At first nothing happened. A candle-flame could be seen burning somewhere beyond the tiny back window, which had been partially covered by a sheet of tanned ox-hide. Suddenly it moved and came closer. Rising as if someone had just picked up the candle and was moving to identify the source of the sound. After a few seconds another low whistle could be heard, this time from inside the cottage.

The candle abruptly went out.

"Come on," Meno whispered.

They began creeping forward into the darkened yard.

When they had passed a crude shed and an empty animal pen, Tagus noticed a high rampart of cordwood stacked against the cottage's rear wall. He watched as Meno began to dismantle the woodpile, methodically gathering armloads of split logs and carefully lowering them to the ground. Aileanor moved to help him, and soon all three of them were in motion, removing the last of the wood until the whitewashed wall was exposed.

Without speaking, Meno pointed to the ground at their feet. In the dim glow of Aileanor's light, Tagus saw a little square trapdoor embedded in the earth. Its formerly white paintwork had faded to a dull grey and it looked barely wide enough for a man to squeeze through.

With a half-smile, Meno fiddled in his pocket for a few moments before drawing out a small copper key, which he lowered to the tiny lock plate on the trapdoor lid. It gave a tiny click and the gnome carefully slid it open, revealing pitch darkness below.

"Ladies first," he grinned at the unresponsive Aileanor.

With her usual catlike grace, she lowered her lithe form through the narrow hole and vanished from view.

When they had all dropped down the trapdoor, with Meno being the last to shove his stout frame through the narrow opening, Tagus could hear the lid being slid back into place. Seconds later, Meno's lantern came on, nearly blinding him with a flash of blue light.

Squinting, he took in their surroundings.

They were in what Tagus at first took to be a simple cellar, its worn stone walls damp with condensation. But as his eyes adjusted to the light, he saw that the basement extended far further than would have been possible for the cellar of a humble peasant cottage, which would not have had the luxury of stone foundations to begin with.

The space beneath the cottage was the size of a barroom at a large inn, and most certainly predated the tiny house by centuries. Perhaps it had once been the basement of a manor or temple. There was a ladder in the far corner, leading up to another trapdoor that must have opened into the cottage itself. The rest of the space was empty, apart from some barrels and burlap sacks filled with grain and other dried foodstuffs. Three sleeping mats had been laid out on the floor nearby, and between them was a large leather bag with its drawstring top pulled shut.

He turned to see that Meno had removed the short sword from his belt and was lightly tapping on the cottage floorboards above his head with its pommel. After thumping the wood three times he set the weapon down and sighed. Then he walked back over to the trapdoor and listened. Tagus could faintly hear footsteps in the grass and the sound of wood being moved, as though someone outside was stacking the firewood back into place against the cottage wall.

"Well, that's that."

Apparently satisfied, Meno returned to the middle of the large room where the sleeping mats were laid out. He stripped off his musty apron and flung it to the floor before practically falling down onto one of them.

"Welcome to our glorious hovel," he said, turning to Tagus with an exaggerated yawn that made his mouth look like a cavern opening.

"A good friend of the Association lives upstairs and the old codger's been sheltering us riff-raff for years in his nice smelly basement. We'll be safe here until morning."

He chuckled and gestured to the bag.

"If you want to change out of that sodden get-up of yours, feel free to take what's in there. I'd let that armor dry if I were you."

Tagus did not reply. He felt like a man who has just been shaken awake, only to find himself in a strange and unfamiliar place. He found himself reaching into his pocket, turning Julia's amulet of Mora over and over in his hand, trying to ground himself amid the confusion, but all he could think of were endless questions. Questions he was too tired to ask and could tell that Meno was too tired to answer.

The alchemist had fallen back upon the sleeping mat, his breath coming out in labored bursts.

Aileanor, for her part, showed no signs of fatigue, casting about the cellar like a she-wolf securing her lair.

He could not figure her out. She had appeared from nowhere to free him, guided him through a forsaken tunnel network, shown the way through along abandoned sewer systems, broke into a heavily guarded merchant headquarters, been seized out of nowhere by some bizarre sickness, yet still fought off an entire band of attackers who had likewise seemingly emerged from nowhere. Then there was that strange woman, Cybelle, who appeared to know her and who spoke of "tests" and former employment with the Inquisition. Who in Gormani's flames was she? And where had she gone?

What were these beings that had attacked them, only to vanish into nothingness? Tagus could only think of the stories, the old wives' tales, of the "nightmare empire"; where corpse-kings reigned over unthinking legions. The slave girl, Nayla, had never gotten enough of scaring him as a boy, with her wild tales of blood sacrifice, dark magic, and things that were once men. But he was grown now, and he knew that real monsters wore human faces and breathed the same air.

These "wraiths" were probably nothing but mortal assassins with a strong gift for trickery and subterfuge, the best merchant league money could buy. Their talents were indeed remarkable, especially this "Cybelle" who had made it look like she had faded away into nothingness…and then there had been the vanishing tapestries and the corpses in the tiny chamber.

It gave him pause remembering how his mother had always left the room whenever Nayla went off on her morbidly silly tales, or told her to be quiet if she was in a bad mood. He had looked into her face once when she put an abrupt end to one of the young girl's more outrageous efforts, and amid the irritation he was sure that he had seen fear in his mother's eyes.

At length he dismissed these wayward thoughts and pulled off his sodden leather jerkin, his weariness dragging him down like a stone onto one of the empty mats.

He exhaled in a long sigh. He was still alive. His quest had begun. But, unlike the legendary trials of Ishan the Founder, it was hardly heroic. A fugitive from royal justice, he barely knew what he was doing. At least the gnome had proven trustworthy, even if his partner was more than a little odd. He thought back to what the alchemist had said, promising to free his people, to never abandon them regardless of what happened. It was a pledge that Tagus had never expected to hear from anyone.

Overwhelmed by thoughts, he soon fell deep into an exhausted slumber.

Tagus found himself dreaming again. His nightmares returned and, just as before, the world around him was consumed by flames, a city on fire. Thatched roofs blazed like torches and molten drops of lead rained from the towers and belfries of the grand buildings.

But there was no Black King looming above and the heavens were godless. Indescribable heat seared at his flesh, but did not burn him, even as the cobblestones melted beneath his feet and a black void swallowed his sight. He wanted to scream, but no sound came from his lips as he rose his arms to shield his face from the inevitable.

When he looked again, Vitus was standing there in full battle regalia, as he had appeared at Fallonier. But there was nothing but shadows around him, a twisting dark mass that writhed like a nest of vile spiders.

As Tagus watched, the stygian darkness seemed to peel back his mentor's plate armor, disintegrating the ornate legacy of the Order's smiths in a heartbeat, and exposing the mangled, broken flesh beneath. The praetor grinned through broken teeth. His tortured body obscured by the clawing shadows from which a hand emerged. Its fingers were snapped and bloody, yet what it held shone with a brilliant yellow light, like the heart of a forge.

It was Julia's amulet.

Tagus extended his hand, trying to reach him, trying to grasp the hand that had once pulled him to safety from dark waters, trying take hold of what his mentor was offering. He was so close.

"All too late."

The broken jaw exploded into hysterical laughter as the mangled flesh disintegrated into the writhing shadows. Tagus covered his ears and fell, his face hitting something hard.

When he looked up, he felt the jolting motion of the slaver's wagon beneath his youthful hands, his ears filled with the rattling of the bars and the rumbling of the wheels.

In panic, he scurried forward on hands and knees to the iron grill of the wagon's door. There was the manor, the road, the high hedges, and there were the two figures. His father wore the same proud and ambivalent expression as his own son was taken into slavery. But it was not his mother who stood beside him now. It was Cybelle. Looking exactly as she had in that evil room as the shadows came to life. Her cruel eyes shone, impossibly bright, above her sneering lips.

"Such a stupid boy…"

Tagus was struck violently from behind and everything spun into darkness.

He awoke, his chest heaving and cold sweat drenching his brow. He was lying on his back on the hard cellar floor, looking up into the blackness.

Meno lay nearby, still snoring contentedly on the mat.

Aileanor was nowhere to be seen. And the only sound was the faint whisper of the wind beyond the nearby trapdoor, clawing at Tagus's mind with the terrors of the past.

****

They left the cottage before sunup.

Tagus's body felt as heavy as a block of stone. His head ached like it had been struck with a cudgel. Meno looked little better. Only Aileanor appeared completely awake and unphased.

After a simple meal of bread and cheese, that Aileanor did not partake in, Meno stood, again knocking three times on the ceiling with the butt of his sword. The response was not long in coming, and soon they could hear the sounds of the woodpile being dismantled outside.

The sun was only just beginning to creep over the trees around the village by the time they had all scrambled up through the trapdoor. Meno glanced once at the sun and nodded to himself, before purposefully marching off toward the woods as though he were late for some appointment.

Tagus followed the alchemist unthinkingly through the trees and mercifully light underbrush, his mind half-dazed from the trauma of his dreams, his legs protesting with every step. But by the time they had reached the broad paved stretch of a south-running road, cutting through the woodland with its high banks and parallel ditches, his senses had returned and he could not contain himself.

"What in the infernal pit are you playing at, gnome?" His voice came out in a furious whisper as he glanced up and down the empty arrow-straight expanse of road, "Are you trying to get us all killed? This is the most heavily patrolled highway in Vinos!"

His blood was racing as survival instinct purged the aches and pains from his tired body. The foolish little man was casually standing in the open beside the Great South Way, the main trade route between Fiore and Trastamere that imperial engineers had cut in a straight line across the Vinosian heartland almost seven centuries ago. They might as well have been standing on a target range. Given all that had happened, the prince's men were surely sweeping the roads around Fiore as thoroughly as the city's streets and sewers. Why in Gormani's flames were they leaving the cover of the woods?

Meno gave Tagus a grumpy and sleep-deprived glance over his shoulder.

"Be quiet," he snapped, "Just get behind those bushes and trust me."

Tagus turned to see Aileanor holding something out to him. A cloak. The same cloak she had handed to him during their escape from the palace, and as musty smelling as ever. He sighed, nodded, and put it on over his now thankfully dry armor, before crouching in the undergrowth.

He still had a good view of the road. Paved with time-worn flagstones, it had once linked the Empire and the distant kingdoms of the southlands. The last time Tagus had traveled it was as a mercenary on horseback, headed out on campaign in the southern marches five years before. But that was not the memory that flooded into his mind as he looked down at those worn stones over which so many feet, hoofs and wheels had flowed across the centuries.

What he recalled was the view of a young boy chained inside a bouncing, rumbling cage, watching the flagstones slip by beneath him, and wondering where he was being taken. His senses aflame with anxiety, he found himself trembling in the cover of the bushes.

Meno, however, remained still. He had backed up slightly and his small frame was half-hidden in a weed-choked ditch. Tagus was still wondering what the gnome was playing at when, from the direction of the city, came a loud bang and the clatter of hooves on the flagstones. He cringed, half-expecting the horrific silhouette of a slaver's prison wagon to come rumbling into view.

But when the source of the noise became visible at the crest of a small rise, he saw that it was a merchant's caravan; a small enclosed cab followed by a large flatbed divided in two, with each section covered with a tarpaulin. A team of four large horses pulled the rig and yet the jovial and colorfully dressed driver seemed to be alone, which struck Tagus as being odd to say the least.

Ever since the enclosures began ten years ago, resulting in the eviction of the peasantry from the lands claimed by the great plantations, the numbers of cutthroats and thieves had risen dramatically. Even with the prince's patrols, any merchant traveling the road to Trastamere was bound to have an entourage of at least five armed men. Many Tarnish merchants moved alongside small armies of mercenaries to keep away those who had turned to vagabondage to fill their bellies. This solitary trader was either mad, dangerously overconfident, or both.

Meno emerged from the ditch as soon as the man had come fully into view. Standing by the roadside as though he had been expecting the caravan and its driver all along.

Upon seeing the gnome, a rather exaggerated look of surprise crossed the man's lips. He immediately reined in his team as Meno called out to him in a loud clear voice.

"Giovanni Lechianno! You are late, my ever so punctual King of the Southern Roads!"

He sounded like he was hailing an old friend.

The man, clad in an outrageously patterned doublet striped in red, blue, green, yellow and pink, his head covered by an equally outrageously patterned hood, looked confused at first. But then his cleanshaven oval face broke into a wide comical grin.

"Well I never! It's the Grandmaster Shortstack himself! Did ye finally decide to become a pedlar after your luck ran out with that cushy court job, Meno?"

"Ha! More like a wandering faith healer with a specialty in getting the warts off of peasant grandmothers' buttocks, but you're not far off. You might be getting some competition as the only alchemist/travelling salesman in these parts if the Holy Church doesn't get me first!"

Meno was grinning wider than ever. It was clear that these two went way back.

The trader chuckled merrily, "Guess I should sell you to the first inquisitor I see then; it would be good business sense, if not necessarily etiquette. Oh, and I assume you, and whoever you've got hiding in the bushes over there, need a lift or something. Planning on appealing to my religious sense of charity, eh?"

"Oh, come on old man!" Meno replied mockingly, "Do you really think I'd put my trust in your spirituality after you tried to sell me on that 'God of Wanderers' horseshit, with its heavenly rewards for you and your fellow pedlars? So much for merchants not being superstitious. I hope they paid you for that little performance by the way…"

His voice lapsed into a deep belly laugh and he had to steady himself before continuing.

"This is pure self-interest, Gio," Meno finally said. "You do still owe me for scaring off those bandits ten years back, remember? You were so sodding drunk you couldn't name your own mother to save your skin when they waylaid you. I even got your little shipment through to Fallonier before the battle and saved your bloody profits for the year. Don't think I've forgotten. Now, being a fair man who always pays his debts because he knows what's good for him, you'll be carrying me and my friends here as far as the Tamus bridge, free of charge."

A smug smile on his face, Meno gestured and Aileanor emerged onto the roadway. With no alternative, Tagus cautiously followed, but not before making sure his face was well hidden in the shadow of the hood.

"Heh, consorting with rogues and scoundrels again, little man?" The trader said, raising an eyebrow as they came into view.

"Hey, I worked with you, right?" Meno laughed. "And seriously, what do you care? They're my friends. So, you'd best be making room, you pseudo-spiritual, multi-hued lunatic!"

Giovanni Lechianno gave a comically exaggerated expression of hurt.

"What disgraceful unprofessional words," he pouted, "to be spoken by an upstanding member of the Eternal Fraternity of Alchemical Sciences and Sorcerous Sundries! You wound me, good sir! Oh, how old Zebulon of Many Colors spins in his grave at the sound of your sacrilegious verbiage…oh, whatever, come on up! You're all fugitives I assume…the sort of people I'd be hanged for consorting with?"

He frowned directly at Tagus.

"Oh well, what did I expect when I agreed to deliver those supplies to your brother and his sewer-rat friends, huh Meno? Do I get any thanks for that?"

"Well, Nicco paid you, didn't he? What more do you want?"

Giovanni's face broke into a broad grin at the gnome's retort.

"I just hope your friends didn't kill anyone too important this time."

Chuckling merrily, his hurt expression utterly vanquished, he climbed over the roof of the cab to the nearest tarpaulin and proceeded to unstrap it.

The stench that struck Tagus's nose was almost as bad as Fiore's sewers and he had to stop himself from gagging. Even Meno's smug face looked a little sickly. Aileanor was as impassive as ever.

Giovanni laughed heartily at their reaction as he stood over the stinking brown mess that he had just uncovered.

"Hey, I promised to smuggle you to Trastamere, and I will! You just might need a little wash once you get there; I hear the river's nice this time of year!"

"Hiding your contraband under night soil again, Gio?" Meno sighed as he clambered up next to the trader, gesturing for the others to follow. "How resourceful. I should have known."

Giovanni was scraping through the muck with his gloved hands, apparently unconcerned about the smell. In no time he had uncovered three large wooden boxes that almost resembled coffins.

"Don't worry, they're well-ventilated!" He grinned, pulling his filthy fingers together deviously. "As an honest businessman, I've got to make a profit if I want to be a do-gooder. And it's been a bloody good year for fireweed! Cleaned out my whole stock back in Fiore! You've got plenty of space, most of my new goods are in the back there, so feel free to stretch out and relax. Would my lady like to go first?"

He opened one of the long narrow boxes and beamed at Aileanor. She gave a brief smirk before gracefully climbing in.

"And you, sir?"

He had already opened the second crate, which Tagus could see was not completely empty.

Tagus's nose wrinkled as he stepped forward, stoically wedging himself between the small wooden boxes, bottles of nameless liquids, and tubes full of coloured powders. But their scent was masked by a wild odor that smelled as if someone had set these assorted ingredients on fire.

"You're lucky, I had a lot of material stowed in that one. Should keep the stink out no problem!"

The trader shrugged and plunged him into darkness.

In a moment he could hear Giovanni fumbling with the lid on Meno's hiding spot and heard the gnome give a loud groan of protest.

"By the pit, Gio! This crate is almost packed, are you trying to drown me you lout?"

"Just taking your personalized space requirements into consideration, my friend and colleague! Now come on, there's a good fellow!"

"I swear Gio, you're a…"

The sound of approaching horses cut him off, and was followed by a storm of muffled curses. The lid slammed down and Tagus could hear Giovanni scrambling back and forth, scraping the night soil back into place as the hooves thundered closer. These were riders, and by the sounds of it, they had just come into view as the tarpaulin was being pulled back into place.

They had been seen.

In the sickly smelling claustrophobic darkness, Tagus's heart began to hammer in his chest, his stomach tightening in knots.

The clatter of hooves abruptly ceased. And a proud, impatiently aristocratic voice hailed the trader alongside the snorting of several horses. There were at least seven of them.

"Pedlar! Your name and your trading pass!" The voice demanded.

The speaker was likely a young noble saddled with the tedium of leading a gaggle of rough mercenaries on highway patrol duty. No doubt he thought it far beneath him, a slight against his honor, and that fact alone probably made him any honest trader's worst nightmare.

Tagus could hear creaking from the cab in front of him and he pictured the crazily-dressed Giovanni turning to face this impetuous knight and his retinue. But his response was not what Tagus expected from a man who just moments before had seemed the most clownish fool this side of the Noctus.

"You know well who I am, soldier."

The trader's voice was firm, certain, are far cry from the foppish idiot who had just packed them in a bed of shit. This "fool" actually sounded commanding, as sure of himself as a lord coming back to his estates.

The leader of the patrol must have been surprised as well, for there was a distinct pause before he replied, anger rising in his voice as though he had been personally insulted. But amid the highborn arrogance, Tagus could now detect a hint of uncertainty.

"You are a fool to take that tone with your betters, merchant. I am Lucius of House Derezzo and I serve His Holiness Inquisitor Fortius in the name of the Most High. Do not insult me with your heretical signs, I am charged with the security of the royal highway and they will not give me pause in my task. Men, search the caravan!"

Tagus's heart skipped a beat. Hirelings of the Inquisition patrolling the prince's roads? Yet another responsibility that the Church had taken upon itself. Perhaps even using his own escape, the "heretic that got away", as an excuse to muscle in on more secular concerns.

Horses snorted violently and there was a clatter of boots as the soldiers dismounted. Tagus's leg began to itch. The sickly smell of fireweed filling his nostrils as he struggled in vain to keep still. The maddening sensation spread rapidly down his leg, and suddenly the back of his neck seemed to catch fire. He could not stop himself from scratching, rubbing his body against the boxes around him, desperately struggling for relief as more and more parts of him became inflamed. He hardly dared to breathe as the heavy tread of multiple pairs of feet approached the caravan and he heard the metallic rattle of armor plate.

"By all means," Giovanni spoke again. Calmly, but no less commanding. "Search my wares, my good man…Sadly, I fear you shall be disappointed, for they are tragically mundane."

"Silence!" snapped the young noble, but the hint of discomfort had not left his voice.

"Get those tarps off!"

Tagus heard the tarpaulin over him being pulled aside, followed by a chorus of retching and cursing as the soldiers uncovered the night soil.

"By the Most…Shit!"

"I told you it would be disappointing, gentlemen…"

He could hear the knight curse before shouting the unwelcome order.

"Start digging!"

"Sir…boss, you can't be serious…" came a gruff voice of protest from somewhere directly above Tagus.

"Do you want twenty lashes waiting for you when you return to barracks, soldier? Move!"

Now he could hear the scrape of something metallic scraping through the mulch above him, probably the soldier probing it with his weapon. Tagus's panic rose to new heights as the point of a sword struck the solid wood of the box lid. He struggled to hold his body still, but it was useless. The fireweed essence continued to attack his skin and he could not stop his irritated leg from thumping against the box's side. Worse, he felt himself getting light headed. The drug was getting to him.

Fireweed addicts could be recognized by their lethargy and the disquieting orange tint to their skin. They spent everything they had on the stuff, down to the last penny, inhaling the toxic fumes until they were dead to the world. An addict would do anything to secure more of the stuff, even kill for it, their lethargy giving way to twitching hyper-active madness. Corrie had told him how in the fire weed dens of the Ox

Guts, it was not uncommon to find people licking the plant's residue off the walls or floors, trying to return to that euphoric state of emptiness. Tagus had known unemployed dockers for whom the drug was a way out…indeed their way into the next world.

"Captain! Nothing but a load of mouldy thatch back here!" Came a shout from the back of the caravan.

Tagus thanked the gods that the soldier's voice momentarily drowned out his continued thrashing.

"I said search, idiot! Not gawk! Get in there!"

"Yes sir, there are such wonders to found in piles of shit and decayed straw…"

Tagus could tell that Giovanni had made this jest with a straight face.

"Shut up! What are you hiding?"

Tagus heard the sound of a sword being drawn from its sheath.

"Sir knight, I think you are…"

"Tell me!"

There was silence, interrupted only by the telltale thump of Tagus's spasming leg as it hit the wood again and again.

"What was that?"

He tried in vain to freeze, catching his breath in his throat.

"Only your men mishandling my property."

Giovanni's reply sounded hoarse. It sounded like he had a blade held to his throat.

"I sincerely doubt that His Holiness would be pleased if you and your clots started tampering with our profits. We enjoy His full protection."

"Damn you…"

"The Most High is Himself a Wanderer in The Sky."

There was a pause. A very long and torturous pause. The only sound was the knocking of Tagus's body inside the box, silently praying for the load of shit above him to deaden the noise. His feverish brain even hoping that a lord of shit truly sat at the side of the earth goddess in the halls of the Celestial Court…and that this great and rotting lord of excrement, whose stench made even the immortal gods hold their nostrils, smiled upon him now.

"Get on with you!"

There were furious stomps as the defeated young noble made his way back to his mount. The caravan rattled as men jumped down, loudly cursing as they followed their irate leader. There was a chorus of snorts as they re-mounted, followed by the clatter of hooves.

Tagus's leg spasmed again. Sweat was pouring down his face as he rolled onto his side, silently begging for the ordeal to be over.

A moment later the caravan began to move off. This was going to be a less than comfortable ride.

Chapter 20 – Trastamere

Nothing interrupted their journey south. Several times Tagus heard riders speeding past, but no one hailed the trader or demanded to inspect his wares. Giovanni was either extremely lucky, or extremely well connected. At least twice the caravan stopped at what must have been a tollgate based on the buzz of official-sounding voices outside, only to be waved through without paying. Giovanni jovially shouting his thanks at the toll keeper as they rolled away. The smuggler must have greased more than a few palms to be able to pull off such a feat. The prince's toll men were notoriously strict.

The light-headedness had been mercifully temporary. But the fireweed's intolerable itching continued to gnaw at him. At least the straining of his nerves in tandem with the pounding of his heart each time the clatter of hooves swept by, had kept the drug's notorious lethargy from setting in.

At last, after what had felt like hours of restless torture, the jolting wagon came to stop. And a few moments later, he could hear the tarpaulin being thrown aside and Giovanni humming tunelessly as he began to scrape away the night soil. He heard muffled shouts and the sound of fists banging on wood before the trader lifted the lid off and let an evidently enraged Meno out from his tightly-packed captivity.

"Damn you Gio!" The gnome sputtered, coughing violently, "You've got some nerve to stuff me like a sardine amid your pedaled trash! I'll apply Demon's Wort to your skin and watch your insides melt if you ever do that again! What in the pit are you laughing for? This isn't funny, you brainless horned toad!"

The sound of Gio's musical laughter filled the air, rising alongside a chorus of colorful curses exploding from Meno's lips.

"Well, you blighter." Meno finally said, his voice filled with all the irritation that his skin must have been feeling, "I don't even want to know how many frothing orange-tinted madmen you've serviced these past few weeks. I can only imagine how much harder Master Eccles would have thrashed you if he'd known just how much of a rogue you'd become! Get the others out already! You've likely turned them into carrots by now!"

Giovanni was still laughing uproariously at Meno's outburst when the lid of Tagus's box came open, greeting him with the brilliant blinding colors of sunset and the awful reek of night soil.

"I assume you were also hoping and praying that the god of entropy and all things filthy would smile upon us this fine day?"

Meno was looking down at him, itching his crotch and looking despondent.

Tagus snorted at this sarcastic remark, trying to rise to his feet and failing as his itchy leg spasmed again.

"Damn it! Yes!" he cried, "If only there was such a god!"

Meno's hand was jittery, but it still had the strength to pull him to his feet.

Giovanni kept laughing under their shared withering gaze as he opened Aileanor's box. She emerged without a sound, looking slightly annoyed as she dusted herself off. But she gracefully turned her back on the chuckling trader and stepped to the ground.

"Oh dear, did my shit offend thy sense of dignity, my lady?" He called after her in mock alarm.

"Leave off, you oaf!" Meno snapped, "Where in Gormani's flames have you taken us? This isn't the Elephant Bridge!"

He gestured at the unbroken line of woodland lining the road. Almost identical to the spot where they had met the crazy smuggler earlier that day.

"Hey, you wanted Trastamere," Giovanni said, crossing his arms smugly across the chest of his outrageously patterned doublet.

"The Elephant Bridge and the castle-town are but half a day's walk down that way."

He pointed to where the road climbed a low tree-covered ridge.

He paused at the stony looks that Tagus and Meno were giving him.

"Oh, don't look at me like that! We're in Trastamere, so I've kept my promise! The boundary marker is half a mile behind us if you please, but being an honest man, I took you in a little further. I can't be letting a thrice-accursed heretic arch-fiend off my wagon in public view! But it's safe enough here. You can camp in the woods tonight and carry on at day-break on foot."

He winked at Tagus, straightened up and climbed to the roof of the cab.

"I, on the other hand, am going to get myself some ale and a nice feather bed over at the Crosskeys Inn. I paid the landlord myself last year to get em' installed, just got tired of sleeping on mouldy straw."

He turned his backed to them and began tending to the horses.

"You are very lucky this 'heretic' doesn't take your 'generosity' out of your hide, pedlar!" Tagus spat, clutching his leg.

Back in his mercenary days, he would have beat the man senseless for this.

"Oh, just forget it, he's been a stubborn ass ever since I met him at the academy."

Meno laid a supportive hand on Tagus's shoulder.

"I figured there'd be some walking involved with you at the helm, Gio. Now be off with you! And, believe you me, I've got more than a few other favors to call in next time, and so does my brother. You'd better keep it regular when it comes to getting those loads of supplies to the undercity!"

"Oh please, Master Shortstack, you know I'm a man of my word. Run along and play now!"

Meno jumped off the caravan just before it jerked into motion, with Tagus following as best he could.

From the cover of the shallow ditch, the three of them watched the wagon wheel around and disappear into the sunset back down the road. Tagus saw the trader briefly turn his head. It was too far away to see his expression.

Then the strange man turned around again and went on.

****

It was full dark night by the time they had found a suitably secluded place in the woods and settled around a small campfire. The swaying branches reached over them like twisted claws in the night breeze. Aileanor, who was furthest from the crackling flames, sat with her back against a tree, seemingly indifferent to the latest ordeal they had just been through together. The itching had finally subsided and Tagus's leg only twitched annoyingly every now and again, drawing the occasional curse from his lips as he doggedly stared into the fire and tried to forget all that was tormenting him. His nerves remained shaky and he spent a long-time glancing at every leaping shadow, thinking that they were about to be attacked by bandits, guards, or things more monstrous.

Meno, for his part, seemed to have recovered from his own harrowing experience under Giovanni's night soil, and was studiously poring over the documents that they had taken from the Seven Moons. At long last, he looked up at Tagus and shook his head.

"Well that answers a few questions."

Startled, Tagus reluctantly shifted his gaze from the flames.

"What is it? Did you find something?"

"Bad news I'm afraid," the gnome replied. "I'd have noticed it before if we hadn't been in such a rush, but your people aren't headed for the plantations, Tagus."

A severe look covered Meno's normally jovial face, the handlebar moustache forming a solid black line in the firelight as he went on.

"I knew that there was something off about this deal as soon as I saw the inflated prices. The slavers could have rounded up the folk of the Asylum, loaded them onto barges and had them in Trastamere within a day. Instead, they hauled them all the way across town in the opposite direction to languish in that accursed compound for days on end. Something else is going on. And this here document proves it."

Tagus's irritated pre-occupation with his leg evaporated in an instant, his face becoming a mask of fear and anger.

"Then where are they being taken?"

"Southmarch. It seems Trastamere is only a transit point. I found this letter between the Seven Moons and a certain nobleman. A nobleman so bold as to go by his real name when corresponding with slavers. His fortress is their destination. I even found the manifest."

Tagus's teeth clenched. Southmarch was beyond the boundaries of the prince's domains, a lawless region of southern Vinos straddling what had been the imperial border. The rulers of that land did not merit the word "noble" in any way. They were warlords, little more than bandits with their own private armies, and merciless in their appetite for plunder; raiding the surrounding domains like a swarm of locusts. No trader passed through their domains without protection money and any traveller without the necessary bribes would surely lose his freedom or his life. The cruel bravado of these robber barons was legendary.

He swallowed hard.

"What is his name?"

"Priscus Scarrus, the same king of thieves who proclaimed himself the re-born Emperor of Five Seals two years ago. Even named his own Hierophant and started his own church from what I hear. It's no surprise he has an appetite for slaves."

That was barely a fraction of this warlord's appetites, thought Tagus. He knew this man. And he knew his work. If there was anything worse than toiling in chains, subjected to the rule of the whip on a Trastamere plantation, it was falling into the hands of this creature.

"I have faced him before," Tagus snarled, looking up at the stars, "And believe me, gnome, we had best hurry. I have seen what he does to captives."

Meno gave only a stony-faced nod in reply. Priscus Lentellus Scarrus was known throughout the land as a most foul murderer. He would kill women and children purely for sport, if he had deemed them too weak to sell as laborers. But he did not just kill them.

Tagus had been a mercenary, hired alongside Vitus and his Falhorne comrades by Prince Chero himself, when they had been sent to the Southmarch border five years ago as part of a force charged with stopping this same warlord's spree of destructive raids into Vinos. It had been his final experience as a sell-sword, and he would never forget it.

On the way south they had passed through still smouldering villages. Everything portable had been taken, the rest burned. Carrion birds and scavenging beasts ran wild among the charred and empty houses. But it was the state of the bodies left behind that had shocked even the most hardened soldier: corpses, eyeless and handless, hung from trees; others had been nailed to door frames, tongues cut out, their faces frozen in agony; whole bodies had been spitted on pikes like roasting pigs.

All of them were children. Not one had appeared to be over the age of ten.

"Where did you fight him?" Meno asked.

"Not a stone's throw from the fiend's fortress. We pursued him right back to his lair. If only we could have burned it in the same way…"

He remembered that day. His fury when he had finally come to grips with those monsters. Even hard-hearted, money-mad mercenaries fought like heroes in that battle, and he had more than earned the title of "young lion" the way he had thrown himself on the foe, his halberd striking back and forth like a living thing. Only after he had personally decapitated the bearer of that unholy battle standard, had he become aware of his wounds and staggered to his knees.

They had driven the bastards behind the walls of their fortress, but lacked both the strength and provisions to maintain a siege in that harsh land. Withdrawing without destroying that accursed place had been the hardest thing. Seeing the warlord's banners still proudly flying above the tall stone battlements had renewed his rage like nothing else. He could only imagine how the Falhorne of old must have felt: fighting and withdrawing, often into foreign lands, knowing that the hated imperium of the Betrayer remained strong in spite of their heroic efforts. The very survival of such a foe was an insult to life itself.

Meno sighed, and looked up at the dark sky, to where it showed through the twisted canopy.

"You're a brave man, my friend. I remember that expedition. No army had ever penetrated so far into Southmarch since the time of Cosimo. The ungrateful brat should have hailed you as heroes rather than cursing you for not doing the impossible."

"That was long ago," Tagus replied, "If I have to return to that place again, for the sake of my people, I will."

The alchemist only nodded, still gazing skyward.

"Tomorrow we'll make for the *Prince's Respite* Inn outside the castle-town. I've got a friend there who can help us reach the southlands."

Tagus remembered that name.

"Callidus said to find him there if I ever passed this way," he said.

"Bold man," the gnome grinned, "It's but a stone's throw from the lion's den. Deepest cellars of any inn I've seen. You know, I treated our Callidus when he looked more like a piece of holed cheese. He's full of piss and vinegar that one. Anyone who would follow such a man would need balls of iron too, even if they were a woman."

Aileanor had been sitting silently this whole time. Her face a blank unreadable mask. When she finally spoke, after Tagus's words had faded away, it nearly had the effect of a cannon shot, with both men turning sharply in her direction.

"Assassin."

Tagus blinked at her.

"What?"

She looked straight at him, those penetrating dark eyes holding him like a vice.

"I was an assassin."

Tagus just stared uncertainly at her. Why was she saying this?

She glanced at Meno, who slowly nodded his head.

"I know you have questions," she said. Her voice was firm, almost defiant. "You have wondered who I am from the time I found you. You have wondered why I risk my life. Why I fight. Why I live with Meno. And so much more. Now I will give you answers, Falhorne."

It was true. He had been burning for answers from the beginning. Frustrated and mystified in equal parts when they had not been forthcoming. But now, sitting by the fire under the dark trees of a nameless forest, Tagus felt the urge to protest, to stop her, to say that she did not have to do this. Part of him did not want to know. Part of him remembered Vitus's chivalrous attitude that it was poor manners to demand such things of a lady. And part of him had heard too many horrific stories. In the end, all he could do was nod his head.

"I was an assassin," she said, brushing her midnight locks from her radiant pale face. "I never knew anything of my parents. I was eleven years old when the Inquisitor Fortius came and took me from the orphanage where I was raised. The matriarch, a pious woman of Austellus, was kind to me, but she would never refuse the will of the Church. Cybelle was like me. An orphan taken by the Inquisition. They always take the young for this sort of thing…"

She paused and looked away into the gloom. Silence reigned for a few moments before she continued.

"I never knew the name of the convent where they took me, apart from that it was somewhere in Braxus. They never told me any more than that. But I was trained. Me, Cybelle, and the others, we trained. And we killed. Some of the girls never came back from the missions they were sent on. The Inquisition does not wait until its murderers are fully grown. As I said, they always take the young."

Again, her dark eyes were boring into him, as Tagus struggled with the mixed emotions that her revelations were arousing in his mind.

"Fortius kept me. Kept us. We served him like we were his daughters, but he made it clear that I was his possession. A tool in his hand. The fathers of the Church are barred from marriage, but the Most High did not deign to take away their lust. I accepted my fate. Cybelle was older, and they always take the young…"

Her voice was as heavy as stone.

"I killed for him. I murdered people in their beds. Took the life of anyone deemed an obstacle to the Inquisition. I even slipped poison into the wine of a Church father whom Fortius deemed to be a radical with heretical thoughts. And I did so gladly. Until what they did to her."

She flinched suddenly, her thin fingers trembling on the grass in front of her.

"Fortius said she was disobedient. A rebel. A heretic who had blasphemed against Solar Dominatus. He said that she must be punished. And me and Cybelle punished her. We did what was expected of us. She screamed. She pleaded. But we were the Holy Instruments of the Divine. Her eyes. I could not look away. 'I was faithful', she pleaded until her last breath. That was when I left. Cybelle stayed. She demanded that I stay. But I could not. There, in that room. In the Seven Moons. That was the first time I saw her since then. I do not know who she works for now…"

She fell silent, her distressed expression fading to featureless marble. The fire crackled and a stick gave way, sending up an eruption of sparks into the cool air.

A look of concern, something almost fatherly, came over Meno's face and he turned his wide eyes to Tagus.

"Forgive me, Falhorne," he said, with an uncharacteristic severity in his voice. "I found her three years ago, on the streets of Fiore. I was at court then, but professional demands occasionally had me in the slums, consorting with rogues to get my hands on some of the more exotic ingredients his majesty required…a dubious task rascals like Nicco and Gio were more than willing to assist me with."

The alchemist stared at the ground, slowly running a hand across the stubble of his bald head.

"She was sick when I found her. She told me she'd been working for a guild of thieves, but had been expelled after her illness took hold and had nowhere to go. I promised I would treat her…"

Tagus sat, rooted to the spot as the gnome's words trailed off. Not knowing what to think. His fury upon hearing that Aileanor had once worked for the dreaded Inquisition itself, had melted away into something approaching sympathy. She was no longer a blank slate, even if her answers only raised more questions.

Vitus's voice sounded in the back of his mind: women had no place on the battlefield, they were not meant to be warriors. What would his mentor think of her? This woman whose skill went beyond anything that he had seen in all his years of being a soldier. He had never known, never even spoken to, the female warriors whom they had infrequently encountered on campaign.

The praetor's disapproval had shown, and he had forbidden all contact between his men and these "wenches-in-arms". Aileanor was the first such woman that he had ever been close to. And he still did not understand her. All he knew was that her past was terrible and it was following her. That was at least something he could relate to, even as the unknown continued to torment and gnaw at him.

He opened and closed his mouth several times, before speaking.

"Thank you."

It was all that he could bring himself to say to her.

****

It was cold and damp the next morning. Tagus could not remember the details of his nightmares, only that they had been terrible. Agitated, he had been barely able to close his eyes, expecting to see Cybelle and her wraiths emerge from the darkness to murder them in their sleep. His back ached from the hard earth as he turned up and twisted his head to look for his companions.

Meno was still snoring peacefully nearby. Aileanor was nowhere to be seen.

In the pale light, Tagus saw that they had been sleeping next to a badly overgrown circle of seven standing stones, a feature he had failed to notice in the dark of the previous evening. The tall oak, whose boughs they had camped beneath, appeared to have grown up inside the circle itself, as if to emphasize the incalculable age of the stones, their corroded sides covered with patches of moss and lichen.

Tagus pulled off the cloak covering his naked body, having removed his clothes to escape the drug-induced itch that had returned with a vengeance as he had laid down to sleep. He slowly stood up, bare feet pressing into the wet grass of the glade.

Something was drawing him to the ancient stones.

He did not bother getting dressed, carefully making his way to the closest of them, a time-eroded horn of rock barely taller than his head. He could not name what he was feeling, his heart beating faster as he lay his palm on the rough surface, his fingers settling over the cool dampness. In that instant, he thought he felt something stirring, not inside the stone but inside of him, somewhere in his own blood, as if a second pulse had started within a second heart.

Startled, he jerked his hand back, and the feeling immediately vanished. Looking back at where his palm had been, he saw the straight lines of the faded Ormus sign starring back at him…unreadable, but clearly recognizable for what it was.

The soft, barely audible, gasp from behind him made Tagus whirl around, reaching for his sword, which, of course, was not buckled to his bare waist.

It was Aileanor.

She stood beneath the boughs of the oak tree, dressed once more in the hunting greens that he had first seen her wear in Meno's cellar. Her mouth was agape, and she was wearing an expression that he had never seen her wear before, one of shock.

Tagus froze as embarrassment flushed his dark cheeks. His mind fumbling for an excuse. Perhaps a rough mercenary would not have cared, but Vitus had taught him well how to behave around women. It was unbecoming of a Falhorne to be seen like this.

He opened his mouth to apologize for his indecency, but it was she who spoke first, and it was Tagus's turn to be shocked.

"Your back…"

Her voice was almost a whisper, a horrified whisper. It was the first time that he had heard fear in her voice since that strange malady had gripped her in the basement of the Seven Moons.

Aileanor stretched out her hand, and stepped forward.

"What happened to you?"

The scars. She had seen his scars. Tagus felt his throat convulse. He did not like to think about them. He did not like to talk about them. Even Tarquinus had known better than to ask. But the genuine concern in her voice made his fear and shame appear meaningless. She knew. There was no point in hiding it. And no matter how hard his mind resisted; he could not stay silent. It was a compulsion that he could not name and it flew in the face of everything he had ever learned about self-preservation.

"I was a slave," he said, lowering his gaze away from the depths of those eyes.

"Who did this to you?"

"The overseer…Ranald. I…I was too slow that day…"

He felt weak before her unwavering gaze. But the hardness of those dark eyes was now shot through with a sense of feeling that he could not describe. Again, it compelled him to speak the truth.

"It was fifty lashes."

"How old were you?"

"I was thirteen."

She fell silent. Her outstretched arm dropped to her side, now clutching the hilt of her sword, anger sweeping over her delicate features. It was not the anger of a courtly lady, but of a warrior. And something about it, something about its unambiguous reality, put his confused mind at ease, although it did not take away the pain of remembering.

"It happened in Trastamere." Tagus said, dropping his gaze to the mould of the forest floor. "I wish that I did not have to go back there…"

When he had finally dressed, he found himself gripping Julia's amulet, holding it as if it would keep him from falling.

Epilogue – Visions

The smoke hovered in sweet smelling clouds, carrying the pungent odor of burning herbs. Corrie sat alone in the wide and empty space of what had once been the cloakroom of the baths, one of the few parts of the ruined structure to be free from the clutter of tents and the clamor of voices. One of the few places to give her refuge from the demands, the responsibilities, the grim thoughts of her husband on his way to that horrible land to the south – where he had been before and that she knew he feared so much. But he would do it. He would do it for his people. And that made her afraid all the more as she tried to focus on the task at hand. It was yet another thing she dreaded. But she was doing it for someone who needed her help more than anyone else in the world.

Corrie knelt before the smouldering contents of the brazier. Head bowed and breasts bared as she inhaled the sacred aromas of that which was once living, now returned to the cycle of the elements and the dance of the seasons. Her eyes closed as it filled her senses, her breaths mixing and merging with the pulse of life.

She began the chant.

"Accccchhhhtttaaaa, uuullllllllaaaaaahhhhhhhh…"

The words, the sounds, the rhythms that proceeded to flow from her lips were ancient, primal, and impossible to translate into the common tongue of Vinos or any other human language. For they flowed through waters unseen, spoke of ages long forgotten, ages where man was not master and other beings and powers ruled the land.

Her voice was not her own. Her mind no longer bound within the confines of the flesh as everything became one, undifferentiated, undivided and whole. The Stream of Life, its twisting course drawn in the pungent smoke, widened into raging torrents, cut through the living rock of sky-flung mountains, washed out over great plains and spread into oceans of undreamed-of vastness as it carried her. The walls and stone of the floor ran like rushing water, the solid foundations of the undercity dissolving into vapor as the cycle flowed around and within her.

Then she heard the voice.

The voice that was not a voice, calling to her as a mother would call her child, bidding her to come home. She embraced it, letting go of all false separation, distinctions, and names. Here, in the All Mother's universal embrace, there was only Her and Her alone. And She knew why Her child had come.

No words were spoken as Corrie acknowledged her oneness with the power that flowed through all things. No words. No names. Everything was already understood and had been understood since time began and the wheel of existence had begun to turn in the cosmos. Images of times and places long since past and far future events that yet might be, blended seamlessly and without boundary. It did not take long to find her.

Jesta was there. Buried within the rock and the foundations of the city where mortals walked in fear of names. Names that bound her teacher to the wooden instrument of torment. Names that formed the ropes tearing into the raw bloody flesh of her wrists and ankles. Names that formed the acid they were applying to the incisions that they had cut into her naked body while she screamed.

But it was not names that Jesta screamed at the white clad figures hovering around her. It was a primal scream. The defiance of raging waters, thunderstorms, and brushfires that echoed in the ether and filled the veins of her Mother with a child's anguish. Corrie's tears were not her own as she listened to those screams, nor was her anger anything less than an earthquake rising from the depths in its sheer fury.

The Inquisition had taken her Soyga. And now they were trying to break her. Using every blasphemous technique of alien cruelty, even blocking the psychic bond that she shared with her sisters. As if that would serve to isolate their prisoner. They were such fools. For the Stream of Life flowed through all things and there was nothing beyond the reach of the All Mother. The Sisterhood never abandoned those of the Craft, and it was with knowing defiance that Corrie met the hateful faceless gaze of that golden mask.

Then she felt it.

A chill like ice but so much colder, so much more inimical to life to the point of being outside of it entirely. Casting its alien pall over all creation. She felt the cycle slow, the Stream of Life scatter and break apart into wild rivulets that proceeded to explode into clouds of vapour, hovering like mist around a gallows tree.

The golden mask was still staring at her as she screamed, purple flames writhing around it like a million tiny claws of bone, the hand of death itself reaching out for her as she fell away into darkness.

When her vision cleared, she found herself lying on the floor, face upturned toward the shadows of the vaulted ceiling. The brazier had gone out and the wholesome odor of burning herbs had vanished into stale nothingness. Only when she had risen to her feet did she recognize the chill in the air, something more than the cold of the undercity as she felt those dead eyes burning into her own.

Terrified, she ran from the room.